CHARITY'S
JOURNEY

CHARITY'S JOURNEY

BETH MCDUFFIE

authorHOUSE®

AuthorHouse™ LLC
1663 Liberty Drive
Bloomington, IN 47403
www.authorhouse.com
Phone: 1-800-839-8640

Published by AuthorHouse 06/20/2014

ISBN: 978-1-4969-2087-4 (sc)
ISBN: 978-1-4969-2086-7 (hc)
ISBN: 978-1-4969-2088-1 (e)

Library of Congress Control Number: 2014910968

For Jerry McDuffie
You Rescued Me

Chapter 1

The Beginning of Time

My first memory is of Heart Speak and the warmth and softness surrounding me. I was far too young to know there would ever be anything more than the gentle nurturing of my mother's womb. Her heartbeat soothed and reassured me. Her body nourished me. There were brothers and sisters with me. We spent days nestled together, nudging and providing each other comfort. It was all we knew. It is all there was. This was our world.

We did not know the food, so freely provided, was depleting our already malnourished mother. We did not understand such things. Pain was not a part of our lives. If our mother hurt, there was nothing to tell us. Her heart beat only for us and we could feel her love and concern with each pulse. We existed and our world was a wonderful place. Our lives, barely begun, were the best they would ever be.

But the world does change with time. We would not always be warm. Food would not always be readily available. Our mother's love would be our only constant. We would soon learn there are terrible, evil beings in the world that hurt and maim.

My first harsh memory is of an incredible cold. My mother's rough tongue was quickly removing the very thing that had provided me with life and nourishment for 62 days. I had never worried about breathing before, but now I fought helplessly for air. But as my mother nurtured me, cleaned me, moved me so lovingly and carefully, I began to breathe. I was nudged to my mother's breast. Then there was the heartbeat I knew so well, and the warmth my mother's body provided. I struggled with my brothers and sisters to get as close to her as I could. Her milk gave me strength. I quickly learned if I pushed against her with my tiny paws as I sucked, the warm milk flowed freely.

I suppose I had an understanding of what was happening. My instincts told me this was the way of the world. This was the way of life. That did not mean I had to like it. I already missed the warmth of the womb and the carefree days spent without concern for finding a breast. But the world had, indeed, moved on. I would move on with it.

Even on that first day I could sense something was amiss. All dogs live by instinct and are born with a strong will and need to survive. There is that thing deep inside that warns of dangers we cannot see and guides us to safety. My instincts were keen and I knew... I just knew something was wrong. I did not know what. But there was a lump in my throat that told me I would find out.

As the first days passed, my awareness increased. I did not understand being too thin, and I was still unaware of pain. But I knew my brothers and sisters were with me and we snuggled for warmth. Being together and provided for was still our normal. We just had to work a little harder for it now. Our needs were still being met willingly, eagerly, by our mother's body. We did not know she had no choice in the matter. But, I really do not think she would have changed it had she been given the choice.

We felt her strength. It flowed through me with an energy I have never since known. I know now that strength she gave during my first days of life was something far more than energy. It was that thing that came from the pulsing of her heart. It was an emotion so pure and strong that nothing else mattered.

Mother's love and devotion for her children was fierce and tangible. As my awareness increased and I snuggled against her, I could tell she was far too thin. She was keeping us warm, but her own body was barely skin and bones. I could feel her shiver against the cold wind that was blowing. Somewhere in my heart of hearts I knew there should be something more here. She was my shelter. She was my strength, my life, my love – where was hers?

She was never away from us for long. Man would come and give her food and water and look us over, making noises I did not understand. He spoke very harshly to my mother and it hurt my heart to see her cower away from him. But always she would rush to us and cover us with her too thin body. We knew she was offering the only protection she could. The scarce amount of food she was given meant the milk provided us was becoming very scarce as well. There were times Man would come and move me and several more of my siblings away from our mother. She would protest and struggle to keep us with her. Man would kick her and hold her head down beneath his boot. He would keep her there as the Chosen nursed greedily. We did not understand about the Chosen then. We just knew this man was pushing us away and we were not thriving as they were. Why did they eat while we were not allowed? We could feel our hunger making us weak while the Chosen grew strong. Our mother's heartbeat always reminded us of her love. Our own hearts beating were an extension of hers and we huddled together, comforting each other, until we could be next to her again.

As for our mother, she loved each of us with the same ferocity. When Man would leave she would make sure those who had been pushed away were nursed as much as her wasted body would allow. While she loved all of us, and we knew this without doubt, my "un-chosen" siblings and I knew there was something she saw special about us. Perhaps it was the same thing that elicited hate from Man. Looking back, I now believe Man would have disposed of us – killed us - in the very early days had his son not been there and been so eager to assume the care for a few pups. While we did not totally understand the words these humans were using, we knew Boy wanted us. We knew Boy was to learn something from us. We did not know what. The day came when Man and Boy came together. He chose two of my sisters and me using those words we did not understand. We would soon come to hate those words. We would know pain and sorrow. And we would know there are things in this world much worse than death.

Our first great sadness came the same day Boy selected the three of us as "his." My mother cried and whined in protest, trying desperately to protect each of her children as Man grabbed and pulled the three of us from her warmth and protection. Boy held us to the side while Man took the others that were unchosen and put them in a box to be carried away. Mother struggled harder than she ever had and she received a boot to her head for her efforts.

Our eyes were barely open and we knew Man and Boy by instinct alone, still unable to see clearly and unable to understand their language. Our mother's mournful howl spoke volumes for us, however. We may not have understood the ferocious barking of dogs we could not see, but we clearly understood the piercing screams of our siblings that had been taken. We knew we would never be with them again as our mother sobbed and fell to the ground on legs too weak to hold her. The obvious grief wracked her body with a pain we were not yet privy to.

Our "un-chosen" siblings would never be cold and hungry and they would never understand what my two sisters and I came to know in a very short time. Those sweet, spirited puppies - young lives that never stood a chance – were the lucky ones. My two sisters and I would wish for death soon enough. And our poor mother already understood that sometimes dead is better. Her unrelenting love for us kept her fighting for her life and ours. It also gave her the strength to let us know so long as there is life, there is hope. I may have never known exactly how she knew this. But the days to come, days past the unbearable torture, would teach me things so many of my kind may never know.

The days beyond a life time of wishing for death would teach me there is charity, hope and faith in the world.

And there is the greatest gift of all. There is Heart Speak. All beings start with the ability to understand this language because it is as old as time. It is the music of an angel choir. It is the music of our spirit when our heart first beats. It is that rhythm that provides life, love, peace and the will to survive before we are born. It is the voice of our souls guiding us in the direction of all that is pure and good. For those who understand it, no explanation is needed. For those who lose the ability, no explanation will bring it back.

Chapter 2

The Journey Begins

I suppose it is difficult for humans to understand the way a puppy sees and experiences time. Our lives are much shorter than humans, so time is always measured accordingly. A day in our lives as young puppies can be like one of your years. I believe that makes a moment far more precious to us. But, it is important to know the experience of hours passing for a puppy is far different than it is for an adult dog. So as I talk of the early days for us, an hour can seem like a week in "puppy time." As such, it is impossible for me to convey with any certainty how much time actually elapsed between events in those early days.

Boy had claimed "ownership" of three of us girls and we began to talk excitedly. We were beginning to have some understanding about our differences. Those puppies that were Chosen were all the same color as our mother. We came to understand that this is a color known as "blue." My two sisters and I were basically black with some white. The other pups that had been taken away were different colors, but were not blue either. So we understood only those puppies that were the color of our mother were Chosen. We had no idea what they were chosen for, but if the condition of our mother was any prediction of what was to come for them, Chosen was not such a good thing. We were hopeful that Boy would be a kinder, gentler companion for us than Man had been for our mother. Oh the ignorance of youth. Yes. We had high hopes. Mother listened to the endless prattle and had a very sad, faraway look in her eyes.

Our eyes had been open for some time, but we were only just beginning to see clearly. Our immediate world was coming into focus, and I now knew that my mother's body was far more than just the "too thin" of my original thoughts. She had many scars on her emaciated body and she was far from healthy. I could tell she had many litters of pups before us. Her teats were tough and worn. Dogs typically have ten teats with single nipples; and of my mother's ten teats, three had more than one nipple. This happens to dogs that are over bred and have large litters. I did not know our mother's age, but she looked very old and tired.

There were times I could feel her pain as clearly as I could feel my own hunger. My heart ached for my loving and devoted mother. Her milk was scarce, and the day came when there was barely enough for any of us.

While our mother loved and nurtured us as best she could, she also confused us. We knew beyond all doubt that her heart beat for us. She protected us to the best of her ability and we could feel her unconditional love. It is so very hard to describe the memory of that love and the warmth and comfort it gave. It was like a warm and gentle afternoon breeze whispering across our hearts ever-so-quietly, embracing us as we played. We could also see it in her eyes when she would look at us. But she had never talked with us. While all of her pups played and prattled endlessly among themselves, she sat quietly, always watching. And always with that sad faraway look. It was a look that now brought a strange, familiar comfort to my curious, exploring heart.

We would get very still when Man or Boy would come. We could not forget the screams of our siblings as our mother cried helplessly. But Mother would come to life when those two humans approached. Even today, I recall the way she would put her frail scarred body between us and them. Of course, the humans could and would do what they wanted with us. This was clear since they had obviously treated our mother so horribly. But we knew she tried her very best to protect us. In fact, as time passed, we came to know she would gladly have given her life for any of us. However, there was a very large chain around her neck holding her to a limited area. That, and the fact she had so little strength left in her tired, frail body stopped her from offering the security that she longed to give. So we basked in that warm whispering wind we knew as her love, and we tried to let her know she, too, was loved. My greatest wish back then was for her to know the way my heart beat for her. And, even more, the way it ached for the pain I could see in her tired eyes.

On my last day of innocence it became my clear understanding that humans must surely be the enemy. My mother and the siblings that had already been taken away were all the proof I needed. What happened next would establish and clearly define the truth of my theory. It would take a miracle for me to learn better. It would take a true miracle and Heart Speak.

Man and Boy came into the old shed where we were housed. We could smell their arrival even before the bright sun shone through the open door. The only good thing about them coming was that bright sunshine. There were windows on the old shed, but they were so dirty the sun could barely shine through. We longed to feel that sunshine on our backs and to play outside the walls of the shed. Though we had never been past that door, our instincts told us there was a wonderful world out there. There was a world beyond those walls, the dirt floor where our mother gave birth to us, and the dirty straw that was never made fresh. We had never seen it, but we could smell it. The world beyond smelled fresh and was warm with bright light. When that door would open, we knew our instincts were right and we would long to go and explore that world.

Man came in first and it was wonderful that he left the door open. Boy came in behind him carrying a box. But we had little time to think about that box and what it might mean because that door was still open and the smells were wonderful. Imagine if you can, for just a moment, if you had never seen the color green, yellow or blue. Think how those three colors might smell. And try to envisage how your mind and heart would "feel" those colors in a dark, dank, cold shed.

Mom was trying to push all of her children beneath her as we fought to see that open doorway. I believe that was the first time I realized just how cruel that chain around her neck truly was. Man grabbed the chain and held her up, her body hanging and twisting as she fought against being strangled to death. Even as the vicious hands of Man held her off the ground, choking the life from her, I could see that the fear in her eyes was for her children. There was neither fear nor concern for herself – just for her children. We could not understand what Man was barking at Boy, but his voice was harsh, cold – as cold as the air in that shed. It made me shake and tremble with fear as my young heart hurt for my mother. I did not understand prayer back then. I would come to know it well in later days. But while I may not have understood, there was a prayer in my heart and soul, begging for my mother's life.

Then, as suddenly as the terror had begun, it was over and our mother was lying on her side gasping for air. As the shed door slammed shut behind the two humans, there was the realization that there were only two other puppies left there with me. My sisters that Boy had chosen as "his" remained with me. But, the greatest joy, our mother was alive.

The memory of other puppies being taken was fresh and we waited to hear the screams of our siblings. We thought they had been "chosen" as special because they were allowed to eat when we were pushed from our mother. But now we did not know what to think. Boy had obviously put them in the box he was carrying. Why?

We huddled against each other and our gasping, weeping mother, waiting to hear the horrible screams. The screams never came. As Mother regained her strength and composure she nudged us closer, something we had come to understand meant we were to eat. Perhaps feeding us would bring her comfort. As we nursed noisily, understanding the removal of our siblings meant there may be enough milk for us, we could feel the sobs rocking our mother's body. But I was so young and the pups I had come to know as the Chosen had never had much time for me. The three of us that were left had grown very close and attached to each other. Being pushed away from our mother's breast while the Chosen ate greedily had given them strength and a courage we did not have. So even as I knew my mother's heart was hurting and breaking yet again for stolen puppies, I sucked nosily and my heart was a bit lighter than usual.

There was something else nagging at me. It was something that made me feel wrong and caused me to drop my head. I felt guilty because my heart was glad when my mother was so miserable. I vowed to make Mother happy. My mission would be to cleanse myself of this guilt by making her very happy. She would always be grateful I was with her. I knew my two sisters felt the same as I listened to their hungry, eager smacks. The three of us ate as we had never eaten, and for once, there was almost enough to fill our bellies.

After our meal, Mother washed us more vigorously than ever before. For a moment my heart dropped with a certainty that she had read my earlier guilty thoughts. I feared for a brief moment that she was going to wash the hide and guilt from my body. But the truth was already in my heart. I knew she was just being a good mother and was putting her all into her work. She was trying to be the best mother possible and trying not to let the three of us know how hurt she really was. A mother always knows what is in the heart of her young. All dogs speak Heart Speak, and well, they just know these things. I was slowly starting to learn about this thing called Heart Speak. Even though our mother had never spoken to us, we could hear her heart telling us we were loved as surely as we could feel her rough tongue cleansing our bodies. Our guilty thoughts did not detract from her precious, eternal love. We did not know the name Heart Speak, but it was a part of our normal. For the first time since our birth we felt a weary peace.

But there was always something nagging, picking, there in the back of my mind. It was something I could not quite touch with my conscious thoughts. I wondered if my sisters felt it too. Mother held us close to her for a long time, keeping us under her belly and close to her heart. Even when Boy brought food out to her, she did not go to it right away. As Boy spoke to my mother, I proudly realized I was getting older, stronger and wiser. I understood Boy's words for the first time. Or perhaps it was just that Man was not there and Boy was not as evil as Man. No matter the reason, I was learning to understand human words and what they meant. This was a point of pride for me, especially when I knew my sisters still could not do this.

I only wished the words were kinder and gentler when Boy spoke to my mother. "You need to eat that food, Bitch. You gonna need ya strength later and them's good scraps tonight. We done had us some po'k chops."

Mother sighed as she forced herself to stand. The gaining of wisdom was bringing a lot of understanding my way and much of it was not good. As Mother struggled to stand and get to her food, left in a pile in the dirt, for the first time I could feel the heavy weight of that chain around her neck. While there was no chain tethering me, I could feel my mother's pain and it was fierce. I felt her sad eyes looking at me and realized I had whimpered with my newfound knowledge. There was a sickness rising in my throat as I remembered eating so eagerly earlier. Even as she had gasped for breath after having the life almost choked from her, and as her heart ached fiercely for the pups taken from her, the first thought for her had been to care for my sisters and me. We had never thought twice about what we were taking and what she was giving.

Now I heard her bones creaking and realized the noise was there because there was bone rubbing against bone in her tired body. How long had she lived this way, in this shed, with her food thrown in the dirt as she struggled to feed puppies? I was learning Heart Speak and what I was hearing was almost too painful to bear. Yet I could hear her heart clearly telling me not to worry. Her eyes were sad as she looked at me, but there was that ever-present glow of love. I could feel her weakness and I willed her to go to the food and eat. For the first time I wanted her to nourish her body for her, and not for the milk it would provide me. And she knew. She could hear my thoughts as surely as I could feel her weariness.

She walked over and began to eat, but there was something yet unheard, that she was telling me. I was learning, but learning came with a price and I fought against it. The torture that came with this wisdom was coming too fast and I was not ready. Even when I knew she was trying so very hard to have me hear her, I fought against it. What her heart was saying to mine was not something I wanted to hear. And I knew she would not say it aloud. I knew my sisters were still too young. They had not matured as quickly as me. They were still totally innocent and she would have them stay that way as long as possible.

With that knowledge came another realization. This was why she had never spoken to us. This was why she had not sat and chatted with us as we prattled on and on. Because of a dog's instinct, even a very young puppy would recognize the sadness and pain in their mother's voice. But this other thing, this language that spoke without words from somewhere deep inside, touched something just as deep inside of me. I could almost hear it and a part of me longed to stop fighting it and listen.

I had understood Boy's crude language and it was nothing like this. This was special. This was a language that had been passed down since the beginning of time. My mother was speaking to me with her heart. I was wise enough now to know "Heart Speak." But as I could hear the pleading from her to hear what she was trying to tell me, I was fighting not to hear. I was fighting and wondering if I would ever be strong enough to shoulder the burden of understanding. But, in truth, I heard her every word. Those words were of pain and despair and blood… our blood and man's evil desire to see it.

It was just before dark when Man came for my mother. When he took her off the heavy chain and led her out the shed door I could hear her Heart Speak. "Take care of your sisters. You are stronger than they are. If I do not come back, take care of your sisters."

The hours that followed had to be the longest I will ever remember. Even when my own pain and torture began some time later, there was never another time such as that night. My sisters were afraid so I told them to stay close to me and I would watch out for them. I could feel them shivering in the dark. The smallest among us was whining and shaking uncontrollably. I put my nose across her face to give her comfort. The three of us huddled there together for a very long time. It was a position we would come to know well. But that night I kept hearing my mother's Heart Speak to me as she was taken away. I knew I could not tell my sisters what I had heard. Mother was right. They were still too innocent.

My sisters slept a little, fitfully, but I remained awake watching and listening for the sound of Heart Speak. None of us would lie down. Instead we leaned against each other sitting there huddled close. I realized the thing coming from my own heart was a prayer. I was praying to hear my mother's heart speaking to me again. But I could only hear the echo of her last request.

It was very late in the night when I heard Man's truck outside the shed. I could hear human voices and excited dogs that I had never met. I knew it was the dogs that had made my lost siblings scream and a shudder ran through me. I strained hard to hear and realized what I was listening for I would not be able to hear with my ears. So I stopped trying so hard and sat quietly, willing my mother to come back, but also willing her to hear my own heart speaking to her.

That is when I heard her, far away and ever so faintly. "I am here. I am alive. Do not be scared when you see me. Just make sure your sisters know that I love them as surely as you can feel the love I am sending to you."

My heart leapt. I heard my mother. I heard her Heart Speak. And I was not afraid. I was terrified. I could hear so much pain and torture. Yet there was that wonderful comfort of her love.

Finally the shed door opened. Man was carrying a cloth bag and I could smell the blood on it. He dragged it across the dirt floor and dumped it crudely at the pole where our mother's hateful chain was waiting. It took a moment for me to realize the lump that fell from the sack was my mother. My heart felt like stone and dropped to my paws. I thought she was dead. But then I saw, even in the darkness, her eyes looking at me, begging me not to make such a fuss for the sake of my sisters.

I tried hard not to cry and to be strong. I tried for her because her heart asked it of me. The one comfort that night was Man did not put the heavy, hateful chain on my mother's neck. It did not matter why at that point. It just mattered that she needed me and I would be there for her. I would not let her die. I did not know what had happened to her. Perhaps I did not want to know. But I knew I wanted her to live and I prayed openly and willfully, deliberately for the first time that the Great Creator of all Life would give me the strength to help make my mother well again.

My mother heard my thoughts. For the first time she spoke to me aloud. "You are a very wise and brave girl," she said to me. "I will call you Charity."

Chapter 3

The Longest Night

My sisters had fallen into an uneasy sleep earlier in the night. They had awaken and were excited, knowing Mother was back. They did not notice the smell of her blood and they could not see the terrible condition she was in. They only understood their empty bellies and saw my beautiful mother as their food source. It angered me and I growled as ferociously as a little puppy can growl. I stood between my sisters and my mother determined to guard her from their greed.

My sisters were confused. But, worse for me, I heard the disappointed sigh from my mother. I understood she wanted us close to her. She would give her last breath to know she had offered her children a small comfort. I was ashamed.

My sisters had stopped in their tracks when I growled at them. Now I did my best to bounce and act playful, pretending it had been a game the entire time. The three of us were soon nestled together close to our mother. There was no milk. I knew this even without trying to nurse. My sisters did not complain. They watched me as I began to lick my mother's wounds and they joined me in this quest. Perhaps they were wiser than I thought. Or perhaps the fact we had never had much made the hunger easier to bear on this terrible night. Their bodies were soon limp and resting, huddled together. For the first time I envied them. I wished I could be as innocent and sleep as deeply without worry.

Mother heard me. And for the first time I really listened when she spoke to me. Tonight had taught me a harsh lesson. As much as I might want it to be true, I could not change the ways of the world with my heart and mind. The horrible things would still happen even if I closed my eyes and did not look. I could not make the man and the boy good people. If they came for my mother again, she probably would not come back. Without Mother, my sisters would have only me to look out for them. So I listened and I heard. I was determined to learn.

She started with the name she had given me earlier. And I listened as she told me what the word charity meant. I must admit it warmed my heart to know she saw this in me. When she began to talk about Heart Speak, I understood this was something I had been born with, and I was proud my soul was pure enough to use it.

I do not know how long this wonderful talk between mother and daughter went on. I forgot that I was in the dingy, cold shed and that my belly was empty. My world seemed right and full for the briefest of moments as my mother's love for me flowed through her words and in to my heart and soul.

But just as those days of total contentment I spent in the womb had come to an abrupt end, my mother's mood changed as she nudged me closer to her and began to tell me things I did not want to know.

She must have heard my resistance. I do not think I sighed or pulled away, but she heard anyway. I could feel the air grow heavier as my sisters continued their slow steady breathing in a peaceful sleep of innocence. Once again I longed for that innocence. We were siblings, born in the same litter, and yet I was so much older. For the slightest of moments I resented that.

"Charity," the name coming from my sweet, injured mother made me stop all thoughts. Heart Speak was not something I could control apparently, and it did give a strange comfort that my mother could hear me. "You cannot resent what peace they have. That peace will not last long. Let them rest while they can."

I knew we could not go back now and what was coming would be hard to hear. But I also knew I had to listen more carefully to this part. This was what would help me to survive. If I listened really well, if I tried really hard, this is what would help me keep my sisters alive.

My mother told me how dogs are supposed to be man's best friend and how we are companions to those who care for us. She spoke of wonderful dreams she had when she was just a puppy and how she had once been a part of a beautiful family.

"Those days no one questioned Heart Speak. It just was," she said. "I had a child of my own to love and care for. I was so happy. There was no reason for me to understand the things I must tell you, Charity. Life was good and we all understood each other... human and dog alike. We were a family."

She told me how her days were filled with the love of her family and how wonderful her life had been. Her favorite of all was the apple-cheeked little boy that she saw as her charge. He would throw a ball for her to run and fetch. They would play for hours. I could feel her shiver slightly at the memory and knew she was back there in her mind, running through the field down to the creek for the "coldest, freshest drink of water that had ever touched her tongue."

"There are still good people in this world," she said. "People who are kind and caring. But as much as my family loved me and as much as I loved them, I had my place out in the barn at night while the family slept in the big house. Dad had grown up without a dog and his family had taught him that a dog's place is outside. He was a good and kind man, and he made sure my needs were met. But I was not allowed in the house except in a bad storm.

"As much as I hated not being able to play with my child during those storms, I absolutely loved the time I spent inside that old farm house."

For a moment I could see my mother as a young dog, running with that apple-cheeked boy. And I could see her settling in for the night in the barn, but not shut in like now. She could come and go as she pleased. There was food and clean water and she was a healthy dog. It was a nice memory to share with her and I wished I could have been born in that barn instead of in this shed. How could something so right go so very wrong? How did my mother end up in this terrible place?

"I was stolen," she said. "I know my family must have searched for me. They would have looked for a long time before giving up. They were fluent in Heart Speak and for the first few days after I was brought to this place I could hear them calling out to me. But their voices soon faded when Man took me and put me on this rack he has in the back of the other barn, the nicer barn where he does things that a dog should never have to know.

"I was brought here to have babies." My mother stated that very matter-of-factly and there was no emotion in her voice as she recounted the many litters she had given the man. The rack was something he used in the beginning because my mother would not "be still" and mate with the dog he had brought to her.

"But I loved and cherished every puppy," my mother said. I have loved all of my children and I have lost most of them to Man. She did not have to say more. She did not have to tell me how he would come and steal the "unchosen" puppies from her and how each loss took a huge piece of her soul. But I still could not understand the rest of it. What exactly did he want with the "chosen" puppies?

It was still very dark in the shed but my eyes had adjusted enough to see that my mother was staring away into a distant past. I could see the pain in her eyes as she remembered, and my heart ached for her. But I never expected what I was to hear next.

"There is such evil in this world, Charity and there is not an easy way to talk about it. Nothing will make it sound any better than it is. I learned that the hard way on that night so long ago. I do not think I did anything to deserve this. Once upon a time I tried to figure out what I was doing wrong so all this hurt could stop. But I no longer believe there is anything any of us can do to change things here. And I do not believe we are supposed to be here.

"The only thing I can do now is prepare you because I do not know what pain may await you. As much as I mourn the loss of my children that were thrown to the dogs, as cruel and horrible as that is, there are things much worse. This is the first time Boy has ever taken any of my children and I do not know what may be in store for you. I fear you and your sisters are condemned to a life like my own."

I did not completely understand exactly what she was talking about. Having babies was one thing, but there was something more that she was having a hard time telling me and I could sense her reluctance to go on.

"I am not a baby any longer," I said. "I am ready to hear all of it, Mother." We both knew that was not exactly true, but we also knew that the truth of it did not matter. We could both feel something was coming; something far worse than all that had gone before. I had to be ready whether I wanted to or not. I was the one that had eagerly embraced Heart Speak. I was the most mature of the three unchosen puppies left alive, so this was my responsibility.

"Can you see me, Charity?" my mother asked.

"I know you have been hurt," I answered. "And I have seen the scars from where you were hurt before. So even though it is very dark and I cannot see you exactly, I know you have cuts all over because I can feel and smell your blood."

"One of my sons did this to me tonight," her voice held a deep hurt that I had not expected. It took a moment for the words to sink in, but when they did, a white hot anger boiled inside my heart.

"Which one?" I demanded. "Which one did this to you, Mother?"

My voice must have held all the determination that I felt at the time. My brothers were all larger than me and healthier, but the hate in my heart right now would be enough for me to win the fight, if only she would tell me which one.

Mother sighed a deep sad moan and she did not need to say more. I understood how foolish I must have sounded and in that moment I realized I still had so much to learn. "It is one of my brothers from another litter," I stated, understanding at last. "And that is what the Man trained him to do. Man wanted him to hurt you so he did."

"Yes," a very simple answer that held a heart and soul full of hurt. "Man is a dog fighter. He breeds dogs and then trains them to fight. And there are people who bet on which dog will win. There is a lot of money to be made and Man loves money almost more than anything."

"But you must not hate your brother or any of the other dogs. Think what it must be like for them. They are treated only slightly better than we are. And they do what they must do to survive."

I found that a little hard to swallow remembering how the "chosen" pups greedily nursed while the rest of us waited. But if I was to understand, I could not get caught up in the hurt and hate that filled my young heart. I had to listen and I had to keep my emotions in check.

"When Man needs to train the dogs to fight, he needs a Bait Dog. The bait dog is helpless and cannot fight back. Man makes sure of that," my mother was explaining her role as best she could. It was hard to understand because it made no sense. Why would anyone want to watch dogs hurt each other?

As she explained things that still make no sense to me I came to understand what evil is. It was becoming harder and harder to hold on to that memory she had first given me of the apple-cheeked boy. Could there possibly be people that lived so differently? I was having a hard time understanding that there could be good people.

I thought about the scars on my mother's legs where she had been tied like a sacrificial lamb. Then she told me how some of the evil people would pull a dog's teeth or file them down so they could not fight back. And others would do things so very painful, but quicker. The man that we lived with liked to do things quickly. He had broken my mother's jaw when she had tried to fight back. She still had her teeth, but her bite was not so fierce with a broken jaw. Of course it had healed all wrong and I understood now why it sometimes looked like my mother's face was not even. That alone kept her from doing a lot of damage should she ever try and fight back again.

Then I felt the most incredible sadness when Mother continued, "The memory of pain often fades when you face pain every day. I knew there would be harsh repercussions if I fought back. It was the first time Man had turned one of my own children against me. I was younger then and I tried to reason with the son I had given life and nurtured. His eyes were so empty and cold, Charity. He was so very hungry and I knew he probably had not been fed for several days.

"When he came at me I dodged him easily and cried out for him to stop. But my son was no longer there. He was an empty shell fighting to be given a pat on the head and a morsel of food. I did the only thing I could think of at the time and I bit him. I thought the shock of it might bring his soul and life back to those terribly empty eyes. I did not do a lot of damage, but I did bring blood and it shocked him. He yelped as if I had ripped his heart out. I suppose he knew who I was after all; he was still in there, and that thought gave me reason for joy. Maybe he was not lost.

"I had no intention of doing more than bringing him back from that dark place I saw in his eyes. He kept yelping and cowered away from me, though. Man was there as quickly as he ever was and I heard the loud noise and saw my son fall to the ground before I realized what was happening. Man had shot him and now was in front of me. Before I could react I felt the blow to my head as he brought the butt of the gun up and down. My jaw was broken and I lost a few teeth.

I did not understand why Man didn't just kill me. In time it became clear that as long as I could give him the puppies he wanted, I would live. Some of the bait dogs are killed on site and never last through more than a few training sessions. But Man always used me for the better trained dogs, and my injuries have never killed me. He always stops them before they can hurt me that badly... or he always did.

"But things have changed. I have had too many puppies and am almost useless for that now. Tonight was bad, and I suspect one more night will be about it for me. If they take me out again, I do not believe I will come back."

I could not stop the tears then. I had listened to all the horrors my mother had lived through. I now understood when she said there are things worse than death. But I did not want her to die.

The long night was coming to an end and the light was just breaking through the dirty window. I could see the wounds that would probably never heal on my mother and I understood then beyond all doubt, she was dying already. It would not happen quickly. But without help she would not survive the wounds. I could see bone on her leg and on her head where a dog's teeth had ripped her flesh. Her eyes were almost closed and I realized how horrible it must have been for her as she fought to see through her own blood.

I knew my mother's mouth was dry and she needed water, so I urged her to move closer to the pail that held our dirty water. The Boy had filled it yesterday so there was enough. She was able to raise her body enough to reach the water and she drank until she could no longer support her own weight.

I worked as quickly and as gently as I could and I licked my mother's wounds. Even though she winced several times, I could tell she was pleased with me. I nudged dirty straw from the floor over her wounds to try and help cover them, knowing she did not want my sisters to see the full extent of her injuries. Clean straw would have been better, but we only had straw at all because my mother had given birth to a few chosen puppies. So this would have to do.

Once my mother was as comfortable as she could hope to be, my sisters began waking and I tried to be cheerful. It was going to be a hard life for all of us and they deserved what little happiness and joy they could find in their innocence. They would know soon enough what I had learned on this longest night.

The place we lived was called hell.

Chapter 4

The Loss of Innocence

My sisters were in a good mood and for a moment, I could feel the anger and resentment rising inside me. How was it so hard for them to see what our mother was going through? They nestled closely against her and complained that there was still no milk. They both began to whine their protest. Looking back, I wonder how I must have appeared to them, standing there almost in an attack position with my cheeks blowing in and out with anger.

Then I felt that gentle breeze tugging at my heart and heard my mother speaking to me. "Listen to them, Charity. Listen to what their hearts are saying."

It was hard for me to hear their hearts over the endless nagging. Finally I turned my back to them and listened hard to that voice that does not come from outside, but comes from somewhere deep within and for the first time I heard my sisters' pain.

The larger one was yowling a bit now, but I could tell she really believed the yowling would make a difference. She still had that hope in her heart that food would be provided and the world would be set right again. And for the first time I really knew her. She was playful and carefree. Her yowls were not so much from hunger, but from not understanding why someone did not fix this problem.

The smaller one has always tugged a bit at my heart, just as I know she did my mother's. She was whimpering, her voice never raising above a whisper. No one was going to hear her and come running to fulfill her needs, but there was an eternal faith in her heart when I turned and looked at her and saw her watching me.

Her almost silent cries made me wander over to the food pile from the day before. There was some moist bread left... quite a bit actually. Mother had not been able to finish her food before they had come for her.

The bread fell apart easily and did not taste as good as the milk from our mother, but there was enough to quiet their cries I hoped. I stood back and watched them as they sucked on the wet bread. My own stomach was growling and protesting at me for not joining them, but I did not think I would be able to swallow with the knowledge that had come to me in the night.

Once again I felt that gentle breeze stirring in my heart and I listened. "Those are wonderful names you have chosen for your sisters. It is my dream that one day you will be able to pass those names on to Good People. Tell them your names are Hope, Faith and Charity and do not respond to anything else. They will know because they will understand Heart Speak. You three will live. You will make it out of here. That is the only dream I have left."

I watched Hope and Faith as they finished eating, and I walked over to the spot and licked the crumbs from the dirty board where the food had been. It was not enough for any of us, but as long as we were in Hell, there would never be enough and I knew that. Then I felt the most terrible pain in my heart I had ever felt.

I looked at that spot where before there had been food, a feast for my sisters... and I realized we had just finished off my mother's food. It had not occurred to me she had left food there so she might have some for today. She was only fed about every other day so it made perfect sense that she had saved some. Oh how my heart hurt with this knowledge. In trying to help my sisters, I had hurt our mother.

It was a bleak moment in my life and I ran to my mother to tell her I was sorry. But she was in a deep, much needed sleep and I did not want to wake her. Instead, I swallowed my guilt, a bitter taste I would soon learn all too well, and I nestled close to her. I did not think I would sleep, but I did.

I was running through a very green meadow, the likes of which I had never seen except in visions through Heart Speak. My two sisters were running with me and my mother was playing just ahead.

The dream ended abruptly when the shed door opened and light flooded the dark place that was my home. I blinked against the brightness and saw that my mother was already trying to shield my sisters and me with her broken body.

I sniffed the air and knew it was Boy before my eyes adjusted to the light. He was carrying something in his hand. He stooped down near us and I could feel the hairs on my neck starting to stand, but he did not seem to know we were there. He was putting something in a pan he had brought with him and was adding a wonderful smelling liquid to it. I knew then he was bringing food. Was this a sign that he would be a kinder person than Man? I hoped so. But more, I hoped he would have enough kindness in his heart to help my mother.

He finished what he was doing and turned towards us holding the pan out to us. "Come on now," he said. "Come on and eat. The old hag there ain't got no more milk and if you don't eat you gonna die."

I didn't understand those words so much as feel the crudeness of them. I snuggled closer to my mother and hoped he would call out to her as well. She needed food or she would not make it through the day.

Hope walked toward the boy wagging her tail as fast as it would go. She smelled that wonderful odor too. I could hear the sound her mouth was making as it watered uncontrollably.

I looked around, trying to find Faith. She was not next to Hope where she always was. I realized then that she was behind me, cowering down. She did not trust Boy. Not even her hunger could make her move from behind me.

The boy took a deep breath and laughed. It was not a pleasant sound, but it was not the worst noise I had heard him make. "Look at that there tail going," he said, directing his comment at Hope. "I'm gonna call you Wiggles."

He watched satisfied as Hope lapped up the delicious liquid in the pan. After she had managed to get a little more than her share down she held her head up high and burped. That amused the boy even more than the wagging tail.

I could hear Man just outside calling to Boy. I closed my eyes and hoped he would leave before Man came in. "Coming," he yelled and was gone as quickly as he had come.

Before he closed the shed door and left us in the darkness we had come to know so well he whispered in our direction, "All ya'll better eat. Don't know when I can bring more."

Then we were alone again. Hope had gone to our mother and I knew she was looking at the horrible wounds, seeing them for the first time perhaps. I could feel tears flooding her eyes, hearing the sadness with my new found Heart Speak.

Faith was standing now too, but her eyes were on the pan of food. That wonderful smell was teasing her, calling her forward. I reached out to Hope with the language I had learned, testing, wondering if she could hear me. She did not. Instead the little girl that would normally bounce her way through any horror looked as if someone had just kicked her in the head.

She looked at me now, eyes glistening with tears, almost accusing, "What happened to Mother?" she asked.

Before I could answer Mother was moving toward her and telling her, "Hush now. I am fine."

There was that warm breeze stirring my soul again and I heard her say to me," There will be time for telling later. For now, go and eat while the food is here."

"I will not eat unless there is enough for you, too," I said.

"There is," Faith was smacking as she said it and she sounded happy. There is enough for all of us here. "And it is good."

Faith was right. The pan was filled with bread and milk. It was a lot more than the three of us could eat. I allowed myself to feel gratitude toward the Boy. Mother could eat and get strong. But would she? I had learned that my mother would give her life for us, and now, would she eat knowing that this might be all there was for a while? I barely had time to form the question in my mind when I realized she had crawled to the pan and was eating. It was the best sight I had ever seen, even in my dreams. I did not know how much extra time the food might give her, but I knew it would help her to live a little longer. And now, more than anything, I wanted Mother to live.

With full bellies we rested with our mother. It was the most contentment we would ever know in this place. And it was the last time I would have any peace here. For when I awoke again, I would gain a knowledge no dog should possess.

The light had moved when Boy returned. Once again the hair on the back of my neck rose. I knew he should not be back this quickly.

He reached in his pocket and pulled out sausages that he must have taken from the morning breakfast table. "I brung something for the bitch," he said.

He bent down and looked at her. "Old Girl, you ain't got a lot left in you. Don't think you gonna be here much after tonight. Here. Brought you something you gonna like." He dropped the sausages at her face as she laid motionless.

"You just gonna lay there? Come on and eat now." He almost sounded friendly.

Mother moved her head slightly so she could reach one of the sausages. I could hear her smacking as she ate, savoring the taste. Boy was satisfied and to my relief, walked away from her. He looked at the bowl my sisters had almost cleaned and then looked at me.

"Come on over here girl," his voice was almost pleasant, teasing. "I brung you a little something extra. You don't eat so good as the other two and I don't want you getting sick on me."

I stayed back watching him as he pulled something from his pocket. The smell was strong and it made my mouth water, but trust was not to be given so freely to one who did not understand Heart Speak.

"What's with you?" he asked. "I know you never eat so much and must be hungry. This here is hamburger and if my daddy knows I stole it he will whoop my ass" He bent down and picked up the empty pan. "Here now. This is for you." When he sat the bowl down my smallest sibling ran forward, eager for a taste of the best smelling food ever offered in this shed. Boy kicked her away, not hard; but, enough to startle her and make her yelp. Before I realized what I was doing, I grabbed his leg with my almost toothless puppy mouth. He laughed at my efforts and picked me up.

"You's a feisty one. I think I like you. I'm gonna call you Bully cause you is one." Boy held me by the scruff of my neck and walked to the shed door to peek out again. The bright light shocked me and caused me to squint.

He seemed to be satisfied that Man was not looking for him as he took me from the shed. Even if I could have fought against him, the shock of the fresh air and bright sunshine held me still. Soon we were walking into darkness again and I knew this was the other shed my mother had spoken of. The air here was fresher than in our shed; it was cleaner but still dark.

I tried hard to see what was happening, prepared for anything. Did Boy know I was too young to have puppies? Was he going to put me on that hateful rack my mother had told me about? Then he put me down onto a low stool and was rubbing my head gently. The soft touch confused me, but I liked it and my tail wagged despite my fear. He let me go for the briefest of moments and had I known what was coming, I may have tried to escape then. But I did not know so I stood there, wagging my tail hoping for a just a little tenderness from the spawn of Satan.

Boy turned me around facing away from him and held my neck until I thought it might break. But the pain from what he was doing behind me was what made me cry out. I could not see what was happening but my butt felt as if it was ripping apart as he pushed against me and made strange noises. It seemed to last an eternity before he finally picked me up and looked into my face.

"There, Bully," he said. "Yep. You is my favorite." And then he took me back to the dingy shed and dumped me next to my injured mother.

My siblings ran toward me, obviously happy I was back. My body ached from the assault I had suffered at the hands of Boy, and when they jumped on me playfully, I winced and yelped. They both stopped and looked at me, obviously shocked. I could hear my mother's soft crying as she licked my wounds. And I could hear her Heart Speak. "Charity, my sweet girl." Nothing more needed to be said. It was clear she knew what had happened to me. And I was now aware of one more indignity we would suffer at the hands of man.

My siblings looked hopeful as I held my nose up toward them. They looked so small now. How would I ever protect them from this new horror?

Mother was clearly upset that she had not been able to save me from this and I fought against the pain so her agony would not be so great. My sisters were starting to play again and the smallest looked at me almost proudly. "Mother has named me Faith," she said. "Do you know what that means?"

Before I could gather my strength to respond, my other sister chimed in, "And I am Hope. Isn't that a fine name?"

"They are just grand names," I said, not telling them I already knew because I had helped choose them. I no longer felt any envy for their innocence. I would spare them the total loss of it if I could.

Mother and I rested together, each injured and each longing to comfort the other. We watched Hope and Faith play and I drifted into a troubled sleep. I dreamt of a world I would probably never know. Faith and Hope were there and I wagged my tail as an apple-cheeked boy threw a ball for our mother to chase. The three of us ran ahead of her to the clear stream with the best tasting water that would never touch my tongue.

Chapter 5

Sergeant Stubby

That day seemed to stretch on forever. The pain in my backside was unbearable and every minute felt like an hour, with the hours stretching into a day. Had I known then what the night would bring I would have cherished every long, painful moment. And I would have certainly stayed awake. But my pain was very real and my intuition was not working at all. So I slept.

It was early afternoon when I felt Hope licking my face. I opened my eyes slowly, feeling the terrible pain that made me want to go back into that deep sleep with dreams of open fields and cool streams.

"Wake up Sleepy Head," she said. "Mother is feeling better and is talking to us. Can you believe it? She is talking a lot."

I blinked against the darkness straining to see. Mother was sitting up near the water pail that always seemed to have just enough dirty water to keep us from thirsting to death. Hope was right. There was a light in her eyes I had never seen before. Could it be my wishes and prayers had been answered while I slept? Had my own abuse and pain been enough to pay the torture gods for her redemption?

I stood slowly and tried to ignore my screaming hind quarters. The soft breeze I had come to know and love as my mother's heart speaking, reached inside my soul and made my pain seem very far away. I stood still and listened from that place deep inside myself. "Charity, go easy. Come and drink water and sit with me. It is time to teach Faith and Hope how to listen and speak as you do."

I licked my dry lips, the smacking sound it made exaggerated in this dank place. Then I moved slowly and deliberately toward my mother. As I got closer I could sense the pain that she was hiding beneath her love for her children. The water pail looked a little different. It was an old rusty thing and I could see now why there was never more than half a pail of water. Someone had come and given us fresh water... clean water, while I slept and it was leaking fast from a rusty hole about half way down. Soon the level would be back to that place where we had to stick our heads in to reach.

Faith spoke and shattered my thoughts. "Boy is better than Man I think. He came while you were sleeping and washed our water bucket. Look, Charity. We have clean water today."

"Yes," added Hope, with a faux wisdom. "I think Boy will be more to our liking than Man. He might even make a decent charge for us. Maybe we can go on walks with him and play in the grass."

I closed my eyes and tried not to shudder at the thought of Boy. He had obviously just left before I had awakened. At the rate that water was leaking from the pail, he must have been leaving the shed even as Hope licked my face to make me wake up. I made my way to the bucket and drank the coolest and cleanest water

I had ever had. It did give me new strength and for the briefest of moments, I forgot the pain and the horror.

Once again there was Hope with her new-found knowledge of the world, "Isn't it divine? Mother says water is the blood of life… or something like that. Didn't you, Mother?"

Mother smiled and repeated her honest words of wisdom that Hope had terribly distorted, "Clean water is cleansing to the soul… and can help to create life where there is none. Water is always necessary and keeps our blood pure."

"See," said Hope. "Water is the stuff that makes blood. We can't live without blood. The blood of life."

How could I argue with that?

Faith watched Hope dancing and prancing about and began to mimic her movements, prancing behind her.

For the briefest of moments they were free and it was a wonderful thing. I wanted to prance and be free too, but the truth would not allow it… not even for a moment. That soft wind stirred my soul and I heard Mother. "Yes you can, Charity. This one moment may be the only time you ever have to forget. It will surely be the only time I ever have to see you as a puppy with your sisters. Let it all go for me, Charity. Just for this one moment in time."

Her words hit my heart like a storm. I knew then she was dying. I did not know how long she might have, but I knew her life was slipping away and I would give her this one memory to carry with her. My pain was forgotten as I fell in behind Faith, prancing in time to an unseen drummer. As Hope said, it was divine.

But it was never meant to last.

I was keenly aware of the ache that would not go away in my backside. That is when I discovered I was great at hiding my pain. My sisters tugged at my ears trying to get me more involved in their games. I might have exposed the truth when Hope nipped my rump just above my tail, but the shed door opened.

I smelled him before I saw him. Man was there. My heart felt like a lump of stone, afraid because we had been caught in the act of being puppies. I did not know for sure, but did not think that was allowed in hell.

To my great relief he ignored us and went to the back of the shed where broken shelves still tried to hold up a few jars and cans. The three of us had almost unknowingly formed a barrier between him and our mother. She was trying to move and place herself in a position to protect us, but my sisters and I managed to stand our ground. I realized then that I had not given my sisters enough credit. They undoubtedly knew our mother was seriously wounded. And they cared every bit as much as I did. They were just better at being puppies... and they were still innocent for the most part.

Man grabbed one of the plastic jars that was just teetering there on the third shelf of five. He opened the lid and sniffed it. I did not understand why he had to stick it to his nose. I could smell the rank odor and I was across the room. I could also feel my mother's fear. And I heard that whispering wind. "Another night of hell."

When man took his stinky jar and left the shed, we still sat in front of Mother, but had turned to face her. We all knew there were things she had to say. My sisters were eager to hear. I was not. But I would listen still and I would learn from her all that she wanted to teach me. It was the most I could do now.

Yesterday I had thought I could protect her from any harm. But today I had learned evil was far too strong and I was voiceless and powerless against it. So I sat with my sisters and I listened. In my heart of hearts I knew most of the teaching was for me.

Once again I listened to the meaning of our names and the speech about Heart Speak. I felt great pride when Mother told my sisters that I had chosen those wonderful names for them... and the names were based on their actions and their strength. For the briefest of moments the old feelings of pride and envy began to surface and I wanted to shout the obvious to them... Mother had chosen *my* name. But as suddenly as the thought entered my head it was gone and I knew I was far beyond all that pettiness now. I could not afford to have those kinds of thoughts. I had to be strong and wise and insightful. I could not be a normal dog. I had to be better than normal or the three of us would never survive hell.

Mother talked for a very long time and I listened. My sisters now carried a weight that I would never again have to bear alone. The previous envy of their innocence was chased away and now I regretted they ever had to know the horror. I prayed this would be the worst of it for them. But there was still so much unsaid. I knew that part was for me only. It would be my job to lead and if I failed, we would all die here.

While it seemed the learning had gone on for days, a mere couple of hours had passed. My sisters went to our mother's side and laid their heads against her oft tortured body. Perhaps for the first time they noticed just how frail she was. The hurt in their eyes reminded me of the pain in my own heart when I had first noticed just how skinny my dear mother was.

I joined the huddle and we sat for a time, the three of us huddled together with Mother there protectively, just behind us. Soon Hope and Faith gave in to the sleep that puppies always need. They looked like normal puppies as they slept.

"They do look so innocent," Mother's voice broke the silence of the dark shed.

"Mother," I began, "We keep talking about innocence and the loss of it. I understand getting older and learning of evil. But if there are such wonderful people in this world, why are we treated so badly?"

The question had been on my mind since my mother told me about her first family. Why had they stopped looking for her?

Wouldn't family go to the ends of the earth for a loved one? I know I would never stop looking.

"Charity, I don't think they really ever stopped. It is just as time passes, they learned to live with my absence. There are evil men and women in the world; and, sometimes it seems as if the evil is all powerful, especially if you live here in this place. My deepest desire is that one day you will know another place, another life. Don't lose hope, Charity. If you lose hope, then you will never know the beauty that is in this world."

How could she speak of beauty and hope after the horrors she had suffered? I did not want to disappoint her, but I was not sure I could ever give my trust to a human being.

"Come and sit with me for a while," Mother said. "There is more I have to tell you, so much more."

Reluctantly, I went to her side. The whispering wind touched my heart and I allowed the peace it brought to flood my soul. I snuggled close to my mother. Anyone looking at us would have thought we were sleeping. They could never understand the conversation that was going on between us, the passing of information from mother to daughter. They could never know... unless they knew Heart Speak.

All the conversations before had been about her past, both the wonderful early days, and the way evil men mistreat animals. But this time she went further back and talked about men of the past and war.

I listened while she talked about good men who give their lives to defend others. She made me understand that peace is not free, a concept that might have confused me had my mother not been so good at explaining. She said all through time wars have been fought so that entire nations can live in peace. She talked about America, the place where we live... a place much larger than this little spot in hell that I knew so well.

I learned that men take great pride in setting boundaries and naming the places they have isolated. Mother spoke of towns and counties and states... and then entire nations. I interrupted her once to ask how she knew these things. She explained that her little charge had gone to school and she had paid attention when he would go over his studies at the end of the day. "But," she said, "Dogs have passed some stories down from generation to generation. Man has his history, and we have ours.

"You have to understand where we have been to know where we must go." And Mother began the story of Sergeant Stubby, a decorated War Hero.

"Time means so little when you are actually living," she began. "And Stubby had been measuring time from one meal to the next on the streets of a place called New Haven, Connecticut. Of course the name of the town meant little to Stubby, other than it was a place where there were a lot of people, and a lot of people meant food for him."

"Sometimes a kind stranger would toss him a bite. But more often than not, Stubby lived from garbage can to garbage can.

He had no permanent shelter to get out of the weather and would spend a lot of time each day searching for a place to spend the night. He was a very young dog, having lived barely two years. He had learned to use his senses to survive among a town of both friendly and unfriendly humans.

"One day he heard strange music coming from an area he had always shied away from. The music made him very curious and there were strange new smells. Stubby wandered on to a place called Yale University.

"A university is a very large school used to educate humans that are just becoming adults. But at this time, when Stubby found the campus, it was being used as a training ground for soldiers. These soldiers were part of a group known as the 102nd Regiment, 26th Infantry Unit. They were training to be deployed to France during a terrible time in history when all of the world was at war.

"Stubby watched from the shadows while they marched to strange music the likes he had never heard before. There was something called a bugle call and he watched the men stand in formation when that bugle would sound. Stubby watched and learned their movements. That is how he found his first real Heart Speak person.

"A young man named John Robert Conroy saw Stubby hiding in the shadows. When he asked Stubby if he was hungry, Stubby took the food the young man offered. Every day the young man would return to that spot and feed Stubby. Soon they were best friends and the former street dog was given his name. I believe it had something to do with his shortened tail that made the young man call him Stubby, but the name fit and Stubby was very proud to wear it.

"He no longer had to search from garbage can to garbage can. He stood proudly at John Robert's side. Stubby was a very good student and learned along with John Robert. He would join formation at the sound of the Bugle Call and would always march in time with the other soldiers.

"Soon everyone was watching Stubby and offering him food. He was called a very smart dog by the humans around him and Stubby felt loved for the first time in his life. But there was always something unspoken and the dog knew what it meant. He knew that the day was fast approaching when this group of soldiers would be leaving for the front lines of the war. He could sense the dread and fear coming from John Robert. The distress that this caused Stubby was greater even than his knowledge that when the group left, he would be back on the streets.

"Stubby and John Robert had a very special connection. The Heart Speak was there and they each knew the other's thoughts. John Robert promised Stubby he would find a way to protect him in his absence, someone to watch out for him. But Stubby had other plans.

"On the night before deployment, Stubby went to John Robert and spoke to him of companionship and forever. The man understood the dog and on the following day, Stubby was hidden safely away and smuggled on to the ship heading for the front lines and France.

"Of course it is hard to keep a dog hidden away for long, even on a very large war ship. Soon Stubby was discovered and the men loved him as much as ever. But one day the Commander saw Stubby and he was not so happy about this stow away being on his ship. John Robert knew that the dog he had come to love might well be thrown overboard if he did not think fast.

"'Present Arms'," he ordered in a great authoritative voice. Stubby stood very stiff and saluted the commander just as his human friends would do.

"The commander was so taken with Stubby that he was allowed to stay on the ship and went forward with his friends. Stubby had a place he belonged at last. And he was determined not to disappoint any of his new friends. He especially wanted to make John Robert happy.

"In the month known as February of the year 1918, the 102nd was engaged in a great battle just north of a place called Soissons. They had been under heavy, non-stop artillery and sniper fire for almost a month. Stubby could be heard barking and howling his rage throughout the battle, always watching out for John Robert and alerting him to the dangerous snipers that would end his life if they could. Stubby soon became known as their mascot, a title he was very proud of... for this was the first title he had earned. It would not be the last.

"Near the end of the battle, Stubby was poisoned by the enemy with a lethal gas. He had inhaled enough mustard gas to kill him, but Stubby was a lot stronger than anyone knew. He survived the poisoning and became even stronger. Now he had a newfound talent. Stubby could sniff out the canisters of mustard gas before the fumes became toxic.

"When the enemy would drop the deadly gas, Stubby would run among his comrades and warn them to don their gas masks. Then Stubby would find a safe place to hide away from the toxic fumes.

"Stubby's acute hearing also allowed him to warn the troops of impending artillery fire before the shells exploded. The German's were no match for his remarkable senses, because Stubby learned the unique smell of German soldiers. He would alert his friends of German ground attacks before they actually began.

"His sense of smell served his comrades well when they had been injured by the enemy as well. Stubby would run through the field of battle and locate fallen Americans, still alive but wounded. He would lead those who could walk to safety. If a soldier could not walk, Stubby would stand his ground and bark until help came for the wounded soldier.

"In the month of April of 1918, Stubby was wounded in battle by a German hand grenade. Many thought this would be the end for the brave dog who had worked so hard to protect his friends. But emergency surgery saved his life and Stubby worked very hard in the hospital to amuse the injured men.

"Stubby healed and returned to the front line and his favorite companion, John Robert. He was there for the battle that would liberate a place called Chateau Thierry and the women of the town were so taken with him, they made him a wonderful blanket. But Stubby's favorite attire was his military jacket that held his many medals. Those medals included a Purple Heart, the Republic of France Grande War Medal, the Medal of Verdun, and medals for every campaign in which he had proudly served.

"While there were many notable moments in Stubby's military career, and he had cheated death twice, there is one event that stands out. Stubby, of course, knew Heart Speak and had taught the age-old language to many of his comrades. It is not a language learned as man learns, but a language of the heart. Many of his comrades were worthy of the language after they acquired the knowledge that dogs and man can work together. But they also taught Stubby many things because he was a willing pupil.

"Stubby soon learned the different languages of men and knew the American English language well. On the rare occasions when Stubby's sense of smell would fail, he would listen for the language differences. The knowledge served him well in the month of September of 1918.

"It was during the Meuse-Argonne Campaign while serving in the Argonne Forest that Stubby discovered the camouflaged German spy. He was mapping out the Allied trenches, a feat that would have caused the death of many Americans. Stubby sniffed him out, easily detecting the smell of a German Soldier. But the dog hesitated, wanting to make sure. When the German spy tried to shoo him away, speaking in his native German tongue, Stubby knew and barked the alarm.

"Stubby began to bark and howl for his comrades to come and arrest the spy. The German soldier tried to chase Stubby away to no avail, and finally decided to make a run for it. The soldier was running very fast and might have escaped, but Stubby launched himself like a rocket, biting into the flesh of the German soldier's calf. The spy fell face-down to the ground and Stubby once more sounded the alarm. The man tried to crawl away, but Stubby was not about to allow him to escape and carry vital information back to the enemy lines.

"Choosing his mark carefully, Stubby bit down into the German soldier's fleshy backside and held on. He stood there, refusing to let go until his own comrades came to arrest the spy. Perhaps that was the first time they had ever truly witnessed the tenacity of a Pit Bull when he chooses his mark. The story spread like wild fire of the dog who had captured the spy.

"Stubby was promoted to the rank of Sergeant for his heroics and now outranked his human, Corporal John Robert Conroy. However, this did nothing to deter their friendship and at the end of the war they went home together... dog and man. Stubby became an instant celebrity back on home soil as the stories of his heroics spread.

"No one knew Stubby's birthday. They assumed he was born sometime in the year 1916 or 1917. On April 4th, 1926 Stubby left this earth for a place called Rainbow Bridge. He was a hero to man and dog alike."

When Mother finished her story we sat in silence for a moment. My mother's pride in Sergeant Stubby was very evident to me. There were so many questions in my head, but three were most important, so I asked in one breath, "What is a Pit Bull... and where is this place called Rainbow Bridge? Can we meet Sergeant Stubby?"

Mother had that faraway look in her eyes again, and there was a gentleness in her voice when she answered, "Rainbow Bridge is the place dogs go when they leave their bodies and this earth behind. You will meet Sergeant Stubby. We will all meet him one day. But it will not happen until our time on this earth is passed."

I do not know how I understood then, but I did. This place we lived was hell, and Rainbow Bridge was a dog's Paradise. I knew the faraway look my mother sometimes had was taking her to that Paradise where her fallen children played at the feet of Sergeant Stubby.

She looked down at me with the greatest wisdom I had ever seen in her eyes. "As for your other question: 'What is a Pit Bull?' well, that is what you are, Charity. You were born an American Pit Bull Terrier. With that title comes great loyalty and responsibility. But, sadly, there is a darker side. That title also brings a great hatred with it. That hatred is what keeps us here in hell."

"But why?" I asked. "Why would that make people hate us when Sergeant Stubby was such a hero to man and dog alike?"

"Because of the evil that men do," my mother answered. "Evil men train our kind to fight and to be aggressive. The dogs do what they are trained, always loyal to their human, just as Sergeant Stubby put his own life on the line for John Robert."

She did not have to say more. I understood now. Too many men see us as guilty of a crime that evil men perpetuate. It would take a lot of Heart Speak to dispel the erroneous myths. I understood why Sergeant Stubby's story was so important to us now. It would take heroes... human and dog together. And the first step after escaping hell would be to find a Heart Speak person that might understand and help. My mission was clear.

Chapter 6

The End of the Longest Day

Telling the story of Sergeant Stubby had been important to my mother. It had also used up most of her energy. She was still very weak, and my own backside, largely forgotten while I was engrossed in the story, was screaming again. I looked at Hope and Faith still sleeping soundly and again thought how easy it had been for them to fall into a puppy sleep. I would never again be able to do that, not with the evil I had lived that morning. My mother knew my thoughts and nudged me very close to her body, just as she had done on my first day outside the womb. It was comforting.

Had I known what was coming next, I would have fought with all I had to stay awake. But I did not know and I snuggled close to her body, soaking up the love from her. As I drifted off to sleep she finished what was begun and told me again of the evil we faced in this place. She wept when she told me she had not known Boy would rape me. She had hoped that was one thing I would be able to escape.

I asked her if Boy had hurt her and she responded with a simple "Like father, like son," and I understood. Just before sleep took me back to blue skies and green meadows with clear creeks, she whispered, "Never forget, Charity. Never forget to remember the hell you have come from and the place you must go."

I snuggled closer, willing the peace of sleep to take me away for a brief time. I know now I was still very naïve on that afternoon. Perhaps I was still every bit as young as my sisters. Had I been wiser I would have known the truth. I would have known my mother was leaving me, and I would have cherished every moment of the time left with her.

My awakening was harsh. Hope and Faith were biting at my ears, willing me to get up and help. I fought against the pain that was waiting for me. Then I realized that Man was in the shed. He was there and he was stuffing our mother into that sack he had brought her home in the night before. I could see her legs were tied together and she was not fighting him. The smell of liquor on his breath told me why he was having such a hard time. My mother had already given up. I could see the look in her glazed eyes that said she had gone to that place inside herself.

"He kicked her really hard," I could hear Faith saying. It was a statement of fact, but the tone held a challenge for me to do something to stop this evil that was taking our mother away. I stood to run forward. I would charge him and bite him. I would hold on to his backside just like Sergeant Stubby had done to the German spy on the battlefield. I would save our mother. The fact I could not reach his backside never entered my mind. Neither did the fact what few teeth I had were just barely coming in. Worse, what should have been a nice restorative sleep had allowed stiffness to set into all my sore spots and I could barely move. Standing had taken all the strength I could muster and my paws would not go forward now. It was all I could do to stay on all fours, let alone charge a grown man.

Still, I might not have given up so easily had I not felt that whispering wind stirring my soul. It clutched my heart and brought tears to my eyes as I stood motionless. Man had succeeded in stuffing Mother into the bag and was dragging her across the shed, but I heard her clearly. She may have gone somewhere far away from the torture and abuse in her mind, but her heart was still speaking to me.

"Stay," her heart cried out. "If you follow Man he will kill you here in this dark shed in front of your sisters. Stay, my sweet girl. Live for me, Charity. Stay alive for me, for your sisters, and for yourself. You have work to do.

"Never forget to remember, Charity. Never forget."

As the shed door closed behind Man I could hear Hope and Faith crying. I managed to get close to them and we huddled together for a time. They never questioned why I had not charged forward and tried to help our mother. My own guilt would cause me to play the scene out over and over throughout the night that was to come. But Faith and Hope knew what I did not. They understood I was just like them. Even though I tried to be grown and often thought I was wiser and stronger, I was still a puppy just like them.

They did not know what I had already lived through. They did not know I would never be so innocent again. But the truth was simple. I was too small and too insignificant to fight Man. My guilt at being so small would almost finish us. Almost. But I would not forget to remember.

"She will come back," said Hope. "It will be like last night and when we go to sleep they will bring her back. She will be hurt, maybe even hurt really bad, but she will come back."

I do not think even Hope believed what she was saying. Still, the three of us tried to sleep, hoping her words were true and our mother would be there when we opened our eyes.

Just as the night before I could not sleep. I had slept most of the day away when I had not been talking to mother and now all I could do was imagine her somewhere with my older brothers attacking her. She would be very still, far away somewhere inside her own head. But I felt the pain for her on this night. I felt the indignation and shame knowing she was somewhere out there lying in her own waste, blood filling her eyes like the tears that filled my eyes. I could hear the cheering crowd she had told me about, wanting to see more blood, more gore. Man was there smiling, gathering money from the crowd.

I was helpless here in this dark place I knew as hell. I was wishing and hoping to see my mother again.

Hope and Faith awoke from their own fitful sleep when we heard Man's truck pull into the yard. We heard the dogs that always seemed to have so much more energy than we ever would. Tonight they sounded exceptionally vicious and strong.

And we waited.

The shed door did not open. There was no man dragging a bloody sack across the floor to dump our mother at the pole she had been chained to for so long. There was no mother to offer comfort on this terrible night.

Once, just for the briefest of moments, I thought I could feel that whispering wind stirring my soul. I sat erect and waited, listening, hoping, and willing it to be so.

I do not know how long I sat there waiting. Just as dawn broke and the dirty window allowed its dim light to filter through, Faith and Hope came to my side and we sat huddled together. I felt that peace that had soothed me over the past day. And I heard once more:

"Charity, never forget to remember."

Chapter 7

Training Day

The hours passed slowly as Faith, Hope and I sat huddled together. Faith's head was dropped down, her position telling how incredibly sad her heart was. I sat as close to her as I could with my nose resting across hers. Hope sat just behind us. She was only slightly taller than Faith and me and her head was resting against mine.

None of us spoke, and we did not sleep. We just sat there, each with her own thoughts of hell and pain. How I longed to protect the two of them from the ugly that lived in this place. They had seen too much of it already. I could feel the terrible pain now that my mother must have lived with every day of her life. I struggled to understand how I could keep my sisters safe when my own body had been violated to the point I could barely move.

Boy opened the shed door and entered our world. We huddled closer and I moved slightly, placing myself between the demon spawn and my siblings. Hope had said he was kinder than Man. I knew better. He was younger, not as strong. But he had learned from his father and I had managed to torture me without a second's thought. I could smell his evil.

My only hope now was to keep him away from my sisters. They did not need to know what he had done to me, and I did not want them to experience it first-hand. Of course, I did not want them to feel that pain; but, I was deeply ashamed and did not want them to know. Looking back, it is easy to say it was not my fault. I know now it was not my shame; it was Boy's. But it wasn't that simple at the time.

He was carrying the pail he had brought in the day before and once again took out a jug of milk. He put three pieces of bread in the pan and covered them with the white liquid. There was not as much as there had been the day before and I felt a stab in my heart, understanding why.

"Ya'll come on over here and eat," he said. He was talking to all of us, but his eyes were on me. I fought against the shame when his eyes looked at me. I thought about Mother telling me it was not my fault. If I could hold on to her words, the memory of that wonderful whispering wind deep inside of me, maybe I would be able to get through this.

The smell from the pan would have been tantalizing on any other day. But today, this first day without Mother, it was not appealing. None of us moved to eat.

Boy walked toward us and I was ashamed of the way I cowered as he approached. My fear seemed to amuse him and he took his foot and easily knocked me over. Faith stayed very still, her nose almost touching the floor of the shed. Hope moved to help me and I cried out to her from that place inside of me. "Stop, Hope. He will only get angry and hurt us both."

To my great relief, Hope heard me. She stopped and tilted her head slightly, listening to hear more. I did not want her to think she had imagined it so I said again, "Stop, Hope. Stay still. Leave this to me."

Boy put his hand against the side of my neck and held me in place. I realized he was examining me, checking his handy work from the day before.

"You gonna be ok, Bully," he said. "You gonna be just fine."

He backed away and looked over his shoulder at the open door nervously. I knew he was looking to see if his father was coming. "Listen up," he said. "I ain't gone be able to slip food out here every day. Daddy says ya'll got to get cut back now that you getting older. When I bring food you need to eat it so I don't get caught stealing."

I hated the way he spoke to us, the way he shared his secret with us as if we were his best friends.

Faith still sat with her nose to the floor. Hope tilted her head again, as if waiting to hear something more. I remembered the feel of that whispering wind across my soul and understood. Boy did not. He thought the look was for him and he moved toward her. I had not moved from the place he had left me, but now I rolled over to put myself between the boy and Hope.

He stopped and laughed. It was the same sick, sinister laugh he had used the day before in that other shed. "You jealous there, Bully? Mighty sorry, but ain't got time for shenanigans today."

Then he turned to leave the shed, looking back once. "Ya'll eat that food now, ya hear me?"

Once the shed door closed behind him I let out a long breath that I realized I had been holding. Hope had moved over to Faith and was talking to her softly. Faith lifted her head and looked at Hope, then moved her eyes to me. "Mother is gone forever, isn't she?"

I walked slowly to stand with my sisters and we once more huddled together. "She will always live within us, Faith. She is in our hearts."

Even though I longed to see my mother, I knew what I had said was true. I could still feel her there, willing us to survive and trying to guide me to do the right thing. Sometimes, when I was not thinking about the pain of missing her or the pain in my aching backside, I thought I could still hear her Heart Speak deep in my soul. I prayed that would never go away. It was my one comfort now.

Thinking of her made me realize there was food available for us and if we were to survive, we would need to eat. I spoke as sternly as I could and told my sisters they had to eat. They did not argue with me, and moved to the pan. The three of us nourished our bodies with the food. It was the same meal that had tasted so good the day before, but today it was bland, tasteless. We ate without joy and our bellies seemed full long before the meager amount was gone.

I was looking over the left-overs wondering how and where to hide them for later when I felt something so familiar it brought tears to my eyes. I stopped and stood very still as that whispering wind filled me. "You have to go on, Charity. You have to eat and you have to encourage your sisters to eat every chance you have. The food will be even scarcer now. Let the food nourish your bodies. And you must find a way to nourish your hearts and souls."

I felt weak and had to lie down for a moment. I knew Mother was gone, but I also knew she was still guiding me. Somehow she had found a way to reach out when I needed her. I looked at the food that was left in the pan and told my sisters we needed to finish it. Faith ignored me and went to lie down by herself. Hope looked at me pitifully and moved to the pan. She used her nose to cover the remaining food with the dirty straw.

"We will eat it later, Charity. Later today when we feel a little better, ok?"

I hoped I was not disappointing my mother when I agreed, "Later today we will need it more."

We rested then. Faith snuggled very close to me as she had always done with Mother. Hope rested her head across Faith's body protectively. Hope and I understood. We were having a hard time dealing with the loss of our mother. But Faith was having the hardest time of all.

It had been a very long night, and even though the food had been tasteless, it had satisfied a hunger I did not know was there. Finally I slept. I dreamt of mother. Her presence in my dreams gave me a much needed reprieve from the emptiness that had settled over my heart since they had taken her away.

In my dreams she was young and spirited. She ran through open fields with a litter of black and white puppies behind her. Sergeant Stubby was there watching over them protectively. It was a beautiful place and a wonderful dream. When I woke up I felt refreshed and was satisfied my mother had made it to a place called Rainbow Bridge. One day I would join her. But for now, I had work to do.

Faith and Hope were already awake and were playing tug with an old piece of rope they had found in the corner. I left them to it, shuddering a bit at the thought of what that rope might have been used for. I walked over to the food pan and made sure it was adequately covered. While none of us would ever be the same carefree puppies again, there was a normalcy settling over the shed and I knew we would go on.

Hope saw that I was awake and came to stand in front of me. "Faith said Mother is okay," she said, her tone a bit defiant, daring me to challenge the truth of it. "She said while you and I were asleep she heard voices in the yard. There was a stranger talking to Man and Boy. She heard Man say Mother was to be taken away."

I did not challenge the statement. I knew either Faith had been dreaming, or she had heard Man talking about getting rid of our mother's body. That thought cut deep into my heart. I did not want Hope or Faith to feel that cold stab. If it brought them comfort, then I would let them have that peace. It had brought a shine to my sisters' eyes that might just help them get through whatever we had to face here.

"Do you think it's true?" Hope asked, obviously wanting me to assure her.

I chose my words carefully, not wanting to bring stress back to those eyes that now looked to me for guidance. "It could be true," I said. "It just could be." I thought of my own dream and knew Mother was safe now, away from all harm. Hope and Faith could not possibly understand Rainbow Bridge, not yet.

"She could be in a beautiful place now," I added, wishing I did not sound so old. I did not want to be the grown-up. I wanted to be able to believe as easily as they did. There was no jealousy in the thought, just a deep sense of loss.

Hope bounced around like she always had, happy that I had confirmed our mother might be safe somewhere. "She is probably in an absolutely grand place," she said. "Come on and play with us, Charity. Let's tumble."

My backside was screaming again and I knew I would not be able to tumble with my sister. Before I could think of an excuse, the shed door opened. Boy stood there blocking out the sun, looking much larger than he actually was. The three of us quickly huddled together. Once again I heard that sick, twisted laughter that filled my heart with dread. I believe that was when I first realized he liked us being afraid of him.

"Daddy said ya'll need to help us train today." He stated. My sisters did not understand and stood motionless. I understood perfectly and moved to cover my siblings, much as our mother would have done had she been there.

Once again I was reminded how small I actually was when he reached down and picked me up effortlessly by the scruff of my neck. I realized he had also picked Hope up with his other hand. Faith was flat on her belly, crawling as fast as she could for the shadows. I said a silent prayer that she would make herself invisible and was very grateful Boy did not have three hands.

He carried Hope and me out into the bright sunshine and a terror gripped me like I had never known before. He was not heading for the other shed as I had feared. He was heading for a very large dog on a chain and I remembered by mother telling me there were things much worse than death. Was that the dog that had hurt my mother? Was Boy going to throw us down in front of him and demand him to attack? I realized I had wet myself about the same time I saw he had bypassed the large dog and was heading for a smaller pen that held our "chosen" siblings.

He opened a cage door that was just outside the pen and put both of us inside, closing it and locking it behind us. I heard Man then. "Where's the other one, Boy? Can't you tote three puppies at one time?"

My heart stopped beating for a moment. Boy was going to go back for Faith and she was all alone there in the shed. I did not want her here for whatever hell Hope and I were going to face, but I was also worried about what Boy might do to her before he brought her out.

Man spoke again, "Leave her, Boy. We will make do with these two for now. Gotta get started while Gertie's gone."

I had no idea what a Gertie was or where it might be. But I was glad for Faith. Now I had to concentrate on Hope and keeping her safe. Our chosen siblings were staring at us curiously, their own bodies much stronger than ours. For the first time I realized there were four. There were three girls and one boy. One of the girls looked so much like our mother it made my heart ache, but I knew I had to get passed that when Man lifted the cage we were in and set it down inside the pen.

He stood and watched as the four sniffed the cage. Then he snarled at Boy, "What ya standing there for? Get the bitches back. Do I got to tell you everything?"

Boy jumped as if startled. "Sorry, Daddy. Didn't knowed you was ready." Then he quickly grabbed the three girls, taking a moment to show Man he *could* carry three at once. He moved them to the other side of the pen where another cage was waiting. He put them in and closed the door behind them.

When he came back, he opened the door to our cage and stepped back. "Stay in this cage," I told Hope. "Whatever happens, you stay inside this cage."

Hope's eyes were very large and I knew she was terrified. She backed into a corner and was trying to make herself very small. I stepped out in front of her, willing to sacrifice myself for my sister if need be.

"Get her!" Man snapped at my brother. "Get her, Killer."

Killer put his head down and his ears back, snarling at me, warning me. I locked eyes with him and refused to look away. If I submitted, Hope would be fair game. I mimicked him with my own stance, forgetting the aching pain that was coming from the abuse I had suffered.

"Look Daddy!" Boy was very excited and actually sounded happy. "Daddy I got me a prize fighter I think. I knowed she was special. I just knowed it."

"You're making me look bad," I heard my brother snarl at me. "If I take you down I will get a good meal. Stand still. I won't hurt you."

"Are you crazy?" I snarled back. "Man is not going to stop until he sees blood. I am not happy about that. But if he has to see blood, I would just as soon it be yours."

My brother laughed at me then. "Never happen," he said. "You are just making it harder on yourself." Then he lunged at me. He was very angry and his fury made it easy for me to dodge him effortlessly. I just moved over and he was tumbling in the dirt.

He recovered quickly and before I knew he had turned around, he was on me, holding on to my neck. His teeth were not fully developed and the bite was without merit. I stood very still, knowing he could still do damage if he started to shake his head.

Boy understood this too and yelled out, "Stop him, Daddy. Don't let him hurt my dawg."

As grateful as I was for the reprieve, I hated the sound of Boy's voice. I was not sure what I was most afraid of at that moment.

Man grumbled a little but then yelled, "Let her go. You stop now."

Killer was not ready to let me go and started to shake his head. I could feel my flesh starting to tear. Then there was the shock of Killer being kicked away from me. Boy had delivered a boot to the side of his head that made him break his hold.

Man was not happy and I heard the command again, "Get her, Killer!"

Boy had stepped away and I braced myself for the attack. To my horror I realized Killer had turned his attention to the cage where Hope was hiding.

I lunged at his backside as he ran toward the cage, grabbing a mouth full of his rump. I worried only briefly about Man and the gun my mother had told me about. I might get my jaw broken or the few teeth I had pulled, but Killer would not have Hope without a fight. I locked on to his butt and held tight remembering Sergeant Stubby.

I heard Killer yelp as I shook my head, fighting to get a better hold and keep him away from Hope. I knew his yelp had been from surprise. My teeth were sharp, but not very strong. Then I heard Boy and Man laughing. "I think you may have you a prize fighter there, son. You may just at that."

There was no gunshot that would kill my brother and no one was going to break my jaw or pull my teeth. It took a minute for me to understand this was just a trial run. Killer would get bigger and stronger. He would get better. One day there would not be anyone to kick him off of me, or Hope, or even Faith.

When Hope and I were taken back to the shed, Hope began to lick the wound on my neck. "I think you saved my life," she said. She stopped licking for a second and strained to see my neck. "It's okay, I think. I don't see blood." Then she repeated, "You just saved my life."

"Not this time, Hope," I replied. "This time was just so they could see what our brother's instincts are like. Man did not intend for anyone to get hurt. Not this time."

"Well," said Hope. "His 'in-stinks' and his 'out-stinks' and you still saved my life."

Faith, still very much afraid, crawled over to us and examined my neck. "Was it just awful?" she asked.

Hope's eyes were shining brightly. "Nope. Not awful. Charity bruised his butt good. Our sister is a prize fighter. Boy said so."

Then the sobs came. Dogs do not often lose control that way and I do not know how long I had been holding them in; but, they were free now and my body almost convulsed as I cried uncontrollably. I cried for the times my mother had suffered at the jaws of her own children. I cried for the lost siblings, thrown to the larger dogs like the big one out in the yard on the chain. I cried for the champion fighters, finally understanding they had no more choice than we did. I cried for Killer and the three sisters I would never really know, that would live a life like my mother. I cried the longest for us... for the loss of Mother and for Faith, Hope and me. But I cried the hardest for the lost little puppy I should have been.

Chapter 8

The Land of Nothing

When the sobs finally subsided, I was very weak. Sleep was already threatening to overtake me when I felt Hope and Faith snuggle next to me comfortingly. I do not remember dreaming. I just remember the blissful peace of nothing.

When I finally woke up it was late in the afternoon of the first day without Mother. Hope and Faith were not tumbling and playing like they usually did. Instead, they were sitting quietly together, watching me sleep. For a brief moment I forgot the events of last night and the morning. I did not remember the sobs that had wracked my body uncontrollably. I was still sore, but there was also a freshness I experienced... a new feeling. I struggled to awake from the peace of nothing and with one blink wished I could go back into that bliss. The memories were there, breaking my heart all over again.

I did not have time to adjust to being awake before the shed door opened and Boy stood in front of me, blocking the afternoon sun. I had barely realized he was there when he lifted me by the scruff of my neck.

"Bully," he said. "You done me proud."

I could hear Faith and Hope crying out for him to put me down and leave us alone. They did not yet understand Boy didn't have a clue what they wanted. Many people can understand a dog's signals and there are Heart Speak people in the world who always understand. But Boy was not aware of what our signals meant, nor did he care. As for Heart Speak, well... the person must first have a heart and soul. I was not sure Boy had either.

Boy was out the shed door and closing it behind him before I even realized we had moved. He did not speak that I recall now. What I do remember is the terrible pain from the awful thing he did in the other shed. When he returned me to the shed with Hope and Faith I was sore and bleeding from my backside. I could not move and this pain was too great to let me fall back asleep. This was the kind of intense pain that would make me cry out from my dreams.

I thought of Mother and the way she would pull us to her in her agony. Then Hope and Faith were there, snuggling, licking and nurturing me. I could not speak to tell them that is exactly what I needed. Somehow they just knew. That was the first time I realized their instincts were every bit as strong as my own. They just had to learn to use them. And that was the first time I actually disappeared.

I went deep inside my head to a place where the pain stopped and there was absolutely nothing. I was not asleep and I knew the world was continuing to move on around me. But I was not a part of it. I was in a place that would allow me to live with whatever Man and Boy wanted to throw at me. I could get lost in this place if I chose. I did not have to return to hell.

It was sometime well into the night when I returned from the Land of Nothing. Hope and Faith had fallen into a very light sleep and as soon as I moved, they both sat erect.

"Where were you?" Hope asked. "We thought you were dead."

Before I could answer Faith chimed in, her voice full of the tears she had cried throughout the night. "It was like Mother when Man took her away that time and then brought her back. You were like her when she thought we were asleep and was hurting so much."

My butt was still throbbing unmercifully. However, Faith's words delivered a stab to my heart that brought with it such a guilty pang, the ache in my backside was all but forgotten. How many times had I envied my sisters their innocence? With that one statement, I realized they had always lived in the same hell as me. Maybe their instincts had not been as sharp. They had not given in to the terrible darkness that had overtaken me on more than one occasion. They had simply went on being puppies, even with the knowledge that all was not right with our world.

Before I could respond to my sisters, Faith's voice changed and was now pleading, "Charity, please don't let them take you away from us like they did Mother. Please, Charity, please. Say you will never leave us here alone."

Hope, always the one to try and make the best of any situation spoke up, "Charity will never leave us, Faith. She just won't do it. One day we will walk out of here together and we will go and see Mother. I think she is at that farm now where she grew up. I bet she is telling that boy of hers all about us so he can come here and take us away to that better place."

I knew Hope did not believe one word of what she was saying. She was giving herself solace, much like the Land of Nothing gave me. I could still hear that thing just underneath the wishing that had always threatened to overtake us. It was more than fear. It was a deep sadness. If it ever escaped and covered us, we would not survive it.

I called them to come and sit very close. Mother had told me the story of Sergeant Stubby while they slept. This seemed like a good time for me to share it with them. They sat and listened eagerly, proudly while I made sure to explain about different breeds of dogs and the American Pit Bull Terrier.

I ended the story with Sergeant Stubby coming home a hero and living with his Heart Speak companion until he was ready to leave for Rainbow Bridge. I sat back exhausted while Hope and Faith took turns pretending to be Sergeant Stubby. Faith would march up and down in time to unheard music. Hope was a bit more zealous and crouched on the floor pretending to attack German soldiers before they could get close to her unseen troops.

Their game went on for some time before Hope launched herself at Faith's backside. She did not bite her, but she did pinch and Faith let out an indignant yelp. Hope ran to Faith making sure she was not hurt. "Oh dear," she said. "Wounded in battle. You have now earned the Purple Heart just like Sergeant Stubby."

Faith's mouth opened in a very wide grin. "It's not my heart that's purple… or *yours!*" And Faith launched herself at Hope who tumbled about on the floor as if she were under heavy artillery fire. It was good to see them playing and I watched and waited for the question I knew was sure to come.

It was Hope who finally stopped, stood up and looked at me as if she had just remembered something. "Charity," she began, "just where is Rainbow Bridge?"

"Rainbow Bridge is Paradise," I stated. "It is the most wonderful place. Everyone there understands Heart Speak because anyone who does not is turned away. It holds every color in the rainbow and there are a lot of streams and rivers flowing with that wonderful water Mother told us about."

"Does it have food, too?" Faith asked.

"Yes," I answered. "There is always food so no one is ever hungry there. And the food is served in clean bowls. It is the most beautiful place you can imagine. And all animals wait there for the one human Heart Speak companion that belongs with them to come join them. Then they spend all eternity together, without pain or fear."

Hope's eyes were smiling when she said, "That is where Mother is. She is there with Sergeant Stubby. And she is not cold or hungry. She does not have places on her that bleed all the time and you cannot see her bones any longer. Mother is there and she will not only wait for her apple-cheeked little boy; she will wait for us too. You wait and see."

I could see Mother just as Hope described, beautiful and whole without pain. Faith, however, became very upset at the image we were sharing. "It is not true," she almost shouted, sounding each word out carefully. "Mother has not left for Rainbow Bridge. Not yet!"

Hope looked at me, a little startled that Faith would not enjoy the thought of Mother in that beautiful place. I was a bit confused myself and sat there dumbfounded, staring at my smallest sister.

"I told you," she said. "I heard Man telling someone she had to be taken away. He said he could not take care of her and was sending her away. She *was* here. I know she was here and she was alive."

"But how do you know it was Mother they took away?" Hope asked. "How could you possibly know?"

"Because," answered Faith, "I heard Mother. She was talking to me in my heart. I still hear her sometimes. She tells me to hide when Boy comes in and this morning she kept me from trying to get out of the shed to follow you when Boy took you away. She told me to stay put and I would stay safe."

I fully believed that Faith had heard our mother. I even understood that she might reach out to us from Rainbow Bridge, even though I was not sure how that worked. There was a part of me that wanted to explain all of this to Faith, but I recalled how she had sat with her nose to the floor, not daring to move. No. I would leave it for now. We each had a way of dealing with the hell we lived in. This was Faith's way.

Hope looked from me to Faith and waited. I knew she was waiting for an explanation that would still have Mother in the most beautiful place she had ever heard of. That is what Hope needed to know in order to cope. I was not sure how I could make it so each sister could believe what they needed to believe, but I had to find a way.

Finally I sent Faith to check the food we had not wanted that morning. I told her I wanted to make sure it was covered and still there. She was happy to help and went to the place we had hidden the pan beneath the straw. I took the opportunity to tell Hope what I already knew. Faith needed her fantasy of Mother waiting just out of our sight, guiding us with Heart Speak.

Hope looked relieved. "So Mother is at Rainbow Bridge? She is not in pain anymore?"

"That is what I believe," I stated, matter-of-factly.

Hope and I huddled then, a shared secret bringing us closer than we had ever been. Soon Faith joined us, after she was satisfied our food supply was still there. She sat as close to my side as she could possibly sit, with Hope's body covering her protectively from behind.

I was glad when I felt their steady, even breathing. They were sleeping soundly at last. The pain in my rear end had become almost unbearable and I adjusted to a position that made it feel only slightly better. I concentrated on leaving the shed and going to the Land of Nothing. It was the only place where I did not feel the pain.

I also knew if I could train myself to go there at will I could leave when Boy came for me again. I would not have to experience the pain and shame of what he was doing to me. It would also make it easier for me to keep him away from Hope and Faith. He had readily thought I was jealous when he had gone toward Hope earlier in the day. I never intended to let him harm either of my sisters. I would take the abuse, but I had to keep them safe.

The sun was coming through the dirty window when I came back. Hope and Faith were still sleeping and I was glad of that. I did not want to explain why I had to go to that place in my head. They knew all about hell, but they had not yet experienced unbearable pain. I did not want to be the one to put that thought in their heads.

The Land of Nothing would be my private place and with luck, it would be a place they would never need to visit.

Chapter 9

Guilt, Shame and Heart Speak

Hope and Faith continued to sleep, even after I managed to move away from the huddle. I needed to make a soft place to sit that would be easier on my backside. I could still smell my mother on the straw closest to that hateful chain; the thing that had held her captive since my time began. Working quickly, I used the straw that smelled strongest of her, longing to have her close again.

Knowing my sisters would not miss a thing, I also worked to make them a soft spot where they could sit or lie down. That was the first time I realized just how truly horrible our conditions were. There was very little straw left that did not have feces stuck to it, and the smell of urine was very strong. I thought back to the short time Hope and I had been outside the day before. We had not had time to enjoy the fresh air and sunshine, but now the memory of it made my heart ache.

When my sisters finally started to stir, I had managed to make three small piles very close to each other. "Look," said Faith. "Charity has fixed us a place to lie down that will not be so hard and dirty."

She ran to the pile she was claiming as hers and used her paws and nose to fix it to her liking. I had made my own pile close to Mother's chain, knowing neither Hope nor Faith would want to be near that. It was not my favorite spot, but it smelled strongly of Mother and the location allowed me to watch over my sisters.

"I am hungry," announced Hope, and Faith readily agreed that her belly was totally empty after a long night's sleep.

"Go and eat," I said, nodding in the direction of the food from the day before.

"You, too," said Faith.

"I am not hungry," was only a half lie. My belly was as empty as theirs, but pain has a way of taking away all other thoughts and feelings. "Besides," I said, "Boy will be bringing more in a bit and we can all enjoy that together."

But Boy did not bring food that day. Nor did he come to give us fresh water. By evening, we were all very hungry. There was still water in the pail that could only be half-filled, but I was not sure how long it would be before he brought more. I did not want to keep Hope and Faith from drinking if they were thirsty, so I limited what I used, hoping that would be good enough.

We passed the time as best we could, sharing our memories of Mother. By evening, we were all very grouchy and fell into a troubled sleep. When the next morning came Hope and Faith were awake before me, very hungry and arguing among themselves. When Boy still did not come and we had to stick our heads all the way into the bucket to reach water, I began to fear we had been forgotten.

I went over to the place where Mother's food had been thrown in the dirt so many times. Suddenly a great shame overtook me. How many days had she gone without food, while she struggled to feed puppies? I remembered her telling me she was given more food when she had babies, and I thought back to how little she actually was fed since my birth. We had empty bellies for a day and were already snapping and biting at each other. How many days had she done without, squirrelling away some of her allotment so she could offer it to us when her milk was so scarce? I was sorely ashamed.

I nosed around in the dirt and straw where she had often hidden a morsel and found a few crumbs. I called Hope and Faith over to eat and listened as they complained that it was dirty and it was not enough. Try as I might I could not stop the anger from boiling up inside of me. "Stop whining!" I snapped. "The food you are complaining about is all Mother had for days on end! Stop whining and eat it!"

Both of my sisters fell silent and finished off the crumbs I had uncovered for them. Faith wandered over to her small pile of straw and curled up in a ball. I could hear her stomach grumbling at her because she had given it so little. Hope was not going to rest as quietly.

"You hurt my feelings," she said. "You didn't have to yell at me."

Remembering how Mother had responded on the occasions I had been angry with my sisters, I dropped my head and said, "I'm sorry. I was just worried."

Feeling the old guilt at my helplessness I continued, "I am just a puppy too, you know. I am no older than you and I miss our mother just as much as you do."

"That's okay," said Hope, still sounding very pouty. And she walked toward the front of the shed where we rarely went. I was in no mood to go after her. I started to call her back but my butt was starting to throb again. I was also feeling very guilty about yelling at my sisters. I walked over to my pile of straw and concentrated on the Land of Nothing.

Sleep never came easy for me in those days and my newfound gift offered what little peace I could find. It is very hard to describe being in that nothing state. There's no memory of time there but time passes. Once I would come back, I would realize I had been away for hours usually, though it only felt like minutes.

It was well into the afternoon when I came back. I fought against leaving again when I felt the now familiar ache spreading from my back all the way down into my back legs and paws. Then there was a terrible sense of urgency to get up. Something was not right. I was sitting when I saw Faith with her nose all the way to the floor and I realized the shed door was open. I remembered Hope had gone to the front and shook myself all the way back into hell then. Hope was at the front of the shed and Boy was standing there.

That is when I realized he was holding Hope by the scruff of her neck. She was just hanging there, not moving, not fighting and the thought hit me like a bolt of lightning that I had to save her. I could not allow Boy to take her outside of this shed.

I do not know how long it took me to realize he was not taking her away. He was bringing her toward me. Relief flooded me and made my legs very weak. He dropped Hope next to the pan where he had put our food the last time he had thought to feed us. I noticed there was something in the pan and could not understand how it had gotten there.

Boy looked in the water bucket and grunted. Not speaking to us, he turned and walked outside the shed and came back with a spouted bucket that he poured water from. He filled our pail and it immediately began leaking from the hole halfway down. Then he left us there. Hope did not move. Faith had not lifted her head and I was very, very confused.

I walked to the pan where he had left bread at some point while I slept. It was not touched. He had not added the milk this time, but the smell of the bread made my mouth water. I looked back at my sisters, still holding their positions, "There is food. Come and eat."

I waited, but neither Faith nor Hope moved to come to the pan and eat. In one heart-stopping moment I realized Boy was bringing Hope in from outside when I had come back from the Land of Nothing. If he was bringing her in, that had to mean he had taken her out.

I rushed to my sister, still lying in the spot Boy had dumped her. I could see there were tears in her eyes and her butt was cut and bloody. A great fury began to stir inside me. My mind was racing as I plotted and planned how I would kill Boy when he dared to come back. Then I heard Hope, her voice little more than a whisper.

"He took Faith first," she said. "He took Faith and I could not make you get up."

My mind would not allow me to believe what Hope was trying to tell me. I turned to Faith and realized she was not just sitting with her nose to the floor. She was crumpled with her nose to the floor and her backside was bleeding.

Hope looked at me with tear-filled eyes. "He put stuff inside my butt," she said. "He stuck things in me and it hurt so bad."

I looked at Faith and realized she had been raped, just as I had been. I did not understand exactly what he had done to Hope, but he had hurt her just as he had hurt Faith and me. My heart shattered when I heard Hope say, "I could not make you get up."

A deep sadness settled over me. The already dank dark shed became an even darker place and my world was collapsing around me. I did not make it to my pile of straw. I fell where I was and could not move. I had failed miserably in the one thing I had vowed to do for my mother. I had let everyone down. This was my fault and the guilt of it could go ahead and swallow me now. There was nothing left for me here. Nothing at all.

I did not leave for the Land of Nothing. Something kept me in the shed in my own private hell. I tried harder than I ever had to leave and just not be. But instead I stayed there in a world of hurt, confusion and pain. The pain that had been aching in my bottom since the first time Boy had raped me seemed very far away.

This new pain was all-consuming and over-shadowed everything else. I do not know how long I lay motionless. There was no daylight coming through the window when Hope finally managed to get my attention. At first, her attempts annoyed me and I wanted her to go away and leave me to die. Then I remembered the words that had brought so much grief. "I could not make you get up."

I sat up, dazed, looking around to see if Boy had returned to do more damage. But we were alone in the shed. "You have to stop this," Hope said. "We need you Charity. Please stop going to sleep and stay here with us."

It occurred to me to ask her why she needed me now when I had failed both Faith and her in one day. But her voice was frantic and there was a warm wind that I vaguely remembered stirring inside my soul.

There was nothing but the soft wind, whispering words that were not yet formed, but it was enough to bring me back to reality. I saw Hope looking at me, her eyes still filled with pain. "You feel it, too?" she asked. "Heart Speak." And she repeated her question, "Do you feel it too?"

My mouth and throat were very dry and while it was hard to answer her, I managed to get out, "Yes. I feel it too."

"It's not Mother," Hope said. "The feeling is coming from Faith. She has not moved since Boy brought her back to the shed and took me, Charity. I am afraid for her. I think she may be dying."

Once more I realized how inadequate a protector I was. It was not just my size. I still had all the emotions and thoughts of a puppy and I allowed them to overtake that part of me that was supposed to be alert and ready to fight for our lives. Today when I should have been looking out for my sisters, I had ran away and hidden from the world.

There was a nagging side of me that was saying Mother would often hide that way as well. But Mother had never left the way I did. She only disappeared totally when she was away from us. She would never have left us here in hell alone and gone away to the Land of Nothing.

Because of my need to escape I had left my sisters to fight alone against evil. Faith had been raped while I was away. Hope had been hurt as well. I had not moved to stop it. They had been hungry when I left them. They had just wanted something to fill their empty bellies and I had not wanted to deal with that.

"Will you stop it?" Hope snapped. "I cannot hear you exactly, Charity, but I can feel your guilt. It is not your fault. Boy would have done what he planned to do whether you were awake or not. We are all three too small to stop him."

Her words made sense, but I was not ready to let go of my guilt just yet. I was not sure what solace the guilt was giving me, but there was a strange comfort in punishing myself. I believe now it was the need to cast blame. Someone had to be responsible for all the misery; someone who could actually feel the disdain and loathing that was always there threatening to overtake me.

Hope finally got through to me and managed to get my full attention. "Fine," she said. "If you have to keep on beating yourself up, Faith will die because I cannot bring her back alone."

She was right. I could still feel that whispering wind with words not forming. I realized what Hope already knew. Faith was fighting to leave us. The pain that her body had experienced was nothing compared to the shattering of her heart. She had been the most innocent among Mother's last litter, the smallest and the weakest. Now her mind was trying to take her away to a place where she could never be hurt again, but her soul was fighting to stay with us, reaching out asking for our help, searching for a reason to stay.

"NO!" I yelled. "Not yet, Faith. It is not time for you to leave. I will not let you go."

I went to Faith, sitting just beside her, and nodded my head for Hope to follow. The two of us sat there, resting our heads on our little sister, willing her to stay with us. I had never reached out like this with Heart Speak before, and I wished now I had been honing that skill rather than learning to go to the Land of Nothing. I could feel Hope tremble just behind me, and I knew she was trying to get to that place inside herself where there was abiding love and peace.

It occurred to me it would be easier to reach Faith if we found a way to do this together, to bring our two hearts together as one and reach out to hers. I nudged closer to Hope, knowing that had little to do with the union of our hearts. Still, the feel of her next to me gave me strength.

I allowed my mind to go back to the day we were born and the feelings of love and unity that Mother had enveloped all of us with. For a brief moment I could smell my mother and feel her heart beating for me one more time.

My own heart was beating faster than Mother's, but still in time, making a music that was warming me from the bottom of my paws to somewhere deep inside me, a place that was still innocent and always would be. It was that place where Heart Speak lives and was so much better than I had ever imagined.

The music our hearts made strengthened and drowned out all other sound as Hope's heart joined the beat. The greatest love I have ever known engulfed me. There was no pain, no sorrow... just an incredible peace and love. I could have easily gotten lost there in that moment.

Then my world filled with color like a rainbow bursting in front of my eyes. In that one second I could feel my mother's pain, Hope's pain and my own. I waited for the love to overtake the pain. It was both terrible and wonderful at the same time. That is when I reached out to Faith and began to pull her into the nirvana our hearts and souls had created.

I could feel my heart beat, still very loud inside my head with Hope's right there beating in time to my own. Then I felt Faith's, weaker, out of time. I fought to find the rhythm that would lead three hearts to beat as one. I could still feel the strength and love of Mother's heart, always keeping us in tune. I realized I could not change the beat of Faith's heart, but I could change my own, so I concentrated on that.

Hope had known my thoughts before I was even aware of them and the two of us struggled to stay together. In another blinding burst of color we could feel the third heart beat joining our own. Faith was there with us and we embraced her, refusing to allow her to pull away.

I do not know how long we sat there together, huddled as we always had, but closer than we had ever been. Mother's heartbeat had all but disappeared in the second color burst, and now my own heart was returning to normal. The tremendous event that had brought us all together in that one wonderful moment was over as quickly as it had begun. Finally I opened my eyes and looked around me. Hope was blinking rapidly, struggling to see against the darkness in the shed.

The thought that coming back would be terrible had crossed my mind, but I was wrong. The journey we had taken left us stronger. It also made me very aware of my sisters' pain.

It took a very long time to get Faith to open her eyes. When she did, I almost wished she would close them again. The pain I saw there was so very strong I felt it in my soul. I went back to her bottom and looked at the damage Boy had done. Her butt was bleeding and raw. None of us spoke for a very long time, each taking time to adjust to leaving that place where love lives.

Finally, Hope broke the silence, "He put stuff inside us."

I understood there was a difference in what Boy had done to Faith and me and what he had done to Hope. But I also realized there was no difference in the pain and shame of it. That was the same for each of us. There was no need to explain anything but the sameness. I said, "I know, Hope. He did it to me too."

It was morning again when we had Faith fully back with us. She was not bouncy and happy, but neither were we. The three of us managed to eat about half of the food Boy had brought the day before. Hope and I had to coax every mouthful Faith took. Though our own bellies were empty, Hope and I also had to force the food past the lump that was in our throats. We did not have as much trouble drinking water. It soothed our parched mouths. As much as I hated it, I had to remind my sisters to go easy on the water. We did not know when Boy might bring more.

Boy did not return that morning and we were glad. By mid-afternoon we were all three resting, each in our own hell. All of us ached from Boy's assault. I knew we would recover. We had to. The memory of that place we had been together with Mother's love surrounding us was very strong. Our love for one another would guide us and save us. But we had to find a way to leave this shed.

When I was reasonably sure Boy was not coming and Hope and Faith were asleep, I walked slowly toward the front of the shed. I needed to know this place well and this was the only way. If there was a way out of here, I needed to find it before Boy killed one of us.

I did not find a way out. But I did manage to find a couple of old bones that had been buried up near the front of the shed. A dog had hidden them there for later a long time ago. I imagined the large dog I had seen on the chain outside drooling and digging in the dirt to hide his prize. I wondered what he had done to earn the two bones and decided not to think about that.

Now they were mine. They would give my sisters strength. I carried both bones back to where my sisters were sleeping. I put one next to Hope and one next to Faith. Then I went over and ate a small amount of the bread we had left earlier. I did not drink any of the water, but went back to the front of the shed. There was one more thing I had found there.

I picked up the small rock and brought it back to my pile of straw. It was not a bone, but it would do. Chewing strengthened my jaw and satisfied a hunger that I did not understand. It made my mouth not feel so dry. Without a third bone, I was satisfied the rock would help me leave more water and food for Hope and Faith.

I forced myself to fall into an uneasy sleep. My pain was back in full force, but I would learn to live with it. I would not visit the Land of Nothing again. The price of admission had proven far too great.

Chapter 10

More Training

Night turned to day and then day to night again without food. Our time was spent holding to each other and trying to understand exactly what was expected of us. We talked for hours about the things Mother had taught, always making sure to remember her boy from before she came to this place. We knew she had never wanted us to blindly accept the things that would be asked of us here in hell.

Sergeant Stubby had become our hero. We often talked about what he would do if he were here with us. It helped pass the long, hungry hours. My stone had kept me occupied while Hope and Faith worked hard on their bones. The bones nor the stone filled our empty bellies, and our water was getting dangerously low.

The only good thing about Boy not returning to our corner of hell was we were not being hurt.

Then, finally, when the water remaining in our pail was so low it would have evaporated before nightfall, Boy returned.

The shed door opened and the three of us huddled together protectively and defensively. At first I was not sure what was happening. My eyes, very accustomed to the dark, began to burn and then closed involuntarily against the brightness. I tried to open them and see, but my nose had already told me Boy was standing in front of me. Instinctively I moved my body in front of Faith. I could feel her trembling uncontrollably. I could feel Hope also trying to push against Faith protectively. I believe Hope and I were probably trembling almost as much as Faith, but remembering the way she sat, nose to floor and so absent, made both of us share in this need to defend her against Boy's abuse.

As our eyes adjusted to the light we could see he was carrying the familiar loaf that contained our bread. I willed myself to remain very still, but my stomach dismissed my command and grumbled loudly.

"You hungry?" Boy asked. I had never realized how totally ignorant he was before then. Did he really think we wouldn't be hungry? I might have felt a little sorry for him had he not been as cruel as he was stupid.

He snickered a little. It was not the sinister laugh that turned my blood cold and made the hair stand erect on the back of my neck; but, his laughter was not a sound that warmed my heart in either case. And right at that moment, it was a laugh of stupidity and ignorance. I remembered Mother telling me about the laughing cheering crowds, screaming for more of her blood. Those were laughs of ignorance too.

I took just a second to fantasize about biting Boy. I could see him in a training pen with Faith, Hope and me. We were grown and he was our bait. All of the dogs Man had ever hurt were watching, cheering. The daydream was making me smile to myself. When I realized it, I shook my head and willed myself to stop thinking like that. No one had to tell me evil is wrong and deliberately hurting others is evil. It doesn't matter who's doing the hurting. It is wrong.

"Me and Daddy had to go and see about some dogs," he said, actually sounding as if he thought we might care what the devil and his imp had been up to. "Gotta find another bitch to have babies since your ma ain't no good to us no more."

His words hit my heart like daggers. Oh, how I wished I could go back to a time when I did not understand this cruel excuse of a human. I knew Hope understood because I felt her stiffen behind me, but I silently prayed that Faith could not decipher his words yet.

Boy tossed our bread into the pan that had been empty for more time than I wanted to remember. When he checked the water he finished his thought about my beloved mother. "She's done and dead now anyhow. So we got to get another bitch."

He did not bring the strange pail in with the spout this time, but took our water bucket outside with him. For a moment I was afraid he did not know we could not live without water. Or, maybe he did not care… but then he returned with a full bucket of water. This one did not have a rusty hole halfway down. It was not new. It was not clean. But it held the water he had put in it and would provide us with water much longer than the other one.

He sat the bucket down and stared at us for a moment. There was a strange look on his face and I wondered if it was because his brain was trying to catch up with his eyes… once more understanding Boy was not a great thinker. In fact, I do not believe he ever had an original thought. His brains and his cruelty were inherited from his father. For the hundredth time I thought about Mother and the abuse she had endured at the hands of evil.

The three of us remained very still. We were very aware of the food and water that we desperately needed, but we also knew if we moved, Boy may decide to take one of us with him. When he turned and walked away, closing the shed door behind him, we all let out heavy, relieved sighs.

Then we walked to the food and ate. I started to remind my sisters to save a little for later, but realized there was not enough to worry about it. We finished the bread and drank water. Then we went back to our corner in the shed and rested together. I fell into an exhausted sleep. When Boy came and took Hope away, she was gone before I realized he had been in the shed again.

Faith continued to sleep and I was grateful for that. I planned to find a way to help Hope and did not need to worry about Faith trying to follow. My body was numb with fear as I ran to the front of the shed and sniffed at the closed door. Backing up, I got a running start and banged against it. It shook slightly, but my small body was no match for the heavy door.

Determination is a powerful force. It kept me moving, looking for a way out, even when my legs were almost too weak to stand. I realized the lack of food and water had depleted me and the small amount we had been given was doing little to nourish us.

But I also knew Hope was far too weak to withstand Boy's abuse and cruelty. I was preparing to run at the door again when I heard Faith behind me.

"He's coming back," she said. Her voice was void of emotion, matter-of-fact. "I can smell him. Boy is heading back this way."

She was right. When I took the time to use my senses I could smell him too. That rotten stench would normally have put fear in my heart, but not now. I was sniffing the air for the familiar scent of my sister and it was not there.

"Hope isn't with him," Faith said. "I don't know where she is; but, she's not with Boy."

My mind was racing and my heart was pounding. Once more I had let my sisters down. I had failed to protect them. That was bad enough, but I could still see my mother's sad face telling me it was up to me to protect us and get us out of this place. I had not only failed, but failed miserably.

Just before Boy opened the shed door again I heard Faith say, "That's not what Mother meant, Charity. That may be what you heard but Mother knew you were just a puppy like us. She would never have told you to do that knowing how bad it would hurt you when you couldn't."

My last thought before Boy grabbed me up by my front legs was that Faith was coming into her own. All three of us were now fluent in Heart Speak. If we could survive this day and Boy, maybe we would find a way to escape hell.

I cried out to Faith to hide and not come out until Hope and I returned. I did not know if she would listen, but I knew she heard me. I could feel her heart stirring through my soul and it gave me a strange peace. Fear had clutched my heart but I was able to remain calm and aware as my eyes adjusted to the light of day. I looked around for Hope, knowing she was alive because I could feel her somewhere deep within myself... just as I could feel Faith. For the first time I realized Heart Speak is not just a language that allows us to communicate. Heart Speak is something far more.

Then I saw Hope. She was huddled in the corner of a pen with our brother watching her closely and pacing in front of her. There was blood on her head and I realized she had been bitten. How much damage would he be able to do with his teeth now? If she made one movement, he was ready to attack again. His name was Killer, I remembered. With our frail, undernourished bodies, we had been no match for his strength the last time we faced him. Now, after days without food, our butts ragged from the abuse Boy had inflicted, he could surely kill us if that was his intention. He did not have the teeth of one of the fighting dogs, but they were very sharp and our skin was very thin. His name was more than fitting on this day, in that moment.

Boy did not set me down in the pen. He flung me toward my crouching brother so that I landed hard on his back. Killer had not been expecting it, too intent on watching Hope. I knew this was the only second I would hold an advantage. If I wanted to survive, if I wanted Hope to survive, I had to act fast. I sank my teeth into the back of his neck and held on. Relieved, I realized my teeth had grown enough so I could hold on. I knew I had the element of surprise on my side and I had to take advantage. He was a lot stronger than me, but I had more heart.

I could hear Hope jumping up and yelling for me to hold on. I did not know how much damage I might be capable of. I did not know how long it would take him to regain his composure and overtake me. But there was one thing I was sure of. If I died today, I would die fighting for my life.

Then, Hope was next to me helping me take Killer down and keep him there. Even if we had been capable, we did not want to hurt him. We were not trying to make him bleed. We just wanted him to leave us alone.

Our attack shocked Killer and he yelped as if we had taken a piece of him. I heard Boy laughing and yelling from somewhere far away. "Look at my dawgs, Daddy. Just look at my dawgs. I done and got me two prize fighters."

I blocked the sound of his voice and tried hard to make my brother hear me. I wanted him to tell me why he was doing this terrible thing. I knew he was doing it for Man but I wanted to hear him say that he really did not want to hurt Hope or me. Instead all I heard were his cries. Then Hope was flying. I saw her sailing through the air and did not understand...

... Until I felt Man's boot make contact with my side and kick me through the air. I landed next to Hope, stunned and bruised. Hope moved her head and looked at me. She looked so very tired and hurt, but she was alive.

"You got to get those two in check," I heard Man say. "If you don't make 'em humble I will."

Once more remembering the story Mother told me about Man and his gun, I waited to see if he was going to shoot Killer and then break my jaw. But he was obviously fond of my brother. He picked him up and looked to see the damage Hope and I had done. He half laughed and half snorted.

"They didn't even break skin boy! What was all that hollering for?"

Boy was muttering something I could not quite make out under his breath. It was obvious he was not pleased with his father. Boy had been excited when I defended myself. Hope joining me had made him jump up and down. But his father had dashed any hope he may have had for a "prize fighter."

Man looked away from Killer for a moment and snapped at Boy; "You humble 'em, or I will. And change your britches. You pissed ya'self"

I saw the stain on Boy's pants and realized he must have wet himself when he got so excited. His father had embarrassed him and Boy started to cry. He did not want his father to know and began making terrible sniffing noises. Had he not hurt my sisters and me so badly, I might have felt sorry for him.

But I was not thinking about Boy's disappointment or even how much Man seemed to like my brother. I was more than a little concerned about what devil and spawn might do to make us humble. Obviously the training sessions Man had planned for Killer had not gone as he intended. If I had ever been naïve enough to think he would let it end with his disappointment, that time was long past. I knew better now.

My sisters and I would be humbled.

Killer would grow and get stronger. There would be more training sessions. How many more training sessions before his teeth would be strong enough to really cause damage?

Once more I remembered Mother and the torture she had endured. How much would Hope, Faith and I have to deal with before Man was satisfied enough to allow us to live... or die... in peace?

Chapter 11

Humbled

Man walked away with Killer in his arms. He was kissing his head and all other thoughts faded in my mind. His gentleness with my brother confused me. I wondered if Mother had ever seen this side of him. Oh how I missed her and the lessons she would never be able to teach me. It occurred to me she would be pleased at least one of her children was being shown kindness in this horrible place.

I had been so stunned at Man's gentle touch with my brother I did not even realize Boy had picked me up and was locking me in the crate just outside the training pen. He went to Hope and lifted her by her neck. He was far from gentle, taking the censure he had received from his father out on her. I knew she wanted to cry out, but she remained quiet. She had gone totally stiff with fear as he carried her into that other shed... the shed where a dog could easily be humbled.

Fear touched my own heart and the world began to spin around me. Dizzy and sick on my stomach, I had to sit down. I was less than adequate as a protector to my sisters. Hope was alone with Boy and I knew exactly how he planned to humble her. I was more than a little relieved when he walked out the shed door. There had not been time for him to do that terrible thing to her backside. But my relief was soon trampled down by more fear. Hope was not with him.

Boy came to my crate and peered in at me. He had a smile on his face that made my blood cold. Smiles are supposed to be warming and welcoming. Boy's smile was putrid.

I thought about biting him when he reached in to take me from the crate. But I knew I could not do enough damage to stop him, and it would most likely only bring more pain for Hope, Faith and me. Then there was Hope still in that shed. I knew he planned to take me there too and I needed to be with Hope. My love for my sister was much stronger than my fear of that place. So I mimicked Hope when he lifted me and my body went stiff.

Considering my life thus far had been spent in darkness, it was surprising to me that my eyes were not quick to adjust when we walked into the other shed. They had only just adjusted to the bright sunshine of the outside world, and I suppose the darkness was an assault as I fought to find Hope. Finally I saw her. Boy had tied a rope around her neck and had the other end fastened to a pole in the center of the shed. She was curled in a ball, trying very hard to be invisible.

Boy never spoke as he sat me on the table that I remembered all too well from my first visit here. He unzipped his pants and the humbling began.

Through the pain, I cried out for Hope to run, but knew she could not. She was as trapped as I was; as trapped as our mother had been on that hateful chain, tied to the pole over in our corner of hell. I had said I would never do it again, but the only thing left for me to do was disappear inside myself once more... and I did.

I managed to control the desire to get lost in that state of nothingness, remembering all too well what had happened the last time I had felt the need to go away. The pain was far, far away... happening to someone else. Then I realized in horror that I had changed places with Hope. Boy had finished with me and had taken her. To my horror, I could see what he was doing. Hope looked so tiny. In that second I knew I was just as small.

Had Hope watched when Boy raped me? Had she felt this same sickness that I was feeling? I did not dare cry out to her, hoping she had learned to vanish from Boy's assault as I had. If I reached out to her, it may bring her back from that place she desperately needed to be at that exact moment in time.

When Boy had finished the humbling lesson he returned us to our own shed. Faith was waiting with a knowledge in her eyes that made my heart ache. I wanted to be angry, to lash out at Boy and Man. I wanted to fight the good fight like Sergeant Stubby had done... but I realized all I felt at that moment was a terrible shame. I was ashamed of my own weakness and felt totally guilty that Hope had been injured. I looked over at her and saw that she was still lost in that wonderful sanctuary of nothing.

When I tried to move every muscle in my body throbbed and cried out in protest. I fought the strong need to scream out in pain for Faith's sake as I tried to reach Hope. My body refused to accept the assault I was trying to force and I dropped to the floor, legs splayed out, unable to move from that position. Then Faith was licking my face, washing away tears that I had not even known were there.

I managed to roll over to my side and that put me closer to Hope. Faith accepted the cue from me and went to our sister who was very far away at that moment. Finally, after a lot of kisses from Faith and the silent prayers I sent up to anyone that may be listening, Hope came back from that place of peace. It was hard seeing her awake to the torture her body was now paying for.

We stayed huddled together for a very long time with Faith assuring us of her presence. Hope and I were too hurt to be hungry, but I knew Faith would be. Sometime in the night she made her way to the food dish where we had tried to save as many crumbs for later as we possibly could. I saw her there nibbling at crumbs, trying to be frugal.

"Eat," I told her. "Eat what is left, Faith. Boy will bring more in the morning." I could not be sure of that, but my sister needed the food that neither Hope nor I would be able to eat. And I did remember Boy telling me when he brought us back to our home in hell that he would see me "in the morning."

Hope was still sleeping, crying out once in a while either from a memory, or from the very real pain that was still very much with us. I snuggled closer to her hoping to give some comfort. I did not see if Faith listened to me and ate or not. My body was sore and tired and knowing we were all relatively safe for the time being, I allowed myself to sleep and feel nothing.

The next time I opened my eyes to the terrible world around us, the shed door was opening and Boy was coming in. He had our food with him and did not speak as he threw our bread onto the dish. Surprisingly, he also took the time to give us fresh water. His face was set and I could not read what evil thoughts he might be thinking.

When he walked over to the three of us he took his foot and kicked at Hope. She moaned. He bent down and looked at her. "What's wrong with you?" he asked, his voice more sarcastic and cynical than worried.

I held my breath, knowing I would not be able to fight him off if he tried to take Hope. My body was still far too sore from his last assault. I was relieved when he turned and walked away. But I had heard the promise that sounded more like a threat to me. "Don't worry. I promise I will be back in a little bit. I will take care of you."

Once he left the shed, I turned my attention to Hope. She had been very stiff when Boy was there with us; but, now she relaxed and let out a tired sigh. Relieved, I licked her face, ignoring the pain even that small gesture brought.

"I'm ok, Charity," she said. "He did not hurt me any worse than he hurt you. I just do not understand what he is doing or why. What can we do to make him stop? What does he want from us?"

Faith had not endured the torture the day before. But she was still very aware of what had happened to us. Her memory from the day Boy had hurt her was not about to fade any time soon. "What are we doing wrong?" she asked. "If we do what he wants, maybe he will not hurt us."

Before we could talk about Faith's question, the shed door opened again. Boy had made good his threat way sooner than we thought he would. All three of us fell silent and still, hoping we could fade into those dark shadows that were always a part of our world.

The shadows gave us no more protection than they had provided our mother and Boy came straight to us. He bent down and looked at each of us carefully, stroking my head when his eyes met mine. I still had enough pride not to avert my gaze. I looked him directly in the eye and hoped there was at least a moment of fear in his heart. I had pondered Faith's question long before she had asked it, and I was not convinced we could change anything to make Boy stop hurting us. I was just a puppy and far from being wise, but I knew there was such a thing as evil... and I knew evil was standing in front of me now.

Even though I may have understood there is such a thing as evil in the world, I still regretted my defiance almost immediately. Boy broke his gaze with me and as he was standing, he scooped Faith up from the floor. "You two ain't fit for training today," he said. "This one will work fine."

And he was gone with our smallest sister.

Fear and shame gripped my heart. I was afraid of what was going to happen to Faith, and I was terribly ashamed that my own body was rejected in favor of hers for today's round of torture. I knew Hope was thinking the same thoughts and we cried together. It was not long before we heard growling and cries. We knew Faith was in the training pen with Killer. The fact

I could do absolutely nothing about it hurt as much as anything that had happened to me.

When Faith had been hurt before, I had been far away inside my own mind. Today I was wide awake and still could do nothing to stop this. Faith had just asked what we could do to make it stop before Boy had taken her, and now I believed with all my heart that only I could have stopped it. I should have surrendered myself and made him leave Faith alone.

Hope's voice was clear and wise when she spoke to me. "Then you would be dead," she said. "Charity, we have to stick together now. They will hurt all of us and none of us know why. The only thing we can do is be here for each other."

I knew she was right, just as I knew my staring contest with Boy had not caused him to choose Faith for today's round of abuse. He probably had not even known we were in a battle of gazes. Common sense dictated Faith was the only one fit to be taken today. But common sense is not so common and Boy did not have any from what I had seen.

Aside from Boy's obvious lack of intelligence, common or otherwise, there was also the terrible guilt I lived with now. Shame is a powerful thing and in my guilt-ridden mind I was responsible for anything bad that happened. It is amazing how many reasons I conjured up for Boy's and Man's evil ways.

I was too small and that is why they picked on my sisters. I showed that I was hurt and acted like I was in pain... so Boy would choose Hope or Faith to give me a break. The fact I was not acting did not enter my mind while I was on this shameful spiral. And now, today, at this moment in time, I had been defiant by staring at Boy. He had answered my challenge by taking my sister instead of me. And I had sat there helpless to stop him.

Now, when I least needed her to, Hope was hearing every horrible, self-despising thought. She looked at me with eyes that had seen the same abuse as me and she interrupted my misery. "If you are to blame, then so am I. He left me here too. Do you think it is my fault?"

"Of course not! You had nothing to do with this. It was me. I should have protected both you and Faith. I have done nothing but sit by while you and Faith have been hurt." I stared at the floor, sorely ashamed of my negligence.

"You give yourself far too much credit, Charity. Stop wallowing in your self-pity and help me think of how to keep us alive. I want us to get out of here and I need your help. If we do not escape, we will die. One of us will surely watch the other two go before her... and I do not want it to be me." Hope's voice was matter-of-fact. It shocked me to hear my sister speak with such wisdom.

I did not have a chance to respond. The shed door opened and Boy was there with Faith. She looked so small in his dirty hands as he held her by the fur on her neck. Her body hung, stiff, and I could see blood on her face and head. My stomach churned and I wanted to be sick; I wanted to disappear to that place inside myself where I would not have to deal with pain and misery. But

Faith needed me here with her, and I would not let her down by disappearing when she needed me the most.

Hope's words had stung, mostly because I knew they were true. But now was not the time to think about anything but making sure Faith was ok. I realized now that Hope and I had both been wrong in trying to shield Faith from the truth of what was happening. She had been raped by Boy, just as we had been... she had endured everything alone while we tried to keep her from knowing how bad things were. When Boy had taken her today she had no idea what he was taking her to. We might have warned her. She might have been more prepared.

As soon as Boy left the shed, Hope and I both set to licking her wounds. She was not lost inside herself like she had been after the rape. Now she was just crying softly and allowing us to care for her. Once we had cleaned her wounds to the best of our ability I asked her if she could stand.

"I am ok," she said, her voice very low and very sad. She curled up tight and allowed us to snuggle next to her. Finally, when her soft weeping stopped, she lifted her head slightly and asked, "What did I do wrong? Why are they hurting me?"

Her words and the shame I heard in her voice cut me much deeper than any of the horrible things that Boy had done to me. "You didn't do anything wrong," I answered. "None of us have done anything wrong. Boy and Man are just very bad people and they do not care that we are hurting."

"They want to see us hurt," added Hope. "I think they like it."

Faith sniffed loudly and covered her eyes with her paws. "I wet myself," she muttered. "I was so scared I wet myself."

"It's ok," said Hope. "I have wet myself during the hurtful things too; and, I am sure Charity has."

"Yes," I responded, wanting more than anything for my sisters to know we were all in this together. "I have wet myself too."

We drifted off to sleep then because there was nothing to do but sleep. In dreams we could be far away from here in a wonderful place. My last thought before running through the meadow in my dreams was that we had all been humbled. I wondered if we had been broken enough for Man.

Chapter 12

Changing

Sleep can help the body and mind to heal when you have been beaten down. Faith, Hope and I had not been beaten. We had been starved, deprived of our mother, attacked by our sibling and raped by the one who was supposed to care for us. That was our life. It was not a life we wanted, and we realized we had choices and decisions to make.

That one day when Faith returned to us with bite marks covering her tiny body we knew there had to be changes. We could not continue the way we were going. Killer was not strong enough to kill us, not yet. But these sessions were not going to stop. There was always the possibility we would be tossed in with one of the larger dogs. Man was angry and small, and he was pure evil.

The abuse Boy was dishing out *could* kill us. The pain was almost unbearable and I could see the damage it was doing to my sisters. I knew I looked just as bad. Man seemed oblivious to the obvious injuries. We knew we had to do something to change things. There was always the choice to just lie down and die, but the will to survive is strong in all of Creator's creatures. Still, death was an option and if we continued living from one attack to the next, death would come soon. Hope's words had seemed harsh when she chastised me that day, but I knew they were not meant that way. I accepted them as honestly as she had said them and decided it was time for a change in the way I saw things and in my attitude. I would change that, and then we would work on the greatest change – getting out of hell.

Realizing both Hope and I had been thinking about getting out of this place led to another realization. We had both been thinking the same thoughts, but separately. We had also left Faith out of our conversations, both thinking she was too small to understand. Even though Hope and I had both been hurt by Boy on our last outing... we had still done much better together, as a team. We might never be able to stop the abuse, but we could at least take a stand together. The thought of Faith... alone... and facing Killer hurt me so much more than anything else I had endured in hell.

Hope had been right. I had "wallowed in self-pity" long enough. While Faith and Hope had been living through the abuse and dealing with it, I had made it all about me. The fact I had been raped also had not played an important part in my thoughts. I knew now I had never accepted or faced my own pain, choosing instead to play the martyr. It was far easier than accepting what had happened to me. Both Faith and Hope had realized it and had tried several times to make me see. Awareness had come slowly, but now it was time to face the truth.

I made my way to the food dish and nibbled on a bit of the bread that none of us had felt like eating earlier. I drank my fill of water and then sat near my sisters. For the first time since I had first been hurt by Boy I allowed myself to feel the pain and realize that I was hurt.

Hope woke up before Faith and I could tell she was hurting. But when I told her she needed to try and eat, she did not argue. After Hope had managed to eat about the same amount I had, Faith woke up. She would not eat, reminding us she had eaten earlier before she was taken from the shed... but she did drink water. I accepted that she was not hungry, but it still worried me that the little puppy who was always hungry did not want food. If she became sick, I was not sure how we would take care of her. The only way dogs have to care for each other is to lick wounds. It is not the best medicine, but it was all we had. That would not work on something wounded inside of her... something that would keep her from eating.

Night was falling. The end to a very tiring day was here at last and I had plans to talk well into the night. But not just to talk... to listen to my sisters as well.

"We are in hell," I began. "And in case you are not sure exactly what hell is... well... it is here. Boy is not a kind person that will take care of us and Man is just evil. Mother knew this and tried to warn me. I have been so busy trying to figure out how to take care of everyone, I have forgotten the most important thing. We are in this together. We will live or die together. And I am ready to listen if you have any ideas."

The three of us talked through the night. We talked about Heart Speak and homes for dogs that did not involve starvation and pain. It was hard to conceive of such a place here in hell, but Mother had said it was out there somewhere so we each believed in it.

We talked about togetherness and our love for each other. We laughed again about Sergeant Stubby and we named him as our hero. Faith became very thoughtful then.

"I have another hero," she said, her voice stronger than I had ever heard it before. "Mother is my hero."

She did not have to say why. Hope and I both knew and we agreed that Mother was the greatest hero of all.

With a new resolve, the three of us slept at last. None of us watched the sun cast a dim light through the dirty window on the following morning because we slept as we had not slept since the abuse began.

We were each hurting from abuse, but we were together. That was the important thing and that is what would keep us whole inside. The night and the conversation had changed each of us, made us stronger. We had never really been alone and now we knew it.

Man and Boy might be able to take our food and water. They could bring us great pain. But they could not take that part if us that remained strong throughout the shame and hurt. They could not take our souls. And they could not take away the Heart Speak.

Our resolve would be tested over the next days. Our lives would not get easier because we had learned the truth of Heart Speak. But we would always be together and we would find a way to leave this place. We would leave here for a better place and each of us knew this now. It might well be the land Mother had told us about called Rainbow Bridge... but we would be together.

Chapter 13

Aunt Gertie

Over the next week the mornings became a time of dread for us. Boy was there with each new sunrise. He always brought bread for us to eat, but there was barely enough for three growing pups. We tried to save as much as we could for later. We still remembered the days Boy had not come, when there had been no food.

While his presence insured we would have something to eat, it also brought hurt and shame. Training for Killer was in full force and we were used as his bait. We endured the pain together, as we had sworn we would.

We learned to use the battle that was always there between Man and Boy. Boy wanted to please Man and would go to great lengths. Of course, evil is never satisfied so Boy's attempts were always met with sneers and curses. We had been chosen by the demon spawn and he did not want us to fail. We were his pride, just as Killer was his dad's. We noticed how Man would mock his son when he would only carry one or two of us, so we made it impossible for him to leave one of us behind. It did not matter which one or two Boy chose for the day, because the one or two remaining would run behind him. Boy had no choice but to take the three of us together.

Our lives became a routine of pain and hunger. At night we would cling to each other and talk about Mother, Sergeant Stubby and apple-cheeked boys. We would talk almost until the sunrise when we would fall into a troubled sleep. Our wounds rarely let us sleep long.

During the training sessions, Killer was always boisterous and proud. We had learned to lie still and get the attack over with. Killer was just a puppy, but so were we. And Killer was fed much better than we were. Killer had sunshine and green grass. His sharp teeth pierced our skin and on the occasions Man would allow him to go a little further and shake his head, our skin would tear and bleed. The attacks were always stopped quickly, but each day brought new scars and we knew we could not survive this long.

There were a few times when Man and Boy had been distracted by each other. Their bickering, and sometimes their ignorance gave us a few smiles. We would take those moments to reach out to our brother, hoping we could touch some part deep inside him that Mother had left - maybe even the memory of her heart beat as he rested against her. We were given encouragement on several occasions. But the glimmer of hope would pass as soon as Man returned his attention to training.

I always worried about the day Killer would not stop when ordered. Remembering Hope's words about one of us watching the other two die before her, I prayed it would not be me that had to see this. We talked about these things together now, and no one had to bear the burden alone. The thoughts and images in my mind could not be stopped and there was a very large part of me that still felt the need to keep my sisters safe. Knowing they felt the same did little to relieve my pain.

While waiting in the crate outside the training pen, we had noticed other dogs on the property. They were all chained and looked haggard and tired. Most were covered in scars and they looked at us with empty eyes. I always tried to reach out with Heart Speak, but there was never a response. I often wondered if these dogs were my brothers and sisters. I also wondered if they had attacked Mother and ripped her skin, leaving the wounds I had licked and cried over.

The training sessions with Killer were not the worst of our humiliation. Man would often leave after the sessions and then Boy would take us to that shed in the back where a dog can be humbled quite easily. I had often wondered why he always took us to that particular shed. Why did he not just hurt us there in the place we lived every day? It would have been much easier for him, I thought. But I realized the back shed had stools and tables he could use. There were also objects in that shed... objects that brought a particular pleasure to him and a lot of pain to us. We knew what he was doing must be wrong on so many levels because he always made sure Man could not see what he was doing.

He would take us in that back shed and tie us to a pole in the center of the room. The two he was not abusing would always huddle together and wait, knowing one or the other would be next.

On those occasions, for some reason known only to Boy, Hope was always chosen for a particularly vile act. Boy seemed to take great pleasure in putting objects inside of her through her backside. She had stopped reacting after the first couple of times, learning the reaction always excited him more. After his time with her, he would choose Faith or me to rape. I would usually try to make myself readily available. Even though we had our pact, something in Faith's eyes died a little with each attack on her. My fear of her leaving us forever made me want to protect her from this abuse. I had tried it with Hope too, of course, but Boy had specific plans for her and there was no stopping him.

One day, after the training session with Killer, Man was in a particularly good mood. He came and looked us over after he had taken Killer to whatever place in hell our brother occupied.

"We need to make sure some of those wounds get some ointment," he told Boy. "They are good bait for Killer. Don't want to lose them too soon."

Boy hurried off as he always did when Man mentioned something that was needed. He came back with ointment and immediately began applying it to our wounds. It smelled foul and was very sticky, but it also eased the sting a lot.

"Take them out of that crate and let 'em play a little in the grass. It'll be good for 'em." Even when he was obviously giving us a gift, Man still sounded evil and vile. But the grass felt wonderful when Boy took us from the crate. The three of us sat huddled together, smelling the sunshine and grass more than feeling it.

"Let 'em stay out for about an hour. They need the sun," and Man left us there with Boy. At first I thought he would hurry us into that back shed as soon as Man left. But Boy would not go against what Man told him and he left us there sitting in the grass, close enough to stop us if we tried to run. Of course, we knew better than to try and make a get-away. Boy blocked the only clear escape and in any direction we would never make it past the large dogs chained along the perimeter of the yard.

"What are you doing with those puppies?" The strange voice startled me and I could feel Hope and Faith stiffen just as I did.

Boy jumped up from where he had been sitting in the grass. "They's my puppies," he said defensively.

The woman sounded very disgusted. "If they are your puppies, then you need to take better care of them. They look like they are starving to death. Are you feeding them? Where is their mother? They look awful young."

"They ain't got no ma," Boy still sounded defiant, but there was a particular whine in his voice now that told me this woman may have some power over him. "And I feed 'em as much as Daddy will let me."

"Stuff and nonsense!" the woman snapped. "Of course they have a mother. Where did they come from? These off of one of your daddy's dogs?"

"You know they is," there was that whine again just behind the defiance. "She died though. She was old and she died."

The woman was not going to let it go so easily. "If she was young enough to have babies she was young enough to feed them. I hope your daddy's not up to no good again. As much as I don't like him, I love my sister and she needs him here to support her and you."

Boy was now simply whining. "If Daddy knows I showed you my puppies he's gonna whoop me." He ignored the rest of what she said, worried about his backside now.

Her voice softened and she said, "I am not going to say anything to your daddy. I know how mean he can be. But you wait right here and I am gonna run to the house and get these puppies something to eat. We won't tell your daddy or your mama. Lord knows what my sister sees in him, but she won't go against him; not even for you."

Boy was now sounding very weak and helpless. I liked it almost as much as I liked this woman who had just wandered into our lives. She had a wonderful new smell that was not rotten, and I could almost hear her Heart Speak when she looked at us.

"OK, Aunt Gertie," he said. "If you promise not to tell."

Aunt Gertie snorted and was muttering something under her breath as she disappeared between the hedges into the yard next door. When she returned she had a large bowl of something that smelled wonderful. Hope, Faith and I sniffed it cautiously and to

Aunt Gertie's delight, began to eat heartily. Our starved bellies could not hold a lot, though and she frowned when we stopped eating.

"You take that and put it where they can get it," she demanded. "They will be able to eat more later. And what are all those sores on those puppies? What have you and your daddy been up to over here?"

Aunt Gertie got closer to us and looked at the wounds on our too thin bodies. She saw the ointment and snorted again. "At least you are trying to take care of them. I will give you that."

Before she left, Aunt Gertie promised Boy she would be watching and making sure he took care of us. "If they need food, you come and tell me," she said. "You hear me, Boy? Don't you let these puppies starve because your daddy ain't got a brain in his head nor a kind bone in his body."

Then Aunt Gertie was gone as quickly as she had come. Boy hurried us back into our shed and put the bowl of wonderful smelling food down so we could eat. He stopped on his way out as if he had remembered something. He took our water pail and filled it with fresh water. Aunt Gertie had helped us that day. I hoped she would come again real soon.

For the first time in a long time, Faith, Hope and I slept deeply. Our wounds had been treated, our bellies were full, and we had not been taken into that other shed. When I woke up, Faith and Hope were tumbling and playing. They were not as energetic as they had been in the days before the abuse began, but the food and the kindness afforded on this day had given them new life. Even though my backside ached, as it did all the time, I joined in the tumbles. It was good to be a puppy, if only for a little while.

We stopped after only a few minutes, all three of us hurting and tired but feeling better than we had in a long time. Without speaking the three of us went to the bowl left by Aunt Gertie. We each ate a small amount, our too thin bellies bloating from the unfamiliar fullness.

"Maybe she will come every day," said Hope. "Maybe our lives will change for the better now."

"Of course she will," responded Faith, her words making the reason for her name clear to both Hope and me. "She will come every day and make sure we are fed. I don't think Boy will be able to hurt us any more now. He is scared of her."

Hope happily joined in the fantasy. "Yes. He is scared of her. And I will bet she sees how badly we are being treated and takes us home with her. We will live wonderful lives with Aunt Gertie."

For only about the hundredth time I wished I could join in my sisters' hopes and dreams for the future. I would not spoil their fantasy, but I had seen Mother and had heard the terrible truth from her. Aunt Gertie may have the best of intentions, but I did not think she could save us. She had never been in this shed and she certainly had not been in the other one. The evil that Man and Boy intended for us would just be better hidden so she would not see.

Boy undoubtedly told Man about Aunt Gertie's visit because the training sessions suddenly stopped with Killer. Boy explained to us as best he could. "Daddy said to let Aunt Gertie forget about you. It won't take long. Don't need her snooping around."

I missed the sunshine and green grass more than I thought I would. While none of us missed the attacks from the training sessions or the abuse from the back shed, the darkness in this place was denser now. The air was thicker and we tried to stay in the dim light that came through the dirty window as much as we could.

If Aunt Gertie sent more of the wonderful smelling food, we did not know about it. Perhaps it was given to Killer and our chosen sisters. In any case, it was not given to us. Our diet returned to bread, and very little of that.

Aunt Gertie had been the topic of some of our late night talks, along with Sergeant Stubby and Mother. We had only seen her the one time, but she had given us reason to hope. Boy skipped two days coming into our shed. We had been without food and the water we had left was filthy when he finally opened the shed doors.

Our lives were getting ready to change drastically. Aunt Gertie would be a huge part of it. We would soon be leaving hell, but the price we paid for freedom would be great. It might well cost one of us her life.

Chapter 14

The Loss of Faith

Boy opened the shed door slowly and walked back to where we were hiding in the shadows.

"Got you some grub," he said as he dropped three pieces of bread onto our dish. We did not move, preferring to wait for Boy to leave before we enjoyed the food he had brought us. But he did not leave. Instead he stood there glaring at us.

"Well," he asked, "you gonna eat or ain't you?"

Had Boy been able to understand Heart Speak he may have heard the answer our hearts were screaming. "Please leave! Yes we will eat! We are hungry! You frighten us and we cannot eat until you leave!"

But Boy did not hear Heart Speak and he stood there staring at us, his look saying he did not like us much more than we liked him today.

There was a smell in the air. All dogs know the odor, and those of us who have lived in hell know it is a strong warning of impending danger. Giving the odor an identity is not easy. You will not recognize it unless you have known great fear, pain and abuse. It is the smell of both fear and anger, but there is an energy behind it that compels anyone who sniffs it to run and hide. If you live in a shed in hell where the light does not shine and where mothers lay dying after being attacked by their own children... you know there is nowhere to run and there is nowhere to hide.

Boy's eyes held pain on this day. But they also held a hate that was stronger than any I had felt from him before. He stood there staring at Faith and for the first time since the night we had said we would be together no matter what, I felt a strong need to put myself between Boy and my sisters. I could not understand the hate that was being directed at Faith. She had done nothing to deserve his disdain. But, then, who can understand an evil so great it leads to the rape of puppies? Boy did not have to have a reason to hate or hurt any one of us.

Today, regardless of why, his disgust and anger was directed at Faith. Hope and I both saw it and we moved together to block her from his view. Faith was aware of the smell and the terrible feeling that was permeating the shed, and she did know fear. However, a small light had started to glow in her heart on the day she met Aunt Gertie. The part of her that had dictated what her name would be was a part of that light.

On this day Faith decided there must be good somewhere in Boy. Or maybe she was just tired of being afraid. Whatever the reason, Faith pushed past Hope and me and stood in front of Boy. I saw the tip of her tail wag, hanging low as it had done since the day she was raped. But the wag was there and she held her head low with her nose up, testing, wanting to trust. I held my breath waiting to see what Boy would do.

He bellowed a huge laugh that sent chills down my spine to the tip of my tail. I could feel Hope shiver next to me and knew she had the same sense of doom that I felt. Faith's tail stopped wagging as Boy scooped her up roughly. I heard a small yelp as his rough hands hurt places already very sore and wounded on her tiny body. Hope and I both ran to follow, determined not to allow him to take our sister alone.

I never saw the boot coming at me, but I felt it when he kicked me hard and my body landed midway the shed, just near our food dish and water pail. I watched in dazed horror as Hope grabbed the leg of Boy's jeans and held on, as ferocious a growl as she could muster coming from between her clenched teeth.

Hope's teeth found Boy's leg beneath his jeans as she bit down. I heard Boy yell a sick, twisted sound, and recognized words coming from his mouth, "You stupid bitch! I will kill you!" but he could not make Hope let go of his leg.

I was making my way back to the front to help my sisters when I heard Faith drop to the ground in a sickening thud. I watched and saw, though she had the wind knocked from her, Faith was moving. Relieved she was alive, I hurried forward now and reached Boy just as he used both hands to grab Hope around her throat. She let go of his leg quickly as he choked her. I grabbed his hand and bit as hard as I could, trying to make him let Hope go.

I do not know if he was choking me before he kicked Hope across the shed or if he kicked and then grabbed me, but I could see the world growing pitch black around me. When I opened my eyes again I almost wished he had killed me because only Hope was with me in the shed. Boy and Faith were gone and the shed door was closed.

We both ran to the door and sniffed for a way out, a way to go out into that large world that we did not know and find our sister. I scratched at a spot where I saw light, and soon Hope and I were both digging our way out of the shed. Before we had dug enough of a hole to even fit our nose under the door, it opened and Boy was standing there.

His hand was bloody and I could see the blood on his jeans where Hope had bitten him. But I did not see Faith and my heart shattered into a hundred pieces. He took both Hope and me back to the pole where Mother had spent so many days and nights tied. He put a rope around my neck and tied me to the pole, then he got down on the floor and he raped Hope, holding her down until I thought she would die.

I fought against the rope to help her but it was no use. When he had finished, he tied another rope around Hope's neck and tied her to the pole next to me. He took a long sharp object from his jeans pocket and for a moment I thought he was going to kill us with it.

Instead, he took the rope from around my neck and sat down on the shed floor, holding me tight, just out of Hope's reach. He forced my mouth open and put something in the back between my teeth. My mouth would not close, and Boy took the long object and began to rub it hard against my teeth. The pain was excruciating long after he had finished filing my front teeth down. When he finished with me, he did the same thing to Hope.

After he had finished this cruel punishment, he tied us back to the pole. He moved the water pail so we could reach it and turned to go. He hesitated and looked us over

His parting words were, "Either of you ever bite me again and I will kill you on the spot."

He may as well have killed us both then because Faith was not here with us. We could not even begin to imagine what her fate might have been. Hope coughed and choked and then threw up. She laid on her side and I moved to lie next to her. We rested there for a long time, not sleeping, and not talking, each in our own private hell wondering where our sister was and what had happened to her.

Just before dark the shed door opened again. This time Boy had Faith with him. Her body hung limp as he carried her by the back of her neck. He dropped her body next to us and I heard a sickening thud as she landed just next to me. I also heard the grunt that told me she was still alive.

We waited for Boy to leave, fearing any movement may set him on one of us again. As soon as the door closed behind him, I moved to Faith to see how badly she was hurt. Her breathing was slow and steady but she did not move. Her mouth was bloody and sore and I knew her teeth had been filed just like ours. I saw the horrible wounds on her backside and knew Boy had done his worst to her. Hope was wounded and sore on her butt from the earlier assault, but there was a lot of blood on Faith's backside and I feared she would never come back to us.

Sometime before the sun came up on our last day in hell Faith finally spoke, "If he comes back, let him kill me. I don't want to live this way anymore."

I heard Hope crying and knew she felt the same. We had fought back. We had given all we had to prevent the sick abuse and torture of our sister, but it had not stopped Boy. If anything, it made the situation a hundred times worse.

I laid my body across Hope and Faith and I cried. Finally I reached out to them and asked them, "Will you fight with me again, or do we just give up and give in? Whatever we do we will do together."

Faith never spoke but Hope finally pushed me away from her and sat up. "I want to bite him just one more time," she said. "I will fight with you, Charity. He will most likely kill us when it is through, but I will fight with you."

Our mouths were still very swollen and I reminded Hope we might not be able to bite him. "But," she told me, "He didn't file our back teeth. Just the front. We can still bite."

Hope and I could not reach the feeding dish to eat, not that either of us were very hungry, and not that we would have been able to eat had it been in front of us. Faith sat on her leg, sideways, so her sore bottom was not touching the ground. She did not lift her eyes when we asked her to please try and nibble a little of the bread to keep her strength up, or to at least drink some water.

She remained with her head dropped low and her eyes to the ground. Boy opened the shed door and laughed when he saw us. "I didn't bring no food," he said. "I don't reckon you ate much of your food from yesterday though." Again he laughed a sick, twisted laugh.

He came over and looked at the three of us. "You are a sorry looking lot," he said. "But I got to get ya'll in shape cause Daddy wants to start training again. You need to get up and stop acting mad."

He actually spoke to us as if the torture we had endured at his hands was our fault. He untied the rope that held Hope from the pole, and then he untied my rope. He started to drag us toward the door, neither of us walking for him. Then he stopped as if he had forgotten something and he grabbed Faith roughly. He did not have to drag us then. We followed him, determined to fight with our last breath to keep Faith from being hurt any further.

When Boy was in the yard with us he took us to the training area and set us down in the pen. "Ain't no training today," he said. "Ya'll can play here in the sunshine. It'll be good for you."

The three of us sat huddled together, not moving. I could hear Hope letting me know she was ready for a fight and I listened hard for Faith to chime in. Faith's head was still dropped and her heart never spoke. She was lost somewhere in that place where nothing could hurt her and she could not hear my pleas for her to come back.

Hope and I looked at each other and decided it was best not to try and get her to come back to us while we were out here. We could try to reach her like before when we were in the dark of our shed. My nose started to burn like it does when evil was getting too close and I quickly looked around. Man was coming toward us. I warned Hope and prayed Faith could hear the warning as well. I was not sure how Man would react to the state Faith was in, but I did not want to find out.

My fears were for nothing. As usual, Man did not see anything that he did not want to see. He looked us over and yelled for Boy to come. "These are a sad looking lot," he said when Boy was standing in front of him. "You need to get them out of that shed some so they don't look so weak. I need you to take care of 'em for another six weeks at least."

"Daddy I am taking care of 'em," I hated his voice and hated the way he whined when he spoke to his father.

"Well, that'll be a first for you to stick to anything more than a week," Man said. "See to it they look better than this when the weekend comes. I got some people coming to see Killer and I want to give 'em a show."

Boy kicked the dirt in front of him and I could smell that despicable odor again, the smell of hurt and hate all mingled together. I could hear Hope saying that trouble was coming and I looked at her in full agreement. Today would probably be our last day on this earth because we were gearing up for a fight. We would not just let him hurt any of us again. We had already lost Faith and I did not know if we could bring her back again. He would not find it so easy to hurt any of us again.

Man left and it did not take long for Boy to turn his attention to us. "I'm just plain old sick of ya'll getting me in trouble," he sneered at us.

Boy walked away then and went into the back shed. Hope and I both knew he would return for us. I reached out once more to Faith and asked her to join us in this fight, probably our last stand. She did not lift her head.

Boy came back and reached for Hope. I was careful to bite his hand with my back teeth and, even though it hurt my mouth, I held on, clenching my teeth against his hand.

He let Hope go and hit me in the head with his fist. He grabbed me and carried me to the back shed with Hope running behind him trying to get a grip on his leg with her side and back teeth. He was doing a strange dance trying to avoid her bite. He kicked her away from him hard and I heard the grunt she made as she landed a few feet away. Then he had me inside the back shed and had closed the door against Hope's further attacks. "Deal with you next, you bitch," he muttered.

Just as Boy held me on the stool just inside the back shed and started raping me, I caught a strange, but pleasant and vaguely familiar smell. I heard Hope's Heart Speak, "Aunt Gertie."

Boy could not see her coming and did not have the benefit of his nose to help him. He was not paying attention to anything except what he was doing to me. For the first time I yelped as loudly as I could and heard the evil laughter that said Boy liked the fact he was hurting me. I was yelping so Aunt Gertie would hear me and ignored that my cries were giving Boy even more pleasure.

I saw light as the shed door opened and I heard Aunt Gertie, "What the hell are you doing to that puppy? You sick little pervert!" And to my great pleasure I felt his body fly away from me as she pushed him and then hit him in the face as hard as she could. I watched from the floor of the shed, and did not care that he had dropped me. The bruises and pain were worth it to see Boy getting attacked by Aunt Gertie.

I heard Hope snarling and growling as she ran through the now open shed door and rushed for Boy's leg once again. She grabbed his pants, now fallen down around his ankles, and began to growl and pull at them, looking for his leg so she could sink her teeth in.

I heard Aunt Gertie laugh and say, "I ought to knock your punk ass down so she can bite off the part you hurt that puppy with. That's exactly what you deserve you twisted little boy."

The world was spinning around me, and I knew I could not stay conscious much longer. Boy's fist to my head and then being dropped hard to the floor was taking its toll. I fought to stay conscious, hoping Aunt Gertie would knock Boy down, and I wanted more than anything for Hope to bite him there in that place. As the world went totally dark and I passed out I heard Boy crying.

Somewhere very far away I heard Faith's Heart Speak to me. "You did it, Charity. You saved us." It was the sweetest sound I had ever heard.

Chapter 15

The Road Out of Hell

The sun was very bright when I opened my eyes. Aunt Gertie was wiping my head with a wet cloth. Her smell was wonderful. At first I was very confused about what was happening. My body ached from head to toe and that reminded me of the incident with Boy.

I looked around and saw Hope sitting close by and very near to Faith. Faith was still staring at the ground, but I had heard her Heart Speak and I knew she was in there somewhere. That had been enough to give me hope and I would hold to that until there was nothing left to hold to.

Aunt Gertie had moved all of us to a shady spot in the yard. It smelled of fresh earth and green, green grass. If someone were to describe the color green in smell, this would be that color. It was the most wonderful spot I had ever been. I realized we were just at the edge of the yard, where the bushes separated Aunt Gertie's yard from hell.

I managed to sit up then and I licked Aunt Gertie's hand. It was the first time I had ever shown affection to a person, but I knew I could trust Aunt Gertie.

She smiled at me and said, "There now Puppy. No one is going to hurt you ever again. Not here anyway. Not if I can help it."

Boy was standing just a short distance away from us and was sniffling miserably. When another woman joined us, Aunt Gertie stopped doting over me and stood up. "Let me tell you what your snot nosed brat was up to," she said to the woman.

"He was doing bad things to this puppy. I saw him, and from the looks of the other two, he has been at them too. What kind of shit do you have going on over here, Marge?" Gertie's voice held a truck load of contempt and she was almost spitting the words.

"I don't think he knew what he was doing. He was experimenting. Boys will be boys, you know." Marge's voice held the same whine as Boy's when he would speak to Man, and I instantly did not like her.

"Oh, you stupid, stupid woman. Don't hand me that bullshit." Aunt Gertie's disgust and anger were both equally evident. "The best thing you can say about this little shit is he is his father's son, and that ain't saying anything good."

"Why do you always see the worst in him, Gertie? He provides food for his family and he is here. That's a lot more than you can say for the no account you married." Marge sounded defensive but her voice still held that aggravating whine.

"Oh shut up, Marge. This isn't about the bum you married, nor the sack of shit I made the mistake of wedding. You always try and change the subject and it ain't gonna happen this time. That boy hurt these dogs. He is sick, Marge. He is a very sick, twisted child and it is up to you to get him some help." Aunt Gertie was obviously not in the mood for the whining and sniveling any more than I was.

It felt wonderful to have someone coming to our defense. I could hear Hope's Heart Speak and could hear the smile… "Aunt Gertie is our Sergeant Stubby."

Marge crossed her arms in front of her. "You just need to go home now, Gertie. Willie will be home soon and you need to let me tell him about this. He will take care of the puppies. You just get on home now and leave my family to me."

"Oh wouldn't you just love that?" snorted Aunt Gertie. "And what do you think he will do with these puppies?"

"I imagine he will be getting shed of them as quick as he can," answered Marge. "They are damaged after all, aren't they?"

"Well, now; just who do you think damaged them?" Aunt Gertie had her hands on her hips now and showed no sign of backing down, much to my relief.

Marge did not get a chance to answer. Just then Man came strolling around the corner of the house and saw the lot of us there at the edge of the yard. He was carrying Killer and stopped in his tracks when he saw Aunt Gertie.

He more marched than walked back to where we were, putting Killer in the training pen as he passed it. "What's going on here?"

he asked, looking straight at Boy as if he knew his son was the one who had brought this unwelcome visitor to his yard.

Marge quickly responded, "Gertie *says* she saw..."

Aunt Gertie interrupted her. "I didn't *say I saw* anything," she said. "I *said* I caught your boy here raping this puppy. Is that what you have been teaching him over here?"

Man cleared his throat, obviously caught off guard. "And just where did you see this going on, Gertie? Over on your land or here on mine?"

"Well, since you asked," responded Aunt Gertie; "he was holed up in that back shed there where I have caught you doing meanness before. And I believe there is a little bit of question over just whose land that shed is on, isn't there? I have never pushed the issue because I knew you needed it for storage. But if you have all this meanness going on in there, maybe we should just let the court decide who owns that shed."

Man was obviously shaken by the threat of court. Rather than acknowledge the debate over who owned the infamous shed, he looked at Boy. "Get over here, now!" he demanded.

Boy walked slowly looking at the ground. "Move it, now!" Man snapped and Boy almost ran to join the small group. He stood just behind Marge's elbow, peeking out at Man. I could smell his fear and I liked it a lot.

"What you got to say for yo'self?" Man asked. "Was you up to no good with these here puppies I gave you, Boy?"

Boy muttered something under his breath that no one could hear. "Speak up now!" Man snapped. "Ain't nobody can hear you muttering through your nose that way. Quit acting like the little prissy ass your ma wants you to be and act like a man for once. You done something then you own it, damn it!"

Marge put her arm around Boy's shoulders. "You leave him alone," she snapped in that sick, whiny voice that I hated so much. "You just leave him alone. He's just a little boy."

Man's face grew very dark and made me think of a terrible storm brewing. I could feel the anger, hate and something else in the air. I realized then that Man was afraid. I was not sure what power Aunt Gertie held over him, but he was afraid of her.

His fear made his anger that much worse and he was prepared to take it out on both Marge and Boy. "You stupid cow. That's exactly what's wrong with the little ass wipe," Man was spitting with each word.

I was very glad Aunt Gertie was there or I was certain Hope, Faith and I would have been Man's first choice of a punching bag. For the first time since this encounter had begun I worried that Aunt Gertie might just go home and leave us there with this terrible family. I did not know if she was aware of Heart Speak. I could tell she had the capacity for it, but having it available and being able to use it are two different things.

With everything I could muster I sent the thought to her, "Please do not leave us here. If you leave, we are all three dead."

I could not be sure she had heard me, but she interrupted the squabble that had begun between Marge and Man over Boy. "I don't have all day for you two to argue over who made this child so sick. I think you both played a hand in it. What I want to know is what you intend to do about these puppies?"

Marge had begun to shrink back from Man's voice and Boy was still hiding behind her. But now Man turned his attention back to Aunt Gertie. "Well I reckon they've been ruined. Ain't no good for nothing after he's been at 'em. I can hit 'em in the head or drown 'em and put 'em out of their misery."

"You will do no such thing," snapped Aunt Gertie. "You are not going to let your child prodigy there hurt these puppies and then kill them to destroy the evidence of his meanness."

Man's face grew darker still and he looked directly at Aunt Gertie. "Well I reckon I can take them down to the pound. But there won't be nobody talking about evidence now, will there? I ain't gonna put up with but so much from you. I think we both know you will be keeping your mouth shut about this and exactly why you won't be talking."

Aunt Gertie's smell changed instantly. Even I knew Man had just made a threat against her. Of course, I had no clue what hold he might have over her, or what she was afraid of, but I recognized the fear I could smell coming from her now. I was just very grateful she was using what courage she had to keep my sisters and me safe.

Aunt Gertie's voice did not falter as she managed to hide the fear that had risen up inside her. I understood if she showed him she was afraid, she would have lost the little ground she had gained then. I could have sworn I heard her Heart Speak then. "Don't you worry Little One. I will not let you die here in this place. I wish I could do more for you. I may can't make things right for you again, but I can make sure you get out of here."

"I suppose the animal shelter is the best solution for everyone since I don't imagine you have the money to take these puppies to a vet."

"That's right," said Man. "And they look to me like they might need a bit of doctoring. The pound is the best place for them."

Man sounded relieved that there was an answer that he could live with. He looked back at Boy who still stood behind Marge, sniffling. "Don't think this is over for you. You will answer for this. I give you three puppies to look after and what do you do?"

Boy let out a loud sob and man snorted, obviously disgusted. "You are what your mama made you." Then he looked at Marge, "I don't s'pose you have anything else to say about this? Take your little girl there and go in the house with her."

Marge moved her hands to her hips, ready to fight for her son. "You stop calling him a girl, Willie. He's a child and he was acting like a child will act."

"I reckon so," snorted Man. "A stupid little boy sniffing after a bitch."

Marge may not have been happy with the way the conversation ended, but she led Boy to the house away from his father's anger and Aunt Gertie's harsh judgment. For a moment I forgot the abuse Boy had dished out to us and I felt a deep sadness. The memory of my mother was strong, and the way she had been willing to lay down her life for any of her children. Boy's mother was protecting her son as well. She may have been totally wrong in her defense of him, but it was clear he had no one to teach him how to be a decent human being. I would never like Boy. But for the briefest of moments I did feel sorry for him.

With Marge and Boy gone, Man turned his full attention to Aunt Gertie. "So, if I take these three to the pound I won't be hearing any more about this from you?"

"I suppose I will have to live with that," said Aunt Gertie, "if you will promise you won't leave that son of yours alone with dogs again."

"You don't have to worry about that," replied Man. "He has ruined these three puppies. They won't much to begin with, but I hoped they would teach him a little responsibility. Guess I'm lucky he didn't get at my good dogs."

Aunt Gertie's disdain for Man's attitude was evident to me, but she managed to keep it to herself. "I guess I will be riding with you to the shelter."

"What?" he asked. "You don't trust me, Gertie?"

"Not any further than I can see you," she snorted.

Aunt Gertie put Hope, Faith and me in a small crate she had brought from her house and carried us into the front of the truck with Man. "Put 'em in the back," he snapped.

"No," she responded. "They are going to ride out of this place up front with me. I hate I cannot do more for them." She paused for a moment and then added, "And I hate that you won't do more for them."

Man did not respond to her last comment, but he did not tell her to put us in the back again either.

I was not sure where we were going, but knew we were now on the road out of hell. I focused hard on letting Hope and Faith know how much I loved them and that we were free at last. I could hear their Heart Speak and was relieved that Faith's heart was singing. It was very far away, but she was still in there.

Chapter 16

Safe at the Shelter

Aunt Gertie was very quiet on the ride out of Hell. Man was muttering under his breath so no one could understand what he was saying. It was clear Aunt Gertie was there simply to see that we went to the promised "pound." I was not sure what that place was. Aunt Gertie had called it an "animal shelter." Faith remained very quiet and I was still a little worried about how we might bring her back to us.

Hope was anxious and I could hear her endless questions about what this new place may be like. I did my best not to sound agitated with her. In truth, I was as nervous as she was and her questions were not helping. Mother had never talked about an animal shelter or a pound with me. It could not be as bad as the place we had just come from.

Man finally pulled the truck into a parking lot. Aunt Gertie opened her door to get out, her hand on our crate. Man reached over and tried to take our crate from her. She pushed him away. "What?" he asked, "Exactly what do you think I will do here? Kill them in the parking lot?"

"I wouldn't put it past you," she retorted. "I will feel better if I walk in with you. I don't want to hear that you have told the officers these puppies have some kind of strange disease that will get them killed."

"They are Pits," snapped man. "And they look sickly. How quick do you think anyone is gonna be to adopt them?"

"Oh, it would suit you just fine for them to just disappear, wouldn't it?" Aunt Gertie obviously did not like or trust Man any more than I did. I would have liked her instantly even if she had not just saved us from hell.

"Do you think I am going to go in there and tell them the filth you say you saw my son doing to these dogs? I know you don't expect me to do that." Man was pronouncing each word carefully as if he was trying to make a clear point about something. I had never heard him speak so well.

Aunt Gertie glared at him. "No. I don't expect you will tell them about the meanness that goes on at your place. Still, I think I will walk in with you."

When she took us out of the truck I could see a long yellow building. It was hard to see everything from the crate, but I could smell dogs. I could smell a lot of dogs. When she carried us inside a woman approached and asked, "What have we here?"

"Three little puppies," Aunt Gertie answered. "Do you think you can find them a nice place to live? I can't afford to take them and I have grown fond of them."

Man walked up behind her. "They are my boy's puppies," he stated. "You know young'uns want everything they see and then don't bother to take care of nothing. I let him have the puppies to try and teach him something. But he ain't looked after them at all. Gertie here called me today and told me she had to chase some of the big dogs from down the road off of these puppies and my young'un won't nowhere to be found. I reckon this is the best place for them now. They'll get killed up there at the house with all the dogs around."

The woman did not look at Man but was looking at us inside the crate while he talked. I could tell that she did not trust Man. When she spoke, she addressed Aunt Gertie. "They do look like they might be dehydrated. I will see that they get food and water and we will do our best to get a rescue to take them."

Man rubbed his hand through his hair then. "You got those rescue people up here now? Didn't know there was any of them in this county."

"Of course we have rescue groups trying to save our furry friends," replied the woman. She had the same smell as Aunt Gertie, but hers was a lot stronger and she was not at all afraid of Man.

I sniffed the air twice as hard as normal to try and find her fear. But it wasn't there. "I think we are safe here," I told Hope and Faith.

Hope was trembling ever so slightly from excitement and a fear of the unknown. Faith just sat there looking at the bottom of the crate. I longed to rest my nose across her head and assure her everything was going to work out for us. But Aunt Gertie was still holding onto our crate and I could not move very well with it up in the air that way. When Hope or I would change position, the crate would rock and gave us the eerie feeling that we were going to be dropped. So I sat still and sent as much love and warmth toward Faith as I could. I could not let her give up, not now when we were so close to having a real life.

I turned my attention back to the conversation outside our crate, trying to figure out exactly what was going to become of us. Man was sounding very much like Boy right now and I could smell his fear and agitation. "I don't reckon none of those groups will want these three. I really don't believe they will live very long. They don't eat much and the one just sits there with her nose down."

Aunt Gertie sounded very defiant, "Well, Willie, I suppose if big dogs had been at you like these puppies have been attacked, you might sit with your nose to the ground too."

I could hear the smile in the pound woman's voice, "There are all kinds of rescue groups now. Some will actually take dogs that none of the others seem to want. They believe all dogs deserve a chance; even scrawny little puppies that sit with their noses to the ground."

The woman reached and took our crate from Aunt Gertie. "You wait here," she said, "and I will bring your crate back to you."

The woman carried us to a room behind a huge door with letters on it. The letters looked like this:

INTAKE
EMPLOYEES ONLY

I still do not know what those words were because I cannot read. But if I could read, I will bet those words said something wonderful like "Welcome to your place outside of hell." We would not see Man again. Aunt Gertie would come into our lives one more time, but for now, we were on an adventure in a new place with lots of strange smells.

Some of the smells were not so good, but there was the smell of hope in this place. There was something else lurking just beneath that hope that made me very uncomfortable. I watched Hope and Faith to see if they had noticed, but Hope just looked very excited and Faith just sat staring. My heart broke every time I saw her like that. I hoped we could bring her around quickly. She would never be raped by Boy again. And now we had a chance at a life. Surely she would understand that and come back to us.

We were taken from the crate and placed on the cleanest floor I had ever seen… one at a time. A man that the woman called 'Tony' stayed with us while she returned the crate to Aunt Gertie. For a moment I thought of Aunt Gertie, the woman who had saved us, riding with Man in that truck. I shivered. The truck was just as evil to me as Man. But I relaxed knowing Aunt Gertie did not live in hell. She lived next door to hell where I had a lot of brothers and sisters still being abused. I sent out a silent plea in Heart Speak and hoped Aunt Gertie heard it. "Don't let Boy hurt any of the other dogs there."

It never occurred to me to send out a plea about Man and the dog fighting. That was something that I had come to accept as a normal part of life. The fact Mother had told me it was different on the other side of hell had not registered yet. It would in time, but for now I had enough to think about with this new place and these new people. They seemed kind, like Aunt Gertie. But I would not give my trust until I was sure.

When the woman returned she began looking us over. She opened our mouths and stuck something down our throats while she spoke in a soothing, kind voice. Hope and I both gagged and coughed, but Faith did not make a sound. I heard her swallow hard and then she went back to staring at the floor.

"Do we have any of the preventative left?" she asked Tony.

"No," he answered. "That will have to do for now. Maybe some of the rescues will donate some more."

"Well," she said, "these three certainly needed something to get those fleas off of them. I am surprised they have any hair left."

"Those sores don't look like they come from scratching fleas to me," Tony said. "What do you think happened to these three?"

"I don't know for sure," she said. "My gut tells me there was something a lot worse than "big dogs down the road" hurting these puppies."

"You think they will make it? Will they stand a chance?" Tony's question shocked me. We were out of hell. Of course we would make it.

The woman answered, "Yes. I think they will be just fine. Rescues can always place puppies. You just take extra special care of these three. Give them plenty of food. They look like they have never had a meal."

"Oh, Joanie. You know I will take good care of them. But there is something wrong with these puppies that food can't fix." Tony's voice was not unkind, but I still did not like his attitude.

Then I heard something that made my heart almost leap from my chest. Someone was talking to me. It was Heart Speak and it was coming from the woman. Her lips were not moving but she was looking at me smiling.

"You will be just fine, won't you little girl? Joanie will see to that." She turned her attention away from me and back to Tony and said, "Why don't we wait for the vet to examine them before we worry about what can and can't be fixed? You just take extra good care of these three."

We were looked over really well and given a shot that they called a vaccine. We each had drops put in our nose. The drops made Faith sneeze and she looked a little embarrassed before she started staring at the floor again. That was enough to tell me Faith was not as far gone as I had believed. Or... perhaps all this attention was bringing her back.

Finally we were taken to our new home. It was something called a kennel and it was in a small group that set away from several long rows of kennels. There was something written on our door. It looked like this:

KENNEL 5

Tony set us inside the kennel and put some blankets in for us. He spoke to us as if we could answer and I liked him immediately. "Those blankets will be good for you when you want to sleep. This kennel may not be like Mom and Home, but we will keep it clean for you and even though the floor is very hard, that blanket is soft."

Before he left he set a water bowl and a food dish inside our kennel. We waited for him to leave before Hope and I checked our food supply. It smelled wonderful, but Tony must not have noticed how sore our mouths were. The food was way too hard for us to eat.

"He will see we haven't eaten when he comes back," Hope said. "Then they will bring food we can eat. I just know they will. They are very nice."

I agreed and the two of us turned our attention to our smaller sister. It was time for her to join us here in the shelter and leave the Land of Nothing behind forever. Hope and I sat near her as we had before. Pure love and Heart Speak needed to work magic for us one more time.

Chapter 17

The Sound of Heart Speak

Heart Speak is a wonderful thing. It is a language all living creatures are born understanding. Those who choose evil and wrong-doing lose the ability quickly. Children usually have the ability to understand Heart Speak unless they have experienced a horrendous evil themselves, and then embraced that evil. It was clear to me that Boy looked up to Man. He gave his father a twisted respect and mimicked him. He wanted to learn Man's evil ways. One day he would grow up. He would breed and fight dogs. And he would probably always be a rapist. As we had said before. Man and Boy were demon and imp; if Boy had a heart it was stone and pure evil. There was no way Boy could understand Heart Speak.

Mother had told me about Heart Speak, but she did not teach it to me. Heart Speak is not something that can be learned; it is something already there that must be accepted. Of course those who choose to accept it must learn to use it carefully. For instance, one who understands Heart Speak cannot just assume everyone understands what is in their heart. And those who do accept it have a responsibility if they want to keep the ability. That responsibility is to remain open-minded and open-hearted. Once you allow hate to enter your soul, Heart Speak will start to fade.

It is easy to want to understand Heart Speak; but, it is much harder to hold on to that ability when evil is all around you. Evil, by its very nature, begs to be disliked and hated. The key is to learn to hate the deed without hating the one spreading the evil. Dogs have a forgiving nature, I believe, because the truth about Heart Speak is instilled within our hearts and souls from such an early age. There are very few dogs who have lost the ability to understand Heart Speak. If you ever meet one, you will know immediately. Their eyes will hold no wonder and no joy. Their tail will not wag... ever. And it would be wise for man to stay away from a dog who has lost all knowledge of Heart Speak.

Faith had not lost Heart Speak. Instead, she had gone somewhere deep inside herself to escape the pain that was all around her. Hope and I knew we could bring her back to us if we could get her to listen to her own heart and soul. In other words, Faith had to remember her abilities and embrace them.

When Hope and I wrapped our love all around Faith there in the shelter... when we finally got through to her, she did come back to us. But she was still not the puppy we had known before she was raped that last time by Boy. She blamed herself because she had approached Boy with trust, extended her paw and her heart to him. When she was given the name 'Faith,' it was because of the very thing inside of her that made her reach out to Boy and offer him her trust. In time, I knew she would once more have the capacity to reach out that way. But I also knew it was not going to happen because Hope and I wanted it to.

Guilt and shame are terrible things to overcome. Hope and I had our own shame to deal with. But Faith was very lost in hers. She not only felt responsible for her own abuse, but also thought she had somehow brought Boy's wrath down on Hope and me. I dealt with that the only way I knew by telling her it was not true. Of course that did little to help ease her pain.

Hope, as always, knew what to say. She told Faith that even if what she believed were true... even if her extended paw had brought all of the pain to bear... then she had to realize that it had also brought our freedom. It was the start of our journey out of hell.

So Faith decided to join us there in the shelter. She would cower behind Hope and me when people would approach. It was going to take something grand to bring my sister back to the faith she had been born with. But it was enough for me to know she had chosen to live, and would not waste away hiding in the Land of Nothing. I understood how hard it was for her to make the decision to come back. I had been to that place inside myself and I was well aware of the peace that nothingness can bring.

Now we had a new life and we needed to try and understand what was expected of us in this place. There were a lot of other dogs here... all kinds and all sizes. Would we be expected to allow some of these dogs to train? Would we have to learn to endure that pain still? I could see a lot of scars on some of the dogs here and it worried me.

Even though the kennels at the shelter are designed so each dog has their privacy while inside the kennel, we could still hear the others talking to each other. There was more Heart Speak in this place than I had ever believed possible. It was a very noisy place for a dog. Even when people may have thought the place was quiet, those who understood Heart Speak could hear the endless chatter.

I had noticed right away that the two people we had met here knew Heart Speak; but the dogs... Oh My Dog... I never understood just how easy it is to communicate with this universal language until we had been in the shelter for about an hour.

When people would come in most of the dogs would forego the Heart Speak and start barking and making noise to be noticed. There was one exception to that. There was a little Jack Russell Mix about three kennels down from us. His name was Thumper. I knew right away how he had gotten his name, because his tail never stopped thumping. We could hear it beating hard against the concrete in his kennel and his heart was singing always. It was clear he felt pretty darn good about himself. I don't think Thumper had ever known a person who did *not* understand Heart Speak. And he was very hurt that his family had left him here in this shelter. He did not seem at all sure why this had happened to him.

Tony came back into the kennels frequently and he would sometimes bring a person with him. It was easy to figure out the people he was bringing back were looking for a dog. So I understood almost from the start all of the dogs here were waiting for a person to choose them. The animal shelter *must* be a place for lost dogs to find their way home. Some dogs had been lost their entire lives and were looking for their first home. I was not sure Thumper realized this. But Thumper definitely knew that it was going to take someone noticing him to get him back where he wanted to be. Thumper would hear the door open indicating someone was coming in and the Heart Speak would start:

"Hey... I'm over here. Come on over here and get me out of this cage. I need to get home. I am missing my treats and my toys and my supper. I know you can hear me. Stop acting like you don't hear me, now. Stop playing. Hey! Hey! I'm over here!"

Thumper would carry on that way the entire time people were present. Then, when the people would leave and it was just canines in the shelter, Heart Speak filled the air. We were quickly learning all of the stories for the dogs in the shelter. I was very curious about why Thumper was here so listened closely to see if anyone would talk about it. It didn't take long.

An old Shepherd Mix who had already been chosen by a rescue that helps seniors spoke up first. "Thumper! Thumper, are you listening to me?"

"I hear you," Thumper said, sounding more than a little agitated.

I could hear the smile in the Old Shepherd's voice when she continued. "Thumper why do you carry on that way? Even if all of those people did understand you, they can't take you out of here. And *I know* that *you know* it. You can pretend all day long that you don't know why you are here. But you know exactly what you did."

Thumper was very quiet for the first time. I waited and listened hard, hoping to hear what Thumper had done to land him in the shelter. This place was a haven for my sisters and me and I was having a hard time understanding why Thumper seemed to hate it so much.

Hope had never been known for her patience, and even though we had all three agreed to remain quiet until we learned how things worked in the shelter, I was glad Hope was as curious as I was. "What did he do?" Hope asked. She was looking at the Old Shepherd Mix. Her kennel was in front of ours so the senior was one of the few dogs we could actually get a good look at.

The old girl looked a little shocked when Hope first spoke, almost as if she had not realized we were there in the kennel just across from hers. She sat down in front of her water pail and took a long drink, then looked at Hope. "He bit someone," she said. "He bit a man right on the backside while he was bent over."

I heard one of the dogs down the long aisle of kennels laugh. Each dog has a unique sound specific to their heritage and I could tell by the sound of the laughter it was a Walker Hound. The senior had a smile in her voice as she continued, "The man was snooping around where he had no business and Thumper is not really in bad trouble. He barely broke the skin on the man's tough rear end. But, Thumper's people could not find his rabies tag nor the papers that said he had a rabies shot. The vet's office where he got the shot is closed so Thumper has to stay here in quarantine until they are sure he is not rabid."

She took another drink of water as if talking was thirsty work for her and then went on, "His family loves him and I believe he will be going home as soon as that vet's office opens up. People do not always realize how important things like Rabies Tags are to a dog. But I do believe old Thumper has had that vaccine and will be able to go home soon."

Hope's curiosity was totally peaked now. "Well, what will happen if he hasn't had that vaccine? Will they give him one here? They gave us vaccines when we came in earlier."

The old senior shook her head sadly. "Oh, I hope you do not have to find out what happens if they lied about him having that rabies shot. I hope they *didn't* lie. Thumper may have just been protecting his property and his people when he nipped that thief in the derriere, but rabies is nothing to play with. If he hasn't had that shot he will have to stay in quarantine until they are sure he does not have rabies. It costs a lot of money to keep a dog that way and if his family can't pay, well, then... poor Thumper will have to go to that room in the back."

My heart sank to my paws. Something told me that room in the back was not a very good place. I suspected that was the room that had the terrible odor coming from it I had gotten a whiff of earlier.

Faith was as curious as Hope now and even though I really did not want to hear the answer, I was happy to hear her ask, "How long will he have to stay in *that* room?"

The senior dropped her head and stared at the floor sadly. For a moment, I thought she was not going to answer. Then she looked at the three of us sitting across from her and answered quickly as if to get the truth out and over with, "The room in the back is the place where dogs go in and never come out. It is the place every dog here hopes they do not have to see."

The three of us sat very still. We all understood exactly what the old Shepherd was saying. Every dog in the shelter was thinking about that room now and for the first time, there was not a sound around us. Then we heard Thumper's familiar voice:

"Hey now! I have had that shot. I remember having it right back there in the old hind quarters. Bet you I gotta scar where they stuck me. It made me yelp really loud when they stuck me. Tell those people to get back here. I will show it to them so I can go on home.

"I remember that tag I was supposed to wear, too. My daddy hung it right on my collar with a tag that had my name and address on it. I lost both of them when I jumped in the lake one time. If they take me to that lake I will swim down to the bottom and find those tags.

"Hey. Do you dogs hear me? Get those people back in here and I will put an end to this nonsense right now I need to get home. My people need me."

I hoped Thumper would be able to go home as soon as the vet's office opened up. He obviously had a family he loved. I said a silent prayer to the Great Creator of All Life that his family loved him enough to make sure he had that vaccine. My life may have been the absolute worst before coming to the shelter, but I still did not want to see others suffer. Thinking about it, I suppose that is one of the reasons my mother gave me the name Charity. That thought gave me great comfort.

The Heart Speak began again in the shelter and, though we could still hear Thumper's complaints, we could also hear a lot of other conversations. The Walker Hound that had laughed earlier announced that everyone in the shelter had three days to get out... to find a home or a rescue... before the room in back became a threat.

The senior was still looking us over, trying to decide if we were going to be friends. "It's not really so bad here," she said. "The people here try hard to make sure we all get out and they will hold a dog long past those three days so long as they have room... and providing there is nothing wrong with the dog."

She took a deep breath then as if about to share some bad news. She dropped her head again and cut her eyes up at us. "Of course, you may not be able to leave here together. You may go to different places."

Faith and Hope both gasped and moved closer to me. I was shaking my head hard and I said, "No. We have to stay together."

The old dog shot me a smile that said I shouldn't worry about it and then said, "My name is Nelly. I sort of got dumped here because my family thought I was too old." She sounded a little sad when she shared that bit of information. Then she added quickly, "But I have a rescue that is going to take me so I don't have to go to that room in the back. I guess I'm one of the lucky ones because I don't have to wonder about it anymore. Of course I have been here for almost three weeks. They just were not willing to give up on me so quick… so see… it's not as bad as the hound down there made it sound. I have seen a lot in those three weeks and you three look like you have seen some bad times. What's your story?"

My sisters looked at me and waited for me to answer. I was not too sure how this old dog would react knowing that we had lived in hell, but I decided the truth would be the best answer. "I am Charity," I said. "And these two are my sisters, Hope and Faith."

I stopped for a moment and then went on, "We came from a very bad place. The man and the boy that lived there hurt us. They let another dog attack us. He was our own brother, but he would do what Man told him to do. But the worst was what Boy did to us. It hurt really bad. He did things to us – back there – back in our butt. It makes me ashamed even though I try not to be. I know it is not my fault Boy raped us."

Once I started talking the words just came out. I could not have lied if I had wanted to, and it felt good to put into words what had happened to us. Even though it made it very real; it also helped me to understand that it was really over. I kept talking and Nelly listened intently. I could hear the words as I said them and realized something was happening to me. The more I talked, the better I felt. But it was not just feeling better; I was feeling more like a puppy than I ever had. I was letting a lot of the burden I had carried go.

I told her about my brothers and sisters and those that had been killed early. I talked about "the chosen" and told her all about Killer and my three sisters that were the right color, so they were going to be used for breeders. Then I told her how Boy had come in and tried to take Faith away.

"We tried to defend ourselves but we were too little," I said. "When Boy came back from hurting Faith really bad, he took a metal stick and did something to our front teeth. Now we cannot eat the food the people here are giving us. I hope they notice because we have not eaten in a while now and we are very hungry."

I told her about Boy kicking us and hitting me in the face with his fist when I tried to defend Hope. As the story spilled out, I was relieved to get to the part where Aunt Gertie had walked in and caught Boy hurting me. I ended it with "And so you see, we have to stay together... no matter what!"

Nelly tilted her head slightly when I finally stopped talking. "You three look very young," she said. "Where is your mother? Do they still have her in that terrible place?"

"No," Hope spoke up. "They killed our mother a while back. They used her for something called bait. The dogs that attacked her ripped holes in her. The sores were very bad on her leg and her backside. They did not try to help her at all and those sores were starting to smell really bad. It smelled like she was rotting. They used our mother that way and when she was all used up they just threw her away."

Hope's voice held unshed tears and she stopped talking before they could start falling. I believe she knew if she started crying now, she might never stop.

"Mother loved us. She did her very best to protect us," Faith added, clearly not wanting Nelly to think our mother had not cared about us. "I am not sure where they threw her away, but I know if she could have been there to help us she would have."

Nelly really looked at us for the first time then I think. I could tell she was sorry she had made us sadder than we already were. But while she looked at us and was really seeing us, I really looked at her for the first time, too. I liked her. I liked the way her voice sounded and the love I could feel coming from her heart. But her eyes were simply beautiful. Nelly had eyes that looked like they could go right through your skin and see your heart and soul. She had a very strange look on her face as she asked, "Do you know the name of the place you came from?"

I answered, "The only name I know is hell. We lived in hell."

"Yes you did," said Nelly. "You surely did. But you three have held on to your Heart Speak and that is very good. If anything helps you get out of here it will be that." Then Nelly smiled a huge, almost toothless smile. "As for your teeth, they were puppy teeth and you will get more soon enough. The next that come in, you will keep forever, so see to it that you take care of them. I am so old I have lost most of mine, so I understand all about the food hurting your mouth."

"By the way," Nelly continued. "What was your mother's name?"

Faith spoke without hesitation, "Her name was Mother. That is the only name she ever had and she told me once, it was the only name that had ever mattered to her."

Nelly went back to her water pail and had another long drink. Then her eyes met mine and she said, "I think I might be able to help you three get out of here together. Yep. I think I just might have a secret or two in my head. You girls leave it to me and let me see if I can't make your lives a whole lot better. You watch Old Nelly use her Heart Speak. Yep. Yep. I think you are going to be very happy you met me."

My heart was feeling a lot lighter just from having gotten the terrible story out. Nelly's gentle manner and her friendly smile made it very easy to like her. She reminded me of what our mother might have been had she not lived in hell. I was already very glad I had met the old girl with the toothless smile. Suddenly I was very tired and I realized that for the first time ever, I felt totally safe. I drifted off to sleep with the shelter sounds all around me. I snuggled with Faith and Hope like a puppy would. It was the most peaceful sleep I had known.

Chapter 18

The Song of Souls

Waking up in a strange place can be scary, especially when you have arrived there from hell. Even before I opened my eyes I knew I was not in the shed any longer. Instinctively I sniffed the air searching for my sisters. The bright light in the shelter confused me at first. My eyes had grown very accustomed to darkness. As soon as I could focus I saw Hope and Faith. They were at the front of the kennel talking to Nelly. They stayed very close to each other and I noticed that each of them kept looking back at me, as if to make sure I was still there.

Hope saw that I was awake and her face brightened. It occurred to me both of my sisters looked more alive and happier than I had ever seen them. From our short time in this place I already understood we had three days to find a home. I did not think the shelter would hang on to us much past those three days. I had not missed the concerned look Nelly gave when she had said they would hold a dog longer 'so long as there was nothing wrong with the dog.' I could not see my own puny body, but I could see my sisters. I knew we did not look healthy. All of the other dogs here looked much better than we did. And I had counted at least five kennels that housed puppies. Who would want a sickly puppy, let alone three, when there were so many others to choose from?

"Nelly is telling us stories from her life before the shelter," Hope said. "Oh Charity, even the worst place out there must be so much better than the shed. We will have a chance to live now."

I hoped that was true, but more, I hoped Nelly's magic was powerful enough to keep the three of us together.

I joined my sisters at the front of the kennel, but before Nelly could resume her story, the door opened and three people came in.

Joanie was leading a man and a woman into the back. The woman's eyes looked way too big for her face and she was sniffing. It looked as though she had been crying, but now she was smiling broadly.

"I don't know why I didn't think to look in the Bible before," she said. "I stick a lot of our most important documents there for safe keeping."

"Well I am glad you thought about it," said Joanie. "Thumper is a happy boy, but he has been very anxious here in the shelter. I believe he wants to go home."

The shelter suddenly came to life with barking dogs and it was hard to hear the conversation past Joanie's last comment. Thumper's Heart Speak was louder than the barking and he was very excited.

"Hey. I smell my mama and my daddy. Are they here? Hey! I'm down here. Come on down and get me now. You are taking me home,

right? I've been waiting forever now. Come on. I'm right down here. That's it. Keep walking, keep walking. Oh My Dog I can smell you getting closer. Oh I love you so much. Come on now and I'll let you give me a belly rub. I'll wash your face, your ears. I'll wash your eyes and your nose if you want me to. Just come on. Oh My Dog! Oh My Dog! I can't wait."

As soon as the trio got near Thumper's kennel and he could actually see his people and they could see him, the Heart Speak filled the shelter. All of the dogs stopped barking and joy filled the air. Thumper's family had found his rabies certificate and they had come for him. I sat quietly; it was wonderful to hear the sounds of happiness.

It was hard to tell who was saying what as hearts sang out and love filled the large room. I had never known so much love existed in the world. It made me extremely glad… but it also left an ache in my heart. The ache was for what Hope, Faith and I had never known and for what our mother had missed in her life. The three of us might get a chance, but our mother never would, and that made me incredibly sad.

"Oh I missed you so much. I am so sorry I lost my tag in the lake. I am sorry I bit that man… well… maybe a little sorry… no… not sorry about that. But I am so glad you love me and are taking me home. You are taking me home, right? Please take me home. Oh you are taking me home. I know you are. Oh I'm so happy. Oops! Sorry 'bout that. Didn't mean to pee on your shoe there. Yowza, and you have those open shoes on. Peed right on your paw there, didn't I?

And you don't even care. You are glad to see me. I know you are. Oh I love you."

And from Thumper's mom and dad: *"We missed you, boy. The house was not the same without you. We want you home before the kids get back from school. We have been so worried about you. So sorry we let you down, boy. We will never lose your records again. We love you so much. We have a very special treat waiting for you at home. Don't worry about that pee. Everybody dribbles a little when they get excited. Come on now, let me give the boy a belly rub..."*

It was simply beautiful. I had never known such love and it made tears sting my eyes. I was not sure if the tears were happy ones for Thumper and the fact that such love could exist... or if they were sad tears because of all the dogs who would never even have a chance to know this kind of love. Mostly I was glad Thumper's people had found that shot record and he would not have to stay in the shelter. And I was extremely happy they had, indeed, gotten him vaccinated so he did not have to worry about that room in the back.

Faith was snuggling very close to me. I could hear her small voice imploring, "Charity, you and Hope bit down on Boy. We didn't have those rabies shots. Will they make you go to that room in the back? If you go, I want to go with you. Please do not leave me here alone."

Faith's words tore at my heart and I barely noticed Nelly staring at me across the aisle. I knew she was waiting to see what I was going to say to my sister. If a dog has any decency about them, they will never interfere in a family situation like this, not unless they are invited. But I was as lost as Faith with regard to what she was asking. I looked at Nelly, begging her to help me out as I gave Faith the only response I could, "I don't think anyone will ever know what we did to Boy, Faith. I don't think Man or Boy will ever tell because then they may have to tell what Boy did to us."

Nelly smiled that toothless smile again and chimed in, "No. I don't think you ever have to worry about that piece of work telling on any of you for biting. There are some mean people in this old world. And I know because I have met a few of them. But the meanest of those I have met would not take kindly to what Boy did to you three. That's just plain sick, and I believe he knew what he was doing was wrong. So don't you worry about him telling anyone. I don't think that will happen."

We got quiet and watched Thumper leave the kennel room with his family. His shorter than average tail was totally erect and wagging uncontrollably when he passed us, walking between his mom and his dad. He had a bounce to his step that spoke of both a great pride and love. Thumper was going home.

Joanie was smiling and watching as she walked behind them. When she passed our kennel she glanced over at the three of us, her eyes lingering slightly on the food dish that had not been touched. For only a second I saw the smile fade and a look of concern cross her face. Then she was gone through the door with Thumper and his family. We could still hear the Heart Speak from the front, even with the door closed. Every dog in the shelter sat quietly, listening to the love. It was a very special moment and every dog there knew it.

The long silence was broken when the Walker Hound down the aisle let out a long howl. The sound vibrated in my ears, but had an even greater impact on my heart. I could feel chills starting at my head and going down my back... all the way to the tip of my tail. It made my heart yearn and ache, but there was also a sense of peace that the strange song imparted. It made me a little dizzy and I knew I could easily have gotten lost in the melody.

I felt a strong urge to join in, but knew if I did, it might frighten my sisters. I settled for a huge yawn and managed to gulp down a bit of air. I could feel the air bubble tickling my belly and I let out a sigh that held a bit of a whimper and a huge burp. Faith and Hope giggled and crinkled their noses, obviously fighting against joining in with the hound as hard as I was.

Nelly let out a couple of short howls that sounded more like extra-long hiccups, and turned her attention back to us.

Several of the dogs in the kennels around us joined in the howling session. Six little fluffy puppies in the kennel next to Nelly stepped to the front and joined in the song. They were all the same color, black with brown around their eyes, on their paws and a spot on each shoulder, and a white chest... no chosen ones there. I could not help but wonder where their mother was and if she had told them how hard life could be. Had their mother been forced to lie in her own waste while children she had given life to were ordered to bite and rip her skin until she cried blood tears? I didn't think so. They looked like they had not missed a meal in their short lives.

Nelly winked and whispered across the aisle to me... not using Heart Speak and obviously not wanting the puppies to know she was talking about them. "They were born to a well-loved dog. Family didn't get her spayed and nature took its course. I imagine she will be going to the vet for a spay job after this. At least her family loved her enough to bring the puppies here and not dump them in a lake somewhere. And they *did* let them get old enough to be weaned."

Faith looked very sad and said, "But I bet she misses them. And they must miss her something awful."

"I am sure there is enough heartache to go around for all of them," Nelly responded. "I lost more than one litter in my life and the most we can do is hope our children will find a good home. It is out of our control once Man steps in."

"Man is a terrible person," said Hope.

Nelly smiled slightly and dropped her head a little. "There are some very terrible men in the world," she said. "But, Hope, there are some good ones as well. Look at Thumper's dad. He was a wonderful man. And Tony, the man who works here, is a good man that understands Heart Speak."

Faith spoke up then, her voice sounded far wiser than I could ever remember, "Yes. There are very good men in this world. I think we have to learn how to tell the difference by what is in their hearts."

The six puppies were in a line now at the door of their kennel. Their noses were pointed toward the ceiling and they were howling with a very unique rhythm. By the time the last in the line started his howl, the first was ending his. The song they sang was mournful and beautiful at the same time, music from their souls. It told of great joy for life and great sadness for hearts parting ways.

Nelly knew what I was thinking and responded to me, "Oh yes. That is a wonderful way to describe it. Howling is a way for us to celebrate both life and death... happiness and sorrow. It tells of past memories and future dreams. It holds both tears of pain and heartfelt hopes."

Faith looked very thoughtful now and looked me directly in the eye. "Howling is the song of our souls," she said. Then she stuck her nose in the air and let out a long, mournful howl.

Hope and I could not control the urge to join in. Nelly smiled that toothless grin and stuck her own nose high in the air. She let go a series of smaller yips and then a very long howl that rivaled any we had heard. Every dog in the shelter joined in as we sang our "fare the well" to Thumper.

As soon as the hound tired of howling, everyone else began a tapering off that was as eerie as the first of the howls had been.

The entire shelter grew very quiet. Obviously, the Walker Hound was the conductor for the shelter choir.

An echo hung in the air for a few seconds after the song ended. It was haunting. And it was something that I will always remember as one of those defining moments in time.

The Song of Souls should be something every dog knows and understands. For those who have listened to the song before, that statement needs no explanation. For those who have never heard it, there is no explanation to define it.

Chapter 19

A Place of Shelter

Once Joanie had Thumper out of the shelter and on his way home, she came back to the kennels. I could tell she cared about every one of the dogs here. She appeared to ignore our kennel and started at the one next to us, on the right. She made her way through the kennel room talking to the dogs with a soothing voice, calling them by name. She ended her journey through the kennels on our left.

She walked slowly to our kennel, looking at each one of us carefully. "Now exactly what am I going to do with you three?" she asked.

We huddled closer together as we had learned to do during our time in hell. Joanie came into our kennel and knelt down on the concrete floor. "Why are you sitting on this hard floor?" she asked. "Don't you know what that blanket is for?" She pulled the blanket Tony had left next to her and folded it neatly. Then she put it on the floor next to us. She reached and lifted me first and moved me to the blanket. Hope began to crawl toward me, putting herself on the blanket. Faith pancaked to the floor and put her paws as far under her as she could without tipping over. She turned her head slightly so she could watch Joanie and then began to crawl away as fast as she could.

Joanie reached out and picked Faith up as she tried to crawl away. Faith began to whimper loudly and Joanie held her very close to her chest. "Oh honey. No one is going to hurt you here. I am so sorry someone has made you afraid." Then she placed Faith on the blanket next to me. I felt my backside being lifted as Faith squirmed between my front legs and was pushing under me.

There were tears glistening in Joanie's eyes. Her heart was telling me that she was aching for us. She knew we had been hurt and she wanted us to trust that no one would bring us pain here in this place... not on her watch.

I wanted to trust this woman who smelled so wonderful. I had never smelled safety before, but if I had to give it an odor, it would be the smell coming from Joanie. I stretched my neck just a little and sniffed her hand. Before I even realized I had done it, I licked her hand. She gasped and I pulled my head back quickly.

"Oh Sweetie; it's okay," she said. "You can lick my hand any time you want. You just startled me is all." She petted me on top of my head and for the first time I got a sense of how very small I really was. Her hand was twice the size of my head. This confirmed that I was not one bit larger than my sisters. I was not exactly sure how I felt about that. I honestly wanted to be a puppy, to feel like a puppy feels... but I had been in hell forever and it is hard not to grow up fast there.

Joanie was smiling at the three of us, but she did not try and pick us up again. I believe Faith's reaction had made her realize we needed to feel safe more than we needed to be cuddled. She tilted her head to the side as if in deep thought and asked, "Now what exactly am I going to call you three? Old man Burney didn't give me names for you." She made a small disgusted 'humph' sound and added. "I doubt he bothers much with names anyway."

Perhaps if I had thought really hard and tried to connect with Joanie she would have gotten our names right. But I was still too afraid to really try Heart Speak out with a person. I had reached out to Aunt Gertie, but had sent that message with a lot of very loud yelps. So Joanie chose names for us that sounded nothing like Faith, Hope and Charity.

She called me Jet. Hope was dubbed Sonic. When she got to Faith she reached out and touched her head very gently. Faith cowered down and Joanie said, "I am going to call you Jo-Jo. That was my little dog's name when I was a child. She was very scared when I first got her, just like you are."

She stood up and moved toward our food dish. "I hope you like your names," she said, and then added, "and I hope the vet can tell me why you are not eating."

She walked outside our kennel and closed the door behind her. "Dr. Martin is coming to have a look at you soon," she said, looking us over one more time. "I know you are going to be just fine."

Tony startled me when he walked up beside Joanie and I jumped just a little. Joanie looked back at me and I moved both front paws, making my back wobble. Hope was leaning against my back, with Faith leaning against both of us. We were so close together when I wobbled, we all did.

Tony smiled as if he had never seen anything like that before and he exclaimed, "Look! They even move alike! They are triplets!"

Joanie smiled and said "Well, all three are adorable, but they don't look exactly alike, Tony. I can tell them apart."

"Bet you already named 'em," he said. "You know you shouldn't do that before Doc Martin has a look at them."

"Yes, I named them," she said. "Dr. Martin will need something to identify them by when he picks their charts up. What was I supposed to do? Put Pup 1, Pup 2 and Pup 3 on their charts? I don't think so."

Tony shook his head, totally disagreeing with what Joanie had done; but he sounded kind when he responded, "You know once you have given them a name it will be hard to do the right thing if they are really sick. You just buy trouble for yourself Joanie. Trouble and heartache."

"Bite me, Tony," she said and turned to walk away. Then she added, "And give them some of the canned food please. I think the kibble is too hard for them."

Joanie walked back out the door leading to the office and Tony went to a small room just over to the side of the kennels. He came out with three small cans and the smell coming from them made my mouth water. I heard Faith and Hope both smack loudly and knew they were smelling it too.

Tony stopped at some shelves on his way back to our kennel and grabbed three small bowls, about half the size of our water bowl. He brought them into our kennel and put the wonderful smelling food from the cans in each bowl.

"I imagine a whole can is too much for each of you," he said. "But I will give whatever you don't eat to Old Nelly over there. I think she will appreciate that." Then he added as if someone had chastised him. "Oh, don't you worry. I will make sure Nelly has some soft food even if you eat it all. Old girl's salivating over there smelling this stuff."

He set the bowls in a row and said, "Go ahead now. Dig in."

We looked at him, waiting for him to leave so we could eat. He grunted a little and then left our kennel. He went back to the little room and brought another can out for Nelly. He put it in the food dish already in her kennel and she was eating before he had finished emptying the can.

Tony turned and looked at us, still sitting there waiting for him to leave. "Look at Nelly eat. That's what you're supposed to do. Dig right in and eat that food so you can gain some weight and get healthy."

We didn't move and he sighed as he left nelly's kennel and walked away. I heard him mutter, "Yep. You three are sure to break Joanie's heart... AGAIN."

As soon as he left the kennel room Hope rushed over to the three bowls and began to eat. Faith went behind her, but kept looking at the door to make sure Tony was not trying to trick her and was going to spring from the shadows and hurt her as soon as she started eating. I joined them after I was sure they were going to eat. I was as worried about their appetites as Joanie and Tony were.

We managed to eat about half of what was in our bowls, and immediately had to go to the bathroom. We were not accustomed to such good food and it was running right through us. We were all pacing up and down in the kennel, none of us sure exactly where we were supposed to go in this clean place.

Finally Hope could not hold it any longer and went right on the blanket Joanie had folded so neatly only a short time before. Faith began to cry, certain someone was going to come and hurt us for messing up the nice blanket. She was so frightened she did not even bother to find a place to go, but pooped right where she stood. I went to the blanket and relieved myself while Faith crawled to the farthest corner in the kennel to hide.

Hope and I followed Faith into the corner, each living in our own private version of hell, waiting for Tony or Joanie to come and start yelling because we had soiled our kennel. I heard Nelly calling to us and slowly stuck my head out of the shadows.

"What's the matter?" Nelly asked. "What are you three hiding from over there?"

"We made our kennel all dirty," I answered. "The food went right through us and we could not wait. No one told us where to go and use the bathroom and we had to go really bad."

Nelly threw her head back and laughed. "You sure you three have never been in a house before for training?" she asked.

"No," I answered. "Our training was all in a pen back behind the shed. And we weren't there to poop. We usually did when Killer would start biting us... but that's not what we were there for."

Nelly stopped laughing. "Oh My Dog!" she said. "You three have really and truly been through hell. I am sorry I laughed. I didn't realize..."

Nelly came closer to the front of her kennel. "You three stop hiding now. Tony will come and clean your kennel for you. They know you have to go somewhere and no one is gonna be upset cause you pooped on the floor."

Then she stepped sideways so we could get a good look in her kennel. "Look over there," she said. "I have deposited a huge pile right there in that corner." Then her voice got a little louder as if she wanted Tony to hear her. "And I sure do wish Tony would come and clean it up soon because it is not smelling so good in here."

Faith giggled behind me. Nelly crinkled her nose and continued, "Look over there in the puppies' kennel. There is a powerful bad odor coming this way from that direction. I can't see it, but I bet you they have just dropped it everywhere, all over that kennel."

I glanced over at the puppies, all snuggled in the middle of their kennel sleeping. I noticed several piles littering their floor and could not help but giggle along with Faith. Hope stuck her head out of the shadows and said, "I smell it. But our kennel smells just awful now too." She crinkled her nose just as Nelly had done, and the three of us laughed out loud.

"No one is going to get mad at us?" I asked, wanting to be sure. "Because... well... we have sort of soiled our blanket too."

Nelly snorted very loudly then and yelled back toward the door as if talking to Tony, "Well I reckon that means Tony will need to bring you another blanket," she said. "Can't have three puppies curling up in their own crap over there, now can we?"

That made Faith giggle uncontrollably. Laughter is as contagious as howling with dogs so Hope and I joined in. Nelly called it the "silly giggles."

Hope walked over to the soiled blanket and squatted over the two piles. "What are you doing?" Faith asked.

"May as well make it count," Hope replied. "I have had to pee since we got here and wasn't too sure where to go. If Tony's going to be bringing a new blanket, a little pee won't hurt this one."

That made perfect sense to me and must have to Faith as well. We joined Hope and felt much better after. Nelly was flashing that toothless grin again. "I think you three need to go over in the corner from now on," she said. "I wouldn't go on the blanket again. They won't yell at you or anything; but, I am not too sure when Tony will be back to clean the kennels and that blanket is for you to sleep on."

She looked around in her own kennel and continued, "I have one of those special beds they put in some of the kennels. But those without beds get a blanket and it comes in mighty handy when you want to sleep. That floor can get awfully hard when you are trying to have nice dreams."

I liked Nelly a lot. She had a way of making everything seem alright. Hell was a distant memory and seemed very far away when Nelly was talking to us. Hope and Faith liked her too. I could tell by the way they listened when she talked. She put all of us at ease.

Faith smiled broadly and wiggled her backside in Nelly's direction... a sure sign of fondness from a dog. It surprised me how easily the show of affection came, considering none of us had ever had reason to do a butt wiggle before. Faith grimaced slightly with the movement and I remembered how badly she had been hurt by Boy.

Faith ignored the pain and announced proudly, "Nelly, look! We have saved you some food. You will eat mighty fine today."

I could hear Nelly's Heart Speak clearly, and when she dropped her eyes to the floor, I knew she was embarrassed by the fact she had not realized before just how terrible our lives had been. She cut her eyes up at Faith and said, "Oh yes. I will eat mighty fine today. Mighty fine, indeed."

The door from the front opened again and Tony walked through, looking toward our kennel. The three of us moved back into the shadows and the safety of the far corner as soon as the door had opened. Tony put his hands on his hips and said, "Well I see you three ate a little something. Relieved yourselves a little bit too; now didn't you?"

Hope stifled a giggle and Faith ducked down further behind me as Tony opened our kennel and entered. He cleaned up our mess and put it in a small pail he was carrying. The thought of a "poop bucket" almost sent me into silly giggles again. Then Tony sprayed something on our floor that smelled really good. He used a large cloth to wipe over it and was back out the kennel door, returning briefly to bring us a clean blanket.

"I'll mop that floor for you later," he said. I liked the way Tony always talked to us and told us what he was doing. Even though he had a gentle nature and we sensed no threat from him, we stayed hidden in the shadows for a time after he left. Old habits are really hard to break, as Nelly had told us. I did not hear the main door open and close and I knew Tony was still somewhere in the kennel room. I moved slowly from the shadows, Faith and Hope right behind me.

I had not seen Tony take the three bowls, but they were gone. I heard Nelly let out a loud burp and I knew he had made good his promise to give our leftovers to her. I took a deep breath and let it out slowly. The air smelled a lot fresher around me. I heard a noise down the row of kennels and knew Tony was making his way down the aisle, cleaning kennels as he went, toting his poop bucket.

Hope moved to dart back to the shadows when we heard Tony start to sing. She stopped and looked at me. "We are safe here, aren't we?" she asked. "We don't have to hide."

The three of us moved closer together, sitting on our blanket. It was in the middle of our kennel, but none of us felt any danger. We were safe and for the first time in forever there was no smell of rot, decay and evil in the air. There was a warmth all around us that reached right through our skin and touched our hearts and souls.

I cocked my head slightly and listened to Tony sing about an 'endless love.' His voice was pleasant and he was staying in tune. The three of us rocked together in time to the music Tony was making. We could sit in the light, a light brighter than any we had ever been able to rest in, and we could enjoy being at peace.

Our bellies were not exactly full, but we had eaten as much as we could. None of us had to sleep with one eye open… we could all three sleep at the same time and not have to worry about someone coming in to hurt one of us while we slept.

We were safe. There was a wonderful feeling flowing through each of us now. It was that special peace we had yearned for since time began.

There was no need to hide in this place of shelter.

Chapter 20

Not Worth Saving

It was hard to believe a full day had not passed. We had lived more life in the shelter in a few hours than we had lived for an eternity in the shed. Faith was looking around our kennel, obviously concerned. I walked over to her and looked around to see if I could figure out what was wrong with her.

She looked at me a little confused and a little agitated. "He took our food," she stated. "What if he forgets to bring more tomorrow?"

I did not know the answer to her question. I did not think we would be forgotten here in the shelter and I certainly didn't think they would forget to feed us. But I did not want to give an answer and have it turn out to be untrue.

Nelly came to the rescue once again. "They will bring more food before the sun goes down. That was your breakfast. Actually, I guess it was more a lunch for you since you missed breakfast. They bring kibble around twice a day here. Once in the morning and then again before the sun goes down."

"But we can't eat the kibble," I said. "Will they remember and bring more of the soft stuff?"

"I am not sure how that will work," Nelly replied. "I have a hard time with the kibble but they still bring it. Tony always slips me some soft food during the day though, just like he did you. I don't think they will let you starve."

Before I had time to ask if she was sure, the door to the front opened again and a strange man came through. "That is the doctor," Nelly said. "He is here to look you over like Joanie said earlier. Don't be afraid of him. He doesn't smell the best; I believe he eats a lot of garlic and onions. But there's nothing evil about him."

She looked thoughtful for a moment and then added, "But... he's not always the quickest flea in the pack, if you know what I mean. In fact, sometimes he says stuff that's a might on the stupid side."

Dr. Martin was a bit larger than Tony, but smaller than Man. He did not look to be very old, but I could sense an old soul hidden behind his unwrinkled skin and his easy smile. I listened closely, but could not hear his heart talking to me. Neither did I sense evil, so I wondered if he had learned to hide his heart speaking abilities, or if he was one of those people Mother had mentioned once who just refused to admit they were there.

Nelly heard my thoughts as surely as if I had spoken aloud. "He has learned to keep them pushed way down inside himself. That happens a lot with people who have to work with shelter dogs. It is his job to send those who cannot be placed in homes or rescues across to a place called Rainbow Bridge."

"I know about Rainbow Bridge," I said. "Mother told us all about it before Man killed her.

"Well," continued Nelly, "it is a beautiful place, as I am sure your mother told you. But it is not easy work for anyone to send a dog there. I don't imagine it mattered much either way to Man and Boy. But, here, where there is such kindness and love, it does hurt the humans when they lose one of us. Dr. Martin is hurt the most I believe because it is his job to help the dogs cross over."

Hope sounded alarmed when she asked, "Why is he here for us?"

"Don't worry," said Nelly. "He comes here to help dogs too. Right now he is going to examine all of you and see what you need to get healthy."

Hope, Faith and I still backed into the shadows when Dr. Martin came to our kennel. He came in and stood in front of us looking us over. He was frowning by the time Joanie joined him.

"They look mighty puny," he said. "And they have sores on top of scars all over their bodies. I imagine they are full of worms, but something else caused those wounds and a few of them look infected."

"So what do we need to do to get them in a home?" asked Joanie. "Or what will a rescue need to be prepared for when they take these three?"

"To tell you the truth," said Dr. Martin, "these three are worse than any puppy I have seen here. They are sickly, Joanie. I don't think a rescue is going to take them when there are several litters of healthy puppies here that need a place to go."

He was bent down now looking at us and I felt the need to shrink further back into the shadows. He was not evil, but his words stung my heart. He stood back up straight and looked at Joanie. "I hate to say it, but I don't think these three are worth putting a lot of time into. Taking care of them will be an expensive endeavor and, honestly, they are Pit Bull puppies. You know with BSL making headlines right now a rescue is not going to invest in sickly Pit Bull puppies."

"Well," said Joanie, sounding as agitated as my heart felt hurt, "what exactly do *I* need to do to help them heal? Forget the rescue and let's start with what we can do here."

Dr. Martin shook his head. "We can put them down and get it over with," he said.

Tony was coming out of the little room where the food was obviously kept. I heard him cough. "Excuse me," he said, interrupting the doctor. "Joanie, I'm getting ready to feed up for the night. You want those three to get canned?"

Dr. Martin raised his eyebrows, obviously waiting to hear Joanie's response. Again, when she answered she sounded agitated, defiant; "By all means, Tony. But mix some kibble in it too so maybe they can get used to it."

She looked at Dr. Martin and then back at Tony. "And don't forget to give Miss Nelly a little of that canned food. The rescue will not be taking her for a few days still and I want to make sure she has some weight on her when they pick her up."

Joanie looked back at Dr. Martin. "You remember Nelly? You had said we should just put her out of her misery and get it over with? Well… seems a rescue decided she deserved to live out her days in peace. Glad we didn't just kill her now, aren't we?"

Dr. Martin closed his eyes and held his head back as if very tired. "You know I do not enjoy the killing, Joanie. But I don't enjoy seeing the suffering when it is prolonged either."

He turned and looked across the aisle at Nelly and continued, "I am glad the old girl got a rescue. But I understand you moved mountains to make sure she got out of here. Do you really think these three puppies will be that easy to move?"

"Why don't you just get me some wormer for them?" Joanie asked. "We can see how they do after that."

She looked away from Dr. Martin and at Tony who was going to great lengths to avoid the conversation. "And Tony," she said, "you will need to go and rent me one of those huge earth moving machines before I talk to the rescue about these three puppies."

Tony cleared his throat and hurried into the next kennel with the bucket of food he was carrying. I heard the kibble rattling as he scooped a huge amount out and into a food dish. "Did you hear me, Tony?" Joanie asked. She was looking for an advocate and was determined to make Tony one whether he wanted to be or not.

"I heard you," he said and went on about his business, hoping she would drop it.

He should have known better. "I hope you heard me," she said. "Make sure you take that earth moving machine out of our vet account, since that is what Doc Martin says it will take to get these three rescued."

"Just stop," said Dr. Martin. "I will get you some wormer." And Dr. Martin walked out of the shelter and out of our lives. We would see him again when he came to the shelter, but he would never examine us and we would never have to go to the room in back with him.

Tony walked down to our kennel and asked Joanie, "Did you have to totally piss him off? These puppies need a little more than wormer."

"Then we will have to see that they get a little more than wormer," snapped Joanie. She stomped off in the same direction Dr. Martin had gone muttering under her breath about lazy vets who don't want to work hard enough to save an abused puppy's life.

Nelly looked behind them until the door closed and then she looked at me and said, "I told you. Not the quickest flea in the pack at all. Downright stupid at times."

Hope, Faith and I sat huddled together, still in the shadows. I believe we were all afraid Dr. Martin would come back and take us into that room in the back where dog's went in, but never came out. We had just arrived at the shelter and had already learned there was a lot of living for us to do. I was very thankful Joanie thought we were worth a chance even if the vet had said we were not worth the effort to even try. I knew he was an animal doctor and I could not help but wonder if he had a clue that we could hear and understand what he was saying. Did it matter to him that his careless words hurt us? I hoped the rest of the people that would come into our lives were like Joanie and Tony. The abuse in hell had been hard enough without hearing we were worthless once we escaped.

Hope whispered in my ear, "I sure hope Tony remembers to order that earth moving machine."

Faith and I nodded in total agreement.

Tony opened our kennel door and looked at us hiding in the corner. He smiled at us and said, "You guys can come out now. Ain't nobody gonna hurt you. The vet is gone and Joanie is going to take good care of you."

Tony scooped some kibble into our food dish. "Try and eat a little of that," he said. "It's a lot better for you than the canned stuff we get."

He walked out of our kennel then and closed the door. He began to walk away, but turned and said, "Don't you worry. Tony's gonna fix you up. I will make sure you get some canned food just like I do Nelly. But you have to try and eat a little of that kibble."

Before Tony could get to the next kennel, Joanie came back through the main door. "I've got the wormer," she said. "You want to help me give it?"

"Here?" he asked. "Or do you want to take them to the treatment room. I still say there is something going on more than worms and even though Dr. Martin isn't going to examine them, it doesn't mean we can't look them over."

"No," said Joanie. "I don't want to frighten them right now. We will have plenty of time to do an exam. Let's get this wormer in them and let them have a good night's sleep. I suspect everyone will feel better in the morning. It has been a long day."

Tony came back in our kennel and Joanie held each of us in turn while Tony stuck a pill down our throats. Hope and Faith swallowed theirs without incident. I gagged and coughed over mine. I swallowed hard, several times, trying to make the lump in my throat go down.

"Drink some water," Nelly shouted across the aisle. "Water will make it go down."

I managed to get over to the water bowl still coughing. I took a deep breath and then took a long drink of water. "See how smart this girl is?" Joanie asked. "She knows what to do to help herself. She and her sisters are *very* worth saving. I think Dr. Martin is

197

just lazy. These puppies are most certainly worth our time to try and save them."

Tony put his hands on Joanie's shoulders and turned her to face him. "I don't think Doc Martin enjoys the killing," he said. "And I really don't think he's lazy. I think he is a realist. You haven't been here very long and have not seen the things Doc has. Rescues *never* take sickly puppies when there are so many healthy ones available."

"I get it," snapped Joanie. "What everyone else does not seem to get is each and every dog that walks through these doors deserves a chance. Even the old ones. Especially the old ones. And the sick ones deserve a chance to get better and know love. You know as well as I do those puppies have been abused. They deserve a chance."

"But," said Tony, "will anyone out there in the real world give them a chance?"

Joanie started to respond but stopped. Her finger was pointing at Tony and she had a very strange look cross her face. She tilted her head a little as if listening. "Did you hear that?" she asked.

"I didn't hear anything," responded Tony.

Joanie shook her head, and put her finger down. She stood very still, listening. Finally, she waved her arm at Tony, dismissing him. "Must have been one of the dogs moving around," she said. "You go on and get your work done. Get these dogs fed so we can get out of here tonight. I need to work with Miss Nelly a bit. The rescue asked me some questions about her and I want to spend a little time so I can answer them."

Tony went back to feeding dogs and Joanie went to visit with Nelly. I liked the way she sat right down on the floor with the old girl. I could tell the two were engaged in a deep conversation. It was Heart Speak and I could have listened had I chosen. But it was obviously just between the human and the old dog. It was private and I respected that.

Nighttime was a very special time in the shelter. The doors were locked early and the people would not be back until morning. Nelly quickly told us that there were special occasions when they would come in at night, but it was rare and always involved a dog in trouble... a dog that needed a place to stay the night.

"How do you know so much, Nelly?" I asked. "You know everything there is to know about an animal shelter. Did your mother teach you?"

"Oh no," answered Nelly. "My mother was something called a Purebred Shepherd. She won prizes in dog shows. One time she decided to have an adventure and got away from her people. When she returned home, she was carrying a litter of pups. When we were born we were allowed to stay with our mother until we were 12 weeks old. Then they sent all of us away to good homes."

"Is that how you found your family?" Hope asked.

"No." responded Nelly. "There were three of us who did not get placed. They took us to an animal shelter. A rescue came in and wanted all of us right away, but there was a family at the shelter looking for a puppy to adopt at the same time as the rescue. The man running the shelter let the family choose one of us and the other two went with the rescue. I was the one the family chose."

Hope's eyes were bright and she said, "So you were sort of like one of the chosen."

"I suppose so," said Nelly, a hint of sadness in her voice. "But being chosen may not have been as grand as you think. I loved my family and they were not unkind to me. But I did live most of my life on a chain out in the backyard. I had a dog house and I was not totally ignored by my family. But there were times I was very lonely."

Faith was listening with interest. "I really hope we can be chosen by a family that will not chain us up," she said. "But I think a chain in the backyard will be better than the shed any old time."

"Yes," Hope chimed in. "And if they have children he must know that he can never touch us in certain places. And he can't do things to our teeth that makes our mouth sore."

"And kicking and hitting is not allowed," finished Faith.

Hope moved a little closer to me. "What do you want our family to be like, Charity?" she asked.

I dropped my eyes to the floor and tried to think of something very witty to say. Before anything came out Nelly coughed a little and yawned a huge yawn as if she were very bored. "Come on, Charity," she said. "Tell us what you want. Stop being such an old soul and dream a little."

I stopped thinking and blurted out what was uppermost in my mind, "I just want us to leave the shelter together and go with the same family."

Then I looked over at Nelly and finished my 'dream,' hoping it would not hurt her feelings, "And when we get old, I want them to love us enough to keep us."

Nelly showed that toothless grin again that I had come to love. "That's a fine dream, Charity; a real fine dream. Just see to it you three take care of your teeth so you don't end up like me."

"I think there are far worse things than ending up like you," I said and Nelly nodded her head in agreement.

"But," she added, "no one ever understands that there situation may not be the absolute worst when they are living it. And I believe you three hold the record for the worst living conditions and the worst abuse."

Faith had fallen silent and had a terrified look on her face. Nelly asked her why she looked so afraid.

"Leaving here together is more than a dream," she answered. "We have to stay together."

Nelly smiled wisely and threw her head back knowingly. "Oh, I think you will stay together," she said "I don't think Joanie is going to let anything happen to you. She has a soft spot right in the middle of her heart for you three."

"Wouldn't it be just grand if we went to your rescue with you?" asked Hope. "Then every night would be like this and we could sit and talk, just like we did with Mother."

"Oh that would be *grand*," said Faith, but her face had a very pained look and she was squirming. Faith stood up as quickly as she could and ran to the farthest corner of the kennel... the one on the opposite side from where we liked to hide in the shadows.

I watched her as closely as I could, worried. The lights had been dimmed in the shelter for the night, but I could tell she was using the bathroom. I glanced over at the food bowls where Tony had mixed some of the soft food with a little of the harder kibble for us. Faith had licked the soft food and left the kibble, just as Hope and I had done.

Nelly ignored my obvious concern and said, "Oh my. That would be grand. But I think you three will be going to a far better rescue for puppies than the Old Dog's Home I will be leaving for."

Hope was beginning to squirm a bit now just as Faith had done and my attention was totally diverted from our dreaming game. Nelly called my name loudly, "Charity!"

I looked at the old girl sitting at the front of her kennel, the dim light from the shelter making her look as if she had a halo. "They will be fine," she said, obviously knowing how very worried I was. "It is the medicine Joanie gave you. You will see soon enough. Stop worrying."

Faith came out of the shadows as Hope was hurrying back to the corner she was vacating. "Charity," said Faith, "you need to see this. There is something really wrong with my poop."

Since the first time Boy had hurt us, going to the bathroom had been very painful and hard to control. And there had always been blood to go with the pain. It was something we had gotten accustomed to. What could be so wrong beyond the blood? I waited for Hope to come from the shadows and I went back to see what Faith, and now Hope, were so concerned about.

My own stomach was starting to churn and ache when I walked back to the corner. I was glad I didn't have far to go and relieved myself. When I came out I turned to Nelly, hoping she was as wise as she sounded. "What is that?" I asked. "Do you know what came out of us?"

"I imagine there's a whole lot of worms over there," Nelly answered. "That's one of the things that was making you so skinny. Well... that and the fact you were almost starved to death.

What little food you did eat was not doing you a whole lot of good because you were full of worms."

Faith smiled a broad smile and Nelly laughed. "Now that's a Pit Bull smile if I ever saw one."

Faith nudged me with her nose. "Oh Charity," she said. "With the worms gone we may be worth saving now."

My heart ached knowing Faith had understood the vet's hurtful words. I must have whimpered with the knowledge and Nelly quickly responded for me. "All three of you have always been worth saving," she said. "Don't you ever believe anything else is true."

I had never heard her sound so indignant, and I knew Faith's words had touched her heart as surely as they had touched mine. "It is not your fault you were with evil people," she finished. "You are all three very worthy. And your mother would be very proud of you."

Chapter 21

The Room in the Back

Our first night in the shelter had been a lot better than we could have hoped for. Nelly had made it wonderful for us, and reminded me of my mother. I knew Hope and Faith felt the same. The only thing missing was the ability to snuggle with her while she told us stories from her past life. We made do by snuggling with each other.

We listened intently as Nelly introduced us to every dog in the shelter. Some of the dogs were awake and greeted us when she called their names. Others were already deep in a dream, running through wide open fields, swimming or chasing rabbits. We could hear the strange noises they made in their sleep.

The loss of the worms had made all three of us feel much better. But we still did not have much of an appetite and the kibble was too hard for us. When the shelter began to come to life I had hopes for a little more of that soft food. We were not nearly as hungry as we had been back in hell, and I knew none of us would be able to hold much more than a few bites. But I had figured out if we showed an interest in food, our chances of getting a rescue or a home would greatly improve.

We had already learned so much in the short time we had been in the shelter. So far, all the experiences had been mostly wonderful. Of course there was the exception of being called worthless by the vet. I had to remind myself often that those were not the words he had used. He had not been a particularly likeable human; but, I thought about what Nelly had said his job was here and how upsetting it must be for him. Maybe if he saw we were improving, he would change his mind.

There was a very loud noise at the back of the shelter. It was terribly harsh and made Faith, Hope and I huddle closer than we usually did. We heard one of the dogs down the aisle yell out, "Incoming!" and saw the shelter go from a dim comforting light to very bright as the morning sun flooded the shelter.

Tony came running through the opening that had appeared where the wall once was. The wall had simply moved upward and there was a truck setting in the new doorway. The truck moved forward slowly as Tony fumbled for keys at his waist. I could tell Tony was upset and I strained my neck to see what was going on and what an 'incoming' was.

Nelly was sitting at the front of her kennel and as usual, I looked over at her and waited for her to explain what was happening.

She sighed. "It is not usually so hectic when a new dog comes in," she said. "Something must be wrong."

I could hear the concern in her voice and held my breath, waiting to see what would happen next. Tony rushed past our kennel and went in the room where our food was kept. He came out with a table on wheels and had a blanket thrown over the top. He was running and the wheels on the table made a clickety-clack sound as he pushed it past us and down the long aisle toward the truck.

Nelly sighed deeply and sadly. "Somebody's hurt," she said. "And from the way Tony is running, they are hurt badly."

The dog in the kennel next to us had been very quiet. I had only heard her once when the choir sang 'The Song of Souls.' I remembered her name was Lucy from the introductions in the night. There had been stories told during the introductions about many of the dogs, but Nelly had only told us her name and she had not spoken to us. The barrier between the kennels kept me from seeing what she looked like, but I could hear her clearly when she spoke. "Seems to me they should be rushing around at a vet's office and not here at the shelter," she said.

"Oh My Dog, wouldn't that be just grand," Nelly responded. "You know the shelter doesn't have the money for that." Nelly's voice did not sound as condescending as her words would imply.

Several of the dogs down the aisle began to whine and cry. They were all younger dogs, but not exactly puppies. One kennel housed four little dogs that Nelly had identified as Beagles. They were getting wound up now and had a particular whine that was unmistakable. Their barks were just an exaggerated version of that whine. Nelly told us they had been a hunter's dogs, but they were 'gun shy.' Apparently if a dog is going to live with a hunter, they cannot be afraid of gun fire. I could never live with a hunter. The sound of thunder terrifies me.

But now, I could tell something besides gun fire was upsetting the Beagles. I listened closely to try and hear Heart Speak in their dismal cries. Mostly what I heard were pitiful cries of loss and pain. It made me very sad.

There was a man I had not seen before walking to the back of the truck and Tony was pushing that table right up close so it was touching the truck. I had a good view of what was going on and when they lifted a large white dog from the back of the truck, I almost wished I could not see so well.

I could tell the dog had large blotches of black and grey on him, but one huge spot around his head had a very strange color. It looked to be a deep red, a color I had never seen on a dog before. I heard Hope gasp next to me and Faith began to cry. They had already realized what was refusing to register in my mind. That 'spot' was far from natural. It was blood and something horrible had happened to that dog.

Our lives in hell began to come flooding back into my memory. Dogs do not often live in the past. That is something humans seem to be very adept at, but dogs prefer to experience the life that is happening in the 'now.' That does not mean we do not remember the past. In fact, terrible experiences have as much of an impact on us as they do any person. I believe the bad times may be even worse for us because we do live in the moment. Just as the happy times are so much better, the bad times can be just as intense and can make a dog feel very alone.

Right at that moment, seeing the terrible wound on the dog's head, I searched my memory, hoping to determine exactly what had happened to the poor soul. I recalled Mother talking about the loud bang and her son dropping to the ground when Man had shot him in the head.

"He was shot," I said, not realizing I was speaking aloud. "He made some person very angry and they shot him in the head."

I could feel Faith and Hope snuggling closer to me, and instinctively, I put my nose across Faith's head, protecting her. Hope rested her own head on top of mine from behind us. It was a position we had taken often back in the shed and offered a strange sense of safety now in the shelter.

Lucy was making sounds of disgust from her kennel and Nelly was hanging her head low, looking at the floor. The Beagles continued their pitiful cries and the six puppies next to Nelly began to whimper and moved back to their blanket, away from the sights so clearly visible from the front of their kennel.

I could not look away. I reached out to the dog and tried to join his heart so he would know he was not alone. I felt the dizziness that often comes with Heart Speak starting to work its magic on me. For a brief moment I wished I had not reached out because the pain was so intense. Then I felt ashamed that I was trying to pull away. The dog was hurting and he needed someone to understand.

"What did I do?" I heard clearly. "I was not trying to get in trouble. I was so hungry and they had thrown the food away. I didn't mean to make a mess. I just wanted food."

For the first time Heart Speak took me to a place I did not want to be. I could see the dog approaching cans outside a green house. There were a lot of trees in the yard and there were chickens pecking at the ground. The dog was ignoring the chickens and heading for those cans. The cans were overflowing and I could smell what the dog had smelled. There was food in the cans. Even though I was only there in a deep part of my mind, the smells made my mouth water.

The large dog turned one of the cans over easily enough and I could almost taste the food he was just starting to enjoy. Then I heard a door slam and heard a man yelling, "Stay away from my chickens!"

Then I heard the loud bang my mother had once described to me. It was far more deafening than she had told me. Since I was deep inside the large dog's memory I actually felt the burst of pain in my head as the dog fell on top of the garbage he had been eating. Then I heard a woman yelling as she ran out of the house, "You shot Spot! Why did you shoot Spot?"

The dog let me go then. He had given me a vivid account of what had happened to him and now I was weeping uncontrollably. I had only wept that way once before, but I could not stop it now. I understood this dog, named Spot, was shot by his own human dad. He had been very hungry, so I knew he had not been fed very often. I did not know how he came to be here in the animal shelter. He had stopped speaking to me past the woman running from the house and I understood he had left for the Land of Nothing. I did not try and reach him there. Sometimes it is really best to let sleeping dogs lie.

Dr. Martin walked through the opening where the shelter wall had been before and came up behind the truck. He stopped at the table on wheels and looked at the dog. No one spoke, but the doctor nodded at Tony and the table was wheeled to the room in the back.

The large dog who had a home where he was not fed very well never came back from the Land of Nothing. His body did come out of the room, but he was no longer in it. His soul had left for a beautiful bridge where a rainbow meets the meadow just beyond. I said a silent prayer to the Creator of All Life that he would find peace at the Bridge.

I also said another prayer that Faith, Hope and I would never have reason to enter that room in the back. A very strange silence hung in the air at the shelter as Dr. Martin left through the back entrance where he had come in. The truck was moved and the large dog's body was taken out the door, wheeled out on that table with a blanket covering him. I do not think we were supposed to be able to see all of that, but we did.

"His name was Spot," I announced as the back of the shelter moved down and became a wall once more,

The Walker Hound began The Song of Souls and everyone joined in. No one interrupted the song with talk this time. This time the song was a different kind of farewell. The echo remained in my heart long after the song was finished.

Chapter 22

"They are Pit Bulls"

Nelly had just finished eating as much of her kibble as she could before her mouth was just too sore to eat more. I could hear Lucy in the kennel next to us still crunching, savoring every bite. Tony had mixed our kibble with the softer food from a can. Hope had licked as much of the soft stuff from her bowl and from the bits of kibble as her stomach would allow. Faith and I both sat huddled together, reflecting on the sadness of the morning. Neither of us felt much like eating.

I suspected Faith had witnessed a large portion of Spot's life through Heart Speak. There is something about the journey made to The Land of Nothing that makes a dog in tune to another's dog's suffering. Faith had spent a lot of time in that place of emptiness. She must have seen the images Spot had sent out through Heart Speak just as I had.

Dr. Martin had left as quickly and as quietly as he had come. The man driving the truck had gotten in it before the wall came back down and he must have driven off somewhere. The only thing left to remind us of the morning's tragedy was the memory that would live forever in our hearts.

Tony had started his rounds, cleaning up the kennels from breakfast. He came into our kennel and looked at the full bowls.

The small amount Hope had eaten did nothing to erase the frown from his face.

"You three have got to start eating," he said. "You put out a belly full of worms last night. That should have improved your appetite."

I did not bother to try and reach Tony with Heart Speak. He was the only kind man I had ever known and I knew if I tried hard enough, he would get that feeling in his chest... something tugging at him, begging him to listen. But I was not sure Tony would ever be able to hear me. He had seen far too much sadness here in the shelter. I knew that now. I understood. I even accepted that Dr. Martin may very well have understood Heart Speak at one time. The morning had taught me a lesson in pain I would have been happy to have never known.

Even in this huge world, with its kind people like Joanie, and even when dogs lived in wonderful homes and knew nothing about a place called hell, there was still evil. There were people who did not want to understand Heart Speak. It was not just that they had lost the ability; but, more than that, they did not want to understand. And I believed there were people who embraced evil. I did not understand why, but it was true none-the-less.

There were other thoughts going through my mind. I was learning more about humans and the strange world they lived in. I had never thought about anything other than good and bad, evil and pure. For a dog it is very simple. If something is good, it is simply right. If something is bad, then it is wrong. But apparently there was no black and white in a human's life. It was all shades of grey. If a dog was lucky, they would land somewhere on the lighter side of that grey. But there were no guarantees. Having a home did not mean a dog would be well fed, or cared for. There were obviously all kinds of homes. It would be a wonderful world if every dog could find a home like Thumper's. But I was beginning to believe that those places were very rare.

Most of the dogs in the shelter had never had a good home, and some had even been dumped by the side of a road to fend for themselves. Those dogs were called 'strays.' Strays had to be extra smart in order to live in a world filled with people that chased them and threw things at them.

But Spot had not been a stray and he still had to search for food in his own backyard. From the vision he sent to me, his human mom loved him and was upset when his human dad shot him. I still could not understand exactly why the man had shot him. He had accused Spot of trying to eat his chickens, but in the vision I saw, Spot was nowhere near a chicken. Had the man just hated Spot enough to want to hurt him? Did he want Spot dead? That is certainly what it looked like, so why had the man ever even bothered to take a dog to his home?

With all of the terrible things I had seen, I knew I would take any one of those homes over the shed any day of the week. But I also knew something else now. I understood exactly what Nelly had meant when she said each dog could not see past the hell they lived in, could not see there might be a situation worse than theirs.

Beyond all of that though I believed we could not stop wanting something more. We could not give up. If we gave up, there was not much point in living. Everything that happened on this day that had begun so badly reaffirmed that thought. It would be a day filled with both good and bad, but by the end of the day we would have a place to go.

Tony had told Joanie about the massive piles of worms he had found in our kennel. She came into the back and headed straight for us. She had a huge smile on her face and asked when she walked through our door, "Feeling better today?"

She looked in the corner that we had designated as the bathroom and the smile quickly faded. "What in this world?" she asked. "Why is there still so much blood? I have to get the three of you out of here so you have a chance. You will not last long this way... not in here."

She touched each of us on the head and felt each of us cower back. She did not push it and left our kennel quickly, muttering about finding a rescue that would get us to a vet. She gave Nelly a long look before she left the kennel room. Then she shook her head as if trying to come back from a daydream.

Faith, Hope and I snuggled very close together, each with our own thoughts. I believed Hope and Faith were both thinking about that room in the back. But I was thinking much deeper thoughts. I was remembering Mother and recalling everything she had said to me about home and family. I had to try and reach some of the people that came through the shelter looking for dogs. Surely one of them would understand Heart Speak. And surely one of them would be willing to give three puppies a chance at a life... even if we had gotten rid of a belly full of worms but still had a lot of blood coming from us. Heart Speak was the only way I knew to reach these people and if we were to have a chance at a good home, then I had to reach out.

When Joanie left the back and went to 'start her day with coffee and a phone call,' Nelly had decided to take a long nap. She had smiled at me warmly and told me, "Staying up all night talking with three puppies wears a body down. Not as young as I used to be and I need my rest. Besides, I want to be ready after Joanie makes that phone call. I think we may have some special visitors today."

Nelly was snoring when the door opened and Joanie came through with a woman I had never seen before. They stopped in front of Nelly's kennel. I could not hear everything they were saying... but I knew Nelly would be leaving the shelter very soon. Someone from her rescue was driving a lot of miles to pick her up.

They went from Nelly's kennel to the six puppies and the woman got down on her knees. Her voice changed as she knelt in front of the puppies and talked to them. "You babies will be out of here tomorrow," she said. "You have a rescue and we are going to get you ready for transport."

I don't think any of the six had a clue what she was talking about, nor did I. But it sounded like something wonderful was about to happen for those puppies and, much to the woman's delight, they wagged their tails in unison.

Joanie looked over at the three of us and bit her lip. When the woman stood again she turned to Joanie and asked, "So what is it you are not saying? I have been around you enough to know when you need me to do something for you."

Joanie turned her gaze away from us and looked at Lucy in the kennel next to us. "I was just wondering if you had found a place for Lucy?" she asked. "Her time is almost up and I really believe she is a friendly dog. She has just never had much of a chance."

The woman sighed, "I think I can find a place for her. But I am going to need a little more time. When they show so much fear of humans it's not easy to get them placed. But at least she is not a Pit Bull."

"But you do a decent job placing the bully breeds that come through," Joanie said.

"I try," said the woman. "You know they are all dogs to me. I do not understand all the fuss about one breed or the other." Then she changed the subject back to Lucy. "Can you hold Lucy a few more days?"

Joanie responded, "The shelter is filling up really fast. But I will hold her as long as I can. It's a shame we don't have a good boarding facility to hold them."

The woman laughed a genuine laugh and they walked away talking about the cost involved with rescuing a dog. Joanie glanced back at us and bit her lip again. I wondered why she had not brought the woman to our kennel. Would the woman have gotten on her knees and told us how wonderful we were? I didn't think so. And I believe Joanie knew it and did not want us to see the difference between her reaction to the six cute little puppies and us.

Nelly was wide awake now and she read my thoughts clearly. "That's how it is with Joanie," she said. "She is one of those rare people who just understands Heart Speak naturally. She would never do anything if she thought it might hurt you."

She yawned and shook her entire body, trying to shake the sleepiness that was left in her 'old, tired bones' from her mind. She had told us when something is 'festering' in your body, you have to shake it from your mind to make it go away. I loved the way she explained things and was glad she was awake now.

"That woman with Joanie," she nodded her head toward the door where the two women had exited, "is a wonderful lady. She works overtime to make sure all of the dogs get out of here. Since I have been here she has managed to find a place for every single dog that had to leave.

"Or... at least every dog that could leave," she added and I knew she was thinking of Spot. "Her name is Silvia. Joanie would have told her all about you; but, I believe there is someone special you three need to meet first. If that does not work out, then Joanie will introduce you to Silvia."

Faith had gone over to her food bowl and was licking her kibble. I knew she was going to try and eat so she could put some weight on. Maybe then Joanie would not worry so much about showing us to the people who came in.

Lost in our thoughts and conversation with Nelly, we had not heard Joanie come back; and, we certainly were not aware there was a strange new woman with her. There was also a little girl clinging to the woman's hand. Before we had a chance to huddle and hide, the little girl had pulled away from her mother and was shrieking in front of our kennel. "Puppies! Look Mommy! Puppies!"

I had taken a good look at my sisters after the woman called Silvia left. I had no clue what I looked like, but knew, other than the places we each had white on our bodies, Faith, Hope and I were the same color and we had the same problems. Looking at them told me exactly what I looked like to others. We were not cute little puppies. We looked pitiful.

The three of us must have looked like triplets with our ears and heads hanging very low, eyes to the floor, backs hunched over from the abuse we had suffered and the tips of our tails dragging the floor a little. We stood with a hunch that made it look as if we were always half-sitting. The little girl was not put off by the sight of us. She seemed genuinely happy to see three puppies. She was very young and she toddled when she walked. But I could tell we thrilled her heart and that made me glad. It was the first time anyone had looked at us without either hurt, pity or something worse in their eyes. I didn't care about her age. She had made me feel alive and I prayed Faith and Hope were feeling the same.

Both Joanie and the woman were smiling when they came over behind the little girl. Her enthusiasm was contagious and I was looking at her cheeks to see if they looked anything like apples. I looked from the little girl to her mother and saw the smile on the woman's face change to a look of total disgust. She crinkled her nose as if we smelled bad and pointed her finger at us. "What's wrong with those puppies?" she asked.

Joanie was clearly not pleased with her reaction and she sounded defensive. "They are just small puppies," she said. "The man who had them did not take care of them. I believe he probably beat them. Then when they needed to see a vet, he just dumped them here rather than doing the right thing.

"They have only been here for about 24 hours. They will fatten up. And they will get healthy. They just need a little time and a lot of love. Besides, your little girl likes them. She can see how cute they are."

The woman frowned and shook her head at Joanie. "I wonder if you have taken a good look at those three," she stated. "There's something wrong with them. They stand all hunched over with their butts almost dragging the floor. And... well... can't you see that something is protruding back there? I will bet they were born with a terrible condition that causes it to look that way. Something must be wrong with their spines."

Joanie squinted her eyes and looked at us as if she had not noticed what the woman was talking about. "They are just exceptionally small," she said. "When they start to put on weight everything will fall into place."

The woman seemed indignant now. She also acted just a little embarrassed. "No. Nothing is going to just fall into place," she said. "And whatever is wrong with them… back there… well… I don't think I'm ready to explain that to my child. In fact, I wouldn't want to explain that to anyone. It looks vulgar."

She snatched her daughter by the hand and pulled her away from our kennel. "Besides," she stated as she looked back at us one more time, "they are Pit Bulls. I don't suppose you noticed that either? I don't think I am going to take a dog home with me that will bite my daughter's face off one day." Then she walked to the six little puppies next to Nelly, dragging her daughter behind her. Her daughter was still looking back at us and pointing. Her little round cheeks did look a bit like apples, and I was sorry she had to live with that horrible woman.

"Now these are puppies," the woman stated, standing in front of the six.

"Well, don't start choosing one of these," Joanie said. "All of them are already spoken for."

The woman turned and started to look at the other kennels. "If you are looking for puppies," said Joanie, "we just do not have any available. All of the ones here are already spoken for."

Tony looked over from the kennel he was cleaning across the way, but decided to keep his mouth shut. He waited for Joanie to lead the woman back to the exit and he yelled out behind her, "Joanie, I need to see you if you have a moment."

As soon as Joanie had seen the woman and child off, she returned to the kennel room. "What do you need Tony? I have a lot to do so make it quick."

"I was just wondering why you didn't try to adopt any of these puppies here out to that woman," he said.

"They are all spoken for," said Joanie. "All except for those three, and she was not interested in them." She nodded in our direction. "Silvia was here earlier and she has a place for every single puppy in the shelter. She has even found a nice rescue for the older puppies."

Tony smiled but his eyes were still frowning. It made the smile look more like a grimace than anything else. "You are going to get yourself in trouble," he said. "You know when the puppies are spoken for by a rescue we are supposed to adopt out locally first. The rescues get to take what the locals do not want."

"I don't have to adopt a puppy out to anyone I don't feel comfortable with," said Joanie. "I did not feel comfortable letting any of these puppies go with that woman. And besides, what kind of rule is that? Silvia does wonderful work for all of the dogs here. She should be able to take the puppies when we have them."

"Joanie, not everyone has a heart as big as yours. You are going to have to learn to compromise. I like you. I like you a lot and I believe the dogs that come in here need you." Tony turned back to his cleaning, finishing his thought as he scooped up a huge pile from the kennel he was working in; "Please don't do anything to get yourself fired. You are the best thing that has happened to this place in a long time."

Joanie turned and left the kennel room then. Nelly was looking behind her and smiling. "Yep," she said. "Joanie *is* the best thing that's happened to this shelter in forever I imagine. And that's because she *does* speak up and she doesn't put up with the bull shit."

Then Nelly turned her attention back to us. "Speaking of bull shit," she said; "do you three understand what Dr. Martin was talking about when he said BSL?"

The three of us shook our heads in unison. "I think it has something to do with us being Pit Bulls," Hope said. "I heard him say something about that."

"Well yes," said Nelly. "It has everything to do with you being Pit Bulls. Let me tell you all about it now. Come and sit down so I can explain it to you."

We took our seat front and center facing Nelly. She looked very thoughtful and said, "Before I start, I want to make sure you know none of the people that have come back so far have been the special guest I am expecting. I don't think Joanie has had a chance to make that phone call yet." She looked me directly in the eyes and said, "You will know when the special person arrives."

The Nelly went and took a long drink of water, preparing for a long talk. She came back and sat down at her kennel door facing us. "Now about BSL," she said. "It stands for Bull Shit Law."

Chapter 23

BSL

Taking a deep breath, Nelly told us to get comfortable on our blanket. "This will take a little time," she said. "And some of it does not make a lot of sense."

Nelly told us how Pit Bulls are known for their loyalty and how some of our kind were used as "Nanny Dogs," trusted to watch after young children. She talked about dogs who served in the military and fought alongside man during wars.

Faith smiled broadly and asked, "Have you heard of Sergeant Stubby?"

"Of course I have," said Nelly. "Every dog with a brain knows about Sergeant Stubby. He did us all really proud. And, as I am sure you know, he was a Pit Bull."

We listened to the familiar story of Sergeant Stubby in the war, winning hearts and medals. We did not interrupt nor did we tell Nelly we had heard the stories before because it would have been rude. But we also wanted to hear them again. When something is good and makes you proud, you can hear it a hundred times over and it never gets old.

When she finished, Faith held her shoulders up proudly and said, "Sergeant Stubby is my hero."

Nelly said, "Sergeant Stubby is a great hero. He showed the world what a good dog can do when he is treated right."

Nelly dropped her head and her voice lowered, "But there are dogs who are abused every day of their lives. You three could probably tell me more about it than I can tell you. Because this part is about dog fighters and, not just the evil they do, but also the evil they create."

We huddled close together. Sergeant Stubby's story was a familiar favorite for us, and this part was just as familiar, but there was nothing about it to like.

Nelly continued, "When I tell you this I want all of you to remember where you are now. You are safe and the people you meet from now on will do all they can to protect you. But you do need to know about BSL."

"Why is it called that?" asked Hope. Then she giggled a little and added, "You know, what you called it before?"

Nelly smiled and said, "I am not really sure what it stands for. I had never heard of it before I came to the shelter. Since I came here I have met quite a few really fine Pit Bulls and they have all had something to say about it. Every one of them have called it a *bullshit law*. So that is what I call it.

"What I know about it, I have learned here. As a matter of fact, before I came to the shelter I really didn't know too much about dog fighting. I have met all kinds of dogs here and heard a lot of stories. Some of the saddest have come from Pit Bulls."

"Like us," stated Faith. "Our story is sad."

"It is," said Nelly. "It is one of the saddest I have heard. But your story will have a happy ending. A lot of Pit Bulls never get a chance for that happy ending."

For a moment we were all quiet, thinking about what Nelly said. Then Nelly continued. "There is probably not a whole lot I can tell you about dog fighters. I am guessing you know more than I do already, having lived in that hell. But you don't know about BSL and the way some people hate Pit Bulls. You do need to know that."

She looked me in the eye and said, "And even though you know more about dog fighting than any puppy should, I am going to tell this the way I have heard it.

"Dog fighters are not only evil people; they are very greedy. They use and abuse the dogs they are supposed to take care of. They believe it will make the dog fight better if they starve him. Sometimes they will starve two dogs for days on end, and then put them together with one piece of meat between them.

"If a dog does not want to fight, they will be beaten, kicked, burned, choked and, one I spoke with, said he was held under water until he came close to drowning. This is not something that happens once-in-awhile. That would be bad enough. But these dogs are abused every day of their lives.

"Then, when they do fight, if they get hurt and lose the fight, the dog fighter may kill them. It depends on how angry the man gets and how much money he loses. That's what it's all about; money. The dog fighter does not work, but has the dogs make money for him."

"That's the truth," said Hope. "Man never worked. I didn't know men could work until I came here and saw Tony cleaning up behind us. Man never did that."

"He sure didn't," added Faith. "There was poop everywhere, and we couldn't hold it. So we had to just try and keep it away from where we slept."

"That is terrible," Nelly said, crinkling her forehead. "It is not healthy either. It can make you very sick."

"And we are sick," I said. "Maybe that is why."

"I don't think that's the only reason," responded Nelly, "but it probably has something to do with it. With all the money these men make off of the backs and blood of dogs, it looks like they would at least give them a clean place to sleep. But most of the dogs I talked to were chained out in the weather without shelter. They never heard a kind word and did not know what treats, toys, or even a belly rub were. Most of them had never had clean water to drink."

I thought of the old bucket with the hole in it back in the shed. That had been Mother's bucket. I remembered the day Boy changed the bucket and how good the water tasted that day. It was one more thing added to the list of injustices my mother suffered. She had certainly given her blood for Man, and he had not even given her a clean bucket for water.

Nelly had stopped talking and was looking at me. I knew she could hear my heart. She smiled a tired smile and said, "One thing that stood out when these dogs were telling me about their lives, most of them had never had anyone to care. They had never known any kindness or love. So, in a way, you three had every reason to fight to survive. You had each other."

"And we had Mother," I said, understanding what Nelly wanted me to see.

"Yes," said Nelly. "And she had you. That must have just filled her heart right up, having the three of you and knowing you were her children. In all of that pain and horror, she had three of the smartest, most beautiful children. And in a world of hate and abuse, your hearts were pure. She must have been just bursting with pride. I have no doubt you three were her greatest joy."

If Nelly was trying to make us feel good, she was succeeding in grand style. Hope, Faith and I had our heads held high, shoulders up and ears as erect as we could get them. I could feel the warmth and love spilling from all our hearts, lighting the room. Our eyes sparkled, and had anyone looked closely, they would have seen each of us had tears. Something we were learning now that we were not being hurt every day, tears can come when you are happy just like they do when you are sad. But only when you are so filled up with love and joy it is spilling over. When you are that full of so much happiness, it has to go somewhere. So it leaks out your eyes.

Nelly smiled when she saw her words had hit us right in the hearts. I guess she thought it would help get us through the rest of what she needed to say.

"These terrible men never have pride in their dogs. All the dogs know is pain and fighting. The small amount of food they get is the only thing good in their lives. And the food is used to keep them doing what man wants them to do."

Again, I thought about Mother in the shed on that hateful chain. I remembered hearing her heart in the early days, and not quite understanding what it was saying. It was not meant for me to hear; she would have thought I was too young. But I knew what she had been thinking. I said it aloud to Nelly now, "And the dogs think about not eating that food when it comes. If they just don't eat, they can die and get it over with, because sometimes dead is better."

A look of sadness crossed Nelly's face. "I suppose that is what several of those dogs were trying to tell me, Charity. But they never put it straight out there that way. I think it is so terrible that a puppy as beautiful as you knows these things."

I wished with all my heart I didn't; but I did know. I told Nelly, "But once you know and you have seen something that terrible, it makes the good even better."

Nelly smiled and went on, "The only chance these fighting dogs have is if they are left for dead and someone finds them and brings them into the shelter or to a vet. Sometimes they are dumped by the side of a road and left to die. The lucky ones make it to the animal shelter."

"And then they can have a wonderful life," said Faith.

Again Nelly looked very sad. "I wish they all could," she said. "But the truth is they do not always make it out. In fact, more die in shelters than will ever find a home."

We stayed very quiet, waiting to hear the rest.

"That is because of BSL," Nelly said. "As bad as the dog fighters are, there are a lot of people who blame the dogs for fighting. They think all of the dogs are bad. And they want all of them killed."

"What about the bait dogs?" I asked. "They don't fight."

"These people want the bait dogs dead, too." Nelly stood and walked around her kennel a couple of times, almost marching. She looked very agitated.

"The truth is they blame all Pit Bulls for the evil and the fighting. Even dogs that have never seen a dog fight, dogs that have homes and families. These people want them all dead and do not want any more to be born."

My heart felt like stone as it dropped to my paws. I remembered the woman with the little girl and knew now she had hated me. That was what made me feel so awful when she was at my kennel. Man had been evil. Boy had been as bad. They had not loved me; but, they had not hated me either. That woman hated me enough to want me dead. It hurt.

I reached out to Faith and Hope, feeling their pain, understanding they must feel as terrible as I did. Faith's eyes were filled with tears, but this time it was not happiness leaking out. This time she was filled with hurt, and it had to go somewhere too.

"I never hurt anybody," said Faith. "I never even tried to hurt anybody. Why does that woman hate me? Why does she want me dead?"

"Oh baby," said Nelly, her eyes leaking too, "It's not your fault. It's not anything you did or didn't do. Some people are just so filled with ignorance and hate they do not know when something innocent and good is in front of them. That hate is her *shame*, not yours. Just like the things Boy did to you are not your fault, this is not your fault either. If you did not need to know about these terrible people, I would not even tell you. But you need to know. You need to know there are people who would hurt you just because you are there.

"One Pit Bull that came here told me about dogs who have been taken from their families and killed just because they were Pit Bulls. They did not fight. They had never even seen a fight. It didn't matter. They lived in a place where people believe in BSL.

"That is why you heard Silvia, Joanie, Tony and Dr. Martin talking about it and saying the Pit Bulls are hard to place. They have to be very careful not to let anyone who may live near one of those places take one of the Pit Bulls from this shelter."

Hope had a look that was a cross between anger and hurt. "But if they were a part of a family, why didn't their families fight for them? How could they just let them be taken away and killed?"

"I wondered that same thing," said Nelly. "The boy that told me about it said the families sometimes *do* fight to get their dogs back. When they fight, the dogs are locked away and held until it is settled; they are not allowed visitors and do not have other dogs to keep them from being lonely. It can go on for a very long time, and many times they die anyway.

"That's crazy," I said. "Those people must be so filled with hate it has driven them crazy. How would they like to be locked away from the ones they love?"

"It gets even crazier," said Nelly. "This Pit Bull told me that these terrible people take dogs based on the size of their heads. They will measure the dog's head and if it is larger than they think it should be, they say the dog is a Pit Bull and is bad."

"Because of the size of their head!?" Hope exclaimed.

"It sounds really crazy, doesn't it?" asked Nelly.

"Pit Bulls have large heads," I said, "and they hate us because of it. I think when people are filled with so much hate, they will find a way to hurt others. Those people should be locked away."

We all agreed the people who hate are the ones who need to be locked away from others. Faith looked totally devastated. She looked at Hope and me and asked, "How will we ever find a home? I want a family to love us more than anything. But with so much hate, how can we ever have that?"

"You listen to me," said Nelly. "You will have a home and family. You just wait and see. What you have to remember is Joanie, Tony and Silvia are not going to let any of those people get their hands on you. They work very hard to stop this BSL. And they are not the only ones. You have seen the worst of the worst. You have seen evil and hateful people in your short lives. But you need to know there are also wonderful people. There are rescue angels who fight every single day and night. That is how you will get your home and family. Rescue Angels will come and protect you. Your life is going to be all you hoped for and more. It is going to be just grand."

Nelly took a deep breath and continued, "You three are not very old, just barely out of the womb, but you have seen things that dogs older than me have not witnessed. And you have endured more pain than any dog should even imagine. I know your mother, wherever she may be, is extremely proud of you."

"How do you know?" asked Faith, a small pout starting as she fought back tears at the mention of Mother.

"Because," said Nelly, "I am not your mother and I am very, very proud of you. It is a great honor to know you. Any dog that has fought as hard as you three to live and to escape hell… well… all dogs should be much honored to know you. Your names will be repeated in years to come just as Sergeant Stubby's is. You have done all dogs proud and you have shown great respect for your mother. Of course she is proud."

I could feel my own heart swelling in my chest and I held my shoulders as straight as I could. Faith and Hope were holding their heads high beside me.

"That's it," said Nelly. "Never drop your heads in shame and do not be afraid to stand tall. There are a lot of people out there who will talk about your bravery, too. And those people are the ones that matter. They fight every single day of their lives to get dogs away from evil places and abuse. They are our friends, but more, they are our voice. Because of them, we can take a stand. Because of them, we will be heard."

When Nelly finished talking we heard the kennel room door open. Joanie was talking to another woman that we had never seen before. They were talking in friendly voices and they walked straight to our kennel.

"These are the three little puppies," Joanie said. "Dr. Martin wants to put them down. I have fought against it and I can probably hold him off for the three days, but after that I believe he will start pushing hard to go ahead and euthanize them."

"Did he examine them at all?" the woman asked.

"No," replied Joanie. "He finally agreed to give me the wormer I needed for them and they have gotten rid of a belly full of those. But there is something more wrong with them. I do not know if it comes from the abuse they suffered or if it is genetic."

She opened the kennel door and both women walked in and knelt down next to us. Joanie frowned and said, "I don't think any of our regular rescues are going to take them. Most rescues just do not have the money to take sickly dogs... especially when there are so many healthy ones that need help."

The woman took a deep breath and lifted my head with her hand. She pushed my lip back and I remembered Boy and the tool he had used to hurt my mouth. I pulled back from her and I could feel my body tremble with fear.

The woman pulled her hand back and turned her body away from me so she was not facing me any longer, but was beside me. It put me at ease and I realized she was not going to hurt me. Slowly she reached out again and began to rub my ear between her thumb and her finger. The gentle massage calmed me and I closed my eyes involuntarily.

The woman sat down on the floor of our kennel and kept massaging my ear. She turned her head so she was looking at me and she asked, "Who hurt you little one? What did they do to you to make such a small puppy so afraid?"

The woman was speaking aloud, but her heart was also speaking to me and I felt tears rush to my eyes. "My name is Beth," she said. "And you are safe now. No one will ever hurt you or your sisters again... not on my watch."

Joanie took a deep breath and let it out quickly. A huge smile crossed her face and she asked, "So you will take them?"

"Of course," replied Beth. "I will take them and I will love them to pieces."

She stopped rubbing my ear and stood up. There was a smile in her voice when she continued. "I am just not too sure what I am going to do with Jerry once he sees these babies."

"What do you mean?" asked Joanie, the alarm rising in her voice.

"Oh, don't worry about him not wanting them," Beth laughed. "He is going to fall head over heels. My problem will be making him let go once we find them a good home."

Joanie smiled broadly, but my own heart began to beat way too fast. Find us a good home? I was not too sure what she meant by that but I had to get my message across to her. I said a prayer to Creator as I sent a message with my heart.

Beth looked back at me than and said, "Of course you three will have to stay together. I wouldn't dream of separating you."

My heart slowed down and I felt the greatest peace I had ever known. For the first time since my life began I believed everything was going to work out for my sisters and me. I stood up and moved slightly away from Faith and Hope, wanting to show this woman how happy she had made me. My tail started to wag and I felt the most incredible pain in my butt. I had learned to suffer in silence back in the shed, but in this moment of peace and love I could not control the cry that escaped my throat.

Beth knelt back on the floor next to me and very gently began to look over my puny body. When she got to my backside I cried out again. She looked very concerned and said, "These babies need to see a vet very soon. When can I take them?"

Joanie closed her eyes in thought and said, "I believe they will have to stay for the three days if we don't want any trouble. They came in yesterday morning so you can take them day after tomorrow."

Beth looked at my backside again without touching me, not wanting to cause me more pain. "They really need medical care," she said. "I understand about the three day hold, but we have to do something for them. If I bring some pain med in, will you give it to them?"

"Since you are putting a hold on them, I don't see any reason why we can't give them the pills," Joanie responded. She made out a card to put on our kennel door as she spoke. The writing on the card looked like this:

EAGLE'S DEN RESCUE
PICK-UP FRIDAY MORNING

I could not read what the card said but I knew what it meant. It meant Faith, Hope and I had a place to belong. Someone wanted us. Unless you have known what it feels like to be hated and unwanted, you can never know how wonderful it feels to know someone wants you.

Chapter 24

Nelly's Story

Laughter had not been something we knew a lot of in hell. The only time we had really laughed was once in the training pen when Killer was having an off day. He was laying around, not feeling any more like training than we did. Man was worried about his prize puppy and had sent boy to fetch a fresh pail of water. Boy had left the pail near some shrubbery. When he reached for the bucket, he tripped and fell against one of the bushes. There was a wasp nest nestled down in the limbs and Boy's hand managed to disturb the nest. When it fell to the ground and nothing happened, Boy reached down and picked it up. Man barely had time to yell "Don't do that!" when the wasps began to swarm. Boy threw the nest into the air and it came down on the back of his neck.

Even Killer had gotten a huge laugh watching Boy strip off his shirt and run through the yard with angry stinging wasps swarming behind him.

We did not think we could laugh any harder until Boy ran straight to Man yelling "Daddy! Daddy! Help me Daddy!"

Man had done some kind of a dance in place as he moved first one foot and then the other, and then he and Boy were running through the backyard together. Within a matter of seconds we were laughing so hard we had a belly ache. It was one of the few times we ever laughed in hell, and the one and only time we ever laughed with our brother.

Man almost ended the fun when he headed for the house and ran inside. But fate was on our side for once and Man managed to slam the door right in Boy's face. Once more around the yard and Boy remembered how to open the door all on his own.

There was another burst of giggles later in the day when Boy came out to return us to the shed. He was not wearing a shirt so we got a full view of the damage the insects had done. He had small brown spots all over his back, chest and arms covering angry welts where the wasps had found their mark. We could not tell if his swollen, red face was from wasps' stings or crying. He was making a strange noise with each breath and snorting loudly, indicating he had been crying very hard. We later learned that the foul-smelling brown stuff was something called snuff. Apparently it is supposed to take the hurt out of a wasp or bee sting.

The incident may not have been funny at all, considering Boy had been hurt. But with all of the pain we had known at the hands of the imp, it was not just funny, but hilarious.

Excitement had been as scarce as laughter in hell. The only excitement we had ever known was the day Aunt Gertie caught Boy hurting me in the back shed. So what we were feeling on this day in the shelter, knowing we had a place to go, we were going to be together, and the person who was taking us actually wanted us had put us in a state of euphoria.

We were all three very excited and the laughter came easily. It was a good day and a good time.

Faith and Hope tried to play like they had done eons ago... back before the pain began. They quickly learned they could not roll around without their backsides giving them excruciating pain. Nipping at each other without the ability to roll around and enjoy it has no purpose, so they stopped playing and chose to prattle on and on about what they expected our lives to be like.

I was too excited to talk and just sat staring across at Nelly. My belly felt like jelly and when I tried to stand, my legs would barely hold me. I was very dizzy, but it was not an unpleasant feeling. The closest I can come to describing the feeling is Heart Speak. Back in the beginning when Mother would speak to me, there was a very similar feeling to this. Finally, when I found my voice again I said to Nelly, "So this is what happiness feels like."

"Oh Charity," Nelly smiled as she spoke. "You are going to have the most wonderful life with your sisters. I just knew Beth and Jerry would take you. And they will love you forever and a day, just like you deserve."

"Nelly, when is day after tomorrow?" I asked. Time still had little meaning for me and was measured by sun rises.

"Well," answered Nelly, "the best way to describe it is two more nights in the shelter. You will be here today, tonight, another day and another night... then you will get to leave for the rescue."

"That is almost forever," said Hope. "How am I going to stand it?"

The question was voiced in an exaggerated pained tone. It made Nelly smile to see us so happy and excited. "I tell you what," she said. "Why don't I tell you some stories? That will make the time pass quicker."

Faith raised her shoulders and lowered them, taking a very deep breath. "Make them wonderful stories like the ones about Sergeant Stubby," she said.

Hope bounced slightly and grunted from the pain it brought her. She ignored the pain and said, "Yes. Wonderful stories about rescue and what our lives might be like."

Nelly agreed she would share a few rescue stories with us if we would promise her one thing. "You must take notice of how I tell you these stories and always remember," she said. "One day you will need to share your story with someone; someone that can be your voice and make a difference for all dogs."

"I don't understand," said Faith. "What do you mean?"

"You must remember all of the bad things that happened to you," Nelly said, very serious now. "As painful as it is to remember, your story must be told so people are aware these things happen. It is the only way to make it stop. No one can stop what they do not know is happening. And you can never get justice if no one knows you need it."

"I promise, Nelly," I said. "I will never forget where we came from and the terrible things that happened. And I will tell the story one day when I find someone who will listen. I will do it so people know and so they can fight to make it stop. But mostly I will remember for Mother."

Faith and Hope had gotten very quiet and I heard the small whimper from Faith. I did not think her tears were for the indignities Mother had suffered, but simply because she missed her. "Never forget to remember," she said, and the words pierced my heart like an arrow.

"Now, what story can I tell you?" asked Nelly, already thinking about the many dogs that had passed through the shelter in her stay there.

"Tell us about you, Nelly. I would love to hear all about you," said Hope.

"Oh *pe-lease*," added Faith, emphasizing the 'p.'

Nelly smiled and said, "Oh I think some of my other stories might be a lot more interesting. My life has not been so grand. Just an average life for an average dog."

"You are far from average to us," I said. "We would love to hear about your life. You know you are our only friend? You have heard all about us. Tell us a good story about you."

Nelly was already looking off into the distance, searching her memory for some part of her past that we might enjoy hearing about.

"Well," she started. "There is one story that I keep close to my heart."

She took a deep breath that sounded a whole lot like a sigh and she said, "This happened when I had been with my family past my puppyhood. My name back then was Shut-Up Girl and I had no friends outside my family. Sometimes I would get this feeling in my bones that I needed to run, but I was stuck on my chain. It took another dog to help me find a little freedom. This is the story about a good friend of mine named Toad and an adventure we shared."

Faith crinkled her nose. "Toad? Was your friend a frog?"

"Oh no," replied Nelly. "Toad was a dog. He was a small boy and was well-loved by his family. He was right proud of the fact he had been born without a tail. He thought that made him real special. Toad told me once that he was a Corgi and being born without a tail showed that he came from a really good bloodline.

He had cats that made sure they stayed close to him when he was out and about, because Toad would look out for them. He wouldn't let any harm come to them if he could help it. And he was just as good a friend to the little Chihuahua that lived in the trailer park down the road from us. We lived in the country and Toad was the closest thing to a neighbor I had. His house was a good 30 barks from my backyard. But once I got to know him, I could see what he was up to most days.

"I believe they named him Toad because of the way he would rest with his back legs stretched out behind him. And then there was the way he would jump and bounce around. There were times he did act a whole lot like a frog.

"Toad was a lot of things to a lot of different people and animals. He was the reason for his dad's heartbeat. The love they shared was so obvious it would make my eyes leak at times. He could be a real pain in the backside to someone who was up to no good. And he looked out for his human mom with a determination that made me proud to know him.

"So Toad was many things depending on who you talked to. That little piece of a tail he had would wag so fast it made his whole body shake. And there are times I could have sworn he was wagging his heart at me. But I guess the best way to describe him is just to say he was my friend, and I loved him. He was my best friend."

Nelly had a very far-away look on her face. The memory of her friend had taken her back to a time when she was a young dog and looking for adventure. "This is a long story about how I met my best friend and how I got my name" she said. "It is also about how he saved his family. And every word is true."

A Dog Called Toad

It was a nice day: not too hot and not too cold. The sun was warm and there was just enough of a breeze blowing to stir the heart. It was one of those days when a good run would not make your tongue hang out, but just sitting beneath the trees was enough to make your tail wag.

I was content on my chain in the backyard. The leaves on the old oak tree that often served as my shelter were making a soft music as the wind danced gently amongst the branches. My family had been out earlier and I had been off the chain for a bit, playing with my little girl. She had given me cheese... one of my favorite treats. I had an entire slice all to myself and now was taking an afternoon nap.

There was a strange noise off to my right, but it was not loud enough or annoying enough to make me lift my head to look. With the sun warming my back and my dream already taking me to a nice pond for a swim... if only in my mind... I forgot all about that strange noise.

I was somewhere just on the other side of dreamland, but not quite there yet. I could feel my legs moving slowly and in rhythm, doing the dog paddle... my mind moving me through the pond while my body warmed nicely in the grass.

When the little Corgi pounced on me I jumped straight up, dropping him in a splat to the ground. He rolled around on his back, legs

248

kicking in the air, tail twisting from side to side, and he was laughing hard.

I stood and stared at him, thinking he was just about as crazy as he acted. "Oh! Oh! My stomach!" he half yelped. "That really tickled my funny bone."

He finally stopped rolling around and laughing when he realized I was not going to join in... and the look I was giving him was not one that spoke of like and trust. I could feel my eyes squinting and following this crazy dog as he wallowed around on his back. I was trying very hard to control my German temper that was rising up in my throat, causing me to throw my ears back and making my tail flick from side to side like those windshield wipers on a car.

Crazy dog finally rolled over onto his belly and managed to sit up. "Oh me. I haven't laughed that hard in about ten meals passing," he said. "Didn't you hear me crawling through that grass? I wasn't really trying to be sneaky."

I glared a little harder at him. I was still trying to decide if he was really crazy, or if maybe he had gotten into some chamomile tea and drank too much. It was common knowledge around those parts that people loved their chamomile tea, and it was often left around for dogs to take a few sips. It was actually good for a dog, but it is also a natural sleep aid and too much could make you act foolish.

Or, there was always the possibility that he belonged to one of those people who enjoyed watching others play this game known as football. People that enjoyed watching that game were known to have parties in their backyards on the day of a big game. If the people they liked won... then they would celebrate with a drink called beer. If their people lost, then they would drown their sorrow with beer. They would get really loud and boisterous, saying their team was number one if the team won. Or they would get loud and obnoxious and say that someone called "Ref" was blind and their team would "get 'em next time," if their team lost. People enjoyed that sort of thing.

Either way, there were some dogs that had been known to sneak some of that beer. Considering how people acted when they had too many of them, I imagined it might make a fella act just as foolish as this crazy dog was acting. I didn't want to pick him up and toss him around if he was under the influence.

He stood and stared back at me after he managed to gain his composure, looking me directly in the eye. Then he dropped his nose toward the ground and patted one paw in front of him... shaking his head. "I can't do it," he said, the laughter coming back to his voice. "You are so funny."

I was glad he did not start the insane rolling and laughing again. Instead, he took a deep breath and let out a sigh. "You have made me laugh until I am just dog tired," he finished.

By all the Rules of Dog Combat, I should have just kicked his butt then. He had come into my personal space, attacked me in my sleep, and then stared me directly in the eye. Once he looked away, I almost felt obligated to toss him around a bit. I might have on another day in other circumstances, but now there were three things stopping me. One: I was not at all sure this dog was not crazy and it is never a good idea to attack a mad dog. Two: He had actually managed to make me a bit curious about him. I mean... was he really trying to be friendly? Or was he trying to find a unique way of getting killed?

The third and most important reason I did not just pick this short-legged little beast up and toss him out of my yard, I couldn't do it. He had stepped back just out of my reach. The darn chain would only have allowed me to get within a tail's length of him. Had I thought he was aware of that fact, I might have been angry enough to snap the chain. But he didn't seem to notice that I was tethered. And I wasn't keen on letting him know by pulling against the chain and looking as much the fool as he did.

Deciding to choose the high road, I sat down. Just to be safe, so he didn't think I was backing down or anything, I took my hind leg and started to scratch just behind my ear. He waited for me to stop scratching and said, "Fleas?"

"A few," I answered. I tried to act totally uninterested in him. I yawned and stretched out full on my belly, paws in front of me. My ears stayed totally erect, listening to every grass rustle. I would not let him sneak up on me again.

"I'll have to see if I can't get you some of the stuff my mama uses for the little boogers," he said. "I'm allergic and she makes sure they don't feed on me by putting some drops right on the back of my neck."

"Hmmm," was the only sound I could think up at the moment. I was beginning to feel self-conscious. This dog, less than half my size, had managed to land on top of me without getting so much as a hair ruffled. He had laughed at me, took a battle stance with me that I had allowed to let pass, and now I had just as much as told him I had fleas. I was not feeling very proud of myself.

My only consolation was this dog acted like he had no clue that he had been offensive. Now he was offering to help me get shed of my fleas. I didn't think he was under the influence of anything. I really didn't believe he was crazy either. So that could mean only one thing. This dog was totally domesticated. He was people-pecked.

Dogs, as a rule, are man's best friend. We love our people and we hope to have kind companions in our lives. But we are still dogs. We do have a code to live by. I had heard of dogs that were so taken with their people they had let all the old ways go. As I mentioned before, we call it people-pecked. I had never given it much thought before this because I had never witnessed it. But now here was a dog standing in front of me that was obviously afflicted with the condition. And if I told the truth, I actually liked him.

He smelled really nice. In fact, I believe he had been able to sneak up on me because he didn't smell much like a dog at all. There was a nice lavender scent about him. In my dream, there had been wildflowers growing close to the pond where I was having a swim. That odor wafting all around him just fit right in my dream.

But there was more than his smell that made me like him. Even though his laughter had been almost insane; he was warm and friendly. He didn't make one hair on my neck nervous; not even one stood up. And when he had mentioned his mama, well, it just gave me goose bumps.

It was obvious he was talking about a human mom when he said she put drops on his neck. His whelping mother could not have done that. I mean, I have not seen a dog yet that can do anything close to that without thumbs. So, he had a human mom and his eyes lit up when he talked about her. When a person is so wonderful they can make a dog's eyes light up that way... like I said, goose bumps all over.

That left the only and final conclusion that this boy was definitely people-pecked. And it didn't seem like such a bad thing to be from where I was sitting.

"So," he said, "how about coming for a walk with me? You can try that dog paddle you were doing earlier in some real water."

The invitation made me uncomfortable. I had lived here for a little less than a year and I had seen this dog before. I had not been able to get a really good look at him from my position, and he was not out in the yard a lot. This dog lived in the house next door; and I mean in the house. Being tethered in the backyard suddenly became embarrassing.

"I am totally forgetting my manners," he said. "Toad here, at your service." Then he sniffed me and turned so I could get a whiff of him.

Apparently, even dogs that are people-pecked hang on to some of our oldest traditions. I mean, it is just good manners to sniff butts when you are making introductions. If it is not possible to sniff right away, then you must do it as soon as you are able. It is just rude not to.

"My people call me Girl," I said. "Or Shut Up. I am not sure which they call me the most. And I can't very well be at anyone's service." I turned then and made the chain hooked to my collar obvious.

"Ouch," Toad yelped as if my chain had hurt him. "I hate it when people do that. How long will they leave you out here? Maybe when they come out to get you, we can take a quick run. It will do you good and will probably do your people some good too. I know my mom and dad always seem to enjoy a good sprint when I dig out of the backyard or take off without my leash."

I dropped my head and looked at the ground; then thought better of it and looked Toad directly in his eyes. "I live on the chain," I said, getting it over with quickly.

"Well that just sucks all the marrow right out of a good bone," Toad said. "You don't get to go in the house, lounge around on the couch, and sleep in the big soft bed with your people?"

"No," I was beginning to wish that I was people-pecked. "My people love me, I think. They spend time with me and all. But dogs aren't allowed in the house. I heard my human dad say that once."

*"That doesn't mean they have to chain you up like a wild animal,"
Toad sounded a bit indignant and he grabbed the end of the chain
hooked to the pole in the ground. He had it locked firmly between
his teeth and was pulling with all his strength and snarling just a bit.*

*I felt the wild throes of desire running through my veins and I began
to pull against the chain, wanting more than anything to feel free.
It did not matter to me what my people might think at that point.
Nothing mattered beyond running and feeling the wind against
my face. Besides, I knew they had left the house earlier and would
most likely not be back until after dark. I had heard my little girl
mention going to see "Grandma." Those visits always lasted a long
time. Chances were I would be back long before they were.*

*Suddenly the chain snapped and I was free. Toad and I took off for
the woods back behind my house. I had been down this way a few
times with my child, so I knew exactly where the pond was. By the
time Toad and I had taken a swim and tumbled about all over the
woods, running and playing among the trees and the underbrush,
the part of the chain that had stayed hooked to my collar was gone.
I was totally free for the first time in my life. It was a good time.*

*We heard voices in the distance calling for Toad. "Uh-oh," he said.
They have discovered my exit. It doesn't take them long."*

*We had not been playing long. It had been a wonderful time for me
and I hated to see it end so quickly. But I could see that Toad was
concerned about his people. We were playing hard and had not
been paying attention to anything else, so we could not be sure*

how long they had been calling out. Toad told me they would get very worried and his mom would cry if he stayed missing too long.

We headed back through the small patch of woods. Before we were halfway through, Toad's dad was in front of us. He saw Toad and said, "There you are, boy. You gave us a scare." Then seeing me he continued, "Oh goodness, who is your friend? Her family must be worried too."

Toad's mom was standing at the edge of the woods wringing her hands when she saw us following Toad's dad into the clearing. She started giggling and crying at the same time. "I was so worried about you, boy," she said, kneeling down to pet Toad. Then she just grabbed him and held him very close.

"I told you," said Toad, sounding a little like he was being squeezed too hard. "She worries a lot. I guess that is what mom's do though and I love her."

I stood back and watched, wishing I had this kind of relationship with my people. Then and there I promised myself I would try harder as soon as I saw them again. Toad's dad looked at me and smiled broadly, "Look who I found playing with Toad."

Toad's mom looked up from planting kisses all over his head. "She is beautiful," she said and I was certain I blushed, but did not think they could tell. Most people cannot tell when we blush.

Heck, the average person cannot even tell what we are feeling most times. But Toad knew and he almost whispered, "You are beautiful. Don't you know that?"

Toad's family welcomed me into their backyard and the fence. When they got to the backdoor, Toad ran in and straight for his bowl. I could see him from the door where I had stopped. He was crunching something very loudly, but said between bites, "Come on in, silly. My house is your house."

I could not move my legs on his say so. I stood there until his mom and dad welcomed me into their home. Toad had finished crunching whatever had been in his bowl and was dancing around me now. "Oh it would be just pawsome if you moved in with me." Then he looked at his dad, "Can she stay, Dad; can she pe-leeease?"

Toad's dad was very good at Heart Speak and he answered Toad immediately. "You want her to stay, boy? Is that what you want? Well she can stay until we find her family. They must be worried sick right about now."

As he talked he was reaching for a box setting on the counter. Toad began to leap into the air, almost turning flips. His dad laughed and said, "You already had your treat. I need to get one for your friend."

Then he gave Toad one of the treats from the box. Toad started crunching again while he smiled. It was a very funny look for him and his mom almost purred over him. His dad was offering me one of the treats and it smelled absolutely dogalicious. I was not sure if I should take it. My mouth was watering to the point I was drooling.

Toad's mom took the treat and put it closer to my mouth. "Go ahead and take it, girl. It's yours." Then she looked at Toad's dad and said, "She is a Nervous Nelly. We will call her Nelly."

Toad danced around and jumped up and down showing his approval. "I like the name Nelly," he told me. "Girl is ok, too. But that's more a label than a name, don't you think?"

I liked the name Nelly much better than Girl, too. And I certainly liked it better than Shut Up. I decided to keep the name and from that point on when I told anyone my name, I was Nelly.

Toad's mom and dad began teaching me things right away. By the time night was over, I had stopped thinking of them as only Toad's mom and dad. They taught me how to go to the door when I had to relieve myself so I could leave my droppings outside. They did this by putting a paper on the floor and leaving it at the back door. Toad lifted his leg on it to show me exactly what they expected me to do. Toad said it was a little strange, but that was what they expected. He was right. I squatted and made a puddle on the paper and Mom was absolutely thrilled.

Dad had looked in the pee paper every day searching for someone that was missing a dog. I was not sure why a missing dog would be in the pee paper. But people are strange sometimes and I do not always question their motives.

"I really don't think they are looking very hard," I told Toad after two nights. "I mean, I have been right next door since I was a puppy. And I am certainly well past my puppyhood."

"Ssshhh. Not so loud," Toad whispered. "Dad and Mom both understand Heart Speak. Don't want them thinking you want to go back next door, do you?" From that point on Toad and I had an understanding. Neither of us were anxious for me to go back to the chain; living together with Mom and Dad was the best idea we could think of.

When I first came to live at Toad's house the moon had been full in the night sky. An entire moon cycle had passed when Mom and Dad began to act very nervous. I did not understand what was going on, but Toad did and he explained it to me. There was a place about a full morning's run from us, as the dog goes, where they kept really bad people. They called them criminals and they had all been in a lot of trouble before. They had broken into homes and taken things without permission, and some of them had even hurt others.

There was this box that had an entire other world inside of it. People call it a TV. Mom and Dad had been watching it when the news came across that one of those criminals had broken out of the bad place. He was the worst of the worst from what Toad said. Mom and Dad were worried because we lived in what was known as a remote area. The people living in that box had said the bad man would most likely be heading for a remote area.

Mom got down on the floor and talked to us in a stern voice. She told us we could not leave the fence in the backyard as long as that man was on the loose. She was afraid he might hurt us. Toad strutted and said if he saw that man, he would give him "what for." Toad always talked about giving someone "what for" when they *were up to no good. I was not exactly sure if 'what for' was even real, but Toad sure did like to say he would give it.*

Toad looked at me and said, "Don't you worry your pretty head about it, Nelly. I will protect you." Then he tilted his head, very thoughtful and added, "But we will not even think about digging out of the fence. I don't want Mom to worry and cry."

Toad and I had not thought much about digging out of that fence since the day I had arrived. We were too worried the family next door... my family... might see us and want me back on that chain. But it made Toad feel good to act all protective, so I let it go.

The full moon began to rise in the sky just after we had our supper. I was watching it out the big window in the room Mom always called 'the den.' Mom and Dad were sitting on the couch with Toad and me between them. Toad was lying on Dad's lap, as usual. I was snuggled close to Mom and she was stroking my head.

Mom and Dad would sometimes fall asleep watching people in that TV. Tonight was one of those nights and they had been sleeping long enough for Dad to start making those funny noises he always made in his sleep. Mom had curled her feet up under her on the couch and had her head lying on the back. She was sleeping peacefully and I was preparing to snuggle down and go to sleep myself.

I heard the bang in the backyard about the same time Toad did; but he was a lot quicker than I was. His legs were like springs as he jumped off the couch and bounced all the way through the kitchen to the backdoor. He was barking and growling all at the same time.

Even though he was shouting and all of his words were almost lost in the barks and growls I could hear, "Let me out! Come on! Hurry up! Let me out! I will give him what for!"

Dad was off the couch and on his feet before Mom. He had run to the hallway and was back by the time Mom had stood up. He had a bat in his hand and was heading for the backdoor. Mom yelled, "It's locked! Please don't open the door! Leave it alone!"

But Dad had already opened the backdoor before she had gotten the words out. Toad was bouncing out before I could yell for him to stop. Mom and I were both very worried about our menfolk and we rushed to the door behind them. Dad was out of sight with the baseball bat, obviously looking around the backyard for the intruder. Toad had disappeared too, and Mom and I were standing near the door when I felt something hit me in the head. Before I had the chance to react, a very large man had knocked Mom down. She landed on top of me, and we were both on the ground with the man on top of us.

I yelped as loud as I could, hoping Toad and Dad would hear me over Toad's barks. Mom screamed, but the sound was stifled when the man put his hand over her mouth. I could tell she was crying hard, but from my position, I had no clue what the man was doing to her. I tried to get up, and was almost on my feet and from under the huddle when Toad rounded the corner and came flying through the air. I swear his feet never touched the ground and he landed square on the man's back.

The man let out a scream that had the words "Damn dog" in it. He had rolled off of Mom and was sitting up swatting at the back of his neck and Toad with both hands. He managed to get on his feet and Toad was biting at his legs. Mom was sitting up by then and crying harder. I was stunned by the blow to my head, but was trying to get in a position to help Toad protect my family.

Everything happened very quickly, but when I think about it today, I remember it in slow motion and can recall every small detail. I was weak from being hit in the head, but I was also determined and I jumped toward the man and my full weight hit him in the chest. He landed flat on his back and my belly was covering his face so he could not see Toad coming at him. Toad grabbed him right between his legs and bit down hard. The man's scream came out long and was very high-pitched. For a minute I thought it was Mom screaming.

Dad was on the scene now and was holding the bat in his hands, ready to swing if the man tried to get up. But Toad was holding on to what Dad later called the "family jewels," and when the criminal tried to move, Toad would bite down harder, causing him to scream with that high-pitched sound again. Just to be safe, and because I wanted a little pay back over Mom being knocked down and the blow to my head, I grabbed the man's arm just below his shoulder. Dad called someone to come and get the bad man while Toad and I made sure he stayed on the ground.

It was a very exciting night and there were cars in the yard with flashing blue lights to celebrate Toad's victory. Some people came and took pictures and the next day Toad and I had our pictures in the pee paper with Mom and Dad.

Mom took that pee paper and cut the picture and the story from it. She put it in something called a Scrapbook and said Toad and I were heroes. The next night, people in the TV had our picture hung up on the wall in that other world and anyone who had one of those boxes could see us.

And that is how my family found me.

They showed up when the sun came up again and were shocked I had been right next door the entire time. I went back to my chain with Mom crying and Dad telling my family if I ever needed anything they would be happy to give it. Mom, Dad and Toad came over almost every day to see me and they brought me treats all the time.

My family never really became too friendly with Toad's family, but my little girl started going over to visit them and would always take me with her. Even though she still called me Girl sometimes, she kept the name Nelly, saying the entire world knew me by that name so she could not change it. My own dad would still call me Shut Up though. He never quite adjusted to my name change.

As life happens, Toad's mom and dad had never taken him for something called a neuter. Mom said it was something she had really never thought about since he was an "only child." I had never been "spayed" according to my family. A couple of moon cycles after my wonderful experience in the house next door, I gave birth to my first litter of puppies. They were amazing, all born healthy. There were eight of them, three boys and five girls. Two of the boys and one of the girls were born with a very short tail, just like Toad.

Mom and Dad... I mean Toad's mom and dad... were allowed to take me home with them until the puppies were older and I stayed in their house while my babies grew strong. They found wonderful homes for most of the little ones and would go and visit often to make sure the puppies were being cared for. My family kept one of the boys with a short tail and to my delight, they took him inside the house. One day they brought him outside and hooked him to a chain next to me. They said he was impossible to "house break." He told me they got very angry with him every time he had to pee. I asked him about the pee paper, but he didn't know what I was talking about.

Two of the little girls came back to Toad's house because Mom and Dad did not think they were being treated right. The girls were named Polly and Anna. I do not know how they got those names, but I liked them just the same. Mom and Dad also took the little boy when they saw him on a chain. My family let him go and said it was best that way since we were getting tangled on the chains. He was named Froggy because he was so much like Toad.

Mom and Dad begged and begged then to be allowed to take me too; but, my little girl was not willing to let me go. I know she loved me and I loved her. But my life could have been a lot different over at Toad's house. She did make sure I was able to visit often, and any time my family went away, I stayed with Toad and the three little ones.

Even though I went back to my life on the chain, things changed a lot for me. My life became better and I was able to spend a lot of time with Toad and my three little ones. They were beautiful children and had a lot of both Toad and me in them. We shared many adventures together.

The last time I saw them they were still as beautiful as ever and even though Toad is getting on in years now, he is still looking out for them. Those first puppies I had were the only ones he ever fathered because he went for one of those 'neuters' shortly after our first adventure.

As for me, I had more puppies over time and Mom and Dad always tried to make sure they went to good homes. I had given birth to five litters, including that first one, when Mom and Dad insisted I go to their vet and get spayed. My family had put up a fuss like they always did when the subject came up. But my little girl said she did not want me to spend my life having babies, and since she was the boss when it came to me, I went for that spay. I was very glad.

Nelly finished her story and sighed heavily.

"Why didn't you move in with Toad instead of coming here?" I asked the question we were all thinking.

Dropping her head very low, Nelly said, "I don't think they know I am gone. The last time I saw them they were leaving on a trip because there was a tragedy in Mom's family. They left the same day I came here."

I thought I saw a tear in her dropped head as she repeated, "I don't think they even know I am gone."

"Where is your little girl?" Hope asked. "Why did she let them bring you here?"

"She moved away some time back," said Nelly. "She met a man that does not like dogs and could not take me with her. She said it would be best for me to stay near Toad anyway."

"Still," Hope said, "she could have stopped them from bringing you here. If she is really the boss over what happens to you, she should have stopped them from doing that."

Nelly looked up and I saw there was more than one tear in her sad eyes. "I don't think she cares any more. She stopped caring a long time before she left." Nelly took another deep breath, and I knew she was trying to stop the tears. "She stopped caring, but still would not let me move in with Toad."

Hope, Faith and I huddled closely together then, sending a huge hug over to Nelly. It would have been a good time to snuggle with her. The kennels kept us separated just as her chain had held her captive for too long. But Heart Speak is filled with love, and it surrounded Nelly then. She stretched out in her kennel and it covered her like a warm blanket. Nelly slept with our love holding her close.

Chapter 25

Heart Speak, Love and Bacon

Nelly was very tired and slept long and hard. I understood now why she had told me I needed to remember the pain from our past, so I could tell the story one day. Nelly's story had many lessons in it and was very important for us to hear. She had shared it with us and had felt all the joy and pain it held for her all over again. She slept through supper that day and was still dreaming when Joanie came in and gave Hope, Faith and me one of the pills Beth had sent for us. Nelly slept long into the night and if she awoke, I do not know because the pills helped us sleep soundly without pain.

When the sun came up, Nelly was up before us and was enjoying a bowl of soft food. Tony was in our kennel holding three bowls and a can.

"I am going to divide this can between the three of you," he said. "Let's see if you can at least finish that."

He emptied the can in the three bowls and left our kennel. Looking back, he said, "I sure hope those nice people at that rescue do not think we starved you here." His voice softened then and he added, "And I sure hope they can love you back to health."

As usual, we waited for Tony to leave our kennel before going to the bowls. Hope and I managed to eat a little more than Faith.

I was really starting to worry a lot about her. She only licked at the food in her bowl and her stomach rumbled much of the time. I said a silent prayer to the Great Creator that she would be okay and that the woman who had come to see us and wanted us would be able to help her.

Even though she was not eating, Faith had a light in her eyes now. She loved Nelly and I was afraid she was trying to replace Mother with the old girl across the aisle. It would not have bothered me so much had I not known that Nelly would leave us soon. I said another silent prayer that the rescue came for us before Nelly left for what she called The Old Dog's Home.

Nelly finished licking her bowl clean and let out a burp. "We will all be leaving after one more night," she said. "My rescue will come for me sometime after the sun rises. And I believe yours will be here about time the sun comes up. They are anxious to get you out of here so they can start working on getting you better."

Hope had found a bug crawling through our kennel and was bouncing at it, playing and amusing herself, but Faith was watching Nelly. "That stuff they gave us yesterday while you were sleeping made me feel ever so much better," she said. "It helped me to sleep last night and my butt is not hurting nearly as much today."

Nelly lifted an eyebrow and looked at me. "Joanie brought pills in for us while you were sleeping," I said. "They were a bit hard to get down, and we all fought against it a bit. But if they bring them again, I think we will give them an easier time of it. Those pills helped us a lot."

Those were pain pills," said Nelly. "I will be willing to bet a nice large bone you get more. When Beth was here she could see that you are hurting as clearly as I can."

"I am glad she sent the pills," I said. "They are miracle pills and are making us better."

"No," said Nelly. "They are not making you better. They are making you *feel* better. That is a good thing because pain is not fun. When you are able to leave here they will find something to really make you better."

Faith tilted her head a little and said, "Well, when we are feeling a lot better and actually getting better too, maybe we can go for a run through some woods with you. We will have an adventure."

Nelly dropped her head. "Faith, you do know that when you go to the rescue you will forget all about me? You will have so much love and care, you will not even have time to think about me. All of the pain from the past will be a distant memory, sweetheart. You are going to have such a wonderful life."

"I will never forget you, Nelly. Never, ever. I will never forget to remember you."

Hearing Faith repeat my mother's parting words to me brought back the image of her too thin body and the horrible wounds. I remembered the pain on her beautiful face and dropped my head so no one could see the tears that were starting again.

"Are you doing okay over there, Charity?" Nelly asked. "You do know your life *is* going to get so much better from now on?"

Before I could respond, the door opened and Joanie was coming through smiling and talking. She held the door open behind her and waited for Beth to enter. She still stood there holding the door and talking to Beth. Beth smiled and looked back through the open door, "You coming, Jerry? I can't wait for you to see these puppies."

I heard a man's voice, "I'm coming. Had to tie my shoe."

When the man came through the door, it frightened me just a little. He was the largest man I had ever seen and I knew this was Jerry from Eagle's Den Rescue. I hoped he was as nice as Beth. I realized if he decided to embrace evil, he could crush me or my sisters without even thinking about it.

Joanie and Beth walked to our kennel right away, but Jerry had seen Nelly and was over at her kennel talking to her. "Does this girl have a place to go?" he asked.

"Yes," said Joanie. "Her rescue will come and pick her up some time tomorrow. They may get here really early and be here at the same time as you and Beth. You will be here early want you?"

Jerry laughed. "I don't think I will be able to rest until we have those puppies," he said. "Beth has been really worried about them. She already has an appointment set up with our vet."

Then he looked back at Nelly. "If her rescue falls through," he said, "if they don't show, please give us a call. Old dogs should not be in an animal shelter."

Nelly yelled across the aisle at me, "See. I told you these are good people."

Jerry and Beth were given permission to come inside our kennel. They both sat down on the floor and began to rub our heads and talk to us. Jerry's heart was speaking extra loud. I still don't think he had any control over it that day. Jerry is one of those people whose heart just reaches out and whatever he thinks is there in his heart. It was sort of like the day Thumper's people came in. That is the only way I know to describe the way his heart reached out to me.

"You poor puppies," is what his heart was saying to mine. "Someone treated you really badly and that is so wrong. I hope we can make up for all the pain you have suffered. We will take very good care of you. Please don't be afraid of us. We will never allow you to be hurt again."

To Joanie, he said, "Do you know where these puppies came from? You don't have to tell me, but if you know, someone needs to watch those people. These puppies have been abused."

Beth was taking pills from her pocket and told Jerry to help her give us the pain meds. He took the pills and gave one to each of us. He was very gentle and we did not resist. The pills went down much easier than the wormer had, and much easier than they had the night before when Joanie had given them. Then I smelled the most wonderful odor I had ever smelled in my life. Jerry had something in his hand he was holding out to me. The smell made my mouth water and drool was dripping so fast I could not smack it away.

Beth laughed and said, "Look. He brought bacon in for them. Joanie, I didn't know he was doing that, but I doubt you will be able to stop him from giving it to those babies."

"If they will eat it they are welcome to it," Joanie said. "I will be happy for them to eat anything. They haven't seemed to have much of an appetite."

Jerry responded, "Their mouths look like they may be sore. They look a little swollen to me. What did the vet say?"

Beth responded, "The vet told her to put them down."

"Nonsense," snapped Jerry and he broke the wonderful smelling stuff called bacon into smaller pieces. I gobbled it down and Hope quickly ate hers as well. It hurt my heart to see Faith's mouth obviously watering, but she still turned her head away.

Jerry turned all of his attention to Faith and he lifted her onto his lap. She was frightened and peed on him. If he noticed, he didn't say anything about it, but kept talking to Faith. She held her ears back and looked up at him, wanting to trust, but so afraid. Finally she opened her mouth and took the bacon he was offering. Once she had it, she squirmed out of his lap and ran to our special corner to eat it.

Jerry's eyes were shining with tears. "Someone did something terrible to that little puppy," he said. "We will take extra special care of these three. We will be here very early tomorrow, Joanie. What time do you open?"

Joanie told Jerry and Beth that a lot of dogs came into the shelter and she suspected they had been abused, but it was hard to prove. "I try and make sure none of our Pits leave here with anyone I am not sure of," she said. "We just never know who may be connected to dog fighting in this county. You know a lot of the shelters in neighboring counties have learned some of their officers have strong ties to the fighting rings."

"There are a lot of sick people in this world," said Beth

"No," said Jerry. "They are not sick. They are just plain evil. A sickness is something a person cannot help."

"Well there's a lot of evil around these parts," said Joanie.

"Maybe it's time someone started cleaning up," said Beth. She looked at Jerry and he nodded, something unspoken exchanged between them.

I tried hard to listen to their hearts, but all I heard was, "We can get the group back together we worked with before." I had no clue what that meant. I planned to ask Nelly as soon as they left. She might not know either, but Nelly was smart and she might be able to figure it out if she didn't know.

When they got up to leave, Joanie asked, "How is Sad Miss Snookie doing?"

Beth dropped her head. "She is not so sad any longer," she said, "but she is still not doing as well as I would like. Dr. Curtis gave me all the medicine she needs to get better and we are soaking that leg every day."

"I thought sure your vet would want her to stay in the hospital for a while," Joanie said. "She was in terrible shape."

"He thought she would do better at home with us," Beth responded. "She was terrified in his office and I couldn't have left her if he had wanted her to stay."

Jerry had been kneeling down in our kennel, sneaking more of the wonderful smelling bacon to us and had just gotten Faith to take another piece. He stood up and looked at Joanie. "Snookie will be fine," he said, as they left our kennel and headed for the door. "She was very hurt and needs a lot of care, but she is getting better every day." He looked back at us and added, "And these puppies will be just fine too. You wait and see. Love is the best medicine."

"Love and bacon," Joanie laughed as the door closed behind them.

Faith, Hope and I watched them leave. I could feel excitement fluttering in my stomach. Faith looked at me and whispered, "That man carries love in his pocket."

Chapter 26

A Song for Lucy

The shelter was very quiet for a long time after Jerry and Beth walked out. Breakfast was over and Tony was almost finished cleaning the kennels. Soon it would be time for local people to start coming in. Some would be looking to adopt a dog, while others would be searching for a pet that had gone missing. But we never saw most of the people who stopped by the shelter. The vast majority were stopping to drop dogs or cats off, and there was no need for them to go in the back where the kennels were.

When a dog or cat was left, we could always hear the Heart Speak from the animal. They never understood what was happening to them until their people walked away and left them. Faith, Hope and I had been happy to come to the shelter, but most of the animals here were not happy. We could not see the cats, but we could hear the Heart Speak coming from their room and we knew it was the same for them as it was for the dogs.

There were some exceptions. There were dogs dropped off that had been abused and most of them were hoping to find a new family and have a fresh start. There were also a lot of Pit Bulls. Most of the Pits were like us. They had come from a really bad situation and were glad to be out of the hell they had lived in for most of their lives. Nelly told us that the Pit Bulls usually stayed longer than the other dogs. They were harder to place because of BSL.

Then there were some that came in really injured like Spot. If the dog or cat was suffering and there was no hope, Dr. Martin would come in and help them cross to Rainbow Bridge. I was glad we did not see any more dogs injured that badly. The memory of Spot had given all three of us nightmares.

When we were in the shelter, Nelly had been there longer than any other dog. She told us Silvia had worked very hard to make sure Dr. Martin did not have to come and help any dogs or cats cross to the bridge. Silvia was the one who had helped find The Old Dog's Home for her. There had been a few dogs that Nelly had thought were not going to get out, but Silvia had managed to pull out a miracle each time.

Nelly had told us about several of the dogs that had come through and found rescue. We loved listening to her stories and on our last day in the shelter, we begged her to tell us just one more story. She promised she would tell us a very special story at bedtime, when the shelter was quiet and the world was ready to sleep.

"Bedtime stories are always the absolute best," she said. "They help us to drift off into wonderful dreams and we always feel better when we wake up if we have had a good story to go to sleep by."

We had tried hard to get through our last day quickly. We watched when Silvia came in and took the six little puppies next to Nelly. They would be examined by the vet to make sure they were healthy, then they would leave for their rescue on something called transport.

While she was there getting the puppies, Silvia stopped by Lucy's kennel and asked, "Are you going to let me give you a walk today?" I could tell by Lucy's Heart Speak she was ready to trust this lady.

"She's wagging her tail!" Silvia cried out, very excited. "Look, Tony; Lucy is wagging her tail and she's come to the front of her kennel so I can pet her."

Tony walked over and smiled broadly. "I knew she would come around," he said. "I don't know what happened to her before she got here, but she had a hard life and had no reason to trust people. I am glad we were able to show her not all people are bad."

"Well she can leave today," said Silvia, still excited. "I have a rescue that will take her, but she will need to be spayed first. I have been waiting, hoping she would warm up. Now that she has, we can go ahead and get her started on her new life."

We watched, excited to get a glimpse of the dog that had lived next to us since we arrived. When she walked out of her kennel and into our view, I must have gasped. She was one of the largest dogs I had ever seen. Her coat was almost totally white and very fluffy. I expected her to be a bit clumsy because of her size, but she was not. She walked so softly it almost looked like she was walking on clouds. I had never seen royalty, but I imagined if I met a queen, this is what she would look like.

Lucy stopped just before she passed our kennel and turned back to look at us. "You are beautiful puppies," she said. "Don't ever let anyone tell you different."

She began to walk away again with Silvia, but stopped one more time to look at us. "You will have an amazing life," she said. "I know you will because you deserve it after all you have been through." Her eyes met mine and I saw something very sad. It made me want to snuggle with Lucy.

Her heart reached out to mine and I heard, "I know exactly how you feel. I know the shame. I was never used as bait, but I understand the rest."

Lucy had kept to herself in the shelter. She had never shared her story. She didn't need to. Every dog there knew she was afraid of people because someone had given her reason. But she had reached out to me before she left, to let me know Faith, Hope and I were not alone. Someone had done something terrible to her, but now she was ready to move past that, and she was going to get the chance because of a woman named Silvia.

Just as she got to the door, I did not wait for the Walker Hound to start singing. I wanted to make sure Lucy heard The Song of Souls as she left the shelter. I held my nose as high as I could and let out a long howl. Then I gave several shorter yips, preparing to let out the longest and the loudest sound I could muster. Even though it was hard to hear myself, I could tell it was a very good howl. I held it as long as I could and let it fade to a stop rather than cutting it off short.

Everyone waited for the extra-long howl to end and then they joined in. We sang long for Lucy. Silvia stuck her head back in the door. I could tell she liked our song and was glad she had stopped so Lucy could hear. The last glimpse I got of Lucy, her tail was wagging and she was a happy girl. She was going to rescue and her new life.

Nelly was staring at me when we finished the song. "You are just full of surprises," she said. "I never expected you to lead our choir." I could tell she liked it even though she did not say so.

"She deserved a good song," I said, very glad I had stepped up for Lucy and feeling extremely proud that Nelly had taken notice.

Nelly smiled and said "Even though she never told us what happened to her, how she was hurt, I think someone did something just awful to her. It took a lot of courage for her to put it behind her without ever having anyone to share it with."

"I think it helped her to know she was not alone," I said. "She heard all the stories here and understood she was not the only one some man hurt."

Nelly nodded in agreement. "I think your story has helped a lot of the dogs here move forward," she said. "They have all heard you talking to me and know what you have been through. I believe Lucy was able to come to terms with her abuse after hearing your story and seeing you struggle to accept help."

The old girl had a look on her face that let me know she had heard the Heart Speak between Lucy and me. I was glad Nelly knew. Some things are too hard to hold in your heart all alone.

I had never even thought about our story helping others and when Nelly said it, my heart filled with both hope and pride. I hoped Mother could see from Rainbow Bridge. Suddenly I yearned to talk to her and tell her all about what was happening to us now. I hoped she had seen Lucy and saw the way I had sang The Song of Souls for her. It was the first time I honestly felt like I might be honoring Mother's wishes and I hoped she could know that I was trying to make her proud.

"I am going to take a nap," Nelly said. "It will be a long night if I am going to tell you a bedtime story." She walked over to her bed and climbed on it. Just before she closed her eyes, I heard her Heart Speak, "I know your mother must be very proud of you."

Hope was standing next to me and whispered, "I think when dogs get older they need to take more naps."

"Yes, I think so," I said. "And I think when dogs are puppies they need a lot of naps too." I nodded toward Faith who was curled up on our blanket sound asleep. The pain pill Jerry had given us was working its magic again and I was glad Faith could sleep. Hope and I joined her on the blanket and we snuggled close.

"I think if it's going to be a long night, I will just go ahead and sleep now, too," she said. I did not answer her. I was already halfway to my favorite dream meadow, running for the pond.

This time there was no apple-cheeked boy in my dream. Instead there was a man named Jerry and I was running behind him, following the smell that was coming from his pockets. Hope and Faith were running beside me. We were healthy and happy, and we were well-loved.

Chapter 27

Nelly's Bedtime Story

Faith, Hope and I slept most of the day away. Nelly said it was because we were not used to the pain pills we had been given. The three of us had missed a lot of sleep in our lives and puppies need to sleep to grow and be healthy. So I didn't mind that the pills made us sleep. But I didn't like sleeping as much as I liked the way I felt when I woke up. The pain was still there, but was so far away I could almost forget it sometimes.

Tony brought our supper in and divided a can between us again. He did not bother to mix any of the soft with the kibble. We were still not eating a lot, and Faith was eating less than Hope and me. Nelly said as soon as we left the shelter and were able to exercise, our appetites would pick up. I was still very concerned about Faith, but was glad she was at least trying to eat now. I think the pain pills helped her with that too.

The three of us were excited about leaving the shelter, but we were also scared. I knew how my tummy felt when I would try to eat and was fairly sure Hope's was the same. It was like there was something in there fluttering around and the food did not want to go down, even though we were hungry. But Faith, well, I was not sure exactly what was going on with her. She had come back from her time in the Land of Nothing, but had come back changed. She had been so innocent, so much a puppy, when she left. Now, she looked the same, but was distant most times. The only time she acted like Faith was when Nelly was talking to us, sharing a story.

Hope and I enjoyed the stories as much as Faith and we loved Nelly. But those times made me happiest because I could see the Faith I loved so much was still in there somewhere. So on our last night in the shelter I waited very impatiently for the lights to dim and everyone to settle down so Nelly could start her bedtime story.

It took Tony forever to finish in the kennels. Then Joanie came in to check on everyone. The kennels where the puppies and Lucy had been were emptied out and cleaned exceptionally well, ready for a new dog to come in. The last dog was given fresh water and the buckets, pails, mops and brooms were put away. Joanie went to each kennel and told every dog in the shelter "Goodnight," like she did every day. Finally, Tony stood at the door, holding it open for Joanie. She walked out and the lights went down.

All of the dogs began talking among themselves and I didn't think they would ever quieten down. The Beagles were the nosiest every evening and this was no different. They would argue among themselves, loud enough for everyone to hear. They argued over who had the brightest eyes, whose tail wagged the straightest, who had the best colors. And on this night, when I wanted them to shut up quickly, they argued over whose fleas were biting everyone. Finally a Lab Mix that was leaving for rescue the next morning just like us snapped at them, "Will you just shut up so we can get some sleep? Some of us have a busy day tomorrow!"

One of the Beagles said "Well, Ex-cuuu-se me," and the shelter got very quiet. For a moment it was almost eerie and then the Walker Hound decided to sing a chord of The Song of Souls before he went to sleep. Several of the dogs joined in, but Faith, Hope and I remained very quiet, waiting. Finally the Walker ended his song and the shelter dogs went to sleep – except for those who were whispering to each other through the kennels. Nelly came to the front of her kennel and was ready to start.

"This is a very good story," she began. "It happened here in this very shelter before I knew I had a rescue and when I was not so sure about the people here. But it is not my story. It is the story of a dog that came in almost starved. Dr. Martin was called to her and he wanted to send her to Rainbow Bridge right away."

"Just like us," Hope said.

"Yes," responded Nelly, "And just like with you, Joanie refused to allow anyone to rob the old girl of a day. She said the dog deserved a chance. It was just before a rescue existed called Eagle's Den."

"That's *our* rescue," said Faith, even more excited to hear Nelly's story now with the familiar name being said.

"That's right," said Nelly. "And I saved this story for bedtime, and especially for your *last* bedtime here, so you would know you are going to a very special place. You are going to be just fine. This is the story of a dog called Sad Miss Snookie."

"The dog Joanie asked Beth about today!" said Hope, unable to hold her excitement in check.

"The very same one," said Nelly. "Sad Miss Snookie was here in this very shelter and right across the aisle from me. She was in Kennel 5, just like you. This is the story of how she found a rescue when no one thought she would. This is Snookie's story," then Nelly ended her intro as she did with Toad's story, "And every word is true."

The Foster

The old dog sat on the cold floor with her head dropped so low her nose was touching the concrete. Her eyes were far too large in her haggard face. Her wounds were obvious and the smell was evident all the way down the row of kennels. Dogs in every kennel came to the front to try and see what was going on with this dog. She had not spoken to anyone and I watched her from my kennel across the aisle. I had seen Tony bring her in and she had not walked to her kennel; he had carried her.

After giving her a water bowl and leaving some food for her, Tony had gone to the cat room to deliver a couple of new intakes. He left the door open and within seconds I could see several of the cats in kennels closest to the door peeking out, trying to determine where the smell was coming from. I heard a loud sigh from the dog as her body dropped to the floor, too weak to keep sitting up. I really did not think she would last until Dr. Martin could get here.

When Joanie came in after lunch, she stopped in front of Kennel #5 to see the new occupant. The smell of rotting flesh made her step backward involuntarily. She had always tried to maintain a positive, happy attitude for the animals here waiting to die. For most dogs in this small, southern, county shelter, it was the only kindness they had ever known.

Joanie had accepted the job as manager of the shelter during a time of change. This shelter had one of the highest "kill rates" in the state of North Carolina and the previous manager had done nothing to help the statistics. In fact, Barry Baden was best known for his cruelty. Joanie had been told the story of how one man had found Barry at the landfill using dogs for target practice. The man had come to the shelter looking for his grandson's missing dog. He had heard shots coming from the landfill, directly behind the shelter and had gone to see what was happening.

Barry had a .22 Rifle and was barely aiming, with each shot injuring one of the five dogs he had taken to the landfill. The dogs had been tied together and could not escape with each running in different directions, and one lying dead. All of the dogs sustained several injuries to various parts of their bodies. The one that was dead had been shot at point blank range between the eyes. Unfortunately for Barry, the dead dog belonged to the man's grandson.

The man had taken his time delivering what local residents called a "Southern ass whooping." Barry Baden had been rushed to the Emergency Room and the man was arrested for assault. Someone had contacted a rescue in the next county before the four injured dogs could be put down. One of the dogs had died on the way to the *veterinarian's office, two were injured so severely they could not be saved, and one recovered from the injuries after a leg amputation. He was living a wonderful life with his new family somewhere in Pennsylvania.*

The unnamed man had been released from jail and all charges dropped when the rescue group threatened to go public and "go large" if the five dogs did not find some justice. Barry Baden resigned his position at the shelter and the search for a new manager began. Ned Carson took over in the interim and he had started to bring positive change to the shelter.

A newly formed, local rescue group had been welcomed in and the "kill rate" quickly dropped from about 98% for healthy animals to less than 50%. Ned began a campaign to have the gas chamber removed from the shelter in favor of more humane euthanasia. After a year at the shelter, he was successful and the monstrosity had been destroyed. The local veterinarian was put on retainer and came in at least once a month or as needed in an emergency. Ned was proud of the work he had done, but his health was failing and he needed the county to find a new manager. He reminded the County Administrators that he had only been hired to fill in. They advertised all over the state and had numerous applicants.

Joanie Bellamy was hired because of her reputation for being a strong animal rights activist. She had not applied for the job when she saw it listed, but had been recommended by Ned. He had gone to see her and had asked her to apply, hoping the progress that had been made at the shelter would continue. She applied for the position and then declined the job offer at first. Joanie did not like the attitudes when she went for her first interview. She finally accepted the job only after she was promised she would have full control over the euthanasia practices.

While the statistics were not official, everyone knew there had not been a healthy animal euthanized since Joanie had taken over as manager. Dr. Martin, the veterinarian, was called in to treat injured animals more often than he was called to euthanize. County administrators were still on the fence with regard to more funding for the shelter. Joanie had never been much of a public speaker and had never gotten very involved with politics; but, she had quickly learned she needed to reach out to citizens in the county if she hoped to bring the much-needed changes for the shelter.

Local residents fell under three categories with regard to the shelter and the changes. There were those who were thrilled and thought it was about time the county "got with the program." There was the group that thought all of the taxes going to support the shelter was a waste for dogs who had no place to go. This same group had not blinked when the story about Barry Baden had been leaked to the press. They were very vocal about saying all of the hoopla was a waste of time and money over a bunch of stray dogs when Barry resigned. Then there was the group who Joanie had hoped to win over... those who had no opinion what-so-ever. She was learning that changing minds in this county was hard work, but she was determined.

Joanie had seen a lot of injured, neglected and outright abused dogs since coming to the shelter. This sad dog tugged at her heart strings more than any she had seen. Joanie removed the papers hanging neatly on the kennel door and attached them to her clipboard. They declared she was a stray 'Boxer Mix,' picked up in Marsh Swamp. Joanie knew the area well and she knew who lived there.

"Stray," she muttered. "Yeah, right."

Joanie had lost count of the number of "stray Pit Bulls" brought in from that area, and she had only been working at the shelter for a year. Most strays came in to the shelter hungry, starving for both food and attention. But the Pit Bulls from that area came in with far worse than an empty stomach. This dog might have the label 'Boxer Mix' but Joanie recognized her as a Pit. Her loose, hanging skin, her slightly crooked mouth and her scarred body made her look more like a Boxer, but this was a starving Pit Bull. The uneven bite indicated a broken jaw, something Joanie had seen many times before.

Joanie had started a lot of people in the county thinking about cruelty to animals and the local dog fighters were suffering as a result. The largest and most destructive circle of fighters all lived in the Marsh Swamp area of the county. The group had started breaking bones rather than pulling and filing teeth to make it harder to recognize the bait dogs that came into the shelter. Broken bones were easier to explain and was a more successful way of keeping the authorities away. This poor dog was simply the latest Marsh Swamp casualty and from the looks of her, she would not make it to the mandatory 72 hour hold when she could be adopted, rescued... or killed.

Bracing herself for the smell, Joanie stepped closer to the kennel. Looking at this girl's legs, and backside she knew exactly where the horrible odor was coming from. Of course her ears looked very mangled and rough, too... but that front leg had gangrene setting in. Her backside was ripped open and there were several oozing wounds. Joanie spoke to the old girl in a soft voice, hoping the tears that so often came on this job would not fall just yet. Tears were seen as a sign of weakness by too many of the people in this county and Joanie could not afford for anyone to think she was weak.

Dr. Martin would undoubtedly have a case to go ahead and euthanize this dog before the hold was up. Her injuries were severe and they could easily justify putting her down early. But Joanie believed every dog deserved a chance. Of course, there were circumstances when she appreciated not having to wait, but if possible, Joanie wanted to give every dog a chance. She looked over at me sitting in my kennel and smiled. "He wanted to kill you, didn't he girl? I wouldn't let him and I am not going to let him kill this sweet baby either."

I whined at Joanie and slapped my paw on the floor. Very few people relate to dogs with Heart Speak these days, and I wanted to make sure Joanie knew she was understood and appreciated. Dr. Martin had suggested letting me go early because I was not only old, but I was also an owner surrender. No one was going to come and claim me. With a lot of stray dogs running around the county, the shelter was frequently full and needed all the space available. My kennel could be emptied quickly. Joanie would not even discuss the option and chastised the good doctor soundly for suggesting it.

Joanie smiled at me and I knew she had gotten my message. Then she turned her attention back to the newcomer. "Hey there girl. What's your name, huh? We need to give you a name if we want to find you a home." She knew all too well no one would want to give this girl a home. None of the rescues she knew would be interested either. With so many lives to save, rescues had to select the most likely to be adopted quickly. Not only was this one not going to be readily adoptable, she was going to have a high vet bill if someone stepped up.

The dog never lifted her head. She just sat staring at that floor with the saddest eyes Joanie had ever seen. Joanie went in the kennel. She usually exercised a bit more caution with the newcomers, but she knew this girl was not likely to be aggressive. This dog was totally spent. Man had thrown his worst at her, and she had somehow managed to survive to make it to Kennel 5 here at the shelter. No one who had seen her believed she was going to survive much beyond that.

The poor girl was too weak to even stand. Joanie noticed right away what little weight the dog had on her came from the way too large teats hanging beneath her. Quickly she looked at the paper she had taken from the kennel door. No mention of puppies being located.

"We looked and couldn't find any sign of pups," she jumped slightly, startled by Tony standing outside the kennel. He had just gone on another call and had a litter of puppies on the truck. He had come into the shelter to see which kennel was open and would best meet the needs of the puppies. "I looked really well and old man Gurney

was not happy with the snooping. He acts like he owns that whole stretch of land there."

"He was afraid you might find something more than puppies," Joanie said.

Tony cleared his throat the way he always did when he was trying to warn the pretty brunette not to get too involved. He knew she had the heart for rescue more than for operating a county shelter, and he was well aware of her sympathy for the dogs that came through the shelter doors. She had a special place in her heart for the dogs like this girl. Usually, with any luck, they died before the shelter vet could inject them with poison. Joanie always fought for them the hardest and she was always sorely disappointed when they died at the shelter without ever having known the love of a family.

As for the man Joanie was talking about, everyone knew old man Gurney was a breeder and a dog fighter. But knowing and proving are two different things. And dog fighting seemed to be very hard to prove in this county. That particular piece of work was also widely known as a drug dealer. The authorities were far more interested in him being put away for corrupting the youth of the county than for maiming and killing dogs.

Joanie's eyes were glistening when she looked up at Tony. The tears were there and so ready to fall. "Did you weigh her, Tony?"

Tony knew when she had walked behind this sad dog she had seen the protruding bones, largely hidden by the folds of skin hanging in the front. This girl had absolutely no meat on her bones, and he doubted she would be able to feed puppies if they had found them. This dog was dying and he hoped Joanie would spare herself a lot of hurt and not even bother to give this one a name.

"Old Doc Martin already took a look at her," Tony responded. "He was here to drop off some kennel cough vaccine that was donated and left at his office. He went ahead and weighed her while he was here and said he would be back after he went and grabbed a bite to eat."

Tony shuffled his feet, leaving the rest of Dr. Martin's comments unspoken. "She weighs about 23 pounds. He thinks her puppies probably starved to death days ago. No way could she feed them."

"And what else did he say?" Joanie asked, giving Tony a sideways look that said she already knew the answer.

Tony shuffled his feet again and thought about ignoring the question. He did need to get those puppies out of the truck, and could easily change the topic to them. Instead, he chose the honest answer. "He said we might want to go ahead and do a mercy euth. She is hurting, Joanie. She's hurting bad."

Joanie glared at Tony and snapped, "You don't agree with that? You know she deserves at least her three days to feel loved."

Tony swallowed hard and looked at Joanie without answering. He knew she didn't want to know what he thought, not really; not unless he could add something useful to the conversation that might be beneficial to a dog that was already dying.

"I don't suppose he left any pain medication for her?" she continued. "And I don't suppose you asked him for any since she is hurting so badly?"

Tony knew there was no arguing with her so he walked away without a response and left Joanie to the sad old dog. The county had wanted her to bring positive change and improve the shelter's image to all of the rescues that had been yelling about that high euthanasia rate. Tony doubted she would be able to help bring any positive change by hanging on to dogs like this one. But it was her call. This one was another that would belong to Joanie. No matter what happened, the dogs that were the neediest would live in Joanie's heart forever. Each day and each tear was another memory of the ones lost.

Then he heard Joanie call out behind him, "Her name is Miss Snookie; Sad Miss Snookie."

Tony shook his head. He imagined Sad Miss Snookie would be dead in her kennel either late this afternoon or early in the morning. No worries. She would at least be out of her misery. He stopped at the last kennel on the side opposite from me. It was a large one and would easily work for the litter of puppies. They would be out of here at the end of the three day hold. Rescues always wanted the puppies.

Dr. Martin returned that day and, as expected, left shaking his head. Sad Miss Snookie would have her three day hold just as Joanie had insisted. He looked at me as he walked past my kennel and muttered, "Old dogs and sick dogs have no business taking up space."

I turned my back to him and stuck my butt in the air. That might be a way to say hello and to welcome another dog, but, I had learned, for a person it holds a strong, negative message. Seriously doubting that the vet understood Heart Speak, I wished I had the ability to make a kissing sound so he would understand what I was saying to him. Several of the dogs in the shelter heard me loud and clear and laughed. A couple of them barked, hoping to emphasize the message that Dr. Martin needed to 'kiss my butt.'

Joanie's tender loving care and persistence paid off for Sad Miss Snookie and she managed to survive for the three day hold. She wasn't the friendliest dog I had ever met, and was very stand-offish with most of the dogs in the shelter. However, I have always been known for my ability to befriend the friendless and Snookie began talking to me on her second day here. She did not share a lot about herself, but it was clear she had lived a rough life.

We shared a couple of stories about our children and we cried over those we would never know, hoping they found good homes. She was saddest about the loss of her last litter. Among other things told in deepest confidence, she told me how her milk had dried up before they were ready to quit nursing, and how she had prayed to the Great Creator of All Life to allow her babies to survive, somehow, someway. On her last night in the shelter, Snookie and I held a very long session and said prayers to the Great Creator that we both would be able to live out our days in peace. Neither of us wanted to die in the shelter. We prayed for a rescue for her, and that Mom and Dad would find me and take me home to live out my days with the family I should always have been with.

On the afternoon of her last day in the shelter, Sad Miss Snookie's kennel door opened and there was Tony with food. It was canned food today. Snookie knew what that meant. Every dog in the shelter knew when they brought around the canned food, unless you are a puppy and have no teeth, it would be a last meal. Her short stay in the county shelter was coming to an end. She kept her eyes averted around people as she had learned over the years. I could see the fear in her eyes, and knew it was more a fear of the unknown and what was coming than it was her mistrust of Tony. The man had been nothing but kind to her in the three days she had been here. This was, in fact, the best her life had been in a very long time.

The smell of the food was making Snookie's mouth water and she made a smacking nose that must have startled Tony. He jumped and then with one of the softest tones he could manage said, "There, there girl. Go ahead and eat your supper. No one will hurt you ever again."

Tony hurried from the kennel. The smell of rotting flesh was strong in Kennel 5; but, that was not what made him rush away. Tony hoped all of the dogs that came into the shelter would find rescue or a good home. Sad Miss Snookie had a very special place in his heart though. Most of all he wished she could find a place to live out her days. He thought she would have been put down that first day, but Joanie had insisted on giving her the three day hold so she could feel love for once in her life. Tony had not necessarily agreed with the choice, but still he had fussed over her. Just like Joanie, he hoped something would change for this dog and someone would take her into their home.

Tony heard Silvia coming through the double doors. We all knew Silvia well. Her work as a volunteer for the local rescue had earned her the respect of Joanie and Tony. And the fact she works overtime to get all of the dogs out and into a rescue that will rehabilitate them and find them a good home has earned her the respect and love of every dog who comes through the shelter doors. Every dog may not be able to show it because of something terrible in their past, but none of the shelter dogs will ever have anything bad toi say about her. On Snookie's last day, she was not alone. She introduced the woman named Beth to Tony, and told him that Beth was a foster for the rescue.

Beth and her husband, Jerry had fostered a few litters of puppies for the rescue before. They had worked in rescue most of their lives and were an older couple. After losing one litter to the dreaded disease known as Parvo, they preferred to care for an older dog. Beth had told Silvia they wanted one that no one else would take. Even though Silvia would lose the spot for puppies, the fact the couple was willing to take an older dog helped. It was a request that pleased Silvia and would be easy to fill. Beth had come to the shelter today to select a dog.

Tony walked with them as they passed by each kennel. They stopped at the kennel that smelled of rotting flesh and Sad Miss Snookie stopped eating and quickly stared at the floor. Silvia's phone rang and checking the caller ID, she determined this was a call she needed to take. She walked outside the shelter so she could hear the caller and left Beth with Tony.

I watched from my kennel and knew Sad Miss Snookie may well be saved. I could hear the Heart Speak loudly and clearly. I tried to send the message to Snookie, knowing her fear might prevent her from hearing what was clear to me. Once a dog has been horribly abused, fear makes a terrible noise inside their head when people are near. Sometimes it is so loud it will drown out the most beautiful sounds, like the song of Heart Speak.

"What is this dog's story?" Beth asked.

Tony filled her in as best he could on how they had been called to pick her up as a stray, and how her terrible injuries had lead the local vet to suggest immediate euthanasia.

"Those wounds can be treated," Beth stated. "She can get better with the right care."

Tony patiently explained to Beth that there were far too many healthy dogs here that needed a place to go, and no rescue could afford to take a chance on a dog like Snookie. He saw the frown on Beth's face and for a moment thought she was angry with him. Had he known her better, he would have known she was already thinking about what she would need to care for the injured dog.

My own excitement was building to a fever pitch and I hoped Snookie was hearing and understanding. It was always good to know a dog had cheated death at the shelter. And no dog deserved to cheat it more than Sad Miss Snookie.

When Silvia came back into the shelter, Beth told her she had chosen the dog she wanted to foster. "I will take Sad Miss Snookie," Beth said.

Silvia's eyes lit up for a brief moment and Beth saw it. There was hope in that look that Silvia quickly disguised with a voice of reason. "She's dying. She has gangrene and is being put down tomorrow morning. You know she must be in pain."

I could hear the excitement just under that voice of reason and I hoped Beth was not given to listening to such logic. I should have known from the sound of her Heart Speak that she had already made up her mind and, like Joanie, once her mind was set there was no changing it.

"I will start her on antibiotics and pain meds tonight and start soaking those wounds. I will cover her vetting; I can see you have your hands full with so many here." Beth's voice was matter-of-fact and she talked as though she had not heard that voice of reason.

Silvia's voice changed slightly, questioning... could Sad Miss Snookie be saved after all? She went over all the reasons she had given herself that it was best to let this dog go, but this time, when she finished the recitation she added, "Do you think you can help her, really? I don't mind one bit helping with the cost; that is not the problem. I just don't want her to suffer needlessly."

Beth's voice never changed. Her husband could have told Silvia, Tony, and Joanie, who had now joined them, that tone was Beth's "THIS IS HOW IT IS GOING TO BE" voice. But no one in this group was going to argue with whatever semblance of logic Beth was willing to offer, if it would save this dog. The way she kept her gaze averted, the empty sadness in her eyes, and the terrible wounds that they all recognized as being 'bait dog injuries' had hurt every heart standing here. And each one had secretly hoped she would find a place to get help and live out her days.

"At best, we will be successful and Snookie will have a good life," Beth said. "At worst, Snookie will have lived in my home for whatever time she has left and will leave this world having known love, even if only for a short time. Even a day, or a half of a day, is better than what she has had"

"Or better than what is waiting tomorrow morning," Silvia added

It was settled that easily.

Sad Miss Snookie finished her canned food as the dreaded humans left her kennel. She had deliberately stayed distant and kept her mind on the food that she would soon be allowed to finish in peace. She had no idea her life was about to change drastically. She had not heard the Heart Speak. But right at that moment arrangements were being made in the office for Sad Miss Snookie to leave the shelter the following morning. She would live to eat more canned food in her life.

As soon as the shelter got quiet for the night, I told Snookie she had been saved. She was excited, and she was afraid. She asked me if I was sure there were good people left in the world, and if I had truly heard the Heart Speak so clearly.

I promised her she would one day learn it was safe to hold her head up high and she would learn that not all people are cruel.

There were many lessons to be learned. There were many changes about to begin. Beth's life was about to change too. But she, like Sad Miss Snookie, had no clue. When she and Jerry arrived the following morning to take Snookie home, Jerry's eyes filled with tears when he saw the dog. They put her on a leash and allowed her to walk out of the shelter. It was hard for her because of the injuries, but it was also important for her to leave on her own and the couple seemed to know this.

It took a long time to get to the car and Snookie stopped and relieved herself on the green grass just outside the shelter. I could hear her calling out to me and telling me how beautiful the world was outside, and how wonderful it was to be alive.

"I can hear the Heart Speak," she called out to me. "I can hear it clearly and I have faith that you will be leaving for your home soon, too. Don't forget me, Nelly. And I will surely never forget you."

The next time I saw Beth and Jerry they were here in the shelter talking about Eagle's Den Rescue. The rescue was just starting and they hoped to continue to foster dogs for Silvia from time to time, but they wanted Joanie to know if there was a need for a dog like Sad Miss Snookie, their rescue was available.

And now, you three will be going to Eagle's Den. I suspect Sad Miss Snookie had a lot to do with that. I believe knowing how close she came to dying made Beth and Jerry move forward with their plans for Eagle's Den. And I am very proud that I was here to see the start of it all.

I loved the bedtime story about Sad Miss Snookie and Eagle's Den Rescue, but I was fighting back tears when Nelly finished talking. She knew, even though I never said a word, and she knew why.

"Charity," she said; "please don't be so sad for me. I did get a rescue and I will be safe. And now, when you get to Eagle's Den you can do something for me that will make my heart very glad."

"Anything," I said. "I will do anything I can to help you and make you happy."

"When you get to Eagle's Den," Nelly said, "I want you to make sure you spend some time with Sad Miss Snookie. You tell her for me that my heart sings every night for her because I know she is safe. And tell her that I am going to a wonderful place."

We all fell silent, thinking about Sad Miss Snookie, Nelly, and what our lives might be once we arrived in rescue.

"I do know that my life will be wonderful," Nelly said, and she turned to climb onto her bed for the night. I had caught the hint of sadness in her voice and I thought I saw a tear in her eye. I would not go to sleep for a very long time because I had plans to make. I had to practice my Heart Speak because there was something I needed to say to Joanie before we left the shelter.

I knew, without a doubt, Nelly had used Heart Speak to remind Joanie of Beth, Jerry and Eagle's Den so our lives could be spared. That is what the conversation was about on that morning when Joanie had gone to Nelly's kennel. Now it was my turn to return the favor for Nelly. I had to find a way to talk to Joanie and tell her about Toad and Nelly's real family. Nelly deserved to go home.

Chapter 28

Leaving the Shelter

The moon gave way to the sun and it was another day. It took me a minute to realize we were safe and in the shelter when I first woke up. I had not slept well at all; trying to figure out how to talk to Joanie had taken up most of the night. When I finally did sleep, my backside was hurting again and I had nightmares about life in hell.

The thoughts that had been in my mind for most of the night had brought a little Corgi named Toad into my dreams. But the pain reminded me of Boy and the torture we had endured. In my dream Toad was trying to help me get out of hell. He would go looking for Boy so he could give him 'what for.' But Boy was sneaky and always managed to get me into the back shed without Toad seeing him. I could not understand how Toad missed seeing Boy when he would walk right past him. But dreams are strange that way.

When I woke up, of course I was safe in the shelter. Nelly and my sisters were already awake. Faith and Hope were very excited and were making absolutely no attempt to hide it. They were prattling on and Hope was doing this strange bounce that I had never seen her do before. She could not be still no matter how hard she tried, and she did try.

"What are you doing?" I asked. "Why are you bouncing that way?"

"I don't mean to," she said. "My butt will not be still. It is trying to wiggle and when it wiggles it hurts really bad. The only way I can stop it is to bounce."

Her eyes were glistening with excitement. The mention of the pain in her backside caused a stabbing ache to hit me in the heart. "Don't worry about it," I said. "You go ahead and bounce."

"I will," said Hope. "I can't help it."

She was walking behind me when she finished talking and I felt a pinch. "Hope!" I snapped. "Did you just pinch me on my butt?"

"I can't help it," she repeated again. "I just can't help it."

Faith was prattling on at Nelly, who was sitting calmly with a smile on her face. I looked at Nelly and shrugged my shoulders. "I think they have lost their minds," I said.

"No," responded Nelly. "They are just very, very excited and happy. They have never known happy before, so they really don't know how to act."

The door from the front opened and Joanie came through. Usually Tony arrived first, and it felt a little early for anyone to be there. Faith and Hope hurried to our shadow corner and huddled. I knew they were waiting for me to join them. I had started in that direction, but stopped in the middle of our kennel. I had spent most of the night trying to think of a way to talk to Joanie. This might be my chance.

Joanie came straight to our kennel and opened the door. She got on her knees and looked at me. "I could not get you out of my mind last night, little one," she said. "Today is the big day for you and I was worried something had happened to you."

I allowed myself to drift then and tried to go deep inside myself to that place where Heart Speak lives. I could feel the warm wind and the tugging I had always felt with Mother, but something was stopping me from connecting with Joanie. Nelly had been able to talk with her, so it must be something I was doing wrong. My heart fell to my paws when she stood and left our kennel. For at least the hundredth time in my short life I felt like a total failure.

Joanie began cleaning the kennels from the night before and had almost finished when Tony came in and began dishing up breakfast. Tony had not been surprised to see Joanie. He told her he had not been able to get "the three pups" out of his mind either. I was fighting with myself, trying to reach out to either of the two people I had come to trust when Joanie said, "Someone is at the front door."

"I hear them," said Tony. "Bet they are trying to drop a dog off and saw your car out there."

"Well," replied Joanie, "I will let them in, but only because I am worried about the animal. If it weren't for that I would tell them they need to come back when we open to the public."

She headed for the door and turned to look at us again. "Eagle's Den will be here to get the puppies in a couple of hours. I want to make sure they have had a chance to eat and have had a pain pill before Beth and Jerry get here. They plan to take them straight to Dr. Curtis this morning."

The shelter was very quiet in the morning and we could hear voices through the closed door. Someone sounded very upset. Tony looked around and spoke to no one in particular, "I guess they aren't dropping off. Sounds more like they are looking for a lost pet."

Suddenly Nelly rushed to the front of her kennel. "I smell lavender," she said.

Suddenly I could feel that fluttering in my stomach again from excitement. Was it possible? "Like Toad," I said. "Toad smells like lavender."

"Yes," replied Nelly. "But he smells that way because of Mom. That is her scent and when she hugs him and holds him, it makes him smell that way." She stretched her neck, looking toward the closed door. We heard the voices coming toward it, just on the other side now.

When the door opened I understood exactly what lavender smelled like because the scent filled the room. But more than the smell, my heart was overflowing with something I had never felt before. I could hear Nelly's Heart Speak and she was saying over and over, "That's Mom. It's her. And I think she has come for me."

The woman coming through the door was talking about a strange dream, but became very quiet as soon as she stepped into the doorway. She could not possibly see Nelly yet, but she was looking at me and her head was tilted slightly as if she heard something. Then she walked into the room and looked over at Nelly's kennel. "That's her!" she said. "Oh thank goodness, it is her."

The Heart Speak was strong and I could hear every word exchanged between Nelly and her Mom. What she said told me that the family Nelly had lived with all of her life had not been very nice. But it also told me that they were never Nelly's real family. This was Nelly's mom and she was here to take Nelly home to her real family.

"They said you were dead," Nelly's mom said. "I didn't want to believe them, but you were not there. The kids have all been so depressed, especially Toad. I am so glad you are alive and I have found you."

Nelly was happy. There is nothing else to explain what I saw on her face. I could use words like ecstatic or exceptional, but the word happy says it all… and she was just happy. I could hear the question she was asking, "How did you find me?"

Her mom did not answer just in Heart Speak. She looked at Joanie and said, "Last night I had the strangest dream. A little puppy kept telling me that Nelly needed me. In my dream the puppy was talking to me as clearly as I am talking to you right now. I told her that Nelly died. But the puppy told me that those people had lied to me. She said Nelly was alive and well at the animal shelter. And she told me that Nelly's time was up some time ago and if I ever wanted to see her again, I needed to come to the shelter."

Joanie shook her head in disbelief. "I guess there are strange things that happen in this life," she said. Nelly has been here for over a month now, and she is supposed to leave for rescue today. If you hadn't come Nelly would be on her way to Upper State New York by this afternoon."

Then Joanie got a pained look on her face. She turned toward the door and said, "I have to call the rescue. They are driving down to get Nelly and that is a very long drive."

Nelly's mom had opened Nelly's kennel and was holding the old girl in her arms. Nelly's head was resting on her shoulder and Nelly looked totally at peace. Her mom said, "I don't care where they are driving from, they cannot have my girl."

Nelly's eyes met mine across the aisle, her head still resting on her mom's shoulder. "I don't know how you did it," she said, "but thank you."

I didn't know how I had done it either. In fact, I don't think I did do it. I think sometimes the Great Creator of All Life intervenes when we pray hard enough for something. It was either that, or a whole lot of luck. Faith had another explanation. She was standing right beside me and she whispered in my ear, "I think

Mother helped. She saw what was happening from Rainbow Bridge and she wanted to help our friend. It was Mother."

It took a while for Joanie to reach the rescue that was coming for Nelly. They were not upset. Joanie told Nelly's mom they were driving down to go to several local shelters for seniors that had been dumped. "They said there was one they did not have room for, and they would give her Nelly's spot. This has worked out really well."

With the time it took to contact the rescue, and the fact Beth and Jerry arrived early to get us, we were able to leave the shelter at the same time as Nelly. When we got outside the shelter we were put in a large wire crate in the back of a van. Nelly was being lead to her car by her mom and a little Corgi came bouncing out of the front seat when the door opened.

"Nelly," he said. "Oh Nelly I knew you would be here. I would not let Mom come without me because I wanted to see you as soon as I could. Don't ever go on another adventure like this Nelly. Never, ever. I missed you something fierce."

Nelly looked up at me in the crate and said, "This is Toad, girls. And he is very glad to make your acquaintance."

She looked at Toad and said, "These are my friends. This is Faith, Hope and Charity."

Toad was walking toward the van and the crate when Nelly said, "Stop. You can meet them like that another day. Don't you dare climb in that van and sniff their butts right now."

Hope and Faith giggled and I stifled the laughter that was rising in my heart. Toad was heading for the van as fast as his little short legs would carry him. His nose up in the air as if he were preparing to make our acquaintance officially.

I had not been around enough people to know how the ones we were with now might react to a strange dog climbing in their van and sniffing butts. But Toad's mom was obviously used to Toad's impeccable manners. "Toad," she said. "Get back in the car. Those puppies are going with these nice people."

She turned and looked at Beth and said, "From what Joanie has told me this morning, I would love to help you with your rescue. I understand you are just setting up?"

Beth confirmed what Joanie had told her and said, "I am really glad your dog didn't get sent away with a rescue. It is remarkable how you found her."

"It is," said Nelly's mom. "I am very grateful to luck or the gods or whatever allowed me to find her. And I am serious about wanting to help with rescue. If we can foster, if you need donations, or if we can just volunteer our time, please give us a call." She handed Beth a piece of paper with her 'number' on it. "Call any time for anything," she said.

We could hear the Walker Hound leading the shelter choir in The Song of Souls. The people heard it too and Beth said, "Wow. I think they are telling our dogs goodbye."

"Not goodbye," said Jerry. "They are telling them farewell and wishing them a wonderful life." Everyone stood and listened until the hound fell silent and the echo died away. I was glad I had heard the song for us. And I was glad my people liked it.

Just before the van was closed, I heard Nelly say, "Don't forget to look Snookie up when you get to the rescue. Tell her I made it home. Don't forget."

I smiled and said, "I won't forget to remember."

And just like that four lives changed.

Chapter 29

A Visit to the Vet

The crate we were in had a thick blanket on the bottom and it was wire, so we could see everything around us. There was a special belt that came down from the top of the van, and Jerry had run it through the crate and hooked it over by the side door. It kept the crate steady. A few of the items around us in the van moved around when Jerry would stop or start. We realized the belt had been used so our crate did not slide around. It was nice to have someone consider that we might be scared and take precautions to make us feel comfortable. We started to relax a little on our first ride in the rescue van, but we stayed huddled very close.

Hope whispered to me after we had gone a short distance, "They are talking about us. They act like they may really care."

Remembering the look on Nelly's face when her mom had shown up was keeping me occupied. I was still not clear how she had known to come to the shelter, but I was very glad she had. Nelly would never have to know what it was like to retire to an Old Dog's Home now. She was with her family, the family she should have been with all along.

Hope's words made me stop daydreaming and listen to the couple who had rescued us. They were talking about what the doctor we were going to see might find. "I worry about their backs," Jerry said. "All three walk with their backs stooped. I don't know what may cause that, but whatever it is, we will tell Dr. Curtis to take care of them. We will not give up on them no matter what."

"Of course we won't," said Beth. "I am very glad Joanie did not give in when Dr. Martin wanted to put them down. I am sure Dr. Martin was trying to do what he thought would be best for them. But I agree with Joanie. Every dog deserves a chance to live."

"Yes," Jerry agreed. "It would be different if they had no chance at a quality life and were suffering unbearable pain. Those puppies have been abused and they know what it is like to be afraid. Now they need to learn what it is like to have hope."

"Dr. Martin wanted to kill Snookie on her first day at the shelter," Beth said, as if Jerry might not be aware the good doctor was prone to making such rash decisions. "I am not sure if it is the hard work or the cost of care that scares him," she finished.

My ears perked up when Nelly's friend was mentioned. I hoped I would get the chance to meet her once we got to the rescue. The news about Nelly going home was too good to have to wait very long.

"Snookie was looking much better this morning," said Jerry. "I think the infection is finally starting to subside."

"First time I have ever had a dog's tail fall off," Beth stated.

Hope looked at me and rolled her eyes. "Oh great," she said. "Now I have to picture that."

Faith giggled and I nipped at Hope and reminded her she needed to behave. She nipped me on the back of the neck and said, "I am behaving. And I am picturing that dog's tail falling off." Then she backed away from our huddle and nipped Faith on the hind end, as if not wanting to leave her out of the pinching.

"Ouch!" yipped Faith and Beth turned to see what was going on.

"I think one of those puppies just pinched the smallest one on the butt," she said. "And I could swear she is grinning about it."

I looked at Hope. Sure enough her nose was crinkled up and there was a definite grin. She whispered to Faith, "That means move it over."

"What for?" asked Faith. "Why do you want me to move over?"

"Cause I can't see out the window passed your big head," Hope answered.

Faith titled her head and put a pout on her face. "I do not have a big head," she stated firmly.

"Yes you do," said Hope. "You have a really big head. And it is Booo-u-tiful. You heard Nelly. All Pit Bulls have big heads and you are one of the most wonderful Pit Bulls I know. So... you have a really big head."

Faith wasn't sure if she wanted to argue with that explanation or not. Instead, she chose to emphasize her decision to ignore Hope by muttering under her breath, "She's a crazy dog." Then Faith began looking at the huge world she had never been able to see before. Her eyes were filled with wonder as she watched out the window.

I smiled to myself. Hope was starting to act like a normal puppy, a very mischievous, normal puppy. It was not a bad feeling to have her act normal. Not a bad feeling at all. And Faith was already acting much better. The longer we were safe, the more I felt more normal, too. I felt more like a puppy should feel.

I was not sure exactly what this doctor would say about us, and after the experience with Dr. Martin, I was a little nervous about it. But my heart told me we were going to be safe at Eagle's Den Rescue. The pain I had lived with for so long was already starting to subside. It might still be there. I was still going to be hurt from what Boy had done to me. But it was not so obvious when there was love all around.

When we arrived at the vet's office Beth and Jerry took three small crates and began moving each of us to one of them. Faith became very agitated at the thought of being separated from Hope and me. She peed herself and moved to the very back of the wire crate, trying to avoid Jerry's outstretched hand.

"Wait a minute," said Beth. "They do not want to be separated. Look how they have always huddled together. Let's figure out a way to take them in together. I don't want to frighten them like that on their first visit to the vet."

"One of the crates may hold two of them," said Jerry. "They are very small puppies. But I don't think all three will fit in one crate."

"That's okay," responded Beth. "They have crates for sale in the vet's office. I will just run in and get a larger one."

She went into the vet's office and came out a few moments later with a crate that was twice the size of the smaller ones. She and Jerry started moving all of us to the new crate. Faith ran in by herself after Jerry put me in and Beth was reaching for Hope.

Jerry smiled. "You were right," he said. That little one was scared of being separated from her pack." I liked that. We were a 'pack.'

They carried us into the vet's office and sat the crate down on the floor. Jerry sat down in a chair next to us and Beth went to the desk and spoke to the woman standing behind it. I heard her give the names, Jet, Sonic and Jo-Jo. We would have to work on that. I had already decided I would be able to get my message through to Jerry.

We did not have to wait long and a woman called us back to one of the rooms off the sitting area. Jerry carried our crate back to the small room and Beth helped him lift it onto a table. "You want to take them out of the crate," the woman asked.

"No," said Beth. "We have their weights already documented for you, along with their shot records. They have been given a wormer and a pain pill already this morning. They are terrified of people and there is no need to traumatize them further. They can stay in their crate until Dr. Curtis is ready to examine them."

The woman grunted and I could tell she didn't really approve of the decision; but, Beth was clearly not going to argue about it. She left the room and Beth watched us through the door on the crate. "You are beautiful little puppies," she said. "And we are going to take very good care of you. I hate seeing you scared."

Jerry busied himself reading something that was hanging on the wall in the small room. Beth was watching us closely and before we could get settled in good with our huddle, Dr. Curtis came into the room.

"What have we here?" he asked, and peeked at us through the door. "There are three of them in there," he said, stating the obvious.

I did not get a bad feeling from this vet, and I stepped away from my sisters and moved toward the door. Maybe if they saw me going out first so the vet could examine me, they would not be so scared. Dr. Curtis opened the door to the crate and lifted me out.

When he stood me on the table, Jerry slid the crate back so he would have room to examine me. I did my best to stand straight and show them I was going to be just fine. Dr. Curtis began to examine me, starting at my teeth. He frowned when he looked in my mouth, but he did not speak.

After he had looked at my backside, he asked Beth and Jerry to go ahead and take Hope and Faith out of the crate. He stood all of us on the floor and we immediately came together in our huddle. "Can we get them back on the exam table and hold them all so I can look at them?" he asked.

Beth took Faith and Jerry lifted Hope, while Dr. Curtis lifted me back onto the table. He did not speak as he examined all of us, starting with our teeth. When he finished he looked at Beth and said, "This does not look good at all."

I could feel Beth's heart beating fast, even though she was not holding me. She seemed to be as frightened at what the vet might say as I was. "I know they have been abused," she said. "And I know they have a long way to go to get better. But I want you to tell me what we need to do to get them better. Whatever it is, that is what we will do."

I knew exactly what she was *not* saying. She would not allow us to be 'put down' because someone had hurt us. But she absolutely meant that, even though she was not saying it. I was grateful we had been rescued by people who were willing to fight for us.

Dr. Curtis cleared his throat. "They do have a long road to recovery," he said. "But I have no doubt if anyone can help them, it is you and Jerry.

I heard Hope let out a breath she had obviously been holding. Faith sat very still, leaning against Beth's arm. Beth rubbed her ear between her thumb and fingers. Faith tilted her head into the massage.

Dr. Curtis looked closely at our eyes and he said the first thing we needed was to start eating better. Once more he looked at my teeth and then felt along my back. "I think I may know what's causing that curve at their hips," he said.

"That really concerns me," Beth responded. "All three walk stooped and I am worried it has something to do with their backs. Do you think it can be treated? Is it genetic? Will it get better?"

She was asking questions very fast. I thought it might be because she was scared.

When the vet did not answer, but kept feeling along my back and then looked at my backside with a light, Beth continued, "Can we at least stop it from getting worse?"

"Actually," Dr. Curtis said, "how serious are you about getting these puppies healthy?"

"We wouldn't have taken them out of the shelter if we did not intend to do whatever is necessary," answered Beth.

"I think they may need to see a specialist. Beth, this is not something I can put in writing and don't ask me to swear to it in court... ever... but I think these puppies have been raped." When Dr. Curtis said the words, my heart fell to my paws. I felt all the shame and fear I had felt every time Boy hurt me. And, now, standing on the edge of a brand new life, a good life, everyone would know. Would they blame us? Would they want us? I didn't think it was our fault any more, but what would these people think? Would they think we had done something horrible to bring this punishment on ourselves?

"What do you mean?" asked Jerry. His skin had turned very pale and he looked confused, as if maybe he thought he had heard wrong.

Beth did not respond at first. She kept rubbing Faith's ear. Then she looked up and stated, "Surely they knew these puppies were far too young to breed?"

Then she shook her head like she was trying to comprehend what the vet had just told her. "Wait a minute," she said. "The man that took them to the shelter told Joanie that the 'big dogs down the road had been after them.' Is that even possible for a puppy this young?"

Dr. Curtis saw her struggling with what he had said. She was starting to sway back and forth and he reached over and put his hand on her shoulder, steadying her. "Beth, Jerry," he began, "I know your mind is fighting against what I just told you. It is hard to believe and harder still to understand. But there are people who sexually assault animals. It is hard to prove unless they are caught in the act, or we can get the dog just after it happens and run DNA. But it does happen. And the injuries on these puppies are consistent with sexual abuse."

Beth grabbed the exam table and hung her head. Jerry put his hand on her back and she turned and ran from the room. Jerry looked at Dr. Curtis and said, "She was going to be sick. She will be back."

"It's a lot to comprehend," the vet said. "And I know Beth and you well enough to know you are going to want to go after the person who did this. No one can stop you from investigating. But be prepared, I don't think even the specialist will give you an absolute diagnosis, not at this late date. There is just no way to prove it. And these puppies are so small. It may have done a lot of damage."

Beth came back in the room. She had rinsed her face and was dabbing it with a paper towel. "What do we need to do to hang the sorry piece of trash that did this?" she asked. "And what do we do for the puppies, to get them better?"

Dr. Curtis shook his head and answered, "I can't answer your first question. But we will start working on the puppies today. We will start with some antibiotics and pain meds, and I will set up an appointment with Dr. Felton. He is a very good vet and has written several papers on intestinal problems with dogs."

Beth held her stomach and for a moment I thought she was going to turn and run from the room again. Her skin had changed to a greyish color. "Are you telling me these sweet little babies were sodomized?" she asked. "And now they have intestinal problems because a sorry excuse for a human being has absolutely no morals?"

"That is about what I am saying," the vet answered.

Jerry put one hand on Beth's back again and he rubbed my head with the other hand. "You may not be able to do anything," Jerry said. "But I want to know who hurt these puppies. That is the first thing we need to do beyond getting them better. There may not be a veterinarian or a court in the world that is willing to do anything, but I know exactly what I want to do."

Dr. Curtis dropped his head. His voice was soft, almost apologetic. "This is not something the authorities want to deal with," he said. "Unfortunately, for far too many people it is still something to joke about. And for the rest of the world it is just uncomfortable to talk about. And there are not adequate laws"

Beth shook her head in disbelief. "Well how the heck do they think the dogs feel?" she asked. "Set up the appointment with the specialist. Jerry and I will work on getting the puppies well to begin with, and then we will see what we can do beyond that. You may not be able to say they were raped or sodomized. But you can say the injuries are consistent with sexual assault, right?"

Dr. Curtis thought for a moment and then replied, "Yes. I can say that and not get sued." He reached over and touched Faith on the head then. Her eyes were averted, looking down at the exam table. "I wish there were laws specifically against bestiality in

North Carolina. Then it would not be so hard for us when we see something like this."

"Well," said Beth, "maybe that is where we start. There needs to be a law."

Jerry was obviously very upset and he looked at the vet and said, "And there needs to be a punishment that fits the crime. The man who did this should have to suffer the same as these puppies have suffered."

When we left the vet's office that day, we were feeling better about our future. The truth was out. It was not our fault. We had not done anything to deserve what had happened to us. And these people still loved us. Now we needed to have a talk with them about our names.

Chapter 30

Faith, Hope & Charity

Medicine is a wonderful invention. We were in something called quarantine at the rescue and had to stay there until we saw the vet called a specialist. This was because of infection, and the risk of getting more infection. It was a safety measure as much for us as the other dogs. We were fighting illness and did not need to be exposed to anything new. Our appointment with the specialist had been made and he had ordered some medicines for us while we waited to see him. He had kept us on the pain medicine that Dr. Curtis had given and that was a blessing for us. We were taking it twice a day. We were also getting special baths with some kind of medicine in the water to help us heal.

Hope and I were eating a little better, but were still having a few problems, and Faith was not improving at all in that area. The medicine was helping her to heal, but she was way too thin and I was getting worried. Mom and Dad were worried too. Dr. Curtis had given Mom and Dad a bag with what looked like water in it. He had told her she could give it to us if we kept having trouble eating. She had given it to Hope and me a couple of times and it made us feel a lot stronger. Faith had to have it a lot more than Hope and me. We did not have to drink it, but Mom took a small needle and put it just under our skin. I had been afraid it would hurt to begin with, but there was no pain at all. We did have to stay still while she gave it to us. Mom called it IV Fluid. I was very happy she had it because I think it kept Faith alive in those early days.

Beth and Jerry had never made us feel scared. If we acted even a little unsure, they would stop and take a little more time with what had to be done. We could feel the love they had for us and our love for them was growing stronger. I am not sure when we started calling them Mom and Dad, but it was a natural thing. It was not something we thought about. It just happened.

We had been in rescue for a couple of nights when a visitor came. His name was Dave and he was a very good Heart Speak person. He had spent the largest part of his life hunting down dog fighters and exposing their evil. He had ten rescue dogs that lived with him. Mom asked him if he might have an idea as to why we were having such a hard time eating. She understood why we could not eat kibble, but we were having trouble with the canned food as well.

Dave told her to try taking a slice of bread and putting the soft dog food on it. "Bait dogs are often given nothing but bread," he said. "For whatever reason, they have trouble transitioning from the bread to good food."

Mom went and got several slices of bread and dropped them on our dish. Hope and I went to the dish to eat, like we always did. To this day I do not understand what made the difference, but we were able to eat the bread. Mom took some more bread and added a little soft dog food. We ate that. From that night on, Hope and I had our eating problem resolved.

Faith was a different story. As soon as the bread hit the dish, she ran to a corner and huddled there. She had grown very close to

Mom in the time we had been in rescue and she did not try to pull away when Mom picked her up and cuddled her on her lap.

"She has to eat something or we are going to lose her," Mom said, tears filling her eyes.

Dave sat on the floor and asked Mom to let him hold Faith, only he used her shelter name, Jo-Jo. Faith cowered away and when his hands touched her, she peed all over herself. Mom held Faith close to her heart then and said, "No. She is afraid and I am not going to force her."

"That's best," replied Dave. "We already know what happened to her to make her so afraid and I would never do anything to make that fear worse."

Then Dave looked at me. I had eaten my fill of the bread with the soft food and was watching closely to make sure Faith was okay. I liked this man, but I was glad he didn't push Faith to let him hold her. Suddenly I felt the familiar tugging at my heart and I was starting to get a little dizzy. Heart Speak always made me feel that way when someone was pushing really hard for me to understand and hear them. I knew it could not be another dog. My sisters and I did not have to try so hard. We were used to each other. And we were in quarantine still so there were no other dogs in the room with us.

I had come to understand Mom and Dad quite well, too. When you love someone and they fill your heart up, it is easy to hear their Heart Speak without having to try. That could only mean one thing; Dave was trying to talk to me. I stopped and listened. Or perhaps saying I stopped and *felt* would be a better way to describe it. One does not hear Heart Speak so much as feel it. The surprising part for me with Dave was that he was deliberately focused on talking to me. Most people, even when they are fluent in Heart Speak, never reach out that way. I don't think it is that they can't do it. They just do not understand that they can.

Dave's heart was very full with love and understanding. I knew what he wanted almost immediately, and I was almost ashamed I had not thought of it already. I went to Faith and asked her why she would not eat. "I know you are hungry," I said. "I can see you trying. But you can never get much down and we are very worried about you."

Faith held her head up from Mom's chest where she had been resting, listening to her heart beat. "I am hungry," she answered. "Sometimes I think I am going to starve if I do not get a bite of food. But then when I try to eat I get this knot in my throat and it drops all the way into my belly. I cannot swallow at all, and when I lick the food and get a taste, I start to feel very sick. I am not trying to starve myself. I want to eat. I just can't."

I knew Dave had understood most of it because he told Mom, "I think I know why this little girl will not eat."

He dropped his head a little and continued, "And you may well have to force feed her if she is going to survive."

Mom had a pained look on her face. "I will do what I need to do to help her live," she said, "so long as it does not hurt her or make her suffer."

"Like I said before," Dave began, "we already know the torture these puppies survived. I have watched little Jo-Jo and she acts like she is hungry. I can see her mouth is watering when she smells the food. She runs away from it because something about it is hurting her, or making her very uncomfortable."

"You mean it is an emotional response," said Dad. "And that would most likely mean something really bad happened to her when she was trying to eat."

When he added the last part, his voice sounded angry and hurt all at the same time. "The piece of shit on two legs gave her food and then hurt her while she was trying to eat."

I could hear the giggle rising from Hope when he described Boy as a "piece of shit on two legs." I gave her a stern look, but could not help but smile a little myself. Hope's favorite thing now was to "picture" things in her mind. When I looked at her then, I heard her say, "Now I have to picture that."

Dad never hid the anger he felt toward those who had hurt us, but we could also feel the love he had for us and knew it hurt his heart when he thought about what we had been through. Mom was better at hiding things deep inside herself when she had to talk with other people. We would hear her crying late at night when everyone was asleep. Dad did not try to hide it and things he said would often make us smile or even giggle, especially when Hope would "have to picture that."

Dave cleared his throat and I knew he was fighting back strong emotions. Most people would cry when they learned what we had been through. They would always get angry; and they would always cry. Dave told Mom and Dad he believed that the person who raped us had lured 'Jo-Jo' with food. When she had gone to eat it, he had grabbed her and hurt her. Now it was hard for her to eat because of that memory.

"She cannot survive on IV fluids," he finished. "If you want her to live, you will have to find a way to get her past that fear of eating. And that may well mean you have to force feed her."

Mom took a deep breath. "I understand," she said. "But with her already being afraid, I will have to find a way to do it so she is not more traumatized."

I was not sure what the word 'traumatized' meant, but it didn't sound good. I was glad Mom was not going to let it happen to Faith.

"There is one other thing I believe we need to do," Dad said.

Dave and Mom both looked at him, waiting to see what was on his mind. "I think we need to choose better names for these three," he said. "I think Joanie chose names quickly and did not take a lot of time to think about it. The names do not suit them."

My heart began to beat very fast with excitement. "Do you have names in mind for them?" Mom asked.

"I like the names Faith and Hope," Dad answered and I held my breath for a minute, hoping he would say my name too.

Before he could say anything else, Mom added, "And Charity."

Dad smiled. "Those are good names," he said. "Faith, Hope and Charity."

"I like those names better, too," Dave said. "They fit much better than Jo-Jo, Sonic and Jet. But which is which?"

Mom took a deep breath and said, "Why don't we just keep them in the order we have already said. Faith is Jo-Jo. Sonic is Hope. Jet is Charity. That works for me."

Hope smiled broadly and said, "That works just fine for me, too. I think they really can hear us, Charity. I think this place and these people are filled up with Heart Speak. Nelly was right. Our lives are going to be just grand."

My own heart was filled up with love. Faith was snuggled closely against Mom's heart and I knew she was going to be okay, too. Mom and Dad would not let anything happen to any of us. I had known we were safe when we came to the rescue. I also knew we were loved. Now, for the first time I understood exactly what home is. Faith, Hope and I were home.

Chapter 31

The Specialist

Those first days and nights in rescue passed quickly. After Dave's visit, Mom worked on a schedule for feeding Faith. She and Faith would go into the room Mom called her office and they would stay for a while. The first few times, when they would come out, Faith would be ready for a nap, and Mom always looked exhausted. Faith never looked upset or hurt, but very, very tired. Hope and I would always snuggle with her, and she began to get stronger. When the day finally came for our appointment with the specialist, Mom was not using the IV Fluid at all anymore. Faith had finally started eating. She could not eat much at a time and Mom fed her small amounts several times a day. We were still thin, but we had all gained weight and were starting to look a lot like normal puppies. We were also loved as much as any puppy has ever been loved. And, for the most part, we had started playing more like normal puppies. All was right in our world.

Mom got up very early on the morning of our appointment. She packed a bag for us with treats, toys and canned food. We had not left home since we had arrived and it was a little scary for us. Mom set the large wire crate up in the van and buckled it in so the crate would stay steady for us. She put a soft blanket in the bottom and we were ready to go.

Our crate was fixed so we could see out the window of the van, and we began to enjoy the ride. Faith called it an adventure and Hope said we were seeing the world from the safety of our home on wheels. I was just glad to be seeing this doctor so we could get out of quarantine. I was ready to meet some of the other dogs back at home. I particularly wanted to keep my promise to Nelly and let Sad Miss Snookie know she had found her way home.

We had not met Snookie yet, but we knew she was still trying to get better. We could hear Mom running water in the big tub so she could soak her wounds. And, of course, we could hear Mom and dad talking to her. We had not heard anything from Snookie though. From what little I could tell, I understood why they called her Sad Miss Snookie. I hoped once I gave her the messages from nelly, she would feel better. Maybe that news would let her know that good things do happen in the world. And I was praying to the Creator that Faith, Hope and I could repay the kindness Nelly had shown us by helping her friend. We certainly knew how it felt to be sad and to feel we had no reason to live. I had heard Dad say her body was healing, and he was trying to find a way to reach her heart and let her know she was loved. Maybe we could help with that.

I already knew exactly what I was going to do when we met Snookie. I had played it out in my mind every night since we had been in rescue. I would tell Snookie that a friend of hers wanted us to tell her a bedtime story. Then I would tell the story of our last morning at the shelter. I would tell the story like Nelly had shared stories with us and I would make sure to let the love we felt shine. That way Snookie could take some of that love and start to feel better. It was something wonderful to look forward to.

But today we were seeing the doctor called Dr. Felton. I was nervous and I knew my sisters were too. But we were not scared like we might have been before we met Mom and Dad. Whatever came today, we knew that Mom and Dad would be there with us and they would never let any harm come to us.

When we arrived at the vet's office, Mom took the crate she had used at Dr. Lockheed's office and moved the three of us from the wire crate. Dad carried us in and told them our names. The woman behind the desk said, "I am sorry. I do not have a Faith, Hope and Charity listed for an appointment today. Could I have your name, sir? Maybe someone entered it that way."

Dad gave them his name and the woman shook her head. Then she said, "Wait. I do have a McDuffie from Eagle's Den Rescue. Dr. Curtis made the appointment. Is that you, sir?"

"Yes," said Dad. "That is our appointment."

"Well, Mr. McDuffie," she said, "the appointment is for three puppies, but not the three you named."

Dad laughed and said, "Oh, we changed their names. It is the same three. The names you have are the names the shelter gave them. As soon as we got them home, they told us what their names really are, so we changed them."

The woman behind the desk did not smile. In fact, she looked rather aggravated. "Well we can't change the names in the computer that easily. Maybe you should have asked them their names before you made the appointment."

Mom said the woman was being something called sarcastic. She raised her voice so the woman could hear her and said, "The puppies were not talking at the shelter. We didn't discover they could talk until about three days after rescue. But don't worry; you don't have to change the names in the computer. We know who they are." Mom smiled and looked at us in our crate. Then she added, "I wouldn't want you to get confused or anything."

A lady sitting next to Mom and holding a small dog on her lap started laughing. She talked in a low voice so the woman behind the desk could not hear her. "I am so glad you spoke up to her. That woman has no business working with people who have sick babies. I have been bringing Roscoe here every week for a month now, and she is just plain rude."

The lady held Roscoe close to her heart the way Mom would hold us when she was worried about us. I could tell even from my crate that the lady was upset and worried about her dog. Roscoe did not look like he felt very well. Most dogs would have at least been curious about who was in our crate. Roscoe hugged close to his mom and closed his eyes.

Mom looked at Roscoe and told the lady he was a good looking dog. "Sour puss behind the counter up there is just upset that she has to work, I suppose. And she is probably jealous because she does not have a dog that is as handsome as Roscoe."

The lady smiled and looked grateful that Mom was being nice to her. "Roscoe is all I have," she said. "We have each other and I am very worried about him lately."

"Is Dr. Felton helping him?" Mom asked.

"As much as he can," the lady answered. "He is treating his symptoms right now, and I am hoping he starts to feel better."

I could tell mom wanted to ask questions, but did not want to upset the lady. So instead of questions, Mom said, "My name is Beth and that's Jerry up there talking to Sour Puss. We have brought our three puppies, Faith, Hope and Charity, for Dr. Felton to help. They were badly abused before they came home with us and they need a lot of help."

The lady held Roscoe closer to her and said, "I am Leigh. And of course, this is Roscoe."

She kissed Roscoe on top of his head and she added, "He has been having bathroom issues. Dr. Felton says he can make him 100% better, but it will take surgery. We are trying some medication right now and I am praying hard that it works."

"Why doesn't he do the surgery, if he knows it will work?" Mom asked.

Leigh looked very embarrassed and kissed Roscoe on top of his head again. Roscoe had a red smudge on his head from the colored stuff his mom had put on her lips. "I wish he could have the surgery," she said. "But it is expensive and I just do not have the money up front. I tried to set up payments here, but they had me fill out an application and said I am not eligible for Care Credit. I can barely afford the medicine, but I do what I have to because Roscoe is all I have in the world."

The woman's voice was beginning to sound funny and I knew she was fighting back tears. Mom excused herself for a moment and walked up to where dad was writing a check for our care. She said something to him and he turned and looked at her, nodding his head. Mom came back and asked Leigh, "Does Dr. Felton know you tried to set up payments for the surgery?"

"I don't know," answered Leigh. "He knows I can't afford the surgery."

Mom told Leigh she wanted to talk with her before she left. She added, "I may have a solution for you so Roscoe can get that surgery he needs."

Leigh took a deep breath and said, "Oh that would be wonderful. I will make sure we talk before I leave."

A woman wearing a white coat came out of the back and called Roscoe's name. Leigh stood up with her dog and looked at Mom. "I will wait right here until you get finished," she said. "If you have an idea that will help my boy, I need to hear it."

A few minutes later the woman in the white coat came out of the back again and called out, "Jo-Jo, Sonic and Jet. The McDuffie Pups."

Dad was still at the counter and told Sour Puss, "Here's the check for the amount we were quoted. If it is more than that, let me know. If it is less than that, put the extra on our account because we will be coming back. My puppies are going in the back now and I *am* going with them. Maybe you can figure out what you need to by the time we come out."

Sour Puss snapped at him, "Your dogs cannot be seen unless the bill is paid. You need to wait a minute."

"Well," said Dad, "no one told the doctor they couldn't be seen until the paper work is in order because they have called them back." Dad left her there with her mouth gaped open and a mad look on her face. He came and picked our crate up and we went in the back to an examining room with him and Mom.

The woman in the white coat took us one at a time and put us on this thing called a scale. Mom seemed very happy with the numbers the woman called out. "They are finally gaining weight," she said.

When we were in our examining room, the woman said she needed to take our temperature and she reached for me. Mom stopped her. "No," she said. "They do not have a temperature. I take it every morning and I have their charts here from home for you to use."

The woman reached for me again and said, "It will not take long for me to get a temp."

Again Mom said, "No." She told the woman that we had been raped and our backsides were sore. I do not want them to be frightened. If the temp has to be taken again, I will take it for you. But when I spoke with Dr. Felton, he assured me that they would not need a lot of poking and prodding before his exam. I would appreciate it if you would wait and let's see if he thinks the temps need to be taken again."

The woman smiled and said, "I remember now. Dr. Felton told me about these three. We won't need a temp on them"

A few minutes after the woman left the room, Dr. Felton came in. "let me have a look on these puppies I have heard so much about," he said. He opened a cabinet under the sink and took out a large blanket. He put it on the floor and then opened our crate. He set each of us on the blanket and stood back to watch us. We huddled together, all three looking up at Dr. Felton. He sat down on the floor next to us.

"I am going to sit down here and watch how they walk and sit," he said. "Then we will do an exam. They sure do look a lot better than the pictures I was sent. You have taken good care of them. And this one," he took my face in his hands, "is the cutest puppy I think I have ever seen. Just look at that face." I think it is fair to say I liked him immediately.

Dr. Felton had Mom and Dad get us to walk around and he watched what he called our stride. Once he watched us for a while and took some pictures, he lifted Hope onto the exam table. He checked her from her nose to the tip of her tail. Then he put her back on the blanket and moved Faith to the exam table. Finally it was my turn.

Dr. Felton looked at my teeth and told Mom my permanent teeth should come in 'just fine.' "Their puppy teeth have been filed down, and it was a very crude job," he said. "Not that there is a good way to file a dog's teeth. But whoever did theirs cut into their gums in several places. That is most likely why they could not eat kibble."

He pointed to several of the scars on my neck and said, "I believe another dog, just a little larger than them, was allowed to attack them again and again. They were probably used as bait for training one of their siblings," he said. "That is something we often see in the dog fighting community. Some of these scars were infected at one time. There's not a whole lot that can be done about them now, unless they start causing these babies trouble. They have healed for the most part. Their skin is going to be really sensitive around their necks and chest because they have a few scars on top of scars there. It is something you will need to keep an eye on over time."

Then Dr. Felton put his hand on my back near my backside. "The way they stand," he said, "with their butts stooped toward the floor and their back legs bent slightly, is because of both muscle damage and pain. I need to get some pictures of what's going on internally before I can say what we need to do, but this is the kind of injuries we see on older dogs who have been sodomized. I have never seen this in a dog so small. You have a real sicko out there somewhere. And I doubt he will stop with these three."

"Is there any way to prove who raped them if we can get the information we need to prosecute?" Mom asked.

Dr. Felton rolled me over on my back and felt my belly. It tickled, so I kicked my feet and wiggled a little. When my backside wiggled, I felt the pain shoot deep inside me. The sharp pain subsided, but my butt was aching. I whimpered and laid on my side.

Dr. Felton looked at Mom. "Unfortunately," he said, "unless they are caught in the act and we are able to get DNA evidence, it is hard to even prove this happened."

Dad was very indignant now. "I think it is obvious it happened," he said. "But as usual, the victim has very few rights. Everyone wants to err on the side of the criminal."

Dr. Felton rubbed his forehead. "Mr. McDuffie, I agree with you. I can look at all three of these puppies and stand here and tell you, I do not see where anything else but sodomy caused these injuries. But if I say that too loudly, the person that raped them will have the right to sue me."

"And he would probably win," Mom said.

Dr. Felton made a noise in his throat that indicated his agreement and his disgust. "He would definitely win. Unless someone stepped up and said they saw him raping these babies, I wouldn't stand a chance. And even if someone said they saw it, without DNA evidence, he might still win a suit against me."

"How do you get DNA evidence?" Dad asked.

"We do a rape kit," Dr. Felton said. "Just like with people. But unless we do it shortly after the rape happened, the evidence is compromised. After so much time the evidence is just gone and there is no way to extract DNA."

"Still, I am not sure I understand why it is so hard to get a vet to say a dog was raped. Saying it happened is not the same as accusing someone." Mom was massaging my ear, a little trick she always used to calm us. It did not stop the pain, but it did help me to relax and made the pain easier to bear.

"There wouldn't be an issue had the dogs been strays," said Dr. Felton. "But you have a situation where the puppies were turned into the shelter as an owner surrender. He obviously knew what happened, whether he is the one who did it or not. We know this because he covered his butt by saying the 'big dogs down the road got a hold of the puppies.' Anyone with a lick of common sense knows another dog did not do this. So saying the puppies were raped is like pointing a finger at the person who accused other dogs. Or, since the puppies were turned into the shelter and a vet actually saw them there, but did not even note a wound or a bruise on any of the puppies, the former owner could very easily say they were injured at the shelter."

"In other words," said Dad, "the piece of trash who did this gets away with it. And as far as the authorities are concerned, it never happened. This puppy is lying there whimpering and in pain, but because the first vet who saw them wanted to kill them, and refused to examine them beyond that, her cries are ignored."

"That's the short version," Dr. Felton said. "On a positive note, I have recorded on their charts that these wounds are consistent with rape and sodomy and I can find no other explanation for the injuries. So if you ever do get proof of who did this, there is a record of my findings. I honestly wish I could do more to get justice for these babies."

Mom shook her head sadly. "The worst news," she said, "the scum who did this will do it again. Another dog will suffer because we cannot prove what he did and have him locked up."

Dr. Felton looked Mom in the eyes and asked, "Do you *really* think anything would be done to the jackass even if we could prove it? You are dreaming."

He finished examining us and ordered some pictures to be taken. We were taken to a room where there was a very special, giant camera. The camera took pictures through our skin and showed the vet what our insides looked like. He knew we were very sore and bloody on the outside because Boy had raped us. He could see that. Now he needed to see how bad the injuries were and how deep they went inside of us. This special camera would take a picture that would tell him.

I hoped the pictures would help him give us medicine to stop the pain. I had understood most of what Mom and Dad talked about with Dr. Felton. I wished that Boy could be stopped from hurting another animal, even if those people named 'authorities' did not want to punish him for hurting us. It would be nice to know another animal was not going to suffer this way. But I hoped and prayed to Creator that our pain could be stopped. The authorities might not want to believe it was real, but the pain was very real to us. It was real and the blood and tears were real. Mom whispered in Heart Speak that maybe one day justice would not be so hard to come by for a dog. I hope she was right.

Chapter 32

Dogs Without Borders

Mom and Dad could not go with us into the picture room. We were terrified, so Mom talked to Dr. Felton. He had the woman wearing the white coat come in the room and play with us for a bit while Mom and Dad were there. Once we knew she was not going to hurt us, Mom said it was okay for her to take us for our pictures.

When we finished, Mom and Dad were talking to the woman named Leigh and Dr. Felton. The woman was still holding Roscoe very tight against her heart and she had huge tears in her eyes. I had missed most of what was said, but I understood from the happy hearts I felt that Roscoe was going to get his surgery.

It made me feel good to know that Roscoe was going to be okay. The medicine he was taking helped his pain, but I could tell he was not really living his life. He was not an old boy and had a lot of good years left. Roscoe understood what was going on and for the first time since we had seen him, I heard his Heart Speak. It would be impossible for me to explain to you what a dog feels and thinks when they first know they are going to be helped. The best way to describe it is to tell you Roscoe's tail wagged.

We were finished for the day and had to make an appointment to come back. Mom and Dad were talking with the woman at Dr. Felton's who handles billing. I had come to understand in a very short time that billing is very important when a dog is getting help. It seems nothing can be done without that thing called money. It was going to take a little longer than it normally would have, because Mom and Dad were working out billing for Roscoe too. We didn't mind waiting if it meant he was going to be helped. They had taken us and gone into a special play room so we would not have to wait in our crate.

Dr. Felton had said it would do Roscoe good to have a friend. They set up a very special fence for us called a portable. It was folded, and when they opened it up, it covered a very large area in the play room. Roscoe was allowed to play with us. He wasn't very active, but he had just gotten a shot for his pain. He told me that the shot made him feel really funny, but once the funny feeling past, the pain was much better. Faith, Hope and I had gotten a pill for our pain just after the pictures were taken, but my backside was still hurting a little so I snuggled with Roscoe while Hope and Faith chewed on either end of a rope toy.

We could hear Leigh, Mom and Dad talking to the woman about Roscoe's billing. Leigh was going to pay the bill over time, but they could not put it in her name because she needed someone to guarantee that they would be paid. I told Roscoe I did not understand why all that money was so important. I told him about all about the place we had come from and how Man had made a lot of money by making dogs fight each other.

Roscoe licked his paw while he listened. When I finished he said, "I know money is important because I can't get help without it. My mom can't come up with all of the money at one time and needs them to let her make payments on it. She can't save any so I can get the surgery because she has to keep paying for these visits for my treatment and medicine. I don't think she would make dogs fight to get money though. She loves me but that seems like it would just be evil and my mom is *not* evil."

"Man was very evil," I said. "I don't think he even liked dogs very much. I only saw him act kind to one dog, and that was my brother. His name is Killer."

Roscoe looked very thoughtful. "Maybe he liked him because of his name."

"Maybe so," I said. "But I don't think my brother was born bad. I think Man made him that way."

We were both feeling a little better and started to roll around on the floor. We had rolled all the way into the side of the portable fence. Leigh saw us and laughed. She said, "Look. Roscoe is feeling better already just knowing he is going to be helped."

The billing woman came over to us and began folding the fence back up. "They don't need any borders," she said. "These babies aren't going anywhere. They wouldn't want to run away from any of you. Dogs know when they have it made."

I still am not too sure what she meant about having something made. But none of us were planning on running away from the love in that room.

When the billing woman sat back down she looked at Dad. "Did you decide what name to put this under?" she asked. "We can't give the discount unless it is under the rescue, and you said you aren't comfortable with making her sign ownership of Roscoe over to Eagle's Den. So what are we going to do?"

Dad smiled. Dad had a lot of different smiles and this one was one of my favorites. It was the one that says he is about to solve a problem and make everything work just fine. "Dogs Without Borders," he said. "And we will not need Leigh to sign a contract. This is a special kind of rescue for dogs who have homes but still need a paw up."

And just like that everything was solved. Roscoe's surgery was scheduled for the next day and the woman in the white coat came to take him to a hospital kennel for the night.

I was ready to sleep on the ride home. It had been a very busy day and I had learned a lot. I told Faith and Hope that getting well was going to be quite an experience. We could learn a lot about people if we paid attention. Just before I drifted off into my dream, Hope asked me, "What did you learn?"

I thought for a moment and answered, "It seems everyone needs money."

"That one's easy," said Hope. "I figured that out before we ever got rescued."

"Well," I said, "I also learned that there are wonderful people who are willing to help dogs in need. And sometimes dogs need help even if they have been loved all of their lives. Roscoe has never been abused, but he got sick and needs help. I am glad he is going to get his surgery. He is a very nice dog."

"But," said Faith, sounding very thoughtful. "There was something else I learned today. Man made a lot of money from making dogs fight. Then the dogs that manage to get out and get rescued have to be given medicine. The places with the medicine make money by treating the dogs. It seems everybody benefits from dog fighting except the dogs and the ones who save them."

Chapter 33

A Day in the Sun

Home is the best place to be. It had been a very long day at Dr. Felton's office and snuggling in my bed back at home was the best feeling ever. We stayed in our quarantine room because it was so late when we got back. But Mom promised us the next day was going to be pawsome.

During quarantine, we had been confined to a small area outside that was covered with concrete. When we woke up the next morning, I could barely get through breakfast. Mom had promised green grass and a long play time outside. It was everything I had thought it would be and more.

Mom and Dad had just fenced an area in behind the house that was connected to the back door. They had not lived in the house long and were working to make improvements. They had a lot of cleaning up to do and let us play in the fence while they worked.

There was a dog house set up near the house with some soft, nice smelling hay if we wanted to get away from everyone and take a nap. The world outside was still a little too large for Faith. She was feeling a little exposed and found a corner next to the dog house where she could feel safe and watch everyone.

Hope and I started slowly, but before the sun had moved much in the sky, we were playing in the grass. Hope discovered she could bounce better outside than she ever could in a kennel. Mom said she looked like a little bronco.

Dad had gone outside the fence to get rid of some trash, and yelled back to Mom that someone was in the front yard. She went into the house, leaving us alone in the fence. When we realized we were all alone it was scary. Faith climbed onto the small porch and called out to us. Hope and I joined her and we formed a huddle that made us feel safe again.

Mom came around the corner from the front of the house and had a friend with her. "Look who's here," she called out to Dad. "Anna came to see the puppies."

The woman named Anna had a very friendly smell. She peeked around the corner of the house and said, "Oh shucks. They are so small. And look how they snuggle together."

She raised her hand and aimed something at us. Faith stuck her head under my nose and closed her eyes. I think she was trying to hide from her fear more than this new person. Anna called out to Mom, "I got a picture of them on my phone. Come see. It's a really good picture."

"What is 'shucks'?" Hope asked. "I haven't heard that one before. That's a fine word I think." And then she said it twice as if she was trying to get the feel of it in her mind. "Shucks. Well, shucks."

Mom and Dad both went over and looked at Anna's phone. We could tell they really liked the picture and Mom asked Anna to please send her a copy. It took a little time, but we got used to Anna being there. Faith stayed close to Mom, but Hope and I started to play in the grass again.

It was a really good day. The only thing that would make it better is for Faith to start playing. She was still a lot smaller than Hope and me, and I just knew if she could start feeling safe and enjoy the green grass, fresh air and sunshine she would get healthier a lot quicker. "Please come and play with us," I called out to her.

Mom had sat on the steps to talk with Anna, and Faith was hiding behind her legs. She stuck her head out and said, "I can play just fine from right here."

Hope laughed and pinched me on the butt. "But you can't do that from there," she said.

I let out a little yip and turned to face Hope, "And now we will do battle," I said in my best pretend voice.

Faith let out a small cry so I stopped and turned to see what had happened. She had her head back behind Mom's legs. "Please don't fight," she said. "I don't want you to fight."

My heart dropped to my paws and I sat and looked at my too small sister. "Oh Faith," I said. "We would never fight. We are just playing. I would never hurt you or Hope, and I don't think Hope would hurt either of us."

Hope had the feel of the sun on her back and was feeling better than she had ever felt. "No," she said, "I wouldn't hurt either of you. But I would do this." And she pinched me on my butt again.

"When your teeth get all better you are going to have to stop that," I told her. "Even with them all short and filed off you are bruising me I think."

"Oh shucks," she said, mimicking the word Anna had said that she liked so much. "It's just a little kiss."

I turned my backside toward her then and ignored her. She reached over and pinched me again and said, "And sometimes it means 'move it over, cause your *butt* is in my *face*'."

Hope began to bounce like a bronco again, ready to play and get the exercise we had always been denied. Even though the pinch had hurt just a little, I knew she meant no harm. "Don't worry, Faith," I said. "We are just playing. No fighting allowed in our home."

Mom noticed that Faith was not joining us in our play and it worried her as much as it did me. She picked Faith up and held her very close to her heart. "No one will ever hurt you again, little one," she said. "Never again."

Mom moved from the steps and went over to the center of the fence. She sat down in a nice grassy spot. Faith was at her heels and she told her, "Now you can at least be in the grass and get some sunshine on your face."

Anna came over and sat down in the grass too. Hope and I walked over and laid down in front of them to show our approval. We couldn't stay still for long, though and we were soon back on our feet with Hope bouncing like a bronco. She told me that there was still pain when she bounced, but it seemed really far away now. I knew we were getting better because I could jog a little without the sharp stabs shooting up my backside.

Going to the bathroom still hurt, but the food we were eating kept everything moving freely, so it was not nearly as bad. With the sun shining on my back and the feel of a breeze against my face, green grass beneath my paws, I almost forgot the ache that was always there, reminding me I had been raped.

We spent that day outside and when suppertime came, we took our food out in the fading sunshine. It had been the best day ever and by the time we went inside, we were ready to snuggle on our bed. Anna told us goodbye and promised to come back and see us again.

"You need to come tomorrow," Mom said. "We are going to introduce them to some of the other fur kids tomorrow. Maybe even Snookie. I think she may get along well with these three."

"Is she doing better?" Anna asked. Her voice sounded very concerned.

"She is," replied Mom. "She will probably always have a limp, but her leg is healing. Since part of her tail fell off she actually seems to be doing better. She wagged her tail this morning."

Dad looked up from the paper he was reading. "She has always wagged her heart at me," he said.

I remembered Nelly saying that Toad had wagged his heart at her and again remembered the promise I had made to tell Sad Miss Snookie that Nelly had gone home. "Tomorrow," I said to no one in particular. "Tomorrow I will be able to keep my promise."

Chapter 34

Sad Miss Snookie

My dreams, for the most part, had always taken me to safe and beautiful places. The night after we had played outside all day, I do not remember dreaming. I had no reason to escape and the day had worn me out. I had been tired before, but it had always been an exhaustion that made my heart ache as much as my body. This time my heart was filled with peace and joy. My dreams could not take me to a better place, so I just slept very hard.

Breakfast was wonderful, with the food hitting a lot of empty spots I had never known were there before. Hope ate heartily, just as I did. Even Faith, who was eating much better these days, but was still not getting as much down as Hope and me, managed to eat most of her breakfast. I could not imagine a day being better than the one before, but I was looking forward to feeling that grass beneath my paw pads again.

"Do you think we will meet Sad Miss Snookie today?" Hope asked. "I hope she is not too sad. If she is, maybe the news about Nelly will make her happy."

I had almost forgotten that we were supposed to meet Snookie and new excitement began to rise in my heart. Faith was watching Hope and me with a look of strong interest. "Are you going to try and play today?" I asked her. "When we meet Snookie, maybe she will not seem as sad if we show her how happy we are."

Faith's mouth puffed up in a bit of a pout. "I play," she said. "I just like to stay close to Mom."

Hope laughed. "Your cheeks are going to stick that way if you keep puffing them up."

"Well... well..." Faith began, obviously searching for a witty comeback. "Well, Hope, if you keep pinching, your mouth will start looking like a butt."

All three of us wagged our tails and giggled. Then Mom was standing in front of us. "Are you ready to go outside?" she asked. All three tails wagged harder and we followed her down the hall to the back door. I had noticed it did not hurt quite as much when our tails wagged now. I was glad about that because we had lots of happy things to make them wag.

Dad was already working in the fence and Mom left us outside with him. "I am going to do Snookie's soak," she said. "When I am finished and she has had her meds, I will bring her outside."

She hesitated at the back door. "Do you think they are ready to meet another dog?" she asked.

Dad looked up from his raking. "They are ready," he said. "I think they have been ready and I know it will be good for Snookie. She should be able to play a little with the puppies. That leg has kept her from playing with the other dogs. The puppies are not so rough."

"I think I will use the leash to be safe. We don't know how she may act around another dog after what she has been through, even if they are just puppies. I really don't want her or the puppies to be frightened, but I don't want an incident either." Mom disappeared into the house and Faith hurried over to her corner next to the dog house.

"You don't want to run and play, Faith?" I asked. "It's really nice in the sunshine. It will help you grow bigger."

"No," she answered. "I don't think I want to grow any today. I'm feeling a little tired. Maybe when Mom comes back out I will feel better."

Faith sat further back in the shadows and leaned her head against the dog house. I wasn't sure if she was trying to show me she was tired and needed to rest or if she just felt safer further in the corner. Once we had realized why she couldn't eat, everything else sort of fell into place. She had walked out of the shadows that day when Boy had hurt her so badly and sent her to The Land of Nothing. It had started when he offered her food, but she had come out to show him she trusted him and wanted to be his friend. Knowing that, it was even easier to understand why Hope and I liked the shadows and corners so much. The shadows had been our safe place in the shed. Every time Boy had hurt us it left a picture on our brain. Those normal things around the pain triggered the bad memory. I tried not to think about it too much, but understanding why we were afraid helped get past the fear.

"Should we go over and try to make her come out into the sunshine?" asked Hope.

I thought for a moment and then answered, "No. When I was afraid I wouldn't have wanted anyone trying to force me out of my corner. She will come out when she is ready."

"Okay," said Hope. "But we need to show her how much fun it is out of the shadows." Hope began her familiar bronco bounce. I let her bounce and jogged up and down the length of the fence several times. It felt good to stretch my legs.

I had run the length of the fence several times before Hope and I began rolling around in the grass. Rolling still made my backside hurt, but not nearly as much as before. For the most part, Hope and I would bounce toward each other and bounce back, but without the roll, it was not nearly as much fun. I decided I could ignore it for a while and have fun playing.

When we were rolling around in the grass, Dad stopped raking and watched us for a few minutes. I could tell he liked to see us play. He looked over at Faith sitting in the corner and he reached in his pocket. He walked over to Faith first. She turned her head back toward the house and closed her eyes. Dad laid something on the ground just in front of her. As soon as he turned away, she opened her eyes and reached her head over to grab what he had left. I could see it hanging out of her mouth. Faith looked both ways like she was afraid someone would sneak up on her and try to take her special treat. She looked at Hope and me, then turned her back to us. She laid down and I could see her head moving up and down. I knew she was eating something and it was very good from the way she was bobbing her head.

Dad had stopped to watch Faith and was smiling. I heard him say, "No one is going to hurt you, baby. And no one is going to take your treat."

He turned his attention to Hope and me and we stood still watching him come toward us. I could feel my tail wagging in anticipation. "I can smell it," said Hope. "And it smells mighty good."

I could smell it too and my mouth was watering waiting for Dad to get close enough to give us our treat. Sometimes wanting something really bad can make it be a letdown when you get it. You think about it so much, and build it up to absolutely beyond compare in your mind. Then when you actually get it, it cannot be as good as what you imagined. That treat Dad gave us that day was *better* than I had imagined. It was *better* than anything I had ever thought of before. It made my mouth feel happier than it had ever been.

Dad asked, "Do you girls like your bacon? Do you want some more?" And our tails wagged the answer for him. Faith even stuck her head out of that corner and took her treat right out of his hand when he walked back over to her.

Bacon is a very good thing. We had enjoyed the piece in the shelter, but I don't think any can ever taste as good as that first piece we ate in rescue. I would never turn a piece down for fear of being disappointed though.

Dad went back to work cleaning up the yard. We watched him for a few minutes and then went back to playing. We did talk a little and decided we were going to have to sniff Dad's pockets every chance we got. We wouldn't want him to forget he had some bacon hid in there.

We were having so much fun I did not hear the door open when Mom came outside. Hope and I both heard a strange and very loud yelp from Faith and we stopped in the middle of a bounce to see what had happened. The sound had made my heart stop for a minute because I was sure Faith was hurt.

Faith was standing in the sunshine staring at the door. I would have thought she was frozen except her tail was nothing more than a blur it was wagging so fast. Still, her feet seemed frozen in place and I could tell she could not move. Then I heard Hope say, "Charity, look!"

I looked at Hope and she was frozen in place next to me, her tail wagging just like Faith's. I followed her gaze to the steps where Mom was standing with a large Blue Pit Bull. "That *must* be Sad Miss Snookie," I thought.

The truth hit my tail before it hit my brain, and my tail became a blur just like Faith's and Hope's. I *knew* that Blue Pit Bull standing next to Mom. I tried to move my feet to run to her but I was frozen in place.

They call it cat-atonia, I believe, because of the way a cat will freeze in place when stalking a helpless mouse. And, yes, even though I like all the cats I have ever met, the mouse is helpless against those sharp claws. If you do not believe they are sharp enough to render a mouse helpless, let a cat swat *you* on the nose sometime when you are just trying to give the old butt sniff hello.

But on this day, in that moment, it was dog-atonia. I could not move my paws an inch. My tail and my heart were going as fast as they have ever gone either before or after that moment. My brain was working overtime and it made me feel dizzy. I had thought she was dead. I had dreamed of her at Rainbow Bridge, watching over us, guiding us in the right direction.

She looked better now than the last time I had seen her. She had gained weight and her coat had a shine to it that had never been there before. Her mouth still had that crooked 'broken jaw' look to it, but her eyes had a glimmer of hope now. Had I not known her so well, known the very beat of her heart that had given me life, I might not have recognized her. But my eyes were sharp, my senses keen, and my heart and soul knew the dog in front of me now. I sniffed the air just to be sure. "Mother!" I yelled out. "Mother it is really you!"

It occurred to me that she must be as frozen as we were, because her tail was swinging just as fast as ours and her nose was in the air going from side to side. Her feet were dancing in place. Then I realized Mom had her on a leash.

Faith found her paws first and headed for Mother at a pace I had never seen her run before. Hope and I bounced back into motion and the three of us were with our mother, licking her and dancing around. Mother was as happy as we were and Mom and Dad must have been so confused. They could not have known they had our mother here the entire time. I am not sure what they thought at that moment, because the only thing on my mind was Mother and the fact she was alive and here with us in rescue.

Mom removed the leash as best she could with all the butt wagging going on. She stepped back and laughed. "Jerry," she said, "they act like they know each other."

"Is it possible?" asked Dad. "They did come from the same area. Joanie said she thought Snookie had left puppies behind somewhere."

"I don't know," responded Mom. "I suppose it is possible. Whether she *was* there mother or not, they certainly have adopted her now."

"And she has adopted them," said Dad. "Snookie has never been that excited."

Mom and Dad sat down on the steps and watched us snuggle and roll around with our mother. If they were listening with their hearts they heard the sound of pure love and ultimate happiness.

Our mother had been named Sad Miss Snookie by Joanie at the shelter. Nelly *must* have known who she was and that is why she tried so hard to make sure we came to Eagle's Den. I thought back to everything Nelly had said about the sad dog across the aisle from her in Kennel 5. The one thing that was clear now, Mother would have a name change. She was no longer Sad Miss Snookie. She would keep the name Snookie, but she was not sad any longer. She was reunited with the children she had been carrying in her heart.

Even though I suspected that Nelly knew, I wished I could have told her. It would have been wonderful for her to see the reunion and know what she had helped to bring about. Thinking of Nelly, I remembered the promise. "Mother," I said, "we met your friend Nelly at the shelter. She helped us get rescued and come here. And Mother, she wanted me to tell you that she made it home with her family and Toad."

Mother smiled at me and I found the old familiar love surrounding me and wrapping itself around my heart and soul. "That's wonderful," she said. "I am glad to know we have all made it home."

Chapter 35

Naptime Story

The day we were reunited with Mother was the best day of our lives. Nothing could ever be any better than that. She had been our entire world when we were living in that shed and losing her had made everything so much harder. I had been glad she was not there to see Hope and Faith being hurt by Boy. I was happy she did not have to wait in the shed and see us when we came back in after a training session with Killer. I knew how her heart beat for us and how much it hurt her to see us in pain.

Mostly, back in hell I had been worried I was disappointing her. She was not there to snuggle with me and push me close to her heart with her nose, letting me know everything would be alright and saying she would love me no matter what. I had believed that it was up to me to keep us safe once Mother was gone, and the fact I could not stand up against Man and Boy had weighed heavy on my heart.

Now that we were reunited, she talked to me the way she had done in the early days. She told me how proud she was of me and that she had always known I would get out of hell and live a wonderful life. She said that she knew I felt bad because Hope and Faith had been hurt; but, she wanted me to remember that I had been hurt too. She looked deep into my heart and knew what I was feeling, and her words eased the guilt I had felt since that day when Boy had taken Hope away and hurt her.

"Charity, my sweet girl," she said. "It hurts you so much because you love so deeply. But I never meant to put such a burden on you. I knew how evil both Man and Boy were, and I wanted you and your sisters to survive. I never thought you could stop the abuse. I knew that your heart and spirit were strong enough to get out, and I wanted you to help keep your sisters strong until you did escape. You did that. You made me very proud. Don't ever doubt that."

And her words made my world feel right. I had not let her down. She was proud of me and that mattered. But what mattered most was that she had survived too. She was here with us now and we could live a good and wonderful life. As Nelly said... our lives would be just grand.

We spent that first day and night just snuggled up to each other and taking in every wonderful moment. Mom and Dad saw how close we were and did not try to separate us ever again. We could hear them talking and they suspected the truth. Mom was very determined to find the truth and she told Dad she was going to go and talk to Joanie.

The next day, Dad let the four of us into the backyard while he worked. Anna came over to talk to Mom and to drive her to the shelter to talk with Joanie. I was glad we did not have to go with her. The shelter had been a very wonderful and safe place for us when we first went there. But now we were rescued and I never wanted to go back to hell or to the shelter. We had all we needed right here at home.

We spent that day talking to Mother. We told her all about the things that had happened after she left. Faith told her, "I always knew you were alive. I told them I could still feel you. But then I thought maybe you were watching from Rainbow Bridge. But, Mother, I never gave up hoping I would see you again."

Faith *had* insisted Mother was alive for a long time. Maybe my sister had a wonderful sense for things the rest of us could not see. I knew I would never just dismiss her thoughts again. She had been right about Mother, and I was very happy she had been right. I licked Faith's ear to let her know I love her and was glad she was my sister. Hope saw what I was doing and she licked her other ear. Faith raised her shoulders and stuck her head down, making a funny face. "That tickles," she said. Mother laughed at us and said it was good to have her children with her again.

Hope laid her head across Mother's back while the sun warmed us. "Mother," she said, "please tell us how you got out of hell. What happened? Tell us how you became Sad Miss Snookie."

Mother took a deep breath and said, "It would have been a wonderful day, leaving hell. But it was a very bad day because my children were not with me. I became Sad Miss Snookie because I was very sad indeed. I did not know what would become of you and my heart was very heavy that I could not protect you."

"But," I said, "I thought Man had killed you when you didn't come back to the shed that night. How did you get away? Please tell us the story, Mother. Tell us *your* story, the parts we do not know."

"Yes," added Faith. "Tell us a Naptime Story. I will bet a Naptime Story will be as wonderful as a Bedtime Story."

"It will be better," said Hope. "It will be a dogzillion times better because Mother is telling it."

Mother sighed, but it was a happy sound. "Okay," she said; "I will tell you what happened and how I got out of hell, but you have to promise you will take a nap. If this is a Naptime Story, then you have to take a nap to make it so."

We promised and settled in next to Mother so we could hear her story. I promised myself I would not forget to remember her story so I could tell it again one day. I knew it would be important. And when something is important, it should be told again and again.

Thrown Away

Back then, when we were all together in hell, I did not want your hearts to ache for me, so I tried to hide my pain from you. That is why I stayed so quiet most of the time. I thought you three might have a chance when Boy selected you as his. I did not know he was as cruel as his daddy. Then he hurt Charity and I knew I could not keep the truth from you much longer. Knowing how evil the place and the people were was the only chance you would have to escape it. So the time came when I knew I had to tell you the kind of world we were living in.

I talked to each of you, knowing my time was growing short. I could feel strength in all three of you and knew if anyone ever had a chance to get out of hell, it would be you. I could feel charity, hope and faith in your hearts and I knew if you had those names, and knew the meaning... you would live. But I still could not bring myself to say goodbye to you. Even though I knew I could not survive much longer, I could not say goodbye to the best thing I had ever done.

The last time I saw you back in the shed, I had been through the worst attack I had ever endured. I had to explain to you about being a bait dog because I knew if Man took me out again, I would not survive it. In my heart I knew you were too young to face all of that, but I also knew I was not going to have a chance to see you grow and to teach you. I knew I was no good to have more babies for Man. I was all used up and he would not have any reason to keep me alive. It might not have mattered so much to me if I had been alone in that shed. Sometimes dead is far better than living when you have lost everything. And there are things that are far worse than dying. But it did matter because I had you there, and I did not want to leave you. I had lost my dignity and every child I had ever nursed, except you three. Leaving you was the hardest thing I have ever had to do.

That evening when Man took me away, we went back to the clearing in the big woods. That was always the worst place for me because I could feel the fresh air all around me. I could see the night sky... the moon and the stars... but I was still caught in Man's trap. I was always tied and that place just reminded me of what I was missing. But on that last night, it was worse than ever. I did not even see the sky or feel the fresh air because my heart never left you in that shed. And, yet, I knew I would never be taken back there.

That night it was not so easy to go to that place in my mind where nothing exists. I was already missing you. Knowing Man would never take me back to my children, I thought the best I could hope for that night was death. I had told you to fight to live, to fight to get away from the life Man had planned for you. But there I was lying in my own waste, blood tears blinding me and running down my face, and I had all but given up. Perhaps had the dog up for auction that night been one of my children, I would have just let him finish me. But it was a dog I had known from the rape rack. He was a Blue Pit, like me and his bloodline was greatly desired. When Man ordered him to attack me, I felt the searing pain in my backside and I felt the bone snap in two in my tail with the second bite. I heard the crowd cheering for more, more of my blood. I felt my bowels let go and heard them laughing at me. Then I heard Man yell for the dog to attack again.

I do not know where the strength came from. My love for you and the need to make you proud was strong, but there was something more fueling me to stand. Perhaps it was the memory of the rape rack, or the knowledge that those children man had first taken from me, your unchosen brothers and sisters, had been killed by this dog. I knew it was true because Man was very sadistic and always threw the children to the dog who had sired them. It was a part of his evil and something he took great joy in. Whatever may have given me the strength did not matter, I was on my feet before the dog got to where I was. The crowd cheered louder and the dog's teeth sank into my neck. He was shaking his head, ripping and tearing. His ear was at my mouth. I knew my bite would barely make contact, an ear is such a thin mark. But then, the dog turned his head at an angle and his face was toward my mouth. My mouth was already open as I struggled to breathe. I could feel myself fading, leaving and with everything I had in me, I bit down and held on. One of my teeth must have hit his eye because he screamed and tried to back off. Letting him go, I saw his eyes then. They were blank; there was no life left in them and it gave me the will to fight harder. When he came at me again, I dropped to the ground and grabbed underneath. He howled again as my teeth found flesh.

My bite was nowhere near powerful enough to do a lot of damage, and I heard Man screaming for him to kill me. The crowd had fallen silent... or I could no longer hear them. I am not sure which. The dog pulled away from me again and I felt his skin tear. I could taste his blood in my mouth and it made me sick to my stomach. I had never wanted this, but I had to fight. There was a force driving me more powerful than any I have ever known. I was fighting for my right to live. But, more, I was fighting for you.

When the dog came at me again, I felt him bite into my leg and the pain was so great I thought he had bitten it off. The bite was low, near my paw, and I knew I would not be able to stand again. His teeth were deep into my leg and he was shaking his head. I think I screamed then. That is when I heard someone in the crowd yelling "Fight! Fight, girl! Show them what you've got!"

I realized I was giving the crowd a thrill, something they had not planned on at an auction. That had never been my intention and it sickened me more to know I was aiding them in their lust for blood *and death. My own pain was fierce, and even with the knowledge of the cheering crowd, my mind's eye was fixed on the three of you, hiding in the dark back in the shed. I heard Man yell, "Halt! Back off!" and the dog let go of my paw.*

I believe that is when the realization came that the dog was listening to Man, blindly obeying him. And that is when I decided I would not give up; even if my paw was bitten off and laying in the dirt, I would not give in to Man's plans for me. I waited, lying very still, feeling my blood soak into the ground. I heard Man yell again, "Attack! Finish her!" and I felt the dog over me.

The command man had given was one that would cause the dog to bite into my neck and shake. My head was turned away from him so he had to lunge over me to get to his mark. In my position, I was not sure what I could do to take that last stand. And I did know it would be my last. I was getting too weak to fight even with the strongest motivation. But the dog was tired and he jumped too far and too fast. He landed just in front of me with his rump in the air. Before he could gather his composure and turn around, I lifted my head then and I used what strength I had left to bite down. Even with a jaw that has been broken and set wrong, sometimes my bite was straight.

For one time fate was on my side. Or maybe it was the Great Creator, cheering me on against the evil that had filled that place in the woods. The Great Creator of All Life had surely intended that spot to be peaceful and serene, a place of sanctuary for wild animals. But Man had defiled it, turned it evil with the blood of innocents. My bite was right on the mark and my jaw perfectly aligned. I heard the dog shriek and howl all at the same time, and could feel him fighting to get away from me. His urine soaked me and I realized where I had bitten him. He might one day father more children, but not until the swelling and bruising subsided from my bite. Had my bite been as powerful as his, had I attacked him with the same ferocity that had caused my blood to be spilled, he might never father children again because I would have ended his ability then and there.

I had no desire to kill or maim, only to survive and to see my children again. I held on until I felt the blow to the back of my head. Man had hit me with something and the world was turning black. I knew then I had lost. I did not believe my death would come quickly. Man would want me to suffer for what I had done. But no matter what happened beyond this, no one could take away the dignity I had gained on that night. The dog may be ordered to attack me again and again until I wet myself and my blood soaked both him and me. Revenge would surely foster his task until I was dead. Or Man may decide to finish me himself, slowly and with great pleasure. I knew he would not kill the fighting dog. He had invested too much in him and, even though he would not be able to sell him on that night, he would want him to live to father more children and to fight another day.

Somewhere in the deepest part of me there was a great sense of pride and accomplishment. I had finally taken a stand against Man. I hoped one day you would know and be proud of me. Maybe this dog would want to instill a sense of pride in his children who had been chosen by Man. Perhaps he would tell them how their mother had fought with her last breath. No one had ever fought for me, not when I was on the rape rack and not when I was in those woods being attacked. No one had ever cared about me, until you. None of the children before you had licked my wounds and cried for me. You had given me new reason to live and to hope. I knew you had the love in your hearts to stand for me and with me. I knew you were all three back in that shed worried and praying to Creator for me to come back to you. There was no one there in the woods to stand up for us. Not one of the people there cared that you were back in the shed alone. Not one person cared about my pain. They would not stand up for me, but would stand on their feet to see my blood spilled. But for once, I had stood and fought for myself. I had done it for love of you, for love of myself and for my right to live. And I had done it against your father. Even though I would be dead, I hoped you would hear about it and know you could take a stand too. If you were able to escape hell, whatever pain came to me from here on, whatever torture Man had planned was worth it.

I blacked out then from the blow to my head, blood loss and sheer exhaustion. It may well have saved my life, because Man was very angry and his desire to make me pay was much stronger than his desire to see me dead. He had put me in the blood-soaked and stained sack he had put me in so many nights before. I was not awake to know it, but from memory of past nights I knew he would have thrown me onto the back of his truck. Even now that I am safe, I can still hear the sound my body would make landing in the back of that truck, tossed over the side like a sack of trash. But on this night, man would not be taking me back to feed children or to whelp more. He had plans for me, painful plans that would totally break any spirit I might have before death took me.

I woke up on the ride home and my body was aching from the night's attacks. Trying not to think about what was in store for me, and needing to escape the pain I was already feeling, I fought to just disappear then. I had done it so many times before it had become easy for me to just leave. But on that night, I could not find the path that would take me deep inside my own mind. I was fully awake and aware when we arrived back just outside the shed doors. I knew you were on the other side of those doors and for a moment, the fear I had promised not to show rose up in my heart. The greatest torture I could think of would be for Man to hurt you.

I never found out exactly what he had planned because when we got back, he wanted to attend his money dog first. Even his desire to see me suffer had to wait for that. He yelled for Boy and Woman to come help and he took the dog inside his house to be cared for. Man had seen the wounds on my body, he knew I was done for and would not be able to climb out of the truck on my own. He left me there in that sack, on the back of the truck for a very long time. Wondering what would come, waiting for it to start was a part of the torture. By the time he came back out the sun was chasing away the darkness.

I heard Man shouting orders to Boy and heard Boy entering the shed where you were. Then I heard another voice, a woman's voice. It was the woman from next door that I had seen several times before. Her name is Gertie, I believe. I knew she was not evil, and I knew Man would not do anything with her there. Once more I prayed and thanked Creator for intervening on my behalf.

Had I not been so worried that Man was going to include you in his torturous plans for me, I might have wanted it to just get over with. But the longer Man had to wait, the greater the chances that I would just die from my injuries. That was the only way I could see to stop him from harming you. So I prayed for death to come and take me.

Gertie was fussing at Man about something; I could not tell what. Man called for Boy to come back out of the shed. He told him to "Leave it and come talk to Aunt Gertie." Boy came out looking pale and scared and I wondered what Man might have done to him and Woman in his anger. I had seen him take his frustrations out on his family before. Maybe that was why Gertie was yelling at him now. I believe Woman is Gertie's sister. I could not know for sure why Gertie was there, but I was grateful to her.

Praying for death was nothing new for me, but feeling life flowing through me, renewing me and giving me the will to stop asking for my end was. At that moment, there was a desire that came from somewhere outside of me, but entered my heart and fed my soul. It was so strong it caused me to sit up in the back of the truck, even though I was in a sack soaked with my own blood and pee.

I heard Gertie say then, "You sorry sack of shit!" and for a moment I thought she was talking to me. But she continued, "What have you got in the back of that truck? What shenanigans are you up to now?"

I knew her disdain was aimed at Man and I held my breath, waiting to see what would come of me now. I felt a blow to my head and heard Gertie yell out, "What the hell do you think you are doing? That's a dog in that sack! Don't you dare do that again!"

The blow had not helped me, but it did not have Man's desired effect either. Whatever it was that was stirring my soul would not let go and I remained sitting up. I did not feel the pain that should have been wracking my body. I was trying to stand, but could not feel my paws. I looked to see if maybe the dog had been ordered to attack me again and had taken all of my paws off. The wound on my front leg was terrible and the sight of it made me cry out. Then I let out a low whimper as I fought to get on paws that were there, but that I could not feel.

I felt the sack being torn away from me then. Man was telling Gertie to stop, to get off of his property. Gertie was ripping and tearing, ignoring Man, determined to see the dog that she knew was in that sack. When she finally could see me she covered her mouth with her hand and let out a cry.

"Willie, you are the devil incarnate!" she said. It was not the first time I had heard the man called Willie, but the realization that he had something as normal as a name still shocked me. Still, at that moment it was fitting for me to know what he was called. The name made him smaller somehow, not so larger than life. He stood with his mouth open, pale and caught in his evil acts.

Gertie was trying to lift me, help me from the back of the truck now that the sack was gone. "This dog needs a vet," she said. "But I don't suppose that is what you had in mind, is it?"

Man turned to walk away then. He obviously did not know what to do. It felt good to see him confused and aggravated. Boy was always his father's son and he spoke up, trying to defend his daddy. "We ain't got no money for a vet. We can take care of the old bitch just fine without a vet nosing around."

Had he stopped after the first statement he might have been more helpful to old Willie. But evil never knows when to stop and, like I said, he was his father's son.

"And why would you not want a vet 'nosing' around? What exactly do you have to hide besides this poor soul?" Gertie sounded totally disgusted and was shaking her finger in Boy's face. She looked back at me then and reached for the rope still tied around my neck. "Come on, girl. Let's get you off this truck."

I managed to get on my paws then with her help. Gertie wrapped her arms around me and lifted me off the truck and to the ground. As soon as she let go I lost my legs and fell, face first. I heard Man snort and laugh, and fought hard to find my footing again. Finally giving up on standing, I sat down and looked at Gertie. I didn't know if she could hear me. I knew she had Heart Speak in her soul, but I did not know if she had lost the ability to use it with all of the evil being so close to her.

My own heart cried out to her, for her to help me, to help you. She tilted her head then as if listening. But Man did not intend to let me get the upper paw. He yelled for Boy to stop sniffling. "Get yourself in the house and call the pound," he said. "Tell them we've got a stray up here and need them to come and get her. Tell them they need to bring their guns cause she may be gone mad."

Gertie glared at Man then. "So that's your answer? Have the animal control people shoot her for you and get shed of the evidence?"

Old Willie snorted and laughed again. He did not intend to be outdone by Gertie or this dog. Especially not this dog... not after the night he had just suffered through. "For all I know she is mad," he said to Gertie. "Found her laying beside the road. Thought she was dead. I put her in that sack cause I had a mind to give her a decent burial. Then I saw she was alive so was gonna try to help her."

"You never had a mind to do anything decent in your life!" snapped Gertie. "Even if I wanted to believe you, I saw you whack her in the head with that board. What exactly was that supposed to help with?"

I heard him snort and laugh again. "By the time she sat up I was already thinking she might have the rabies. Didn't want her to bite you and make you crazier than you already are."

Boy was still standing there, listening. He let out a holler that was supposed to be laughter. "That's right," he said through his sadistic glee. "Didn't want nothing to make you crazier than a loon."

Man turned his attention to Boy; "I thought I told you to do something. What you still standing around here for? Get yourself in the house and make that call before this bitch dies and they leave her laying."

Boy ran toward the house to obey his father. Man looked at Gertie and said, "And since you like her so good you can help me get her outside my fence. Help me get her out there to the road since you tore the sack up I might have carried her in."

Gertie shook her head. "I will not. There's no reason they can't come up in the yard and get her. No reason to leave her out there beside the road."

"There's plenty of reason," said Man. "She ain't my dog and I don't want them trying to lock any of my dogs up cause they think she might have made 'em mad like her. She looks like she might have the rabies and my dogs ain't gonna suffer cause I had a thought to help out a stray dog."

Gertie looked totally disgusted now. "You wanted to help her as much as she wanted to be in that sack. I know better."

"Well I reckon you would have to prove it," Man said. "And if you don't help me get her out to the road I will just put a bullet in her right here in the yard. I told you, I don't want them pound people messing with my dogs. They won't have no call to if she ain't in my yard."

"I don't like it one bit," said Gertie. "You are throwing her out like yesterday's garbage. But I will get her out of your yard for her sake. She doesn't look like she's got long to live, but better she die with people who might try to help her. I wouldn't wish you on a poisonous snake."

Man laughed again and walked away, leaving Gertie to get me to the road on her own. She stayed with me until Tony, from the animal shelter, came and got me. I had tried to talk to her heart again. I wanted her to know you were back in that shed and needed help. I couldn't be sure she had heard me, but when I was in the back of Tony's truck, she put her hand against the bars on the crate and said, "Don't you worry, girl. I plan to keep a real close eye on this place from now on."

Once I was in the animal shelter, I met Nelly. She told me her story one night when we couldn't sleep. I liked her and I trusted her, so I told her all about you and the hell I hoped you could escape. We both wished with the deepest of Heart Speak. First we both wished for you to be safe. Then Nelly wished for me to find a home and to get better. My wish was for Nelly to get to go home to her real family... to Toad and her three children.

I guess you know the rest of the story. And I hope you understand that Heart Speak caused all of these wonderful things to happen. As bad as things can be, where there is Heart Speak, there will always be faith, hope and charity. Where there is Heart Speak, there will always be love.

Chapter 36

Wait and See

Rescue had turned out to be so much better than anyone of us had dreamed. Our bodies were healing and our spirits, once almost totally broken, were stronger than ever. Hope and I were gaining strength with each passing day and we would run and play in the sunshine. Faith was not quite as strong as we were and had a bit of growing to do so she could catch up, but her coat was shinier than we had ever thought it could be. She also had put on enough weight so no one thought she was starving any longer.

Mother was still a little thin, but was not a bag of bones any more. Her skin was stretching over muscle that was developing where before there had been nothing. She walked with a limp, and just as Mom and Dad had said, about two inches of her tail had fallen off. I had remembered a white tip on her tail back in the shed, but now it was not there. It didn't matter. The absence of a tail tip is nothing compared to being alive and being with the ones who love you.

The day came when it was time for us to return to Dr. Felton's. We were nervous and did not want to leave Mother behind. Mom and Dad had noticed the way all of us had started to heal faster since we were together. They suspected the truth, but could not be sure. To our delight, when they took us to the van, the crate was gone. In its place was an enclosure that covered the back of the van. There were pads on the sides and a large blanket for us to snuggle on. But the absolute best thing about it, Mother was already in the enclosure, waiting for us.

The drive to the vet's office did not seem to take as long with Mother there to snuggle us close. When we arrived, Mom did not take a crate out to carry us in. She had collars on each of us and we walked in on a leash. Dad walked in front with Mother. Mom held our leashes and we stayed close to Mother's back legs. Once inside, Dad went to the desk to check us in like before. Faith, Hope and I got into our favorite huddle and waited for Mother to come sit with us when she and Dad finished at the desk.

The woman in the white coat came out and called us back almost right away. Mom asked about Roscoe and the girl told her his surgery had been very successful and both he and his mom were doing well. The woman said she needed to weigh us. She weighed Mother first and Mom stood by the scales holding her leash while the three of us got weighed. It was not nearly as scary with Mother there.

Finally Dr. Felton came in. "Is this Snookie?" he asked, looking at Mother.

"It is," Mom replied. "Can we get the DNA test done today?"

"I can collect the samples for the test," he said. "But I can't give you the results today. It will take about a week. I can call you when the results come in."

"That would be great," Mom answered.

"Let's go to my office and go over what I learned about the little ones first. Will that be okay?" When Mom said it would be, Dr. Felton led all of us to his office. It was a small room and was a bit crowded with the whole family there, but no one seemed to mind. Mom and Dad sat in chairs across from Dr. Felton's desk and we huddled at their feet near Mother.

Dr. Felton had stepped out and now came back with a large envelope. He sat at his desk and gave it to Mom. "Those are your copies," he said. "I will, of course, be their veterinarian. But if there is ever an emergency, this will save a lot of time."

Mom sounded concerned. "What kind of emergency?" she asked.

Dr. Felton smiled at her and said, "I really don't think we are going to have to worry about it. But I like to be prepared for anything when we are dealing with dogs so small... and so young. They have a lot of developing to do and will need more testing for a couple of years to come."

He leaned back in his chair then and laced his fingers across his chest. "The fact is, right now, I don't see anything on the pictures that indicate a need for surgery. As they grow, that could change. There may be weak areas in the intestines that will require further action later on. Right now we need to keep them on medication for pain, of course. Antibiotics and antimicrobial therapy are indicated. You may start to see some skin issues as they get older. Some of it is just genetic with the breed, but you need to watch their backsides very closely. Because of what has happened, their bodies' response may cause problems for them. What the body is producing naturally to deal with a problem can lead to complications if not kept in check."

The four of us stayed quiet and listened. I asked Mother once if she knew what the vet was saying. She told me she did not have a clue, but it must be important because he sure charged a lot to say it. She pointed to Dad's hand with her nose. He was holding a piece of paper in it and Mom said it had our bill on it. She said when Dad had gotten it from the woman behind the desk, he had said a bad word so she knew it was a lot.

Dr. Felton picked several books up from his desk and handed them to Dad. "I am giving you a copy of several books that will help you understand what is going on with them. I don't normally do that, but this is not a normal situation. I can recommend several other readings, but I believe these will address any problems we may see. It will help you know what to look for. One of the major problems we will need to keep a close eye on is their ability to synthesize proteins. Their intestines are damaged and that is one of the problems that can arise."

"What are we going to do about the damaged intestines?" Mom asked.

"And what about their bone structure?" Dad added. "They are doing a little better now, but they still walk with a stoop. They don't look like they are walking while sitting any longer, and if it is just a matter of aesthetics, it is not a problem. But if it is uncomfortable for them or if there is anything we can do to help, we want to know."

"The answer to both questions is about the same," Dr. Felton replied. "We wait and see. They are healing and they are healing well. We need to let them go as far as they can on their own and we will hope they never need surgical intervention. You will continue the medicated baths, of course. They will be on a special diet to keep their bowel movements soft. And we will do dietary supplements to help them with prevent any deficiency."

He turned his attention fully to Dad, "And as for your question, again, we wait and see how this develops. I suspect they began to walk with the stoop because of pain. Keep giving them plenty of exercise and they will grow stronger. There is some muscle damage on the smallest one... Jo-Jo..."

"Faith," Mom corrected him.

"Okay," he said, "Faith."

He paused for a moment; I think he was making a note in his head to remember that name. Then he continued, "She *may* always have weakness in her hind legs. I do not know how pronounced it will be. She will never be able to enter any jumping or pulling competitions. But she will be a normal companion dog. I think if you give them time, they may surprise all of us. These puppies have a strong will to live. They were very young when this happened to them, and I would not have thought they could have survived it. Not trying to be graphic, but the person who did this must be very small. Otherwise I don't see how they could have survived."

We had been very quiet all day, listening and trying to understand what was being said. The most I got out of it was that they thought we were going to be okay. We were looking good. We needed to be careful what we ate and they needed to watch us to make sure we didn't get sick. Faith would never be able to jump like a bronco, but she would still be able to feel love and to give it, just like any dog.

And I understood they believed Boy was a very little person. I was not too sure what they meant about the "little" part. Mother said both Man and Boy were very small people. She said the word 'small,' when used that way meant they were not very good people at all. So I could have told Mom and Dad that and they would not have had to pay me a dogzillion dollars.

When I said that to Mother, she smiled and told me she thought the vet might have meant something more than what she had told me. I thought he probably had meant something else and I might have figured it out if I had dwelled on it for a while. But I let it go. I would rather not even think about that small, small person.

When Dr. Felton had finished talking, he called the woman in the white coat in to his office. She led us to another exam room and took a long stick with cotton on the end of it to run in our mouths. She did it three times on each of us, even Mother. When she had finished she told Mom and Dad, "We could not have done this a few years ago. DNA Research has come a long way for people and for dogs."

After the woman in the white coat put the last swab in Faith's mouth, Faith whispered to me, "I think they are going to fix our teeth now. Maybe we will be able to eat kibble."

Mother smiled and said, "I think your teeth are going to be just fine. They will need to wait and see for that too."

It had been a good day at the vet's office. Dad took all of us outside while Mom went and got our medicine and some other things the vet thought we needed. There must have been a grocery store nearby because when Mom came out she had three very large bags. Dad said it was our groceries.

We walked around on the grass at Dr. Felton's office and Dad gave each of us a treat. Faith turned her nose up when Dad offered her the treat. When he tried to give it to her a second time and she didn't take it, Dad stuck it back in his pocket. Faith blew her cheeks out in a pout. She had been hoping he would pull out a piece of that bacon.

Dad looked at Faith and said, "You really are becoming the Pouting Queen. He took the treat out of his pocket and offered it again. Faith took it, and she kept it with her when we got back in the van. She went to sleep nibbling on it.

The ride home was the perfect time for all of us to take a nap. Except for Dad. Mom told him he couldn't nap and drive at the same time. It had been a long day and I felt bad that Mom wouldn't let Dad take a nap. I asked Mother why she didn't want Dad to sleep. Mother told me it would be very bad to try and drive while napping. She wasn't sure what would happen, but she said, "I believe driving is one of those things that you have to be totally awake for and you have to pay attention to what you are doing."

That was a good answer and I was glad Mom had told Dad he couldn't sleep and drive. All things considered, it had been another good day. I slept peacefully all the way home with my head snuggled next to Mother.

Chapter 37

Old Friends and New

Time really does go faster when you are enjoying your life. After our visit to Dr. Felton, we developed a routine. Our days always started with a walk. Faith, Hope and I did not like to go too far from our own yard. There were lots of things to see right there, and even though Mother was with us, we just felt better at home. We still did not like it when strangers would come either. Mom and Dad never forced us to see anyone if we didn't want to. Mother told us we would always be safe now, but she didn't push us to leave home either. She would go for a long walk with Dad and a couple of the other dogs that lived with us, but we chose to stay home.

We would wait in the backyard for Dad to come back with Mother. We would watch until they were just little specks on the road behind our house. And then we would watch them grow big again as they walked back home.

After the morning walk, we would always get breakfast. Then it was out in the back to play for a while. Dad always had a few pieces of bacon in his pocket, and that was our favorite time of the day. Mom would know when we were tired and ready to go in. Faith would walk up onto the porch, then Hope and I would follow. We would huddle together on the porch until Mom came to let us in. Usually Mother would go in with us, but there were times she would want to stay out in the sunshine. We knew we were healing because it was okay when she wanted to stay outside. We knew she would be coming in soon and we were all safe.

One day while we were in the house and Mother was still outside, someone came to the front door. Mom opened it and Aunt Gertie was standing there. It surprised us, but mom acted like she was expecting her. Mom had talked to Joanie about us when she was trying to find out where we had come from. Joanie had taken Aunt Gertie's information on the day we were left at the shelter. She had called her and told her Mom wanted to talk about the puppies that had been dropped off.

Mom called Dad into the house and Mother came in with him. When Mother saw Aunt Gertie, she came to where we were sitting and stopped in front of us. It reminded me of the way she would put herself between us and Man back in hell. She looked all around the room, making sure Man and Boy were not there. Then she walked over to Aunt Gertie and licked her hand.

Aunt Gertie looked surprised to see Mother. She said, "This dog came from Willie's too. Did you know that?"

"We figured it out," Mom said. "And we believe she may the mother to these puppies."

Aunt Gertie told her she couldn't be sure, but it was certainly possible. Then she told Mom and Dad the story that Mother had told us when we were first reunited. "I suspected then she was a bait dog," Aunt Gertie said. "I knew he hadn't found her beside the road. He may have dropped a few on the roadside, but he certainly never picked one up."

"What about the puppies?" Dad asked. "What can you tell us about them?"

Mom offered Aunt Gertie some coffee and she waited until everyone was sitting down again to start. I watched Mother while she told the story of how she had found Boy in the shed with his pants down, and she had come in just in time to see what he was doing to me. "He was raping that puppy," she said. "I don't remember which one it was because they all looked alike to me back then. Well, all, except for the smallest one with all the white on her. It was not her. She was sitting out in the pen in the yard, by herself."

Mother's face had a very hurt looked as she listened to what we had been through. Faith, Hope and I snuggled closer to her. It made me feel good to have her next to me and I hoped she was comforted feeling all three of us near.

Aunt Gertie continued talking, telling about the day she had caught Boy raping me. "One of the other two pups was scratching and whining at the door of the shed," she said. "She was trying her best to get in. I honestly believe she knew what he was doing to her sister and wanted to help. I could hear the other puppy yelping and it sounded like she was hurt. I opened the door and there he stood, his britches down around his ankles, holding that puppy down on the stool in front of him. I can tell you it made me right sick on my stomach. That little puppy's eyes were the biggest thing about her and she was just helpless there in his hands."

Aunt Gertie took a big swallow from her cup. Mom and Dad were very quiet, waiting for her to finish. Faith's head was dropped and she was staring at the floor, very much like she had stared down at the ground on that day so long ago. Hope had her head buried at Mother's chest. She had put her head behind Mother's front leg and I could not see her face at all. I sat as close to Mother's heart as I could get and could hear it beating. Just like when I was a little puppy, I knew that heart was beating for me.

"I knew exactly what he was doing. Couldn't miss it," Aunt Gertie said. "He was in the act when I opened that door. So I politely asked him what he was doing to that puppy, then I marched across that shed and knocked him away from her. He bowed his chest out at me and I popped him right in the face. I saw him the next day and I am pleased to say he had a shiner from where I cold-conked him."

Then she added quickly, "I don't want you to get the idea I go around hitting children. But I did hit him because he deserved it. And I enjoyed hitting him, too. I won't lie about that. The only thing that would have made it better is if I could have knocked his daddy out right there beside him."

By the time Aunt Gertie left that day, Mom and Dad knew who had hurt us. Mom was upset that it was a child, but she said that didn't change the fact that we had been hurt. The next day she called Dr. Felton and told him all about Aunt Gertie.

Back in our early days in rescue, Mom stayed gone a lot. I believe she was trying to find a way to get that thing called justice for us. We didn't care about all that. We were just glad to be safe and loved. Aunt Gertie's visit had reminded us of all that had happened, and for a little while, we were very nervous again. I mean, if Aunt Gertie knew where we were, Man and Boy might be able to find us too.

When visitors would come to see Mom and Dad, we would watch really closely to make sure it wasn't Man or Boy. Mother was worried about all those other people who would show up at the fights and cheer when she was being hurt. If we thought there was danger, we would find a corner to hide in and we would huddle. Mother would always stay near us, but she could see we had a very strong bond. She was happy we were so close.

I was always very worried something would happen to cause Faith to go to The Land of Nothing again. Hope had moved on and was doing really well, so I made sure to keep a close eye on Faith.

We went to see Dr. Felton a lot. There were times when Mom and Dad would get worried about something and they would call and tell them they would be bringing us to see the doctor. That place was almost like a second home to us. We got to know everyone there and they liked us a lot. I could tell the woman in the white coat felt left out a lot. She was always the one that had to take us to get things done we didn't really like. I felt bad for her so I started letting her rub my belly when she would come in the room. I would bump her leg with my nose to get her full attention, then I would roll over and wait for the belly rub. It was our special thing and she knew it was an honor. I didn't trust everybody enough to show them my belly.

Aunt Gertie was not the only old friend who came to visit. One day we were inside and we could tell there was excitement in the air. Mother had gone for a long walk that morning. Faith, Hope and I had stayed in the backyard like we always did. When Dad came back from the walk, we went right back in the house and that was different. Usually we would stay outside and play for a while.

Hope was worried because Dad would give us our bacon while we were outside, and we had not gotten it yet. She thought Mom and Dad might be excited because we were out of bacon. Hope said we had eaten a lot, and there were other dogs around, so maybe it had just run out.

Dad saw that we were nervous and pacing so he came in and said, "Did you girls think I had forgotten you?" Then he pulled out the bacon. I had told Hope she was crazy when she said we had run out, but I was very relieved to see that bacon.

We heard some of the dogs that were outside playing start barking. Mom said, "They're here," and she and Dad walked outside.

Mother jumped up in the chair near the window to peek out and see what was going on. She got so excited she could not even tell us what was happening. She jumped out of the chair and ran to the door. She was pacing up and down. Finally Hope jumped up in the chair so she could see what all the fuss was about.

"There's people out there," she said. "I don't know who because I saw them walking behind the house. They are all in the backyard now. They have left their car in our front yard."

Mother was still dancing at the door and all I could hear from her Heart Speak was a lot of words running together. It's like that sometimes with dogs when they get excited. Heart Speak is really wonderful, but don't expect to learn much if a dog is excessively happy. You are going to have to let her calm down before you can understand a word.

When Faith heard there were people walking around our backyard she was worried it might be someone evil from our past. I was not sure about that because Mother was acting all happy. I could not think of one reason why Mother would act that way. It could be Anna. Mother liked Anna.

Hope was still in the window and was worried about that car. She said, "I hope they don't just leave it there. It's blocking my view."

"Well pinch it on the butt and tell it to move over," said Faith, mocking Hope just a little.

"I think they will move it when they are ready to leave," I said. "People have to leave their cars somewhere. They can't drive them in our backyard."

"Well," said Hope, "they may need to wash their tires. The dog we have seen that mom says needs someone to take care of him just peed all over their tires. Do you think maybe they have come to take care of that dog?"

"No," I said. "That dog lives down the road at someone's house. He runs around the neighborhood all the time, but he has a home."

I heard Mom come in the backdoor and call out to Mother. She was still pacing and rambling. Mother could not really run well because of the place where her paw had been hurt so badly. She would gallop like a pony when she was in a hurry, and she took off at a gallop for the backdoor.

Now we were really confused. I was just a little wounded by all of this. I mean, we hadn't even been invited. I could understand them not taking Faith. She was scared. Hope had started pinching Mom and Dad on their butts just like she did Faith and me, so I understood her not being invited. We had been in rescue long enough now that our teeth were better so Hope could really bruise a butt.

But why didn't they invite me? I can tell you I was very confused and my feelings were hurt. I decided I would not speak to them when they came back in. I would just turn my back to them and let them know they were rude. I had all kinds of things in my head to do so they would know their behavior was just not acceptable.

Then I heard Mom at the backdoor again. "Girls, come on out and play. You have company."

I forgot all about telling her she was rude and took off for the backdoor. Hope almost knocked me down running past me. Faith was heading to the backdoor too, but was hanging back just a little. But she always did that when she was unsure of something. She was just being careful.

Of course, Hope got outside first. Her legs were longer than mine or Faith's. We had argued more than once because she said she looked more like Mother so Faith and I must look like our father. Faith and I knew it was true, but we couldn't let her get away with saying it. She would tell us how both her nose and her legs were longer, like Mother's. I would say something witty like, "Faith and I still have to hit a growth spurt and we will catch up."

Faith was not nearly as diplomatic. She would usually say that Hope's nose was longer because she needed more room for her "super dooper boogers." Then Hope would insist Faith had just said Mother had a lot of boogers. It would usually end with a name-calling session and Faith would, of course, pout. Then Hope would always say, "Look at the Pouting Queen."

Faith could not leave it alone and would come back with, "Look at Hope's big head with the big nose and the super, dooper boogers."

There were entire days spent name-calling. Mother would always go and sun herself on those occasions and leave us to it.

She always said, "A good debate strengthens the wit and dogs need all the wit they can get in this world."

Honestly, I think Mother would get tired of hearing it, but she was so happy to be with us again, she didn't want to waste one minute making us behave. She wouldn't allow us to outright fight, but name-calling was acceptable so long as we did not get really nasty with it.

Since I am telling my story and I need to be honest, Hope and I did get into a bit of a brawl one time. Hope had been in a particularly good mood and had been bouncing around all day like a bronco. The sun was setting in the sky and Mom and Dad were putting all the work stuff away. Dad had planted a really pretty bush with yellow roses on it and we were all trying to see it. Faith, of course, stepped right in front of Hope. Faith was smiling and talking about how pretty the rose was when Hope pinched her hard right on the butt. Faith was totally surprised and, even though I am sure it left a bit of a bruise, she let out a howl that was a lot worse than the pinch. Of course Hope had been aggravating me all day calling me short legs and short nose, so I took the opportunity to jump to Faith's defense.

When Faith saw I was going to stand up for her, she hollered a little more and actually managed a very hurt-looking pout. Hope insisted Faith was making a fuss over nothing so we started arguing. I was trying to show how grown-up I was by telling Hope she had to remember Faith was smaller than her and we needed to protect her.

Hope told me I was being a real pain by acting like a preachy dog trainer. That really offended me so I got in her face and told her, "Just behave!"

She walked behind me and pinched me on the butt and from there, it was on.

Mother was totally disgusted with us and tried to break it up. There was no real biting going on, mostly a lot of paw slapping and growling, but it could have gotten worse. Mom came around the corner when she heard the racket and she punished us for fighting. Mom has a time out crate, and she pulled out another one for the occasion. Hope and I both got put in a time out crate, and Faith sat there grinning and looking innocent. She looked a lot like the dog that swallowed the cat that swallowed the canary. It was the first time we had ever been punished and I was totally humiliated. The next time we were all looking at something, I remembered that look on Faith's face. I walked behind her and pinched her right on that butt. She thought it was Hope and pouted at her for the next little while.

But I was telling you about the day we had company. Where was I?

Oh yes! Hope got out the back door first with her long legs. I heard her yell out, "Nelly's here!" so I picked up the pace and so did Faith. We almost tumbled out the door together.

Nelly looked absolutely beautiful. Her coat was a lot shinier and cleaner than I remembered and she had put on some weight. She looked at us and was very surprised. "Your mother is looking really wonderful," she said. "Rescue has certainly agreed with her. But you three... Bow-Wow! You are stunning. You have more than doubled in size! And look how shiny your coats are."

"We are walking a lot straighter, too," said Faith. "The pain back there is not nearly as bad. Some days I almost forget it hurts."

Hope smiled one of those huge grins that Mom calls a Pibble Smile and said, "Yes, we are walking much better and our butts are not almost dragging the ground now. And *some of us* have gotten taller."

Mother gave her a disapproving look and said, "Don't you start."

Hope dropped the subject immediately, but when she walked past me she whispered, "Only because Mother said so..."

She added something to it that I am sure was meant to provoke me, but I chose not to hear it. I would not let her draw me into a debate on that day. We had good company!

Nelly introduced us to her family. Her mom and dad were really nice people and after they had met us, they went and sat down with our mom and dad to talk. Toad looked just like Nelly had described and, even though he was older, I could see the mischief dancing in his eyes. Polly and Anna were both beautiful and regal-looking, just like their mother. Their legs were shorter than hers, and they looked like smaller versions of her. But Froggy was our favorite.

Polly, Anna and Froggy were definitely not puppies. They were a lot older than we were. But Froggy was very funny, bouncy and he could not be still. He looked like his father. I could tell Nelly was his mother because his eyes looked a lot like hers. When he looked at me it was like he was seeing right through my coat and skin, straight into my heart and soul.

Mother, Nelly and Toad found a nice spot in the shade to watch us while they talked about how wonderful their lives had become. Toad stared at Nelly like she was the only dog there and I knew he loved her a lot. I was very glad she had found her way home to him and their children. Polly and Anna played with us for a little while, but they were older and tired out quickly. They went and rested with our mothers and Toad.

Froggy was the same age they were, but you would never have known it. He bounced like he had springs in his feet and when Dad gave all of us a piece of bacon, he jumped up and down in one spot about three times, and then turned a flip. Nelly said that was his special trick. I was amazed. When he jumped that way he was jumping higher than Dad's head. I was sure if he had wanted to, he could have jumped right over our fence.

Hope was as amazed by Froggy as I was and she tried to bounce right along with him. But she looked a lot like a bronco when she would bounce, just like Mom said. Froggy did not look like a bronco. He looked like a frog with very springy legs.

While Hope and I were fascinated with Froggy and loved his energy, Faith was over the moon for him. She gave him the puppy dog eye big time. She acted a lot different than I had ever seen her, prancing around and doing major butt wiggles. One time she actually got down in the grass and rolled around on her back. I had never seen her do that before.

It started bothering me a little because Froggy was giving Faith as much attention as she was begging for. He played with Hope and me, but he acted like Faith was a delicate little lap dog or something. I realized he was showing off for her as much as she was showing off for him. That bothered me. Mother saw I was acting a bit upset and sent me one of her special heart messages.

She told me, "You have to remember Faith cannot bounce around like you and Hope. Think about what the doctor said. Her muscles are weak in her hind legs and hips. Sometimes I think that is why Faith doesn't join in your play so much. Right now she is doing the only thing she can to join the fun. Don't ruin it for her."

After that I looked at it differently. When Hope came to me upset and said, "Look at Faith acting like her head isn't as big as ours. It is every bit as big as yours, and bigger than mine. And there she is acting like a Poodle or something."

Hope had met Anna's poodle and thought she was very prissy. In fact, her name was Prissy. So every time she wanted to say a dog was acting prissy she would say they were acting like a poodle. I let the comment she had made about the large heads go and told her what Mother had said. From that point on, we enjoyed watching Faith have fun.

When the day was over and we were talking about all that had happened before bed, Hope said, "We have seen several old friends lately. Aunt Gertie came to see us and she is an old friend who saved all of our lives. And today was the best. Seeing Nelly made me feel so good."

"And seeing that she is beautiful, well-loved and with her family made it so much better," I added.

Mother looked at Faith and asked how she felt about seeing old friends. Faith sat up and got that puppy dog eye look again. She said, "I was a little scared on the day Aunt Gertie came. It was nice to see her, but it made me remember how we met her, too.

"Seeing Nelly was really good. I didn't even know I had missed her until I saw her today. But my best time was meeting her family. Seeing old friends was grand, but having your old friends and making new ones too is even better. I think I will remember today forever as one of our best days. And I hope Froggy comes back to see us again."

"And Polly, Anna, Toad and Nelly," Hope added.

Mother smiled a very large Pibble smile and said, "Old friends are always the best." Then she looked at Faith and said, "And when they come back, Froggy will be an old friend too."

Faith curled up and went to sleep with a huge smile on her face. It was a pawsome time.

Chapter 38

Trust and Fear

Seeing Nelly and her family was enough to keep us happy for days and days. We each had our own special memories of the visit, and we could pull them out any time we needed a pick-me-up. Sharing the memories was a good way to feel the joy all over again. It is always important to let the bad memories go and relive the good as often as you can.

That is a secret that all dogs know from birth. When a puppy is born, the mother whispers the secret in her baby's ear. It is the first thing a puppy hears besides a mother's heartbeat, so it is something we never forget. That is why dogs will not hold grudges against all people when they have been hurt. When a dog is treated so badly she forgets that secret, her spirit fades away. But it never dies. So if someone can love her enough to help her remember to let the bad go and relive the good, her heart and soul will shine again.

Something else all dogs know: it is important to make something nice last as long as possible. The longer it lasts, the more good memories there are to relive. Reliving those good memories can get a dog through a lot of bad days. So, if you rub your dog's belly and suddenly stop, do not be surprised when she takes her nose and starts pushing your hand. That is also why a dog will come to you when you call while on a walk, but will take off and run just once more around the dog walk. You chasing behind makes for a better memory. Dogs love to spend time with their people. The extra run is a grand way to spend a little extra time with you, and to make a longer memory.

Some people will get angry after a run. This is especially true when the dog takes that extra lap around. I guess it's because people only have two paws and cannot run as fast or as far as a dog. And when people get tired, they do get cranky. But try and remember your dog may not have a clue why you are angry. It doesn't mean your dog isn't smart. Not all dogs have had the experiences I have with people, so they may not be able to figure things out the way I do. The best thing for you to do is when you get tired, sit down and take a break. You will never keep up on your two paws against your dog's four anyway. If you have been a good best friend, you will not have to sit there alone for very long. Dogs always stay close to the people they love. How else can they keep you out of trouble?

One of the most important reasons I know to hold on to every bit of good, it always helped me deal with the bad.

Sometimes I would see something that reminded me of all that abuse and it would be scary and hurt all over again. Faith and Hope went through that too. Faith would hide in a corner. I would try and find Mother because she always made me feel better. Hope would bounce it away as best she could, and if that didn't work, she would just freeze in place. The huddle we liked to get in was about being scared and feeling safe.

Certain things will always force me to remember the terrible things that happened. Seeing Dr. Felton would bring the bad to the surface every single time. We talked about it one time and it was the same for Faith and Hope. But it couldn't be helped. All the hurt places had to be touched and looked at if we were going to get better. We just tried not to dwell on it so much.

We went through a lot on our trips to the vet. Some of the tests they did were not easy, but the pain was over really quick and we knew it was for our own good. We had always behaved really well no matter what tests we had to have. And we always got a very special treat when we left. Dad always had bacon in his pocket. Smelling that bacon was very helpful. It kept us behaving by tempting us the whole time and making our mouths water.

Sometimes Hope would walk really close to Dad and almost have her nose stuck in his pocket. I think she did that to remind herself not to pinch any butts. I saw her looking at Dr. Felton's rump a couple of times, and I knew exactly what she was thinking.

I always thought Dad would have given us the bacon no matter how we behaved. Dads are that way, you know? They act all tough on the outside sometimes, but they are all fluffy stuff inside. He knew how much that bacon meant to us, and he would not have been able to keep it from us. I believe he liked watching us eat it as much as we enjoyed having it in our mouths.

The point is, even though going to the vet was not fun, we tried not to dwell on the things that we didn't like. Everything they did at Dr. Felton's was to help us. For instance, when I think back now I remember the good things that happened first.

I remember Dr. Felton was always really proud of us and how we were growing. Mom and Dad always told him wonderful things about us. Everyone there knew our names when we would walk in, and they gave us all kinds of love and good attention.

Now sometimes one of us would get a little scared going in the door. Faith would get down on her belly and crawl in once-in-awhile. She did that mostly when there were a lot of people waiting in the office. Faith always worried that Man or Boy might be hiding in the crowd so they could dognap us. And she also worried that there were a lot more evil people in the world. Some of them might be standing right in that crowd. Crawling was her way to feel safe. Mom and Dad were very patient with her when she would do that.

Then there was one time when Hope got really scared. It was early on when we were still trying to gain weight, and we had only been to see Dr. Felton a couple of times. Mom got really worried because Hope was having problems. She had been sick for more than a day and Mom thought it would be best if we went and got checked by the vet. We didn't know exactly what to expect since Hope had been throwing up her food. What she didn't throw up went right through her and out the other end. We were still sore when that happened and she was afraid Dr. Felton would have to do something to her butt.

Hope had been really quiet for the entire ride there, and when we got to the door to go in, she just laid right down. She wouldn't budge. Dad tried to stand her on her feet and they just folded right under her. Finally he picked her up and carried her in. She would have never walked in. She was too scared.

It turned out okay that time and every time we went. But going to the vet still caused a lot of bad memories to hurt our hearts and make us scared.

After a really scary memory, it was good to know we would always wake up at home. Mom always told us, "Home is that place you belonged all along, but got terribly lost along the way."

It was good to have friends. It was good to have a home and family. And it was good to be found.

Chapter 39

Puppies Come to the Den

Mom and Dad were still making a lot of plans for Eagle's Den Rescue. They did not have everything ready yet, even though a lot of people knew them and would call them for help when there was a dog that needed them. Anna was working with them a lot to get everything set up. Hope, Faith and I were never sure what they were talking about. I heard them say they were not really Eagle's Den yet. They were very real to me and that is all that mattered.

Mother told me once that their name had been something else before. They had lived somewhere else, and when they moved they had started making plans for a name change. Mom was working on that and she was trying very hard to find out what to do about Man and Boy. She wanted them stopped from hurting more dogs and she wanted justice for us. I never quite understood what was going on. I just knew we lived in hell once. We were abused. Then we went to the animal shelter and were rescued. Now we lived in the opposite of hell and we were safe.

One of the things Mom and Dad talked about a lot was finding a home for dogs who did not have one. One day Mom and Anna left very early in the morning. They were gone a long time. The dark was already starting to chase the sun away when they got back. When they came in the door they were carrying a box.

Mom was smiling and Anna was carrying a bag. There were five little puppies in that box. Mom said they were Border Collie puppies. I am not sure what happened to their mother, but they needed a lot of help. Their eyes were not even open yet and they were very hungry. I heard Mom tell Dad that the woman who had them could not figure out why they were crying so loud all the time. The woman said she had been trying to feed them every time they cried, but they were crying all the time.

By the time we saw them, they were very quiet and resting in that box. Mother explained to us that one of the things a mama does for her babies is help them go to the bathroom. They cannot go without that help. She said the babies had been crying when they didn't have a mother any longer because, even though they were being fed, they didn't have anyone to help them with the rest of it. Mom had known that and had helped them.

There was a dog in rescue then named Roxy. She loved puppies a lot, but she didn't have any milk to feed the babies. Mom kept feeding them and Roxy would take care of the rest of their needs. Mom would get up all during the night and feed those babies. With five babies, Mom was not getting a lot of sleep, and she didn't have time for much else other than those feedings.

She had been getting up to feed them for two nights when someone from the animal shelter called. There was a dog there who had come in with babies. Her babies were older and a rescue had taken them. They took the babies but left the mother behind. The mother still had a lot of milk and Mom was going to get her and bring her home.

To begin with, they told Mom to bring the babies to see if the dog would feed them because they did not want her to get "stuck" with a dog that would not feed those puppies. That made Mom really mad. She was already upset because a rescue from very far away had taken the babies and left the mother behind. She didn't like that.

Mom told the person at the shelter that she would not take the puppies with her. She said if the dog fed the babies, that would be wonderful, but if she didn't, there was no way she would send her back to the shelter.

That is how we met Beauty. She came into rescue and she did feed the puppies. But she never really wanted to spend any time with them. Mom would sit with her when it was time to feed and she would let the babies nurse. Then when they finished, Roxy would take them back to her bed and take care of them. It worked out really well because Roxy wanted to be a mother and Beauty did not.

Beauty was a very large Black Lab. She was the largest dog I have ever seen. Mother said she thought she might be mixed with something like a Great Dane. When she first came she seemed very sad. She liked Faith, Hope and me a lot and started spending time with us and Mother. One day I got up enough nerve to ask her why she didn't want to take care of the five little puppies.

"Do you see that my muzzle has some white coming in?" she asked. "Well, that's because I am a senior. I spent my whole life having babies and the people who were supposed to take care of me would always sell my children before they were ready to leave."

I noticed then how sad her eyes were and I did see that she had some white coming in around her mouth and nose. "Did they make your babies fight?" I asked. "We lived in a place called hell before we were rescued and they would make dogs fight."

"I have heard of that before," said Beauty. "That is terrible. But, no; they didn't make dogs fight. They did make money when they would sell my puppies though. And they would take them away before they were old enough to leave."

She had a very faraway look in her eyes then like Nelly would get when she was ready to tell us a story. I got comfortable and she started telling me about her last litter.

"I had a very hard time with it this last time," she said. "I am really too old to be having babies now and there were ten in my last litter. As soon as they were starting to eat a little on their own, they sold four of them. But no one came for the last six and they were getting very impatient to get the puppies gone."

She looked at Mother who was never very far away from us and continued, "It was nice to have those six with me for so long. I was beginning to think maybe they would actually let them stay until they were old enough to go to new homes. But I should have known better. They were not feeding me very well... not that they ever had... but the food was really scarce in those last few days.

"Then they came out to the barn where they kept me and started taking my babies away. They took two at a time and I couldn't do anything to stop them." She lowered her voice then like she was ashamed. "I lived on a chain out there at the barn so there was never a lot I could do."

Faith had been lying next to Mother, listening to Beauty talk. She sat up now and leaned toward the old girl. "You don't have anything to be ashamed of," Faith said. "They are the ones who should be ashamed for keeping you tied up that way. I used to be ashamed because I was abused, but I have learned in rescue it is not our fault when people do wrong. We don't have anything to be ashamed of. The people are wrong and should be punished. You wait and see. Mom will tell you all about being innocent and getting justice. She wants to get justice for us. I will bet she wants to get it for you too."

Beauty looked very tired when she responded to Faith. "That is very nice of you to say. It would be good if it were true, but they always told me I was a bad dog."

"See," said Hope; "that is just wrong. Mom says there is no such thing as a bad dog. There are just bad people who are supposed to take care of the dogs."

Beauty looked thoughtful and I could see a glimmer of life coming into her eyes. Then she continued with her story. "After they had taken all six of my babies, they unhooked my chain and led me to the truck. My babies were in the back in a crate. The crate was too small for all of us, but they put me in there with them anyway. It was a terrible ride. I was afraid I would crush one of them and tried to stand the entire way. Then when they took us out, we were at the animal shelter.

"I actually thought it was a good thing. I was treated better than I had ever been while I was at the shelter. Then someone came in from a rescue and wanted my babies. They had said they would come back for me once they got the puppies to the vet. Said they didn't have room to take me too right then. Of course, once they left with the puppies we never saw them again. I began to get very depressed. They kept talking about how I am so large and I am a senior. Then they added the fact that I am a black dog and that meant I probably would go to the room in the back.

"I sat with my head hanging down all the time. The kibble there was really too hard for me, but I didn't much feel like eating anyway. Then your Mom came in. I didn't look up when she came to my kennel. But I could hear her Heart Speak and I knew she was not happy that I had been deserted in the shelter. That is when I came here.

"I really don't mind helping out and feeding those puppies, but I still miss my own and am worried about them. Seeing they had another dog to help look after them suited me fine. I love my babies and I miss them, but I hope I never have to give birth again. I am just too old. My teeth are almost totally gone. That's why I couldn't eat the kibble at the shelter. Your mom has been so good to me. She has given me food I can eat and I am actually starting to feel better. I will hate to leave this place when the babies are weaned."

Mother smiled a very sad smile at Beauty and said, "My friend, I know exactly how you feel. But you will not be sent away. Mom and Dad would never do that. You are safe here. You are in rescue. And they are *your* mom and dad too."

Beauty began to change after that. She was a really good friend to Mother and we liked her a lot. She said we reminded her of those babies of hers. She said her babies were always really large and we could have been hers at about the time they were weaned. Faith's eyes got very huge when she said that. She said, "Those *were very large* babies."

As soon as the Border Collie puppies were old enough to eat on their own, Mom did not ask Beauty to feed them any longer. Beauty liked to sit in Mom's chair. She was so tall she could sit on the chair and hang her paws down to the floor. We liked it when she would do that. It would make us laugh. She looked almost like a furry person sitting there.

Roxy did not mind taking care of those babies at all. She loved being a mother. In the afternoon, Mom and Dad would both take several dogs for a walk. Mother was always ready to go and would be the first in line to get her leash on. Roxy also enjoyed a nice walk, as did beauty. Faith, Hope and I never wanted to go on the long walks in the morning or the afternoon. We would go out into the play yard and have fun while we waited for everyone to come back. The puppies were too young to go for a walk, and they were still too young to be out in the play yard without Mom or Dad. They would stay in the bedroom with a gate at the door while everyone was outside.

One afternoon Mother did not run to get her leash when it was time. I could tell it worried Mom and Dad, and it sort of bothered me too. I was afraid Mother was getting sick. She had been getting up a lot at night. I would wake up when she got out of bed, and then I would wake up again when she came back. I never knew where she was going on those nights because I believe every dog needs their private moments. I thought she might be going off by herself to think and to pray to the Great Creator of All Life. She had taught us those prayer times are very personal and we should never interrupt someone who is praying.

So on the afternoon when she didn't feel up to going for a walk, Mother went to the couch and climbed onto it. She was resting her head on the arm. Mom touched her nose and announced that it was cold and wet. She looked at her eyes and said they were bright; checked her gums and said they were nice and pink. Mother just didn't feel up to a walk that day. I was going to stay in with her, but she insisted I should go outside with my sisters. She said she just wanted a few moments to herself.

I figured there was something she must be praying for really hard with all the late night sessions and now this, but I respected her privacy and went outside to the play yard. It was a really nice day, and I was glad to be out in the sunshine and fresh air.

Mom always took something called a fanny pack with her on the walks. I don't know why they call it a fanny pack, cause it doesn't look at all like a fanny, and it is a terribly small thing... so none of the fannies around our house will fit in it. If you tell her I said so I will deny it, but Mom's most certainly will not! She would carry a few things in it to make the walk better. One thing she always carried was her camera for what she called cute moments, and a bottle of water. On that day she had her camera dangling on her arm, and she left the house so quickly, she forgot the fanny pack.

Since they were just at the beginning of the path they always used, Mom had dad and the dogs wait for her while she ran back to the house. I saw her run in and then in just a minute, I heard her squeal.

Now there are all kinds of squeals. For instance, when Faith squeals you just know that Hope has probably done a butt pinch and there will be a very strong pout following the squeal. Mom gives a bit of a squeal with one of Hope's butt pinches too, but she never pouts. She just says Hope's name very loudly and then Dad giggles. But, mostly when Mom squeals it is in delight. And this definitely sounded like a delighted squeal.

We might not have seen what she was squealing about, but she still had the camera hanging on her arm. Never one to miss a Kodak moment, she made it last forever with a picture. We saw the picture.

My mother had gotten across the barrier to the bedroom. No one knows how she did it because the gate was intact and the door was still locked. That means she had to climb it, or she figured out how to open it and close it back. I cannot tell you which. My dog bone is on climbing. She does have that bad front leg, but when she gets determined.... And even if she managed to get the gate open, I am not sure she could lock it back. That is one of those things that requires thumbs.

Whatever way she may have gotten in, when Mom found her she was sitting there with a huge grin on her face. It was one of those grins that go from ear to ear and is so big your eyes close automatically. Those five puppies were all tucked up under her and they were trying to nurse. Now I can tell you my Mother did not have a drop of milk. And if you don't believe me, you can ask Faith because she had been trying to nurse every night since we were reunited with Mother. Oh... she was slick about it. She would snuggle up all close and close her eyes like she was asleep. Then you could hear the sucking noises. Mother never made her stop any more than she made those Border Collie puppies stop.

With Faith, Dad called it a "pacifier session." Hope called it a brat session and I called it dreaming. I don't think any of us figured out what to call it with the Border Collie puppies. I guess they saw Mother was well endowed for feeding puppies and could not possibly know there was no milk. They had missed their own mother and grabbed the opportunity. It made Mother happy because she felt good about helping those puppies, and she had missed so many feedings with her own children. I guess she loved being a Mother every bit as much as Roxy.

From that day on Roxy and Mother both looked after the puppies.

The puppies were growing fast. They were starting to explore and needed a lot of help to keep out of trouble. Mother said puppies had to be taught how to get along with each other so they wouldn't fight. She gave Hope and me a stern look when she said that. Then she added, "You girls did really well on your own because you *had* to. Once you were safe, well... you know."

I blushed because it made me embarrassed I had misbehaved. Hope gave her best innocent look like she never did anything wrong. I wanted to tell her she was not innocent, but I bit my tongue. I don't think that was the right time to say anything to Hope cause she would have tried to fuss. She always tried to fuss with me when I was trying to teach her something.

The three of us spent time playing with the puppies so we could teach them how to act right. Faith told Mother we would teach them how to be good dogs. Mother shook her head and smiled. She winked at Beauty and Roxy and said "I would say the blind leading the blind, but my girls are very special, don't you think?"

Beauty and Roxy both agreed that we were very special.

While we are talking about puppies and habits there is something else I need to share with you. Mom had this very strange habit. Every time we would poop, she would run to look at it. I don't mean she just looked at it either. She would actually examine it. She would take a stick and stir around in it. I never could understand that, but it made her happy so who am I to judge?

She did that same thing to the Border Collies' poop. But she was never as intense about theirs as she was Faith's, Hope's and mine. Our poop was very special to her. Sometimes when she would look at our poop she would dance. Don't ask me why. The only thing I can think of is it must be some strange ceremony people have over poop. Mother said she didn't understand it either. Sometimes after she would dig all around in our poop and do that strange poo-poo dance, we would go and look to see if we saw anything special about it. It just looked like it always did. So I have no clue.

I would not even tell you about the poo-poo dance and all because I think that is a very private thing, but there was this one thing that bears mentioning in our story. Sometimes when Mom would look at the poop, she would pick some of it up and put it in this bottle. Dog only knows what she wanted with it, but who can explain people. I looked around the house one time to see if I could find where she was keeping it. I did worry that someone might find the bottles and, not knowing what was in them, open them up. Wouldn't that be embarrassing?

There was this one time she had taken poop from all three of us and put it in three different bottles. That's something else... she never mixed the poo-poo. It always stayed separated and she would follow us around if she had to so she would know whose poop she was examining. Like I said, our poop was very special to her.

That day, I walked in the house behind her and watched to see what she would do. She stuck the three bottles in this little bag that looked a lot like an envelope. I think it was one of those things like a transformer that can change. You know. It is a bag, then it is an envelope if you want it to be. Oh My Dog people are strange. This bag/envelope had green-colored writing on it that looked something like this:

LABCORP

Anyway, she sealed it all up like an envelope then took it out to the car and drove off with it. I have no clue where she took our poop. She wasn't gone that long, so she couldn't have taken it very far. The writing on the envelope may well be a clue, but since I have never learned to read I can't tell you.

But then something really strange happened. The day after she took our poop for a ride in the car, she was on the phone talking to Dr. Felton.

Get this! They were talking about our poop!

Mom seemed really pleased with what Dr. Felton was saying. I went straight to Faith and Hope and told them that our poop made both Mom and Dr. Felton happy so we needed to make sure we gave them nice, large piles. Faith did not understand what I meant and dropped a huge pile in the hallway. It didn't faze Mom. She picked it up with a paper towel, mopped the floor with a little bit of that strong smelling stuff that burns my nose, then when she took that poop in the bathroom I can only suppose she played in it because she came out dancing.

There is one other thing I need to share about the poop. This is something I will tell you for your own good. One day Mom gave the Border Collie puppies some of that medicine for worms we had been given at the shelter. When they had to rush to the bathroom after taking it, they came back looking all scared. I had a very strong memory of the fear that had hit me like a brick when I saw my poop that day at the shelter. I was glad we could put their minds at ease.

Now I had not noticed at the shelter because we had never seen a lot of different things, but that poop looked very much like those spaghetti noodles that Dad likes so much. Considering how Mom handles the poop, I decided not to ever eat spaghetti again. I believe this is something you may want to think about as well.

Chapter 40

The Pond

It was very hard to tell how much time had passed since we had been safe. Once we were reunited with Mother we lost all track of time. I mean, time didn't matter at all to us. Every day was better than the one before. We were taking trips to see Dr. Felton. I heard Mom tell someone once that we had to go see the vet every two weeks, so I guess that is how often we went. We were gaining weight and filling out really well. I still could not see myself, but I knew from what everyone said that Faith and I almost looked like twins, except she had a white chest and white paws. Mom called her a Tuxedo Pup.

At one time it was very easy to tell Faith from Hope and me, even without the white. She was about half our size. But as time passed and our hearts and souls were filled up, Faith blossomed. It did not take her long to catch up with us. Dr. Felton was very pleased. We were still eating special food and had to be watched closely. Then, not too long after the Border Collie puppies came to stay, Dr. Felton said he wanted to take some more special pictures of our insides.

I know we were a little over four months old then because I heard Mom say so. She was talking to a woman in the vet's office who was asking what was wrong with us. The woman had said we looked so healthy, it was hard to believe we were seeing a specialist. Mom told her, "They do look wonderful, don't they?"

and she beamed with pride when she said it. Mom never failed to let us know she was proud of us, and it always made my heart swell up real big in my chest.

The woman said, "Yes. They look like perfect puppies. They have bright eyes and shiny coats."

That's when Mom said, "We got them when they were very young. We don't know for sure how old they were because someone had taken a file to their teeth about the same time they came in. But they did have teeth so we know they were over six weeks old. And now we know they are over four months because their adult teeth are coming in. That started a couple of weeks back."

That is how we found out how old we were. And that is when Dr. Felton took pictures of our insides again.

When we went back to see the vet after he took the pictures, he showed them to Mom and Dad. He told them he could tell which pup he was looking at by the picture.

We wanted to see them too, so we could see what our insides look like. I saw the pictures, but couldn't recognize who the insides belonged to. All of the pictures looked alike to me so I guess Faith, Hope and I all look like twins on the inside. Except Dr. Felton is very good. That must be why they call him a specialist.

He showed Mom and Dad something called scar tissue on the pictures and said each of us had scarred differently. "As they get older, these patterns will change. These are the areas we need to watch."

He talked about the parts that can't be seen getting stronger with age, just like the muscles that can be seen from the outside. They had to watch the inside very close for signs of weakness. And we had to keep on our diets. We could have peanut butter and that made Faith very happy.

The thing Mom and Dad had to do was just keep an eye on us, bring us back for our check-ups, and if they felt uncomfortable about anything they could always bring us in to see him. Mom and Dad did take us to the vet a lot I suppose. We would have something called infections from time to time and were always having to take some kind of pills for it. Then there was the thing with our poop. While I cannot say for sure, I would like to think Mom's looking at it had something to do with keeping us well. I would hate to think she was just a poop inspector. That is not a job anyone should have for no good reason.

Dr. Felton also told Mom that she should watch Faith especially close. I think he was worried about her not being able to jump like Hope and I could. Then he got down on his knees and gave each of us a good rubbing. That was his version of love and we could feel it. We wagged our tails for him and Hope would give him her best Pibble smile. That would always make him happy.

He told Mom each of us had strengths that we would build on. I was the strongest over-all. That made me feel proud. I would stick my chest out and hold my head back to show him how strong I was. He said Hope was something called a prankster and was the most active. I know Mom was worried about Faith because of what he had said, and she asked him what Faith's strength was. He thought for a minute and then said "She has the strength to overcome."

I could have told him Faith had the strongest heart. I knew where she had been and what she had come back from. It takes a lot of heart to come back from The Land of Nothing when you have been hurt and gotten trapped there the way she was. I know because I had been to The Land of Nothing several times. It was a place I never wanted to go again. It was a place I never wanted to *need* to go again.

There was one other thing I heard Mom and Dr. Felton talk about during that visit. Mom was concerned that we were in pain and what the pain may mean. She talked about pain pills that helped us live, but was worried about the pain wearing some kind of a mask. I am not sure about all of that. I know I did hurt sometimes. But when your life is filled with love and your days are filled with sunshine you learn to live with a little pain.

The pain was still there and sometimes, when it was bad, Mom would notice we were hurting and give us a pill to help. But most of the time it was just something that had become a part of our lives. We had gotten used to the pain. Dr. Felton couldn't tell Mom and Dad we were hurting because he didn't know. He didn't see what was hiding under all that scar tissue in places where the camera could not reach. I guess sometimes there *are* sore or wounded places inside us that wear masks. But the happy faces they saw were as real as the love they had wrapped around our hearts. And that is what was important to us.

It was always late when we got back from a vet visit. We would always be really tired too; so we would usually go straight to bed. That day when we got home mom gave all of us one of the special peanut butter cakes she would make for us. They were very good and Faith would always make hers last a really long time. We could hear her smacking on hers long after we had taken our last bite. Even Mother would sigh and groan and make faces when Faith would do that. It made our mouths water. But Mother would not say anything to her and would not let us bother her. She said it was Faith's greatest pleasure, and everyone needs a greatest pleasure.

The next day Mom hooked our leashes on and took us for a walk around the yard. Mother did not have a leash on and took off at a gallop in the field next to the house. She yelled for us to come with her. Mom and Dad began walking us slowly in that direction. We knew they wanted us to leave the yard and they knew there was a better chance of that happening if Mother led the way.

Mother had stopped and was looking in front of her, then she looked back at us and smiled really big. Then we heard a splash. Mother was swimming in a pond that was in the middle of that field. She called out to us, "Swimming is good for the heart and soul. It touches that place where Heart Speak lives. You girls need to come on in."

Hope began dancing in place like she really wanted to go. Then Mother yelled out, "The water is just right today." Hope pulled against her leash and Mom let her go. Then we heard Hope splash in the pond. We could hear her heart barking out loud. When the heart speaks, you always know there is love. But when a dog's heart *barks,* well that is about the finest sound in the world. It means the world is filled with love and peace and light. But, more, it means the world is a very happy place to be.

Mom and Dad dropped Faith's and my leash. We didn't run to the pond, but we did walk to it with Mom and Dad close by. Then we jumped in and all of our hearts were barking out loud. From that day on the pond was the one place we would go outside our yard. It wasn't very far away and we didn't go that often. But sometimes, on very special occasions, we just needed to bark out loud.

Chapter 41

These Dogs Are Home

One thing we knew about a lot of the dogs we met in rescue: they would be finding homes of their own and leaving. The Border Collie puppies were getting old enough to go to their forever homes and Mom and Dad were looking for the perfect families for them. There were a lot of people that wanted puppies. Mom said those puppies would not leave unless she found the home where they belonged.

Beauty was like us and had a lot of problems. She had problems because she was getting older, but most of it was because she had been abused and neglected. She was scared when strangers would come into the yard, just like we were. One day while we were in the play yard a man came to visit and said he was looking for a dog. He stood at the end of the fence and was looking at all of us. He saw Beauty and liked her a lot. He wanted to take her with him right then. Dad told him he would have to fill out an application and it could take a couple of weeks to get approved. Mom and Dad always made sure it was the perfect home before they would let any of the dogs leave.

That man got really pushy with Dad. He yelled out, "I don't need to *adopt* a BLEEPING dog. It ain't no baby!"

Mother covered my ears when he said that bleeping word so I don't know exactly what he said. I told her I had heard much worse from Man and Boy when we lived in hell. She said, "That was then and this is now. We have moved on from that place and we are just going to leave all those bad words there in hell."

Then the man told dad he was looking for a Lab to hunt with him. Mom heard what he said and saw he was getting really ugly with Dad. She walked over to them and looked that man right in the eye. She had her hands on her hips so I knew she was about to say something really important. Faith saw it too and said, "OOOOHHH... he's in trooou-ble now."

We all knew Mom could get really bossy when she put her hands on her hips. Dad always said that meant people needed to get moving fast. That day she put me in the time out crate for fighting with Hope she had her hands on her hips so I know it's the truth.

She stared that man right in his eyeballs and she said, "Our dogs don't hunt. They are retired from any kind of work they might be asked to do for a human."

The man didn't realize he couldn't just have what he wanted. I don't guess he was used to being told no. He said, "Well that big black dog right there is a hunter. I can see it in her eyes. Dogs like that ain't happy unless they can hunt."

Then before Mom could answer him he looked at us and said, "And you got a yard full of them fighting dogs right there. You're gonna ruin them dogs babying them. You need to let them do what comes natural."

I couldn't see Mom's face, but I saw Dad's eyes and they were laughing. So I knew Mom was getting ready to do like Toad and give that man "what for."

I can't tell you what she said to the man because Mother covered my ears.

That man decided it was time for him to go, and he left pretty fast with Mom walking behind him all the way. My ears were covered the whole time so I can't tell you the good parts. I asked Faith and Hope if they had heard any of it, but Roxy and Beauty helped Mother out and had covered their ears. So you will just have to fill in the bleeps I guess.

Once the man was gone and Mom had calmed down, she came over to us with Dad. That day we all knew we were safe and would never have to go to a bad place. Mother said she believed some of us were just home already. I could hear the Heart Speak just fine and knew we would never leave. I didn't think Beauty was going to leave either. Mom said no one would leave unless the place they were going was better for them than the place they were.

Did you catch that? Anyone who wants to make a dog work for them need not apply. And if anyone thinks they might find a fighting dog around Mom, well... BLEEP, BLEEP, BLEEP, BLEEP, and BLEEP.

After that, when anyone would come up that was what Mom and Dad called an "unsavory character," Mom would just look at them before they could get started talking and say, "These dogs are home."

Chapter 42

Finding Homes for the Babies

A lot of people wanted Border Collie puppies. Mom was on the phone a lot trying to check references and trying to find someone to do a home visit several states away. The puppies were older and were a lot more fun to play with, so we kept them occupied for most of the day. They would fight going to sleep. They told me one time if something important happened, they needed to be awake for it. Mother had been frustrated with them for some time, and even Roxy was getting to the point where she said they needed a time out crate. Beauty would hide in the bedroom when they started acting up.

I was always very careful to keep an eye on them. Mom and Dad thought I was such a very good girl... so responsible. And I was very glad they were proud of me. But honestly, it was self-preservation rather than a sense of duty. Those puppies were thieves. And worse, it was hard to tell who was stealing the treats, toys, or whatever they could get their mouths on and run with, because they all looked alike.

There was one little girl that was different. Border Collies are black and white mostly, but once-in-awhile one will be a light brown and white. Annabelle was the only one of the five that was light brown and white. And she was the only one that was not a thief. So if something got missing and I saw a tail turning the corner, I never could tell whose rear end it was. And those four babies would sit in a line and look at you with a "Who me? No not me!" expression. What's a dog to do?

Faith had taken to hiding her stuff really well. She would put it in her bed and then lay on it. She knew better than to get up and walk away because it would be gone when she got back. And then, of course, there would be a huge pouting session.

With Hope it was always one of her toys. Hope never had a treat left. She was a gobbler and those treats disappeared before anyone had a chance to steal them. And she was a little more paws on when it came to those puppies stealing her stuff. Actually, it was more like teeth on, cause she pinched their butts more than one time when she caught them stealing. And if they lined up and gave her that innocent look, she would just pinch all of them on the rump. She would go right down the line and you would hear four little yips.

They never stole anything from Roxy. They didn't have to. Roxy would give them anything she had if she thought they wanted it. She was a tender-hearted girl. She would defend anything smaller that needed help: puppies, cats, rabbits, squirrels, even birds. Roxy did not like to see anything hurt.

So in the beginning, Roxy would lecture Hope about pinching the babies. She would tell Hope she was a lot bigger than they were and as Hope would say, "Yadda, Yadda, Bark, Bark, Snarl, BARF!" She never said it to Roxy's face, but she would mutter it under her breath when she was walking away. That was Hope's way of saying she had heard it all before and she was tired of hearing it because her stuff was still being stolen.

Roxy had this one toy that she kept on her bed. It was a stuffed puppy and it looked real. Mom called it Roxy's "stuffie." No one touched that toy. It was the one thing that Roxy did not want to share. Mother said it reminded her of one of her puppies that something bad had happened to before she came into rescue. It didn't matter why as far as I was concerned. It belonged to Roxy and no one had the right to take it. But, of course, those puppies saw something and wanted it so they were not about to keep their paws or their mouths off of it.

One day two of them went and grabbed that toy off her bed. I think the only reason Roxy didn't totally flip out and just totally ignore those babies from then on is because Mom caught them stealing the stuffie and put a stop to it. They had already grabbed it and were playing tug with it. Mom had to do surgery where they had sank their teeth into it and pulled. From that time on, Roxy would give those puppies lectures about stealing. She was frustrated that they wouldn't listen. I know she was totally fed up cause one time she saw Hope pinching their butts and all she said was, "Carry on."

Faith, Hope and I talked about how tiring puppies could be. We thought about it, and there were a few times after we got rescued that we acted out. We went to Mother and apologized for all the times we were pains in the butt.

One day Mom was especially busy with finding their homes. No one wanted her to get interrupted. Those puppies were ready to go to their homes and no one wanted to hold them back. I mean, we loved them. We loved them a lot and liked to play with them. We hoped they would have wonderful lives in their homes with their families. And we were all ready for a break.

Well, on this day those puppies got very quiet. I knew they were up to something so I ran and checked my stuff. They had not bothered it. Faith was laying on her bed with her treats and toys up under her, so I knew they hadn't been in her stuff. Hope was walking around with her favorite toy in her mouth to protect it. I asked Mother if she had seen those puppies and she said, "No, thank Dog!" Then she looked a little embarrassed because she had said it.

Beauty was outside with Dad so I couldn't ask her. I didn't get a chance to ask Roxy. She heard me asking Mother and she jumped up and said, "Those puppies are into something. We need to find them."

Roxy was really good at finding anything. She put her nose to the floor and started sniffing. I ran behind her thinking she might need help, and her nose led us right into the back room where Mom kept the dog food. All five of them were back there, even Annabelle. Annabelle was really not doing anything but watching the others. I think they made her be lookout because as soon as she saw us she started barking.

Three of those puppies were in the trash and they had it scattered everywhere. They had ripped the used paper towels to shreds. What a mess! And we couldn't find the fourth puppy anywhere.

Annabelle's barking had caused Mom to come running. It's a good thing she had her camera with her cause she got a picture of those puppies caught in the act. And she found the fourth one. All you could see was his backside hanging out of the top of a bag of dog food.

That was the day things changed for the better. Mom decided she didn't want to risk those puppies getting into something that could hurt them. She got one of those portable pens like they had at Dr. Felton's. Those puppies had their own little play pen and our stuff was safe again.

Mom worked for days looking for the perfect families for those babies. Finally she had found all the homes where the puppies belonged. She set it up so they would all be leaving about the same time. She didn't want any of them to get lonely. She had their rides worked out so everyone was leaving on the same day, except Annabelle. But no one was going to be left behind because Annabelle was leaving a couple of days before everyone else. She was going to a very special home and her new mom had worked out her ride. Mom said Annabelle was one of those adoptions with a very special story that had touched her heart. It was one of those where as soon as she talked to Annabelle's new mom, she knew that was where she belonged. Of course she had checked her out and she was just simply wonderful, so Annabelle's mom was waiting for her to come home.

We celebrated all of the puppies getting homes with peanut butter cake and we spent the whole day outside in the play yard with them. It was a really good day. They were all very excited and didn't get into trouble even once. Hope was very happy and bounced like a bronco most of the day. Even Faith was playful and she and Annabelle spent some time together rolling around in the grass.

I saw Mother watching us and my heart swelled up with love for her. I went over and rolled around in the grass in front of her. She wrestled with me just a little and then we snuggled up close. It was one of those times when I had Mother all to myself and I enjoyed every minute of it. I think everyone needs a little time alone with those special people and dogs in their lives.

Watching the puppies play, I remembered they had lost their mother. I knew what that felt like too. I was lucky; my mother had been saved and had come back to me. She knew what I was thinking just like always. "They did have Roxy to help them along," she told me. "And they were so young when they lost their mother, they may not even remember."

"They had you, too. And I know how wonderful that was for them. But a puppy always remembers their mother," I said. "And no matter how many others come into their lives and love them, they will never forget to remember."

She snuggled very close to me then and said, "You are my very special girl. And you have always made me very proud. Don't ever forget to remember that."

It was such a wonderful and warm moment, it made me feel very safe and sleepy. It made the day perfect.

Chapter 43

The Day Before Tomorrow

After we celebrated all of the puppies finding homes, Mom called Dr. Felton. She said we were supposed to have a surgery called 'spay.' We had heard them talking about it with the vet one time. He had said he would check us when we were six months old to see if we were ready. We would need to go in for an exam, and he would test to see if we could stand the medicine that would make us sleep through the surgery. It was time for us to have that exam.

I heard Mom tell Dr. Felton on the phone that she thought we might need to wait a little longer. She said she didn't want to take any chances that something would go wrong. We were all a little nervous about having surgery so we were glad to hear her say that. Still they made an appointment for us to go in and be checked by Dr. Felton. Mom wrote the appointment on her reminder board in the kitchen. She had a lot of reminders on it for different things. It looked like this:

Annabelle, Transport
Thursday, July 15
Burger King Parking Lot @ 9 am

BC Puppies, Transport
Friday, July 16
Call Robin Thursday Night for Time

The Girls, Dr. Felton
Monday, July 19 @ 11 am

Once again I will tell you, I can't read so I didn't have a clue what that said. But I knew we would not go to the vet until the Border Collie puppies were all gone to their new homes. I was glad about that. I was a little nervous about leaving all my stuff at home with them. We had been to the vet since they had been with us, but that was before they turned into thieves.

We had celebrated those babies getting a home, but they hadn't left yet. I was beginning to wonder if they were really leaving at all. Then one day we all woke up and did our morning routine. We didn't stay out in the play yard that day. Dad was putting three of the big blue swimming pools out there and filling them with water. They would do that on hot days because we liked to climb in the pool and cool off. Since he was filling three with water I knew it was going to be a fun day.

We couldn't really swim in those pools because they were too small. But the water felt good to us. We also had games we liked to play. The Border Collies were jabbering among themselves because they knew they were going to get to go in the water too. They were staying out of trouble for once.

The one thing that got me really excited was I could see Mom was making some of our peanut butter cakes. I knew there was going to be a party and that was enough to get me excited. Faith was sitting in the kitchen watching every move Mom made with that peanut butter. She would stomp her paws once in a while to make sure Mom knew she was there.

I saw Mom slip Faith a bite so I went and sat beside her. I made sure to stomp my paws just like Faith had done. Mom smiled and gave me a bite of peanut butter right off the spoon. That is how I liked it best. Hope would take it off a spoon but she liked the peanut butter cakes. Faith liked it anyway she could get it. When she saw Mom coming with that spoon of peanut butter, she opened her mouth and actually smacked like she was tasting it too. Then, of course, once she had stopped slobbering, the cheeks blew out in a pout. Mom said Faith was the only dog she had ever seen blow her cheeks out that way.

Mom laughed and gave her *another* big spoon of peanut butter. She grabbed it very fast like she was scared I would take it from her. The spoon slipped out of Mom's hand and Faith ended up with peanut butter all over her mouth and nose. She made a "nom-nom-nom" sound while she smacked over it. She licked and licked and licked over that peanut butter.

Mom was getting the peanut butter cakes ready to take outside. Hope was standing at the backdoor looking out and stomping her paws just like Faith and I had done over the peanut butter. I ran to the backdoor to see what she was excited about. Dad was setting up a table with some cups and people treats. And he had put two more pools in the play yard. He also had some special dog treats on that table. Hope pointed them out to me.

I asked Mother if she knew what was going on. She was as baffled and as excited as we were. Mom took the cakes outside, set them on the table and came back in. She closed the door so Hope and I could not see out any longer. I tried really hard to do a pout like Faith but it didn't work.

Finally, after what seemed like a few years, she opened the backdoor and let us out. All I can say it's a good thing that was a very large play yard because there was Nelly and her family! Faith ran out to see Froggy and almost fell down the steps. The Border Collies came out too and everybody had a really good time.

I thought it was a special occasion because our friends had come, but Mother told me that it was also Annabelle's last day with us. That date Mom had written on the message board was tomorrow and this was the day before tomorrow. That meant this was her farewell party. I spent as much time with her as I could and told her I would really miss her. She was happy to be going to her home and her mom. She said she had this fluttering in her belly. I knew all about that.

Playing in the pool was fun at first, but I decided I wanted to go and spend some time with Mother and Nelly. I was not feeling well. My butt was hurting and I could feel it starting to droop a little. I saw Mom watching me. She looked worried.

Later on Mom came over to where I was laying with Nelly and Mother. She felt my nose and looked at my eyes and gums. Then she gave me a belly rub. I rolled over and kicked my feet in the air to let her know I liked it.

It was good to see Nelly and her family again, but by the time they left, I was feeling really tired. I went in the house and climbed up in Mom's chair. I liked getting in her chair because I knew she would sit with me when she came in. I liked it when she let me be a lap dog.

I stayed on her lap until bedtime. I heard her tell Dad she thought I was feeling bad and she wanted to have Dr. Felton check me. Dad said maybe it was just all the excitement from the day. I could feel something changing. I wasn't too sure what it was but I felt dizzy and was very sleepy. Mom was looking really worried so I made sure to lick her face a little and my tail wagged at her.

Bedtime came and I went to get on my bed. Mother, Faith, Hope and I would often snuggle at night, but we were getting too big to all sleep on the same bed. We had not done that in some time. That night we curled up together like we had done when we were puppies and Mother was feeding us.

Sometime later, I got up and went and sat by Mom's and Dad's bed. There was a mirror near the bed and I sat and looked at myself in it for a bit. I had always known the mirror was there, and I had barked at the dog I saw in it before. But that night I realized it was me staring back from the mirror. Finally, I could see what I looked like. I did look a lot like Faith. In fact, I realized I was growing into a very good looking dog.

Mom woke up and saw me staring in the mirror. She climbed off the bed and sat there with me. I laid across her lap and she rubbed my belly. It felt really good and I dozed off. When I woke up Mom had put me in the bed with her. It was really strange that I didn't remember getting in the bed. I shook my head a couple of times trying to think clearer. Finally, I climbed back off the bed and sat and stared at myself in the mirror again.

Looking in the mirror, I could see all of my past. I saw the abuse and the pain from my first weeks of life. The mirror showed me how very tiny I had been. Nelly had called me an "old soul" once. Remembering how I thought it was my responsibility to save the three of us, I understood what she meant. I was an old soul. I saw the days we spent at the shelter and understood that is really when our lives began to change. For the longest time I had been upset over the way Dr. Martin had dismissed us. But looking back, I believe he was trying to do the kind thing. If no one had come for us, if no one had cared, we could not have survived.

Then I saw Mom and Dad rescue us. They had looked at us with so much love, I felt my heart flutter with happiness all over again remembering that day. The memory of seeing Mother again was one of the best. She had told me once, a long time ago, about Rescue Angels. Back in hell it was easy to doubt their existence. But seeing Mother alive, knowing how long she had suffered and how badly she had been hurt, there was no more doubt. The one thing I could say absolutely, even though the abuse had determined many things about my life and had brought so much pain, my life was wonderful. More, it was grand.

When Mom woke up I was still sitting there.

The day before tomorrow was over and it was tomorrow. Mom got Annabelle ready to go and told Dad when she got back he should be ready to take me to the vet. She told him I had sat looking at myself in the mirror all night and she was worried about me.

Dad came over and looked at my gums and my eyes. He felt my nose. Then he said, "I don't see anything wrong. But she's not quite herself today. If she didn't sleep, maybe she is just tired. Yesterday was an exciting day. That could have caused her to be a little restless."

I could tell Dad was as worried as Mom, but he was trying to find reasons for me to be okay. When Mom left he put me up on the bed and sat with me. He offered me a piece of bacon and I took it because I knew it would make him feel better. He thought I had eaten it, but I put it under the pillow on the bed. He laid down next to me and I rested my head on his chest. We waited for Mom to get home.

Chapter 44

The Greatest Love

Mom came in the front door and I heard her call out, "Are you ready to go? Where's Charity?"

She came back to the bedroom and Dad was sitting next to me, rubbing my head. "I think she is very tired," he said.

Mom came over and looked at me. She looked at all the things Dr. Felton had told her to check if one of us ever got sick. "I have no clue what's going on," Mom said. "I know she didn't get in to anything that hurt her. All of the dogs stayed together yesterday. She is the only one that acts sick." I could hear tears in her voice and I knew she was scared. "I am going to call Dr. Felton. I don't like this at all."

As she walked out the bedroom door she turned back and said, "It's a very long drive to Dr. Felton's. We may need to take her to see Dr. Curtis. Get her records ready."

She left the door open when she went out. Dad got up to close it, but Mother, Faith and Hope were standing there. He let them in and sat back down on the bed.

Hope walked up to the bed and rested her nose just in front of my face. "Are you going to be okay?" she asked. "I heard you get out of bed and followed you. I saw you looking in that picture thing on the wall last night. You didn't hear me when I called out to you." And again she asked, "Are you going to be okay?"

I didn't know how to answer her. I felt okay. I was worried about Mom and Dad being so scared. I didn't like seeing Hope so worried, "I believe I am going to be just fine," I said. "I am not sure what exactly is happening. The one thing I do know is your life is going to be just grand, and that makes me very happy."

"But," said Hope, "I feel you leaving us. I don't want you to leave, Charity. Do you need me to help you? I can help you fight, you know?

Hope's words reminded me of our last day in hell, how she had tried so hard to get through that shcd door to hclp me. Looking back at the past, Hope was the one who had stepped up to fight first. I sent her the warmest smile I could and hoped she could feel the love coming from my Heart Speak.

"Do you know how much I love you?" I asked. "We would probably have never made it out of hell had it not been for you and your courage. I tried very hard, Hope. The burden was very heavy on me back then, until you stepped up and let me know I was not alone. Faith would have been lost forever, her spirit totally broken, without you. We let her know it was safe to come back to the world together. I could never have done that without you."

I felt the warmth of her Heart Speak glowing inside of me. "I want you to come back now, Charity. I love you."

Hope stepped away from the bed and then I saw Faith standing there. "Have you decided to go back to The Land of Nothing, Charity? Did something make you scared or sad?"

Faith's eyes could still get to me. She had the saddest eyes and I wanted to comfort her now. "I promised I would never go back there again," I answered. "When you came back from there last time, I promised and I will not go back to that place. Nothing scared me. Nothing made me sad. I am happy, Faith. I am happier than I ever thought I could be."

"But you are sick," said Faith. "Mom is calling Dr. Felton because you are sick."

For the first time since I had begun to feel funny, I realized exactly what was wrong with me. I wanted to put Faith's heart at ease. I wanted her to know it was going to be okay. So I told her the truth.

"It's not that, Faith." I said. "I don't think Dr. Felton can give me what I need. I don't think there is anyone here that can change the path I am on now. And it really is going to be okay."

Faith looked confused and for a second I thought she was going to pout. Instead, I could feel the tears flowing freely from her heart. "Oh, Faith," I reached out with my own heart and held her as close as I could. "I am going to be okay. It is going to be... just grand. And no matter where I am, no matter where you are, my love will always be deep in your heart and soul. As long as you hold me there, I will be with you."

"Then you will be with me always and forever," she said. "I love you."

She stepped away and I knew she would be okay. I could rest knowing she was going to be okay.

I felt the old familiar love swirling through my entire body. It was almost overwhelming. I could feel the bright light and the warmth lighting my heart and soul. It was the best feeling I had ever known. I knew Mother was there in front of me.

Mother looked at me with so much love and pain, it hurt my heart. She did not speak. She didn't have to. "Mother," I said. "I love you so much."

She dropped her head and said very softly, "And I love you. I have given birth to many children, and I have loved every one. But, you, Charity; you are my heart and my pride. You were born a very old soul. I knew from the first time I felt you move inside me there was something very special about you. There are no words that can say what is in my heart. But you know. You have always known."

"I will be with you always," I said. "And one day we will be together again."

"Charity, yes," and I could hear the tears in her heart. "As much as I would love to have you here with us, as much as I will miss seeing your face every day, I must give you the greatest gift I can and tell you, safe journey. Until we meet again... safe journey."

Mom came back into the room then and my mother and sisters stepped aside so she could pass. The room was full of more love than I had ever believed possible. Mother had set my heart and my mind at ease. I could not have left with a free spirit had she not said it was okay. But there were two people who were holding on with their hearts and souls. They wanted to make me better... one more time. I could feel the Heart Speak and knew they would do anything they needed to do to help me.

They sat together on the side of the bed, holding hands, and each had one hand on me. I could feel the prayers and the love and it filled me up. I raised my head, tried to sit up, but I was so very tired and my head fell back on the pillow. I did not mean to sigh. I could feel the fear and the pain coming from my human mom's and dad's hearts. If I could ease their minds at all, I wanted to. When my head hit the pillow I sighed very loudly.

Mom got very quiet then and laid her head against me. I thought of all the times she had comforted me by rubbing my ears, how that one act of love had been her way of reaching out when I hurt or was sad. I thought of how much that had meant to me and what it said to my heart. If I could have, I would have rubbed her ears.

I felt Dad's heart reaching out to me and thought about him and the bacon he carried in his pocket. I had heard his Heart Speak many times and loved the feel of it. I knew he had been hurt as a child, just as I was hurt and abused. I knew he had been very lonely when he was a boy. He and I had taken many journeys together with our Heart Speak and I knew the sound and the feel of his heart as well as I knew my own. Any time Dad was upset or worried, he would eat. He had never failed to share his food with me, or any of the other dogs who lived in his heart. And Dad had a very large heart. That bacon he gave us was his way of giving a small dose of love and happiness every day.

I thought of the love in Dad's pocket. I moved my paw against that pocket. Tears rolled down his face. I knew he was listening to me. I knew he could hear me.

Mom and Dad both could hear and feel my Heart Speak. I knew they could. They lifted their heads and looked at one another. Mom whispered to Dad, "She's tired. She is so very tired." Dad nodded his head in agreement.

I could feel the tears in their hearts, but the fear was gone. They had heard me and I had helped them not be so scared. They had been praying for me, and I had prayed for them. I believe all of our prayers were answered. Mom put her mouth next to my ear and whispered, "I love you sweet girl. More than anything, I want you to stay. I want you to get well." She paused for a moment and I waited for her to say what I needed to hear most. "Charity, I love you. If it is too hard, if you need to let go, it is okay. We will be okay."

I held my breath for a moment and I listened closely. She had said it, and I needed that. But there had to be more. I needed one more thing before my heart and soul could be at peace.

Then I felt the glow. My heart filled with love and peace. The words Mom had whispered in my ear had reached her heart, and they had reached Dad's. They had not been just words to make me feel better. They meant it.

Reaching out, I needed to touch every heart in that room. I knew they were all waiting. The room filled with a beautiful light as our love united through Heart Speak. It was beautiful. It was grand. They loved me enough to give me the greatest gift of all. They loved me enough to set me free.

Before I went to sleep, I looked at all the faces around me. Everyone had moved closer and I could see them now. I let each face sink deep into my heart, where I would always hold them. I whispered, "Don't forget to remember," and I closed my eyes. The journey continues. My heart speaks from Rainbow Bridge.

Chapter 45

Message from an Angel

Dear Rescue Angels,

This is Charity. If you are reading this, then you have been on a long, and sometimes painful, journey with me. I know some of it was almost too much to bear, and I am glad you stayed on the path with me. I know our journey together ended very quickly, almost without warning. But that is how things are sometimes.

I suppose I knew I was ready to move on, somewhere deep down. But no one else knew. I remember the fear they had, the shock, but mostly the hurt. I think you may be feeling some of that too. So I want to reach out with Heart Speak and say a few things just to you.

There was a time when I did not believe in you. I must be honest about that. It is very hard to believe in angels when you are sitting in hell, and you know there is nothing but pain coming every day. So the first thing I want to say is thank you. Thank you for being real and for standing up day after day to protect those who cannot protect themselves.

You helped to show me there is a lot of good in this world. You helped me to believe in the things that always make life just grand. Thank you for that. Thank you for loving me and my sisters and for helping us to live and know love. Thank you for being a voice for the voiceless. Thank you for being a Rescue Angel.

So many people cared about me and the love lives in my heart and soul. When I came to Rainbow Bridge, Mom and Dad wanted to know what had happened to me and they got the answers. While the pain was better and the wounds were healing, the damage was most likely done the first time Boy hurt me. All it took was a small place in my intestines to be too weak, to let poison out and into my body and the damage was done.

What had happened to me... to my sisters... was not something vets see every day. Most of the time the dogs never make it to the place where someone is trying to help them get better. My death did teach them that things may look okay on a picture, but an injury can be hidden. It is important to look above where the actual damage occurred because things change with growth. The only way I know to tell you so you may understand, if you get hurt and get a scar on your knee when you are a child, when you get older, the scar may be on your thigh.

Mom had said once she was worried about the pain. Pain is a symptom of something wrong. I was in pain, especially when I went to the bathroom... but that was expected. There was other pain that was hidden. There was other damage that did not show up on the pictures.

The pain had begun at a very young age for my sisters and me. It became normal to us. A lot of things looked normal because of how young we were. The vets operated on Hope and Faith and found a lot of damage they had not seen on pictures. If anything good came out of my death, it helped to save their lives.

Rainbow Bridge is a beautiful place. I am very glad I was able to find a home and to know the love of a family, my family, before I came here. Some arrive here having never known that. They are okay, but there is always a little something missing for them. One day someone will arrive here and help them. Rescuers always take the ones who need them the most, even here at Rainbow Bridge.

Of course, there is another good that came from my death. It made people aware. Awareness is the first step in stopping evil.

Now there is more work to be done. There was a time when I did not think it would do me any good to say that. But I know better now. I know I can come to you, and while everything might not ever be perfect, you will stand and fight to make the world a better place for all beings to live. You cannot fight every battle. There is far too much evil in the world for one person to fight all of it. But each of you together can choose one battle and stand up to be heard and counted.

If you have been on this journey with me, you know I lived through three very great evils. I was born into a world where many people hate me. I was born an American Pit Bull Terrier (APBT), and while I think that is just a grand breed to be, a lot of people want to destroy the entire breed. Sergeant Stubby was an APBT. He was well-loved and he was very brave. But his heroics have been long forgotten by too many.

My sisters and I were very lucky to be dumped in an animal shelter with people who were fluent in Heart Speak. Had those people not been there, we would never have made it out of the shelter. There are thousands of dogs who die in shelters every day. The breed of dog most frequently killed in a shelter is the APBT. Dogs who have something wrong with them and who are black also are quick to be killed. So a black, APBT who has an injury and is taken to an animal shelter will most likely never see the light of day outside that shelter again.

It was hard for me to understand in the beginning. I had not done anything that I could think of to cause people to just hate me. The hell I was born into was a sadistic world of dog fighting. There are many people in this world who see nothing wrong with making dogs fight. Many think it is natural, that dogs want to fight. I can tell you because I was there: Dogs do not *want* to fight. They fight because they are taught it is what they must do to live.

No living being wants to be hurt. No man, cat, rabbit, bird or dog wants to be hurt. There are people who believe the only beings who should not be hurt are humans. A dog's pain does not count in their world. Some are even worse. They cheer when they see a dog's pain. They laugh when one is hurt. They cry out for the dog's blood to soak the ground. Those dogs who can fight the best and cause the most damage to another are sought after by these people.

Because so many people love to see the blood and gore, and see nothing wrong with it so long as it is "just a dog," there are men who earn their living breeding and training these dogs to fight. That is the world I was born into. At one time I thought all people were that way and life could not be any different. I know better now. And I know not everyone enjoys my pain.

The final evil, the one that eventually ended my life: I was raped. It is hard for some to believe there are people who want to rape dogs. It is real. It happens more often than anyone thinks. The dogs who are living through it do not know there is any other way to live. They are waiting for someone to save them. No one hears their voices and their cries. Too few people in this world even know about Heart Speak. So many of the dogs who are raped will die and never know the love and peace that I had in my life.

Your voices are needed. Will you stand and be heard? Will you be a voice for the voiceless?

You may not think you have anything to give. Trust me, you have so much... so many things you can do to help.

The first thing you must do, before anything else, you must see the abuse and know it is real. If you close your eyes, you will not see it and maybe you can sleep at night and not think about it. But it will not go away. If you think it is okay to close your eyes, and you believe it stops because you cannot see it, then you are just like those people who do not believe a dog's feelings matter. You are making your world comfortable and forgetting the rest.

Trust me, closing your eyes does not make it stop. I closed my eyes when Boy raped me and it still was just as bad. Closing your eyes may make an imaginary evil go away. But when the evil is real, closing your eyes and refusing to see it just makes it worse.

The ones who *are* evil... those who hurt and maim and kill... are counting on you closing your eyes.

Once you know the evil is real, you must never keep quiet. You must yell, shout, scream, and holler... until you are heard. Those who do not know Heart Speak will never hear unless you do. They never heard me. Some never cared. You have to make them hear you and you have to make them care. And you have to teach those who do not know any better.

Remember, at Rainbow Bridge I can watch and see things a lot better than I could when I was trapped in hell. And there is something that you do that bothers me. Those of you who really care, I have noticed, will get all upset when you see things on your computer that support dogs fighting and dogs being raped. You do scream out as loud as you can and it makes you angry. It should. But there is something you are doing that makes it worse. I know you do not mean to do that, so I thought maybe if I tell you, it will get better.

You go to the authorities at Face Book or the internet site that is allowing these people to share the stuff and you scream for it to be removed from the computer. And it usually is. But do you think those people stopped doing evil because they made them take it down? I can tell you they didn't. But it got a lot worse because when they took it down, it became a big secret again. Remember: Once it cannot be seen, people become blind to it.

You should leave the site up and get in touch with someone who will fight against the evil. That way, when the site is finally

459

removed, it will be because someone has stopped that group of evil people. There are places you can go to learn how to report this stuff on the internet. While they are not the only ones, my friends at Eagle's Den rescue would be happy to help you and give you the information. You can find them on Face Book, or you can email them at EDR.PETS@YAHOO.COM

There are many other things you can do to make life better for those without a voice. Every person should have animals in their lives. You can adopt a homeless dog or cat. You can adopt through a rescue, or go to your local animal shelter and take one or two home. One favor, please, if you go to the animal shelter and see a mother there with her babies, have a heart. If the puppies are old enough to leave their mother, remember: those puppies will get out. Someone will take them. The mother may not. If you work with a rescue: NEVER EVER TAKE PUPPIES AND LEAVE THE MOTHER BEHIND.

Always make sure to look at the seniors, too. They deserve a home where they can live out the remainder of their days in peace. If they are in a shelter, chances are you will give them the only real home they have ever had.

You can foster a dog or cat for a rescue. Rescues are usually filled and cannot help more until the ones they are caring for find a home. Offer your home as a temporary shelter. You will give them love and care and they will carry a piece of your heart with them for the rest of their lives. The rescue will usually provide for their medical care. You will feed them and give them love. Toys and treats would be nice too. But if you have a heart big enough to foster, I know you will not deprive them of treats and toys. And sometimes, you may find that you are a terrible foster and cannot let the dog or cat you love go. That is called a "failed foster," and rescues love those.

If you cannot adopt and you cannot foster, maybe you can give some of your time to help. Go to your local shelter or a rescue near you and offer to walk the dogs, to feed them, to clean up after them; or, maybe you can even give a dog a bath and a really good belly rub.

There is something else you can do that is important to every rescue. Rescues always spend a lot of money to care for the dogs they help. You can donate money, food, treats, medicines, toys, beds, or anything else that dogs and cats must have to live good lives. Even if you can only spare a dollar, dollars add up and you will be making a difference. Sign up to donate monthly. Most rescues would be happy if you would give even one dollar a month. Your dollar may well help to save a life. Most of the rescues who need your help the most cannot send you a t-shirt or a magazine. But they will send you their thanks and the Heart Speak joy from every animal they have saved.

There is one more thing that is very important for rescues. They need your love, support and prayers. Words of encouragement will often help them when they are feeling really down. There are days when people in rescue find it very hard to put one foot in front of the other. They have vet bills due, dogs to feed, more dogs that need to be saved… and nowhere to turn. You are their support system and can make the difference with a kind word.

The one thing you should NEVER do is argue and bicker among yourselves. If you are in this to save lives, that is what matters. One person may not be able to do the same things you do, or they may do it differently. None of that matters. You do not even have to like someone to help them save a life.

If you search the internet and Face Book looking to criticize or condemn others, if you find fault in things others do and always feel the need to point it out, you are not helping anyone. There are much better ways to spend your time. If your aim is to hurt anyone or any group who is advocating for an animal, you are helping the abusers. Your intentions may well be good at the start, but when you start hurting those who are helping... you are on the wrong path.

Roll your sleeves up, put a little love in your pocket, put your hip boots on... or kick your shoes off... and climb down in the trenches. That is where the abused, deserted and lonely animals are. Climb on down in there and get them out.

Love, Hope & Heart Speak,

Don't forget to remember...

Charity

A NOTE FROM BETH, AT THE DEN:

Charity died on July 15, 2010. She was approximately six months old. I miss her every day.

This book has been a long-time coming. Many of my friends asked me to write it after Charity died. I said, "One day... maybe;" and put it on the old back burner. I had more important things to do, or so I thought.

After Charity's death, I wanted revenge. That is about as honest as I can get. I had to get past that and it wasn't easy. There are still days...

But, once I got over myself I knew recording Charity's Journey was important.

Faith and Hope had numerous surgeries to repair damage to their intestines. Faith suffered muscle damage that makes it impossible for her to jump to this day. When Faith needs to go to the bathroom, she needs to go NOW. She has some control and she can go on her own. But holding it is not much of an option for her. We keep pads handy for nights and for those occasions when she just cannot make it to the door.

Hope had objects inserted inside of her that were embedded in her intestines. They were hidden by scar tissue and normal tissue and were found during surgery. The girls were so young when the abuse began, as they developed in the first weeks, a lot of the damage was hidden. The first 18 months of Faith's and Hope's life was spent having medical procedures done so they could live quality lives. As long as we had the hope and promise for a quality life, giving up was not an option. From the day we first met them, our hearts were invested.

Once the two girls were better and the surgeries were over, we were told their diet would always be very important. They could live quality lives, but they might not live long lives. We watched for any sign of trouble. We knew they would have trouble absorbing proteins. That is one of the dangers when the intestines are damaged.

As I said before, there are days... and one of those days when the revenge monster reared its head was April 17, 2014. Hope passed away from complications related to her abuse. She was four years old. She lived a good, quality life for almost three years. I miss her every day.

Some, who probably do not know better, have asked me if all the time and money spent was worth it. YES! I would do it all again.

Faith is still here. She soaks up all the love we offer and gives it back tenfold. Since the day Hope passed away, every night somewhere between 9 and 11 o'clock Faith begins singing *The Song of Souls.* She goes outside, does her business, and then the howling begins. By the time she is finished every dog here has joined her. This is where the idea for the song was born.

Snookie is also still with us. I know many of those who have followed the girls for a long time did not know Snookie was their mother. The book should have been published a long time before this and I was saving the news. We suspected for some time and a DNA test confirmed it.

While <u>*Charity's Journey*</u> says we had the DNA test done early, in truth, it was done after Charity's death. We learned the test was available during one of the numerous surgeries and had it done then.

We saw the reaction of all four on the day they met, and we knew they had come from the same area. Snookie began to heal very quickly after the girls' arrival, and they would not leave her alone once they saw her. Faith *always* attempted to nurse from her. There are times she will still try today and she is as large as Snookie. Snookie never tries to stop her.

This story is written from Charity's perspective, and is based on events surrounding her rescue. In some cases, there were changes that made no difference to the outcome of the story, or changes that were made for creative purposes. The story and people surrounding the animal shelter are the culmination of several incidents and several people at different shelters. The same is true of the veterinarians. The ones in the book are products of the author's imagination. I want to be clear that all of the veterinarians we use for rescue are wonderful and work very hard to save lives.

Before I leave this alone and say it is done:

There are many people who have my heartfelt thanks and gratitude. I wish I could name everyone, but that would take more pages than there are in this book.

Thank You (in alphabetical order) Anne Housley & hubby Norm, Besty Roth, Jonathan Ezzell, Kat Sutherland, Lori Paquin, Marti & Paul Jones, Richard Stack, Sheila McLean, and Tammy Williams for being a part of Eagle's Den Rescue. We couldn't do it without you. You are our family and Jerry & I both love you.

Thank You Beverly Lussier for the pictures you created for the girls, including the cover for Charity's Journey. Mostly, thank you for your dedication and for always loving Charity, Hope and Faith.

Thank You Brandy Rock & Ray for the benefit you held for the girls. Knowing you are there for me is sometimes all I need to remember to get up in the morning and keep going. And Ray, just for you: *Oh hell yeah!*

Thank You Brian & Mary Krajewski. You have made it impossible for anyone to "forget to remember" the girls with The Charity, Hope & Faith Foundation for Abused Animals. For all you have done, there are not enough adequate words...

Thank You Glen & Beth Williams for taking Gabe home and teaching another rape victim it is safe to trust. You have put a light in his eyes that I never thought I would see. And thank you for the work you do to help stop this terrible crime.

Thank You Cynthia Schlichting for telling Bella's story in the book *As Bright as the Sun.* And thank you, Brian & fur-kid Jane for loving Bella and Tyler enough to give them a home, and for your never-ending fight to raise awareness for bait dogs. Your dedication inspires me. I know Foster is with Charity at Rainbow Bridge and he is very proud of his mom and dad.

Thank You Letha Garrison for making Buddy's eyes shine again, and for loving him to the moon and back. You are right; he belonged with you all along.

Thank You Richard & Robin with *The Lexus Project* for saving so many lives and for bringing Tigger into ours.

Thank You Mike Albanese Jr and the entire Puppy Doe Pack. You humble and inspire me.

Thank You Silvia Kim & *A Shelter Friend* for Snookie and for your tireless efforts in rescue. Thank You for the three little puppies who never had a chance. I still remember. Thank You for trying. You made the rescue of three more possible.

Just a few more, and I trust each will know why. They do, after all, understand Heart Speak:

Alison Housley, Amanda Housley, Ann Bridges, Anna Brisson, Beth Housley, Bob & Tamara Nolan, Carrie Dennison, Cissy Prestage, Claire West, Corrie Toffoli, Denise Damanti, Denise McGuire, Donna Taylor, Dot Kirby, Erica Podjasek, Gena Green, Jean Schmurr, Joan Marion, John, Jessie & Alyssa Price, Kristen Price, Kristy Waldo, Miranda & Frank Cron, Nancy Bartow, Nina Pollard, Samantha Housley, Stacy Cain, Teresa Lash and Treena Kilgore...

You keep the Heart Speak flowing.

A very special thank you to Dr. Ronni LaVine and her entire staff. You have worked more than one miracle for our victims. Without you so many would never have had a chance. And thank you for bringing Tyler and Buddy back to us. When no one thought they would make it, you believed.

Thank you Dr. Doug Gensel and his entire staff for always caring enough to do it right.

Thank You Jerry McDuffie for the Heart Speak. You rescued me.

And a huge thank you to over 43,000 Face Book friends. You Sustain Us.

~Beth McDuffie~

June 9, 2014